THE DARK

WORKS BY JEREMY ROBINSON

THE
DARK

JEREMY ROBINSON

BREAKNECK MEDIA

For those with PTSD and chronic ailments,
fighting every day to overcome the dark.

1

I move through the grocery store the same way I do life.

Backwards.

Earbuds wedged in place. Missy Elliott's *WTF* in my ears. I strut through the aisles against the natural flow of traffic. A snowplow through a fresh foot of white. I delight in the agitated sideways glances. The eye-rolls from old men putting me into one prejudiced label or another. The look of revulsion when a young mother sees my purposefully unkempt hair, wiry frame, eyeliner, and my KISS T-shirt.

I'm a happy enigma. Like a dark Dr. Seuss creation come to life. Outwardly horrifying but good natured.

Passing the pharmacy, I give the staff a smile and a two fingered salute. I frequent the Hannaford enough that the employees either know me by name or by reputation. I'm a nice guy. They know it. I know it. But the pharmacy folks...they give me a fierce stink eye, like it's the only thing keeping me from diving over the counter and Cookie Monstering their Oxy supply.

Lucky for them, I don't partake in hard drugs. Or even alcohol. I'm faithful to Mary Jane. She's always been good to me, and thanks to a dose of post Army grunt PTSD, I'm not even breaking the law.

I'm somewhat disappointed in the level of attention I'm getting tonight. Hardly a second glance. Everyone seems to be in a hurry. Probably some kind of sporty event. But it's the middle of August. There aren't any big sports events now. I think.

The Olympics, maybe?

Do people still watch the Olympics?

They must.

But not with Pats in Superbowl fervor.

When I pass the paper product aisle and see two women in a tug of war over an eight pack of Quilted Northern Ultra-Soft, I cross out the sporting event theory. What does toilet paper have to do with sports?

Then again, half the people in here probably have an Uncle Steve, or John, or Peter or whatever, who can't hold his booze and hot wings. Toilet paper must be in short supply, or nature produced an excess of Uncle Steves.

I watch the match for a moment, wondering if it will come to fisticuffs. It's like Tyson versus...whoever Tyson used to fight. I don't know. Can't hear what they're saying, but it's not hard to read their exaggerated lips, cussing with the energy of Hitler giving a speech.

"Go, Susan!" I shout, pumping a fist over my head.

Both women pause. Glare at me. Sneer in disgust. Then the smarter of the two uses the distraction to her advantage and yanks. Instead of pilfering the posterior-destined paper, she tears the package open. Rolls spill to the floor, skittering away like anthropomorphic hedgehogs staging a breakout.

"Scatter!" I say, giving a high-pitched voice to one of the fleeing rolls. When the two women forget each other and drop to their knees, I have a good chuckle and leave the aisle behind. Missy whisks me onward. I'm bopping when I round the corner into the last aisle in the store—home of eggs, dairy items, and bread.

I give the cart a little push and follow it, doing a jig, fists clenched in front of my chest, grooving to the music. I'm in the flow. Feeling the vibe and a little bit of the edible I had at lunch.

Then I open my eyes and see the shelves.

I feel like I'm in one of those movies, where the main character has seen something shocking, zooming in while the camera pulls back. *The vertigo effect.* That's what it's called. That's what's happening in my brain right now.

Because the bread aisle...is empty.

I laugh again, but this time like a man who's just discovered he's pregnant.

Everyone who smokes a joint, tokes a vape, or chokes on an edible gets their own particular kind of munchie craving. For some, it's anything crispy, salty, and fried. For others, it's fast food. For me, it's big, homemade sandwiches. Soft bread—any kind will do—stuffed with deli meat, pickles, lettuce, and enough mayo to make it look like an eviscerated éclair.

And I'm out of bread.

Because of Rich.

Fucking Rich. My mother's live-in boyfriend. She says he contributes to the family, but I'm pretty sure all he provides are various indefensible odors, toxic masculinity, and a vacuous hole into which all of the food *I pay for* is absorbed. The man eats with total disregard to his health and everyone else in the house—my mother, my sister, and the dog included.

What kind of monster would steal food from Sanchez? He's a four-pound chihuahua with a heart of gold. Granted, he doesn't really need to eat raw meat. He's as far from a wolf as any dog ever has been, but Mom insists. Problem is, that means he's sharing food with Rich, whose last name might as well be Hoover. Come to think of it, I don't know his last name.

Who cares?

My eyes flick from the aisle to a young man wearing a telltale red vest, which identifies him as an employee. One I've spoken to several times before. Brad. He's stocking jars of peanut butter at the far end. I pluck Missy from my ears, put the buds in my pocket, and launch down the aisle like a Viper attack fighter launching from *Battlestar Galactica*.

I scan the shelves as I roll toward Brad, my inner child growing nervous as I approach the end without spotting a single loaf, bun, or English muffin.

"Brad, my man," I say, sliding to a stop.

Brad is tall for a seventeen-year-old. He's what you might call a galumph. His spaghetti hair hangs partially in his eyes, and he's constantly flicking his head to the side to clear his view, which he does when I stop beside him.

"Oh," he says, tilting his chin up at me in greeting. "Hey, Miah."

My name is actually Nehemiah, but that's Biblical as hell, and I'm not. So, I make sure people call me Miah, which is at least a little cool. I'm named after a great, great, great grandfather, which, for the record, is a horrible way to pick a name for a modern-day child. It's not even retro. It's ancient.

Brad's brow furrows and he gives me a visual once over. Before I can wrap my head around the idea of grocery store Brad coming on to me, he adds, "Nice kilt."

"Nice...kilt?" I look down. My tight black skinny jeans are missing, replaced by my sister's yellow and brown plaid skirt. I try to hide my widening eyes by not looking up. *Holy shit.* The new edibles must be more potent. I search my memory for the events leading up to my grocery store venture and mostly come up blank.

What the hell else did I do today?

"Yes," I say, trying to act casual, like I meant to put on a damn skirt. "Turns out my family has a rich Scottish heritage. This is the Tartan of Edin...brodeen."

A lie obviously. My ancestors were Romani. Some would call us gypsies, but I grew up being taught the word was pejorative. Now, nothing much ruffles my feathers, but my extended family, whom we never see, finds the term offensive and derogatory. After all, it's a misnomer that grew from the belief that gypsies were from Egypt, when it's more likely they originated in India—not that you can tell from looking at us now. Fifteen hundred years migrating around Europe and mixing with various cultures has lightened our skin to a pleasant, non-threatening tan. I don't know a lot about the Romani people of my lineage, except that they must have been handsome.

I pause for a moment, focusing on the cool draft rolling away from the refrigerated side of the aisle and assessing its prickling on my skin. Yes...like the good faux Highlander that I am, I have gone commando, balls in the breeze.

I make a mental note to not impersonate an ice skater whilst riding the grocery cart—as I'm prone to do—and then I press forward to the important query.

"Pray tell, Bradley, where are all the breads?" I sweep my arm out to the empty shelves.

"Uhh," he says. "People bought them."

"Clearly," I say. "Why?"

"Happens sometimes. When people think something bad is coming."

"Something bad?"

"Like a storm. Blizzard or something. People buy bread, milk, meat, and toilet paper."

"No veggies?"

"This is New Hampshire."

"Mmm. Well, I don't suppose you have any loaves lingering in storage?"

He shakes his head. "Put them out this morning."

"When did the great loaf purge start?"

"Last night. People started coming in, buying enough food for weeks. I mean, we get folks like that on occasion. Families with eight kids or whatever. But some of the people coming in definitely don't have kids." He leans in close like the next part is a secret. "And they all seem squirrely."

"Squirrely..."

"You know. Like afraid."

"Afraid of what?"

He shrugs again. "Beats the hell out of me. But we'll be stocked up again in two days, and all of them will feel stupid for blowing their money on perishables."

I feign a laugh. "I know, right?"

"Hey..." He backhand swats my shoulder. "The bakery is tapped out too, but check the gluten free section. Over by the veggies. Could be the apocalypse tomorrow and no one would buy gluten free bread. Or vegan shit. Meat alternatives. Some of them are pretty good."

"With enough mayonnaise, anything can taste good."

He nods like I've just spoken an ancient truth.

"Well, thanks for your help, good sir." I tilt my head and roll my hand out. "My quest continues."

I stroll around the aisle's end feeling more nervous about what I've just learned than I'd ever admit. Missing bread is bad enough, but now I'm thinking that there's some kind of impending doom I should know about. I look around the store with new eyes. Some people are rushing, stuffing baskets full of food. But they're in the minority.

Like they know something the rest of us don't.

I pause by the toilet paper aisle. As with the bread, the TP is now completely gone. "Huh..." I scan the shelves stopping at boxes of Kleenex. Feeling paranoid, I pick up a box. "With lotion. That will feel nice on the tush."

I smile at the old woman standing beside me, and I carry on, finding gluten free bread—thank you Brad, you titan of grocery store knowledge—and faux deli meat made from pea protein and 'natural flavoring,' which I generally read as something like 'extract of dung beetle anal gland.' If it tastes good, I don't care where it came from. After collecting mayo, lettuce, and pickles, I head for the checkout, which is mobbed.

I slide to the end of the shortest line and nearly tune out the world. A flurry of motion draws my eyes to the checkout number eleven—the last in the line. My friend Laurie is there, waving me over like she's trying to put out a fire with her hands. I scoot out of line and roll to the end, steering my cart into the empty space between registers.

"Yo," I say, unloading groceries.

"Sup, bitch," she says. Laurie and I have never hung out. It'd be a little weird. She's not yet eighteen and I'm twenty-seven. We're kindred spirits separated by a decade.

"Dig the skirt," she says, recognizing it for what it is.

"I'm starting to, as well." I look back at the long lines and realize that Laurie didn't officially open her lane. The light is off. This is just for me. "Thanks for saving me from grocery purgatory."

"It's been nuts here all day," she says.

I nod. "Brad told me. You know what's going on?"

"People be cray-cray," she says, smiling. "They'll believe anything. Doesn't matter if it's bullshit or not."

"What bullshit are people believing?" I ask.

She leans over the register. Points to the magazines. "*That* kind of bullshit."

The first magazine features an airbrushed supermodel. I read the headline aloud, "Enhance your butt with—"

"Beneath that," Laurie says, ringing me up.

It's a tabloid paper. The front page reads:

THREE DAYS OF NIGHT STARTS ON THURSDAY!

Today is Wednesday. I take the tabloid and hand it to Laurie.

"You sure?" she asks.

"Toilet reading."

"Tik Tok is for the toilet," she says. "This..." she rings up the paper, "...is good for wiping your ass."

"Let's hope I don't need to resort to that."

She finishes ringing me up, bags my grub, and sends me on my way with, "Don't forget to trash bag your windows."

No idea what she's talking about, so I laugh, give her a wink, and head for the exit. I step out into the summer air, thankful again for the skirt. A steadying deep breath results in a lungful of Taco Bell, Burger King, and McDonald's scented air. My stomach awakens. I pop my earbuds back in, restart Missy Elliott, put one foot on the back of the cart, and launch myself through the lot with the skill of a Jamaican bobsledder, oblivious to the stream of people headed in the opposite direction.

2

You wouldn't know it from looking at me, or my old red Trans Am, but I live in McMansionville. The lawns and landscaping get the mani-pedi treatment once a week. The houses are equally nice and similar, but each with a different flair. Brick work here. Cobblestone driveway there. Granite posts in place of a fence. The only thing special about one of the houses is that it has a bright red door. That's it. But my mother comments on that damn door every time she passes it. The perfectly smooth street is like a catwalk, the best homes of ten years ago strutting their stuff, inciting envy in those who pass through.

I mostly feel disgust at the neighborhood. The people who live here are shallow and materialistic. The ecosystem that existed before we all showed up was pristine. And I'm stuck here, like a wolf in a trap, because I'm too emotionally weak to conquer my personal demons and escape.

Could also have something to do with being comfortable.

Because for all this neighborhood's faults, it's also pretty nice. Pools in the back yards. More than a few good-looking ladies with whom to flirt. And a total lack of outward strife...until you pass through my front door.

Then all bets are off. Could be fun. Could be quiet. Could be World War Three.

At night, the neighborhood looks like Christmas all year long. Not because people have decorated, but because the light posts are old school, sporting flickering bulbs like they're flame-lit—like this is London in the 1800s and the lamp posts are oil burning. And all the homes keep their outdoor lights on all the time. Heaven forbid you pass through in the dark and miss out on the modern art installation representing gluttony and repressed rage.

I might be a little bitter.

In part, because my stint in the Army opened my eyes to how people in other parts of the world really live, but also because my father paid for all this and didn't get to enjoy it.

Because he died.

No one's fault but his own. And genetics. Had a heart attack two months after we moved in, shortly after my eighteenth birthday. Life insurance paid off the house and supports my mother. Puts a roof over my head, too. Dad was good like that. An old school provider, even in death.

Rich showed up just a few months after Dad died. Quick enough that Allie and I thought Mom might have been cheating on our father before he kicked off. That's when I joined the Army and shipped out to solve my problems by avoiding them entirely. Thing is, I came home with more problems than when I left.

It's like that Alanis Morrissette song.

Ironic.

My eyes snap to two people walking in the street. For a moment, my heart flutters with anxiety, but then I remember where and when I am. Sidewalks line both sides, but most people here walk down the middle of the road. Bunch of extroverts looking for conversation. I'd normally roll up behind them, give a two fingered wave, and drive on by—most people here are uncomfortable talking to me anyway—but tonight is different. Because the two people in front of me are Jenny Gearhart and her younger sister, something-or-other Gearhart. Don't really care about her. She's fifteen. But Jenny. She's twenty-two, fresh out of college, and according to my online stalking efforts, available.

I slow down to match their pace. Manually roll down my window.

They turn to face me.

Jenny smiles. Her sister sneers like she's got dog shit smeared across her upper lip.

"Jenny," I say. "Salutations."

She lets out a laugh. "Anyone ever told you that you're weird?"

"Every day."

She shrugs. "Weird is good."

I've never had the chance to get to know Jenny very well. But she's got a streak of pink in her blonde hair, and just last week I learned that she went to art college, and I'm pretty sure weird is a prerequisite for people who spend their days drawing naked people.

"Jenny, can we go home now?" the sister says.

"In a minute, Emma."

Emma rolls her eyes and scuffs away, kicking an acorn that somehow survived the weekly detritus purge. Jenny leans her elbows on the car door. Tilts her face down. She's just a foot away now. Smells like coconut. Well, fake coconut. Fauxconut. It's intoxicating, mostly because it's coming from her.

She gives me a once over.

Doesn't even flinch when she sees the skirt.

"I knew it," I say.

She squints at me, waiting to hear the second half of my thought that I didn't actually mean to say out loud.

"You're weird, too."

She grins. "I'm not weird. I'm freaky. There's a difference."

"Is it too soon to profess my undying love?"

Her smile becomes a laugh. "You watching the meteor shower tonight?"

"Who isn't?" I lie. "Remind me. What time does it start?"

"3:00 am."

"Holy sh— Already have an alarm set."

She sees through me. How could she not? Only a madman would get up at three in the morning to watch little lights streak through the sky. But a very sane man—with significant emotional baggage—might take advantage of said light streaks to spend the wee hours of the night with Jenny. "You want to join me?"

"You have weed?" she asks.

"I'm wearing a skirt," I say, garnering another laugh. I really shouldn't share my prescribed medication, but it's 'use as needed.' No one will miss a gummy or two, and I've never shared them before. Never had the opportunity. Despite my outward charm, I'm something of a loner. Don't deal well with loss. My solution is to not be close to many people, but I'll make an exception for Jenny. "But...you're not just using me to get high, right?"

"Might be," she says, and I can't tell if she's joking.

I shrug. *Who gives a shit?* It'll be fun, either way. "How about 1:00 am? My yard. If we're found out by my family, I think they'd be relieved. But your dad is—"

"Scary. Tell me about it. He was a Marine, you know."

"Was he?"

"Killed a bunch of people, I think. Once said, I shit you not, 'You never feel more alive than when you take a life.'"

"That's...an interesting perspective."

"I'm agreeing with you, BTdubs. I don't want you dead. Yet." The threat is a joke, but she nearly slays me on the spot with that smile.

She reaches out and gives my chin a shake. "Tonight, then." She leans back, steps away from the vehicle, and gives me a wave.

Knowing when I'm dismissed, I waggle my fingers at her and drive away.

In the rear view, I watch her approach her now grumpy younger sister and attack her with tickles. Jenny might be a freak. Might be a pot-head, too. But she's definitely also a good person. If she actually shows up, I'll try to hide my surprise.

I pull into the driveway, still smiling. Including mine, there are now three cars—all of them outside. Rich doesn't let us use the garage during the summer months, because he likes to sit in the shade with his friends, sipping light beer and watching the neighbors walk by. Not that it makes a difference to me. I don't get to park in the garage even when mother nature barfs up a foot of snow.

Three cars means everyone is home. Which also means there could be drama ahead. If I wasn't planning on getting high with Jenny tonight, I'd chew a gummy now. The old stress-o-meter is approaching the red zone. I don't want to go in, but I've got food in need of refrigeration and a stomach still growling for mayonnaise and pickles.

I take a few deep breaths, heft my grocery bags, roll out of my personal trench, haul myself across the perfectly trimmed battlefield, approach the door, and enter enemy territory.

3

The front door opens silently to a two-story, cylindrical foyer with a chandelier, all sparkly and lit up behind the tall windows, announcing to the whole world: This house has shit to steal! Curved staircases on either side lead to the second floor, where three bedrooms are occupied by my mother and Rich, Allie, and a craft room.

By the time I finished a few tours of duty and decided a lifetime of emotional scarring wasn't the future I wanted, my room had become home to crochet needles, acrylic paint, and a thousand half-used hot glue sticks.

So now I reside on the first floor, above the basement level garage. The space is large, but unfinished. There's no closet. No nearby bathroom. No molding on the floors. At least they put in a cheap rug.

I should be grateful. They didn't need to let me move back in. I came home funny looking and emotionally damaged. But I pay my own way, and I try to stay out of theirs. When they let me.

The house is uncommonly quiet. I'm normally greeted by the scritch of tiny claws scrabbling over the hard wood floors, and high-pitched barking. Pretty sure Sanchez loves me the most. But I don't hear Sanchez. Don't hear reality TV blaring from the living room. And no one's fighting.

"Huh..." I kick off my shoes, place them by the door, and slide my way toward the kitchen. As I approach the back of the house, bags in hand, I hear the distant bass *whump* of music. Allie.

At least that's normal.

But it's not.

The thump isn't coming from the home's far end—the Allie wing. It's coming from right above me.

The lights flicker in time with the thumping.

"Oh my god," I say, realizing the nightmare that I've walked into is far worse than I'd feared.

Ear buds back in, I crank up the music and hurry to stow my wares in the fridge, shoving it all to the back, like a pirate hiding his booty. Then I pull half of it back out and make myself a towering sandwich, doing my best to ignore the hump-generated strobe effect in the recessed lighting.

Food once again hidden well enough to require a map to find, I pick up the sandwich and head for the double doors on the leather-furnished living room's far side.

A twitch of motion to my right sends a shiver up my spine. I nearly drop the food, as I yank a leg off the floor and lean away from the aberration, shouting, "Shit!"

When the small, brown creature flinches away from me, I know exactly what I'm looking at. "Sanchez. Man. What are you doing?"

He's curled up in his living room bed, which he generally uses only when someone is watching TV. He's as small and fragile as a gerbil and somehow aware of his own mortality. The dog is afraid of the sound his piss makes when it hits the pavement.

I lean down and talk like I'm speaking to a baby. "What are you doing by yourself, dude?"

The lights flicker.

"Ahh, right. There are worse horrors than loneliness, huh?"

He wags his curved vanilla stick of a tail, but he seems unsure.

I stand and tilt my head toward my room. "C'mon."

Sanchez lets out a snort as he springs to his feet and follows close by my side. He's usually a bullet. Bounding back and forth, yipping with the energy of a larger dog contained inside a stuffed animal. Now he's like a well-trained show dog, matching my pace.

"You're interested in the grub," I guess. "Don't worry, dude. You know I share."

I open the door, allow Sanchez to enter first, and then follow him inside, sealing us away from the evidence of Rich plowing my Mom. Both doors are windowed, top to bottom. I've tacked blankets over them, providing me a semblance of privacy. A sliding lock, poorly installed by me, keeps people from walking in on me at inopportune times.

I face the room, take a deep breath, and exhale the anxiety that comes with leaving my den. I put on a good show, but inside I'm jumping at sounds, twitching at chemical scents, and wishing my limbic system would take a damn break.

I've been to therapists, psychiatrists, naturopaths, and a few different neuro-whatevers. Each and every one of them has come to the same conclusion: 'It's all in your head.'

Not really. That's a coarse way to say it.

The limbic system is a network of brain structures. The thalamus, hippocampus, amygdala, and a few more. They're responsible for processing emotions. And sometimes, when they endure chronic stress—the kind that comes from being stationed in a forward operating base constantly under attack—physical and emotional symptoms can wire together. Couple that with the chronic Lyme disease I picked up last year, my neurology has been bitch-slapped into a permanently confused state. So now, when I'm overwhelmed by the world, I don't just feel it emotionally, I feel it physically, too.

Feeling anxious, Miah? Here's a huge dose of electricity running through your body. That helps, right? No? How about I make your skin so hyper aware that a gentle breeze makes you nauseous?

If my limbic system were a dude, I'd kick him in the nuts, stuff him in a box, and throw him from the Empire State Building. Then I'd rush to the bottom to laugh at his demise.

That's not how I'm supposed to think about it, though.

The limbic system has the emotional maturity of a three-year-old.

I laugh at the mental image of me kicking a three-year-old in the nuts. "The hell..."

I fall back in my lounge chair, ignoring the lumps of discarded clothing.

I'm going through this program. Honestly, it's beyond cheesy. Involves me talking to my imaginary toddler limbic system, cooing that everything's okay. To let it go. Calm down. I'm skeptical, but hopeful. Seems to be real science behind it. Logically it makes sense. I just wish there were a way to get there without doing laughter yoga...because good Lord.

I manage with the pot. Wish I could say it was just for fun. But it keeps me on this side of the fence, where life is worth living. The other side of the fence is a hundred-foot drop into the afterlife. Heaven or hell, it can't be as bad as constant nerve pain.

But I'm feeling okay now, safe in the den, featherweight dog on my lap, sandwich ready to be devoured. I break off a piece of the crust and hand it to Sanchez. He chomps down, but then looks confused.

"That good, huh?" I say, and I take a bite of my own.

At first, it's a confusing mash of flavors and textures. Then the mayo and pickles kick in, and I don't give a shit about the rest. Sanchez and I collectively shrug off the newness of this food and chow down in silence.

Ten minutes later, the munchies that were powerful enough to pull me from my cave have been satiated. I lean back in the chair, gently petting Sanchez, who's curled up on my belly.

Might as well get in some mental work, I tell myself. In addition to having conversations with the malfunctioning part of my mind, I'm also supposed to recall past events where I was happy and healthy, and then envision future events where I am once again free of PTSD and its effects. I generally struggle with this bit. The happier the memory, the greater my sense of loss. I'm supposed to come out of it feeling better. I usually just cry.

How the hell did I ever make it through boot camp? I'm a fragile flower now, smoking pot, wearing skirts, and giving pep talks to pretend baby me.

Screw it.

Eyes closed, I drift to the past.

It's summer. Like now. Blue sky. Fluffy cumulus clouds in the distance. Green pine forest everywhere. I'm in the Berkshires of Massachusetts. At a summer camp. Thirty kids are gathered at the base of a long, sloping hill, where cut grass meets a sandy beach.

I don't know the pond's name. Might not even have one. All I really know about it is that no one swims in these waters—because leeches. But we take canoe lessons here, and today we're partaking in a team race involving two rowboats. Each team needs to row out and around a buoy and then come back. The trick is, two different people are rowing. With practice, coordinating such a feat would be simple, but to seven thirteen-year-olds who met just days ago, it's chaos.

Both teams shove off, the four rowers putting everything they have into it. It's clear, from the get-go, that our team is in trouble. Even when the girl and boy rowing my boat are in sync, he still out-powers her. For every stroke of his, she needs three to compensate.

We're halfway to the buoy as the other team begins rounding theirs.

This is unacceptable.

I don't like losing, especially when I'm a passenger.

But who says I have to be a passenger?

I shout back to the counselor overseeing the race, "Do we have to stay in the boat?"

She smiles back at me like she's proud, like the three days she's known me have shaped me in a way she can claim partial responsibility for. Thing is, this is who I've always been.

I've got a collection of trophies and blue ribbons at home.

Not because I love competition. Or sports.

Losing just doesn't agree with me.

"No!" she shouts back.

Without a second thought about leeches, or drowning, or snapping turtles, I hurl myself into the water, clasp on to the back of the boat, and kick like a human motor. Instantly, we're on track, and gaining. Seeing that it can be done, I put everything I've got into it, imagining my legs moving faster than is possible, the same way I do when crushing sprints.

We pass the competition before they can fully round the buoy. Seeing us take the lead has thrown them into disarray. Inspired, two of my teammates join me in the water, kicking hard. With a considerable amount of the boat's weight now in the water, we cruise toward shore, leaving the other team floundering by the buoy, even as a few of their team jump into the water and kick.

We reach the shore in record time.

My heart pounds.

Breathing is difficult.

My legs are numb. I make it three steps and fall to the ground.

It feels like death.

But I'm smiling.

I'm alive.

And I'm desperate to feel like that again.

My eyes snap open. I'm tense. Ready for a fight.

On my stomach, Sanchez growls.

Something woke me up.

My nerves awaken. Pain crawls up my arms and digs its talons into my back.

And then my phone blares the *Stranger Things* theme song. Love the show, but the theme song as a ringtone hits my nerves wrong every time. I never remember to change it, though, because no one ever calls me. I pick up the phone.

It's two in the morning.

Two. In. The...

Jenny...

I'm late!

I answer the phone. "Coming!" And then I hang up.

Sanchez isn't happy about being uprooted, but he's back on the chair, enjoying the warmth left behind by my body. Barely notices me open the sliding door to the back deck. I slip into the pitch-dark night and whisper, "Jenny?"

The hissed, "Above you..." that follows strikes me like a full body attack on the funny bone.

4

I fall to the deck in a conflagration of nerve pain.

When Jenny starts laughing, I'm glad that it's too dark to see the look on my face.

"Hot damn," I say, trying to sound fun, despite my overreaction. "Be still my beating heart."

I look up. She's standing above me. High above me. A silhouette against the night sky. "Are you..."

"On the roof," she says. "Yeah."

Distraction dulls my nerves. The funny thing about nerve pain is that if you forget about it—one way or another—it fades. Sometimes it goes away completely, without medicinal aid. "How did you—" I see the ladder before I finish the question. "Did you bring the ladder or was it already here?"

"Here. Geez. So many questions."

I let out a laugh. It carries my nervous energy away.

"Now, get your ass up here." She waves me up and backs away from the edge.

I haven't used a ladder since I was thirteen. Not for lack of need. Things always need climbing when you're a teenager. I stopped using them out of fear. A friend from back in the day found himself locked out of his house. Rather than wait, he decided to climb a ladder to a second story window. When he reached the top, the base slipped over his driveway. He and the ladder fell fifteen feet to the ground, where the ladder bounced up and collided with his chin, leaving him an unconscious, bloody mess. I didn't see it happen, but the visualization of that event was enough to turn me away from climbing ladders any higher than I can jump.

But for Jenny...

I'll make an exception.

And hopefully get to the top without feeling panic's cold grip.

Jenny's humming calls to me like a siren. Two steps into my climb, I forget about my fear. It comes back three rungs later, when I reach the top and somehow need to transition from ladder to roof.

I know it's possible. It's just not something I've ever done before.

Bullshit, I tell myself.

I used to climb from the fence at our old house to the roof of the shed, which stood at the precipice of a twenty-foot drop. All to win at a game of manhunt. This is nothing. The worst-case scenario outcome is that I'll somehow embarrass myself.

Leg hoisted to the shingle roof, I lift with both arms and one leg, rising up more easily than I'd imagined. I roll over onto my butt and stop just short of pumping a fist in victory.

Weird is good. Corny...probably not.

It's strange how life changes. I wouldn't have seen any significance in this during my younger years. Now it's a major victory, worthy of telling my therapist about.

I smile at Jenny, wondering how many victories are in store tonight. Then my foot slips, striking the ladder and knocking it to the deck with a rattling crash. I freeze, muscles locked, ears primed, searching for signs of movement inside the house.

When I'm sure no one is coming to inspect, I give Jenny a thumbs up and shuffle closer, stopping when I notice she's got a blanket spread out, which is great because I'm still free balling in a skirt, and shingle tar probably chafes like a sonuvabitch.

"Hey," I say, sitting beside her.

"That was slick," she says.

I shrug. "It's a lot of work to be this cool."

"That skirt have pockets, or did you forget something?"

"Forget..."

Shit. The pot.

I pat my sides and feel a lump. "Aha!" I pull out the emergency Zip-loc bag of edibles I keep with me at all times, even though I'm really not supposed to carry it around. Just knowing it's there eases my nerves. "Pockets indeed."

She holds out her hand.

"Straight to the point, huh?"

"I'm not a fan of foreplay."

I swallow. "Nor I."

"Also, I want it to be in full effect by the time the light show starts."

She might not admit it, but I think Jenny is a closet nerd. There's a slim chance she's partially here for me. She's definitely got a hankering for the pot. But the main attraction for her is actually what's going to happen in the sky. A quick yank and a shake drops a gummy into my hand. I place it in hers.

"Just one?"

"One is definitely enough, and you'll feel it quicker than three jiffies and a jig or two."

She inspects the gummy. "I have no idea what that means."

"I'm sure no one does." I deposit a single gummy in my hand. "Bon appétit."

We place the gummies in our mouths and chew.

"Mmm," she says. "This doesn't even taste like weed."

"Nothing but the best for you," I say, smacking on the flavor. "Watermelon."

"I think mine is apple," she says, crushing the little pot leaf shaped gummy between her teeth.

We lie back on the blanket, looking up at the night sky, which isn't as impressive as I'd like it to be, mostly because, despite being the wee hours of the morning, the neighborhood is still on display. As if the creatures who lurk in the night might stop to appreciate the trappings of the American Dream. Hell, if we want a nice view of the night sky, we can put on the Discovery Channel.

The next hour is spent laughing, joking, and loudly shushing each other lest we be discovered. I'm not sure what we're afraid of. I mean, yeah, we're not really supposed to be on the roof. And I'm not supposed to share my dope. But we're looking at stars.

No harm, no foul.

The real danger is Jenny's father, Beefcake McMurderMarine. So, there's that. But he's currently snoozing, ten houses down the road. If she can sneak back into her house, then we should be...hold on.

Jenny is an adult.

One would think she can come and go as she pleases.

I can.

But then I'm not daddy's little girl all grown up.

Stop, I tell myself. Part of PTSD is obsessing about things. Aches and pains, fears, the future, the past, whatever keeps the limbic system feeding its trauma loop. *Stop.*

I'm about to repeat the inner command again when Jenny's hand rests on my wrist, disintegrating the fledgling fixation. "It's starting!"

A streak of light cuts through the sky.

I'm not sure what I was expecting. Not a whole lot. But something about the light strikes a chord with my ancient reptilian brain, unleashing a sense of wonder. Of not being alone. Of a higher power.

Might also be the pot.

I settle in for the light show, and for the next hour, we watch the sky in silence.

Jenny's hand never leaves my arm.

This...is bliss.

All my fears forgotten. All my pain some distant memory.

I am whole again.

The full Moon creeps higher into the night sky, further obscuring the meteor shower with its brightness.

"Go away, Moon," I say. "You big, glorious ball of reflected light."

"Do you think Buzz Aldrin peed on the Moon?"

I laugh. "Like full on whipped it out? Wouldn't his dick have frozen off? Oh my god, does Buzz Aldrin have no dick?"

"Oh... Oh God..." After a tirade of snickering, she says, "I mean, like, they must have worn space diapers or something, right?"

"Or pissed before they went out," I point out. It's obvious, but less fun.

"I guess."

I stand and pretend to urinate.

"One small dick, one giant piss for mankind."

We laugh loud enough that anyone awake would definitely hear us.

I'm still laughing when I sit back down, but Jenny is not.

I turn to her, smitten by her personality now as much as I was by her good looks earlier. Her upturned face is lit by the Moon.

This is it. The right moment to transition into something more. I inch closer, eyes locked on hers, which are locked on the Moon.

Her face begins to dim. *A cloud,* I think. Soon there will be nothing left to distract us from—

"Miah."

"Yes," I say, sounding a little breathy.

"The Moon."

Begrudgingly, I turn to the sky once more. A dark circle is sliding across the bright face. "A meteor shower *and* an eclipse?"

She shakes her head. "You'd think it would have been front page news."

"You'd think," I repeat. "Guess we just got lucky."

She snuggles up close. "Very."

As the Earth's shadow blots out the Moon, the meteor shower grows in intensity. White streaks become orange. It's dazzling, and we fall silent once more. I can't remember ever feeling more content. So much so, that I slowly drift off to sleep.

5

I wake up feeling a mixture of physical pain and emotional bliss. Jenny is snuggled up against my chest. Somehow, my arm is around her. But...the rooftop is not a bed. My back is stiff, and she groans as I shift just a little bit.

The Moon is gone, having slid out of the Earth's shadow and plummeted behind the horizon. But the stars are bright, and I take a moment to appreciate the night sky. The meteor shower is over, too, but a sense of connectivity to something greater lingers. I feel miniscule, but not insignificant.

Through my early morning bliss, a message from my subconscious arrives, urging me to run through my morning routine.

Too early, I tell it.

A pang in my bladder sides with my subconscious.

As does a rumbling in my stomach.

I didn't fall asleep until somewhere around 4am, which isn't uncommon for me, but I don't normally feel like this until 10am, when the sun is already shining. And since the sun rises around 6am right now, this must be closer to five. If it weren't for the uncomfortable roof, I'd have slept through the morning.

One way to find out.

Careful to not jostle Jenny, I dig into my pocket, extract my phone, and lift it up. I tap the button at the bottom, and the screen comes to life, showing the time.

"What the hell?" I say, rousing Jenny.

"What's wrong?" she asks, sleep softening her voice. If I said nothing, she'd probably nod back off.

"My phone is messed up. Is it daylight savings or something?"

She stretches and sighs. "That was back in March, dummy."

"Then my phone set itself to England time."

"What time does it say?" she asks.

"Eleven. In the morning."

Her eyes open, brows curled up in worry until she sees the night sky. She sits up, arms supporting her. "Yeah, your phone must be borked."

"Is that even a word? Borked?"

"Also, you need a new phone." She takes my caseless, cracked Android phone—I'm not really sure what model it is—and slathers it with disdain oozing from her eyeballs. "This thing is a doorstop."

She pulls out her phone. The newest iPhone. It's like a sparkling gem compared to mine, but it's the custom case that catches my attention. I take the phone from her, looking at the back rather than the front. The image is surreal and dark, like if Salvador Dalí and H.R. Giger collaborated. Six dark eyes glare out of the gloom, clawed hands grasping the sides of a wooden doorframe. It's sinister and beautiful. "Is...is this your work?"

"You like it?" she asks.

"It's frikkin' amazing. Why aren't you famous yet?"

"Working on it." Her voice carries enough weight to say that the life of an artist probably isn't all sexy and easy. She's young, and new. Despite being talented, she still needs to pound the pavement or whatever cliché artists do when they're working hard. Squeeze the tube? Brush the...brush. I don't know.

I flip the phone over and the screen winks to life, looking for Jenny's face. It only sees me, so it displays the time.

11:01am.

"Umm." I hold the phone up for Jenny to see.

She takes the phone, unlocks it, and flicks through a series of menus and options, the weight of what she's finding tugging her smile into a frown. "What the... This can't be..." She looks at the sky again. "Which way is east?"

I hitch a thumb over my shoulder to the rooftop's far side. "The coast is that-a way." And then I understand what she's really asking.

If it's eleven in the morning, where is the damn sun?

We stand together and climb to the roof's pinnacle.

"I uh... Okay..." Words escape me. I've seen a lot of shit. Dead friends. Limbs lying on the ground like they were forgotten by someone in a hurry. People living in bombed out homes. But nothing the U.S. Military has done in its long history has ever filled me with as much shock and awe. Even my limbic system doesn't know what to do with what I'm seeing.

"This is insane," Jenny says.

"That... Yeah."

The night sky stretches out before us—except for where the sun should be. That part of the sky is blotted out.

"Solar eclipse?" I guess.

"The day after a meteor shower and a lunar eclipse?" Jenny is dubious. "And no one was talking about it?"

"Then this is some real Biblical shit," I say. "Seven plagues and all that."

She has no idea what I'm talking about, which is too bad, because I've just exhausted the depth of my knowledge on day turning to night.

"What I mean," I say, "is that this is supernatural. Like a God thing."

"You *believe* in God?"

"Well, I've been debating the subject for the last few seconds, and I find myself woefully unprepared for an event of this magnitude."

"Yeah," she says, "but I don't think it's a God thing."

Before I can ask why, she points to the horizon. A wavering orange glow stretches from North to South as far as I can see. "Looks like fire."

"Which makes this more of a Devil thing."

My limbic system understands that. The nerves in my elbows light up. Had I been wearing a long sleeve shirt, it would have become intolerable.

"Someone must be talking about this," she says, swiping open her phone.

I do the same with mine.

While she heads for social media, I look for actual news. Ten seconds later, she announces, "Nothing is loading. The cell network must be down."

I scan the neighborhood like I'll see some kind of evidence to support her conclusion. What I do see is a fully lit neighborhood that is uncommonly active. People are out of their houses, looking at the sky. Some, like us, have taken to the rooftops for a clear view past the trees.

"Power but no cell network..." I check my news feed, but the loading icon is just spinning. A quick glance in the phone's upper right-hand corner tells me why. "No WiFi, either."

"I should get home," Jenny says, sounding worried.

I nod and head for the roof's edge. When I reach it and look down, I remember our predicament: The ladder is lying on the deck. The only obvious option is to slide down onto the deck railing, but it's unsteady. We need the ladder. And that means we need help.

"Could we jump it?" Jenny asks, beside me, looking down.

"If you're a ninja," I say. "It's not going to kill you, but it looks like a leg breaker to me. Given our current circumstances—" I glance back to where the sun should be, but isn't. "—I think mobility is important." I hold up a finger. "I have an idea."

I tiptoe across the roof to the home's far end and lie down on my stomach. I inch toward the edge, feeling the pull of gravity inside my head. "Whoa..." I have second, third, and fourth thoughts about this until Jenny takes hold of my ankles.

"I got you," she says. "Also, dude, no underwear?"

I suddenly feel the cool night air washing across my backside, fully exposed. "Just don't take a picture," I say, and I slide my head over the edge.

I've got an upside-down view of my sister's window, which is, as usual, open. She's not a fan of air conditioning. Says the freon is making people sterile.

"Allie," I say. "Are you home?"

I hear her sigh, stomp across the room, and open her door. A moment later, she grumbles, closes the door, and flops back into her bed, saying, "Dick."

"My dearest sister, I'm not at the door."

"The hell?" she says, scooting over to the window. She looks down. "Miah?"

"Up here," I say, garnering a yelp of surprise.

"Miah, what the hell?"

"Alas, I am a damsel in distress."

"Two damsels," Jenny says.

Allie's surprised face is easy to see inside her well-lit room. I'm probably a dark blob against a dark sky to her. "Who's up there with you? Is that Jen?"

"Hi, Allie," Jenny says.

"You two know each other?" I ask, and then to Jenny, I ask, "Wait, do you prefer Jen?"

"No one has called me Jenny since I was ten. Except you. But I like it. It's cute. And yes, we know each other. She's my sister's friend."

"Huh." I look back to Allie's confused face. "What do you say? Give your brother a hand?"

"You know what's going on?" she asks, like it's a prerequisite to getting rescued. "We don't have WiFi. No cable, either. Or phone. Only thing that's working is the radio, and that's mostly just static."

"Haven't the foggiest," I say. "Just woke up."

"You were sleeping? On the roof?" A smile blossoms. "With *Jen?*"

I grin and give my eyebrows a double tap. "I know, right?"

"What do you need me to do?" she asks, on mission now.

"There's a ladder on my back deck. Just stand it back up." She ducks back from her window.

"Wait, wait, wait," I call.

She reappears. "My bedroom door is locked. You'll need to use the deck stairs."

She looks out into the daytime night, unsure.

"It's like thirty steps from the back door to the top of the deck. You'll be done in a jiffy."

She sighs.

"Fine."

Then she's gone.

Her thumping footsteps move through the house below. Jenny... *Jen*...helps me back to my feet, and we scurry our way back across the roof. I'm not sure why we're sneaking. Allie is going to tell everyone she can, starting with Mom and Rich, but I'd prefer that happens after Jen has left.

As we near the garage roof, a bright light to my left makes me trip. I lose my footing for a step. Then Jen grasps hold of my shoulders, steadying me.

"My hero," I say, turning. Her face is lit in orange light. We look into each other's eyes for a moment, lost, and then we both notice that we're illuminated in orange.

"The sun," I say. We face east together.

A ball of light, miles across, is frozen on the horizon like a rising sun that isn't the sun at all.

Jen takes my hand. Squeezes. Whispers, "Miah..."

The ladder slaps against the gutter behind us, making both of us jump. Gripping each other, we hurry down the sloped roof. "Go," I say. "Go, go, go."

6

"What the fuck was that?" I ask myself. "What *was* that?" I slide over the roof, dangling my feet toward the ladder. The shingles cling to my skirt, hiking it up as I lower myself down. "Oh! Oh, geez." I inchworm my way down, careful not to drag my man bits over the rough surface.

If I wasn't afraid that the ball of light might expand and envelop us all, I'd find another way to do this. But getting off the rooftop feels more important than preserving what little dignity I have left.

I pause before hoisting myself fully onto the ladder. "Sister?"

"I have a name," she grumbles.

"Allie, best you avert your eyes."

"I can't see shit out here. Wait, are you not wearing pants?"

"Indeed," I say, and I make my move, lifting myself up over the ladder, placing my feet on the top rung. I climb halfway down, steady myself, and reach a hand up to Jen. "My lady..."

"I appreciate the chivalry," she says. "But just...get out of the way."

I hop off the ladder and step to the side. What took me nearly a minute of grunting she does in seconds, sliding onto the ladder, stepping down three rungs, and then hopping off.

"Well, don't I feel like a wimp," I say.

"About time you realized it," Allie says.

Jen remains silent. She's barely here. While I was worrying about scraping my nether regions, she was concerned for her family.

"Seriously?" Allie says, noticing her skirt.

"I don't know how it happened...but I kind of like it."

She sighs. Allie puts up a grumpy younger sister front, but she's actually okay with my eccentricities. And while Mom and Rich don't want to hear why I am like I am, Allie listens. And she puts up with a lot.

"I'll walk you home," I say to Jen. "Just...hold on."

I open the sliding door and enter my bedroom. I'm greeting by a yipping bark and the smell of dog shit. And piss.

"Sanchez!" I say, crouching down to the little guy as he approaches, both excited by my return and apologetic that he couldn't contain his tiny bowels. "It's okay, buddy. My fault."

I pick his quivering body up in one arm and then head to my dresser. The top drawer contains the detritus of my life, pre-military. Batteries. Action figures. Nemesis cards. And a pair of unused walkie-talkies, courtesy of my father, with whom I never got to use them. It takes a moment to slide batteries in one handed, but I get the job done, pick them up, and head back outside where—

—Allie is climbing down the ladder. She's stunned. Has tears in her eyes. Meets mine.

I shake my head. "I don't know what it is. Just...stay inside. I'll be back soon." I hand Sanchez to her. "And if you feel like being benevolent, he dropped a deuce somewhere in my room."

Allie rolls her eyes, but heads for the door.

I hand Jen one of the walkies. "Just in case. If the radio is working, this should let us talk between houses. You know, in case there's an emergency."

"Thanks," she says, all of her good humor now gone. She pockets the device and heads for the stairs. We move around the house together and emerge on the front lawn, bathed in the light of American excess.

The neighborhood is buzzing with energy. At first, it seems strange, this many people being out in the middle of the night.

But it's not night.

It's approaching noon.

I turn my head skyward. A splotch of empty blackness, covering a patch of sky four times larger than the sun, looks back at me. I feel the weight of it, crushing down on me.

Nothing will ever be the same.

I reach out and take Jen's hand. She accepts it. Squeezes tight.

Neighbors that I recognize but don't know, stand in their yards. In the street. All of them looking east, where the sky glows a sinister orange. All of them afraid for their lives but drawn to the mystery of it.

I try to ignore it all. Lest I get obsessed. Last thing I need is to get fixated on something for which there is no answer. Better to spend the time I have left living, whether that's forty minutes or forty years.

Easier said than done when everyone I see is staring at the same thing. And for once, it's not me.

I look at Jen instead.

Her eyes are locked on our hidden destination, like she can see though the towering homes and trees to her house.

"I'm sure they're fine," I say. "Your family."

She nods. "Dad will keep them locked down. I'm just...I feel bad about not being there. He's probably freaking out about me."

We walk in silence, following the sidewalk's slow uphill curve. It occurs to me that we'd have a better view of what's happening to the east from the roof of her house. Not only is it three stories tall, but it's also at the neighborhood's peak. Can probably see the ocean from up there.

Apprehension slips into my muscles, each step closer to Jen's house harder than the previous. These are not the ideal circumstances to meet your...hookup's parents. I have high hopes that it will be more than a surreal, possibly end-times hookup that didn't go very far—but worried parents won't see it like that.

I'm the guy who endangered their little girl.

I'm the asshole who gave her drugs.

Who probably defiled (but didn't) their baby.

"Jen!" The voice booms.

It's Rambo-Dad.

He's a gorilla of a man dressed in shorts, a tank top, and a tactical vest. An AK-47 rifle hangs over his back. There's enough body hair protruding from his arms and neck to classify as a forest. But...he doesn't look scary.

He looks...scared.

Jen's hand slips from mine as she races toward her father. I'm tempted to turn tail and run, but that wouldn't be right.

"I am calm and capable in any situation," I whisper to myself. "I am calm and capable..." I suck in a deep breath, fending off lightheadedness. "...in any situation."

I stand awkwardly nearby, wondering if Jen will forget about me, but knowing her father definitely won't. Before the hug comes to a conclusion, his cold blue eyes open and drift in my direction.

My nervous smile does nothing to placate his grim visage.

He leans up and away from his daughter, focusing on me like a bird of prey. I half expect him to unfurl wings, the feathers patterned like glaring eyes.

If my attire has any effect on his opinion of me, negative or positive, he doesn't show it.

Instead, he says, "You're the Gray boy."

I nod. "Yes, sir."

"You served, right?"

"U.S. Army."

I expect an eyeroll or a grunt of disgust, but he surprises me with an affirming nod. Like he's pleased to hear it.

"How many tours?"

"Three."

"You see action?"

"I was stationed in the Helmand Province."

That tidbit slips through a chink in his armor. He softens. "You lost people?"

I nod. "Most of them."

He approaches me, somehow shedding everything about him that's terrifying. Puts a meaty hand on my shoulder. "Most people couldn't wade through the shit you did and come out clean on the other side. Your body might be okay, but for you, the wounds are up here, yeah?" He taps my head.

I don't reply.

The big galoot is going to make me cry.

"I get that, and it's all good. Men who are twice the soldier you are—or I am—have been broken by less. You standing here while all this..." He looks to the east. "...is going on? You should be proud."

I smile.

Never thought of it like that.

His face darkens again. Back to business. "You have a firearm?"

"No, sir."

"What can you handle?"

"Anything," I say, and it's true. There isn't a weapon I haven't fired.

"Glad to hear it." He slips the AK-47 over his shoulder and holds it out to me like he's presenting the reformed longsword, Andúril, to Aragorn after the high council at Rivendell.

Obviously, I accept. The weapon's ten pounds are made heavier by my past. I try to hide it, slinging the weapon over my shoulder. Three magazines appear in his hands, offered to me.

"Don't you—"

"He's got an arsenal inside the house," Jen says. "Never know when the Russians might invade, right?"

It's a joke, but Dad doesn't hear it. He just looks east again, grim.

Is that what this is? An invasion? Does Jen's father know something we don't? He's retired military, but maybe he still knows active-duty people.

I take the magazines and move to load them in my pockets, but then remember I'm wearing a skirt rather than my usual cargo shorts. Dad notices. Grimaces.

"Change when you get home," he says, and I sense I'm being dismissed. "Not that I mind, but strategically... You know."

"Mind...what?" The question slips out, as the thought springs from my head.

He claps my shoulder. "You being gay. Now go home, protect your family. If trouble finds you and it's more than you can handle, come find me."

He nudges me along. Gets me walking down the sidewalk back the way I came, befuddled and amused. I survived that encounter because Papa Bear believed I was more interested in him than in his daughter. Good on him for being tolerant, but what's he going to do when he finds out the truth?

At least I now have an AK-47 to defend myself.

I glance back as I leave, and I catch a glimpse of Jen waving goodbye. I do the same, and I continue my brief downhill journey as the light to the east grows brighter still.

Halfway home the pine scented forest surrounding the immaculate neighborhood is invaded by something new.

An odor.

I take several quick sniffs like a dog. No idea if it helps people smell things better, but the new scent is impossible to miss.

Sulfur.

7

I quicken my pace for a few steps, until my heart starts racing. Out of fear. Not exertion. My legs slow. And then stop. I lean forward, hands on knees, willing myself to calm down. To keep moving.

I don't know what the hell is happening but outside feels unsafe. Could be the smell. Could be the slowly building light on the horizon.

Something rustles in the woods to my left.

It's nothing uncommon. This is New Hampshire. Eighty percent of the state is forested. And every inch of that terrain not maintained by human hands is covered in layers upon layers of leaves, twigs, fallen branches, and deceased trees, all of it slowly transmogrifying into soil.

Unless you've got wings, it's impossible to move through the trees without making a racket. In the still night, even a mouse is easy to hear.

I'm probably hearing a squirrel. *Are squirrels nocturnal?* I see them running around all day, but that doesn't mean they're not scooting around at night. The owls gotta eat something. Doesn't matter. The sound is moving away, and with it, my anxiety—

A branch in the woods across the street snaps, crushed under the foot of something heavy.

My breath catches.

Pin pricks of electricity race up my spine and flare out through my arms, crackling inside my fingers.

A shadow emerges. It's a mirage of a monster, there and not.

And then it lumbers into the flickering streetlight.

A black bear.

Its dark body heaves with frantic energy, froth dangling from its mouth, falling away as the beast huffs.

It's rabid, I think, willing myself to run, but unable to overcome the fear locking me in place.

Then I notice the look in the bear's eyes as it crosses the street toward me. Some people think animals don't have emotions. Anyone who owns a dog knows otherwise. Reading the look in the bear's eyes is easy.

It's terrified.

The heavy breath and tendrils of drool aren't signs of mania—the animal is exhausted.

How long has it been running?

And from what?

As the bear passes me, just a few feet away, we make eye contact. In that moment, we are connected.

Why are you just standing there? I hear him ask with his eyes. *Run, fool, run!*

And then, he's gone, crashing through the woods to my left.

While people are terrified of black bears, they're generally skittish. If you happen to see one, it's usually their backside as they dash away. But there was something primal about this bear. It didn't have the look of a predator in its eyes.

It looked like *prey.*

A rumbling slowly turns my eyes back across the street to the dark woods. Sounds like a train. Or an avalanche. A strange kind of energy fills the air.

"Run," I tell myself, managing to lift a single leg.

Instinct tells me it's too late. My jackhammering panic isn't going to let me move.

So, I need to fight.

Stand my ground.

If I know how to do anything, it's that.

I slide the AK-47 off my back, chamber a round, and turn to face the forest on the street's far side.

Slow down, I tell myself, slipping a finger around the trigger.

Training takes over. My breathing smooths out. Muscles stop quivering. I've been here before, facing down the rumble of impending death, gun in hand.

Branches snap. A chorus of snorting chimes in. It's like a thunderstorm, contained within the trees.

I look down the sight, weapon tight against my shoulder.

And then, it emerges.

They emerge.

Deer. Hundreds of them. They're as panicked as the bear, but faster and more chaotic. I maintain my aim. The deer swerve around me, re-entering the forest at my back, but if one of them doesn't see me, I'll have to drop it. Getting trampled by a Bambi stampede is not how I want to die.

The storm passes as quickly as it arrived.

The rumble fades as night and forest consume the herd.

The rifle's weight tugs my aim down.

I take a breath.

And then I laugh.

"Holy shit, guy!" shouts a man from one of the two homes directly across the street from my house. I don't know much about him other than he's new to the neighborhood, his license plates are from Massachusetts, and his accent says he grew up in or around 'Bahstin.' I think his name is Danny... Danny Patton maybe? Or is it Danny Cannon? I don't know. One of those two.

I stand, feeling the strange kind of exhilaration that comes from a brush with death.

"You almost got run ovah by a hehrd of frickin' deah, bro."

I laugh again, this time at the man's accent. There are few things more entertaining than an excited Bostonian.

"Yeah," I manage to say, slinging the AK back over my shoulder, and then I decide to mess with the city boy. "It happens."

He's confused. "It does?"

"Welcome to New Hampshire." Free of panic's grip, I give a wave and resume my journey.

Five steps later, adrenaline starts to wear off and fear creeps back in, bringing with it a host of questions. *Were the deer chasing the bear?* I don't think so. They seemed equally scared shitless. *Was something chasing the deer?* I don't think so. It didn't feel like that either.

It was more like an evacuation.

Like they're fleeing the area. Not a specific threat.

I pause and look east to the glowing sky, then straight up to the starless void where the sun should now be.

What do they know that we don't?

Whatever is happening, I don't think we can outrun it.

Further ahead, beyond my house, a smaller herd of deer sprints across the street, disappearing into the woods.

I look west. The sky is dark. As far as I can see, anyway. Most of my view is blocked by trees. But I don't see a distant glow. *What's west?* Barrington. Northwood. Eventually Concord. A lot of empty space and trees. I'm not sure how being in any of those places would be better than Dover.

The god damn sun is blotted out.

Whatever is happening here... It's happening there.

Happening everywhere.

I trudge across the lawn toward the front porch, and I'm surprised to find Allie, Mom, and Rich standing together, eyes east.

Rich notices me first. Double takes on my face. "You okay?" He sounds genuinely concerned.

"Never better." I feign a smile.

"Miah!" Mom runs down the steps. "Where have you been?"

"On the roof," Allie says. "With Jen."

Mom throws her arms around me. Squeezes me tight. The last time she hugged me was when I came home from the military for good. Before that, it was the day I shipped out. She's not an affectionate person unless she's shaken. She feels small in my arms. Skinny. Fragile. Her curly black hair tickles my cheek. I feel like I could hurt her if I squeezed too hard, but I return the embrace until she flinches back, looking over my shoulder.

"Is that a gun?" she asks. Mom is opposed to guns of any kind. Probably because she's a Californian import to New Hampshire. Most people here either own a gun or don't mind them—unless they're originally from some other part of the world.

Rich is a Granite Stater through and through. Looks more interested in what I'm carrying than afraid.

"I just walked Jen home," I say, as Rich inspects the weapon. "Her father gave it to me."

"Why?" my mother asks.

"In case that—" I point east, "is an invasion."

Her eyes go wide. "An invasion? From whom?"

"Russia," Rich says, like he knows, like he's part of some ultra-secret cabal that knows all the world's secrets. "North Korea. China. Hell, it's probably all of them. Venezuela and Cuba, too."

"None of those countries know how to block out the sun," I point out.

"It's Harvard, then," he says.

"Harvard?" I ask. "Like the school?"

Rich nods. "They have scientists there. Working on ways to block out the sun. Geo...geoengineering or something. To reflect sunlight. Control the Earth's temperature. Because of global warming. It *has* been hot."

Amazingly, this crackpot theory is a little less insane than invading Russkies from the Mother Country. But it doesn't explain the light on the horizon, or the media blackout, or the freaked-out animals.

Or the smell.

Something is coming, and it's not an invading country, or Harvard scientists.

"I think I know what it is," Allie says. She's on the top step, Sanchez in her arms, still looking east.

"What?" Rich asks, with the kind of machismo that insinuates a teenage girl couldn't possibly solve two plus two, never mind decipher what the hell is happening in the world.

She looks him in the eyes, defiant, and then addresses me.

"I *know* what this is."

8

Back inside the house, Allie storms into *my* room, of all places.

"Allie," I say, apprehensive. There's a long list of secreted items hidden in my room that would be rather embarrassing should they be brought into the light of day, or the non-light of day as it is now. "There's nothing in there that could—"

She emerges, holding the tabloid paper I bought from the grocery store.

"Oh. Carry on."

Allie joins us around the kitchen's granite island. Slaps the paper down.

Rich must only see the publication's title because he instantly scoffs, waves his hand, and turns away to fetch a beer from the fridge.

But Mom sees the headline. Same as I did in the grocery store.

"Three Days of Darkness," I say, eyes widening. "They knew. How could anyone know about this?"

"It's a prophecy," Allie says. "It's an esch... an escha-something-logical."

"Eschatological?" Rich asks, holding his unopened lite brew.

Allie nods. "Yeah. That."

"You know what that is?" I ask. Despite Rich's know-it-all attitude, he rarely speaks with actual authority on anything beyond the Patriots, Red Sox, Celtics, or Bruins.

"It's Catholic," he says. "End of the world stuff. Like Revelation. But not part of the Bible. It's more like...personal revelations. You know, to saints and priests and nuns. That kind of thing."

"So, run of the mill superstition." I say.

He takes offense at that. "Catholicism is *not* superstition."

Rich was raised Catholic. Still attends mass on occasion, but I've noticed these visits tend to coincide with holidays, playoff games, and Super Bowls. For him to know anything about this weirdness suggests that, once upon a time, it meant more to him than it does now.

"Anyway," Allie says, "there was this nun. Anna Something…"

"We need to work on your reading comprehension, Sis," I say.

She flips me off. Mom pushes her hand back down without taking her eyes off the paper. "Anna Maria Taigi. Listen. 'There shall come over the whole Earth an intense darkness lasting three days and three nights.'"

"That's like Jesus, right?" Allie says. "When he died. Three days in the grave."

"That's right," Rich says. I can see his mind searching for some greater significance so he can share it with us.

"Just…" Mom takes a deep breath, closes her eyes, and calms herself. She usually just lets her anger loose. This is different. She's terrified. "Everyone shut up and let me finish reading this."

We fall silent and wait.

She picks up the paper and continues. "Nothing can be seen, and the air will be laden with pestilence, which will claim mainly, but not only, the enemies of religion. It will be impossible to use any man-made lighting during this darkness, except blessed candles. He, who out of curiosity, opens his window to look out, or leaves his home, will fall dead on the spot. During these three days, people should remain in their homes, pray the Rosary, and beg God for mercy. All the enemies of the Church, whether known or unknown, will perish over the whole Earth during that universal darkness, with the exception of a few, whom God will soon convert. The air shall be infected by demons, who will appear under all sorts of hideous forms."

She lays the paper down. "This can't be real, right?"

"But it's dark out," Rich says. "In the middle of the afternoon."

"I was outside," I say. "We were all outside. And we're still alive. It's paranoid horseshit."

"There's another bit," Allie says.

She's nervous. Falling for the whole thing like all the toilet paper pilferers at the grocery store.

Mom speed reads a little bit, tracing her finger along the lines of text. There're a few images included with the article. A wood carving depicting demons chasing people through the woods. A pen and ink drawing with a mishmash of religious symbols, including a pentagram and a goat skull.

"This is from another woman. Marie-Julie Jahenny. She was a stigmatist."

"That means she had the wounds of Jesus on her—" Rich starts.

"We all watched Stigmata last Halloween," I point out.

Mom ignores us, distilling the article's revelation. "She said the three days of darkness would take place on a Thursday...Friday and Saturday."

"Today is Thursday," Rich says.

"Thank you, oh wise font of knowledge," I say.

"*Miah,*" Mom grumbles. Then she returns to the tabloid. "During these trying days, people should only light their homes with candles of pure beeswax, blessed by a priest because...the gates of hell will be opened on Earth."

Allie throws up her hands. "Who the hell has a three-day supply of blessed beeswax candles?"

She's buying it.

They all are.

I think I might be, too. But...

"Still horseshit. Obviously, something is going on that the editors of this paper knew about and are taking advantage of. To scare people. To sell papers. For all we know, they invested in blessed beeswax candles."

"C'mon," Rich says.

"I'm just saying, this is all explainable without conjuring demons. What happened to the Harvard scientists? Maybe there was some kind of solar storm, and the government did something to prevent us from baking? Solar radiation might explain interference with cell networks and WiFi. Maybe the damn magnetic pole is shifting. That happens. And I didn't read about it in a tabloid. This isn't the middle ages." I look each of them in the eyes, challenging them to disagree. "We've evolved beyond superstition. Boogeymen and the Devil? Give me a break. The scariest, most horrible thing on this planet is other people. Also—" I lift my hand toward the halo of recessed lighting above us. "—the power is still on."

They look up at the lights like they need to confirm this fact for themselves. After a moment, they all settle down a bit, shoulders relaxing.

Mom sits down, still looking at the tabloid. "But so many other things fit..."

"Does it say what we should do?" Rich asks, still a newly converted true believer. "Beyond the candles. I mean, are we just supposed to stay here?"

"The alternative is falling dead on the spot, right?" I'm joking, but Rich nods.

"That's right."

"We need to cover the windows," Allie says. "Look." She points to a side panel article with instructions on how to cover your windows. There's a drawing of a person tacking blankets up over the windows. "Says you can cover the windows with blankets, tarps..."

"Trash bags," I say, recalling Laurie's parting words.

"Yeah," Allie says. "We should do it, right? Just to be sure? You know, in case—"

"You know what," I say. "If it will make you feel better, I'll help you do it."

Allie smiles with relief.

"But we're all going to feel stupid when the sun comes back out and we don't know, because we're too afraid to look out past our trash bags."

"Better stupid than dead," Rich says.

"In the 'feeling stupid' scenario, all of this is B.S. and no one dies," I point out.

"In the 'this is real' scenario," Rich counters, "you feel stupid while you die. I'd rather be wrong and feel dumb living, than wrong and feel dumb dying."

I smile. "That...actually makes sense." I clap my hands together and give them a vigorous rub, like a lumberjack about to pick up an axe and fell a tree with one mighty swing.

I point to Rich, "Trash bags and tarps."

I point to Allie. "Blankets. Thick ones no one is using."

"It's summer," she says. "I'm not using any blankets."

I point to Mom. She doesn't notice. She's just staring at the tabloid, picking at her fingers like she does when we talk about Dad. "Mom." She doesn't hear me. "*Mom.*"

She flinches. Looks me in the eyes. "We need tacks. You have tacks, right? Up in the craft emporium?"

She nods, slowly, like she's on her deathbed. Then she looks me in the eyes and says, "Thanks. I know this must be hard for you. Because—"

She motions to my body. She knows all about the emotion/pain connection.

"Actually," I say. "I'm doing okay. Now *vámonos*. Let's go!"

The group disperses, everyone on task without realizing that I didn't give myself a job. I leave with the same urgency, though, entering my room, closing and locking the door behind me. Hands shaking, I open my prescription pill bottle, do a quick count, and drop a gummy into my mouth. I sit down in my recliner, close my eyes, breathe in, and let the marijuana dissolve under my tongue where it is rapidly absorbed by my system.

Calming down, I turn my mind to the problem I'll face in two days' time.

It's not the devil or hell. If I can't somehow get a refill, I'll be out of gummies on Saturday, even if I ration them carefully.

That's what I get for sharing.

For now, I let my mind and body relax, repeating my neuro retraining steps in my mind. "I'm calm and capable. I'm calm and capable."

Then the power goes out.

9

I stand in the pitch dark, like nocturnal prey trying to stay still despite my pounding heart.

It's just a power outage, I tell myself. They happen all the time. This is totally normal.

I inhale for four seconds, hold it, and exhale for five, mimicking the ancient Japanese meditation technique created by some monk or wise man or whatever they have in Japan. All I remember is the number of seconds. Everyone has their own version. Four seconds. Five seconds. They all do the same thing.

And none of them work.

"Miah!" It's Allie. She sounds panicked. That she's calling for me instead of my mother puts a weird kind of pressure on me. Like I'm somehow responsible for her. I suppose I did put myself into a leadership position. I did give everyone orders. And they listened.

But that doesn't mean I'm in charge.

"Miah!" she calls again.

"In my room!" I shout, flicking on my phone, glad to see that it still works. Basking in the glow of electric light, my brain chugs back to life.

What was I doing in here?

Right. Pot. Mission accomplished.

Knowing I've already taken a hit allows me to calm down. My limbic system will be wrangled into submission and I'll feel back to my normal self soon.

A warbling light moves through the kitchen, headed in my direction. "I got the blankets," Allie says.

You've been through worse.

You're still alive.

Suck it up and get it done.

I stand up tall and squelch my fear for my sister's sake, and I join her in the kitchen. "We'll need them for the big windows."

Mom returns from the second floor, a plastic case full of tacks jangling with each step. As we reconvene around the kitchen island, our cumulative phone lights illuminate the space.

"Here," Mom says, still looking a bit dazed by everything. "Tacks."

A staple gun slides onto the island. "Got this, too," Rich says, emerging from the dark without the assistance of a phone light. "Thought it might be faster and more secure." He places two boxes of black trash bags and a roll of duct tape beside the stapler.

I don't say it aloud, but Rich's haul is enough to keep nuclear fallout at bay. Has he secretly been preparing for something like this? Would be nice if he had some food stored away, now that everything in the fridge will be thawed out and spoiling within 24 hours.

He motions to the hallway behind him. "Tarp is still in the garage. We can use it to cover the foyer window."

Holy shit. I forgot about the massive foyer window.

"But," he says. "I can't find the ladder."

"It's on the back deck," Allie says.

"Why is it—"

I point to the ceiling. "Roof, remember? I'll get it."

"Are you sure you should go outside?" Mom asks.

"Hasn't been fifteen minutes since we came in," I point out.

She crosses her arms. "The power wasn't out then. Things are different now."

She's not wrong. The ladder is just to the side of the sliding door, but I'm terrified to retrieve it.

It's nothing, I tell myself again. Paranoid bullshit spun by a tabloid paper trying to make people freak out over something that is strange... but probably harmless. "I'll get it," I repeat, more for myself than for her, and I head back into my bedroom.

When I pause at the door, I'm surprised to find Allie by my side.

In response to my confused glance, she says, "I'm staying with you."

"Why in the world would you do something like that? I'm a mess, Sis."

"You've done this before," she says.

I take hold of the sliding door handle. "Pretty sure this is a first for everyone."

"You know what I mean. You're...here, despite. I'd be in a padded cell if I'd seen what you did. If I survived it. But you..." She smiles. "You're badass. Dad would be proud."

And just like that, there are tears in my eyes. I wipe them with the back of my hand. "Stop," I say. "I won't be able to do this fast if my eyes are blurry."

"Just... We stay together, okay?"

I nod, sniff back my emotions, and count down. "Three...two...one!"

With a quick yank, I nearly pull my arm from its socket. For a moment, I think the door is supernaturally sealed. Then Allie says, "Shit! I locked it earlier."

A quick twist unlocks the door. Then I give it a slow tug. All of my frenetic energy was spent on the first failed attempt. This time, I'm going for stealth. I mean, even if hell has been let loose on Earth, there're still rules, right? There can't be enough demons to cover every inch of the Earth's surface. And I'm pretty sure they lack traditionally God-like attributes, like omnipresence and omniscience. One guy opening a sliding door in the McMansioned backwoods of small-town New Hampshire shouldn't be noticed.

Shouldn't.

Then again, the prophecy was pretty clear. He, who out of curiosity, opens his window to look out, or leaves his home, will fall dead on the spot.

The door slides open. Just enough for my head to slide through. I lean out into the warm night. Everything seems normal, ignoring the fact that it's still lunch time. Insects chirp. Wind hisses through the trees. It's peaceful.

Until I breathe through my nose and get a whiff of sulfur.

It's more potent now. Makes my nose scrunch up. The stench helps me overcome my fear. I slide out onto the porch, pull the ladder away from the roof, and then maneuver it down and around so I can carry its eight-foot length through the door and—

The ladder bumps a chair behind me, knocking its back legs over the staircase leading to the yard. I listen in abject horror as the aluminum chair thunders down the steps. Each thump hits my body like the recoil of a rifle, until the chair lands in the grass at the bottom and silence returns to the darkness.

I stand frozen. Listening. Waiting for demonic doom to swoop from the starry sky.

But nothing happens.

"C'mon!" Allie says from the door. If she's waving me on, I can't see her. She's got her phone light aimed at my eyes. When I squint and scrunch my face up, she lowers it. Following the green dot now floating in my vision, I guide the ladder into my room, safe once more within its musky confines.

Allie closes the door behind me. Locks it. "Did you see anything out there? Or hear anything unusual?"

"Aside from the chair harumphing down the stairs?"

"I don't think 'harumphing' means what you think it—"

"To grumpily express dissatisfaction or disapproval," I say. "I'd say the chair was displeased at being knocked down the steps during a supernatural apocalypse, wouldn't you?"

The green spot in my vision hides her face, but I'm sure she's rolling her eyes.

"Now then," I say, "Onward."

We return to the kitchen with our prize to find Mom pulling shades and Rich stapling trash bags over the windows. "Think it's good?" he asks me.

The question forces me to reassess Rich. He's always been a thorn in my side. A cheap replacement for the original. But his desire to please me, the son of his partner, is on full display. Or maybe that's not it. Maybe...he sees me as an equal? A fellow adult?

I had honestly never considered that. Because for most of my time with Rich, I have been a screw up. Well, maybe not a screw up, but *screwed up.*

"Perfecto," I say, like I know. Like the military gave us secret training on how to combat the armies of hell and their farty air.

"Mom and I will start on the windows," Allie says, taking the initiative. "You guys hit the foyer."

"The matriarch has spoken," I say, and I head for the foyer with the ladder. Mom doesn't say anything. Doesn't remark about the matriarch comment. Just keeps bustling around, drawing shades.

"Should have gotten curtains," she says.

"Bed, Bath & Beyond has light blocking curtains, but I don't think they have the Beelzebub-proof variety," I say, hoping for a smile, but I get nothing. She's in shock. Which is understandable. The human mind doesn't always deal well with Earth-shattering new paradigms of existence, like prawn-cocktail flavored potato chips or Baconnaise.

Rich follows me to the foyer. We stop in front of the door, looking up at the large window, ten feet above us.

"So high..." I say.

Rich extends the ladder and leans it up against the wall to the side of the window. Holds the staple gun and the corner of the tarp out to me. "Up you go."

"Me?"

"Whoever stays at the bottom needs to keep the ladder steady. And keep it from slipping. I've got, what, seventy-five pounds on you?"

He has a point. "Fine. Just...don't drop me."

"Son," he says, "if you get hurt, and I could have prevented it, this three-days-of-darkness bullshit will be the least of my worries."

I take the staple gun and the tarp, heading up the ladder without saying another word, not because I no longer object, but because I don't know how to respond to Rich calling me 'Son.'

"So," Rich says, "'Beelzebub.' Isn't that like from a Queen song?"

"Uh, yeah. 'Bohemian Rhapsody.'"

"Riiight. *Wayne's World.*"

I pause on the ladder, close my eyes, and sigh. "Yes. What about it?"

"Why did you say it?"

I continue my upward journey. "It's one of Satan's names. Abaddon. Apollyon. Mephistopheles. I like that one. Mephi*stoph*eles."

Aww, shit. This is not the best time for the gummy I ate to take full effect. Then again, it's probably the only reason I agreed to scale to the summit of Mount Foyer.

"I played a lot of Diablo when I was young. Man, I miss that game. Timmy the Great. That's the name I used when I—"

"Miah," Rich says. "Are you high?"

I look to the floor. "Uncomfortably so."

He sighs.

Both of us know that's not what he meant.

"Just keep it steady." I lean out, position the corner of the tarp above the window, and staple it in place. "*Diablo* is also a name for the devil, by the way. *En Español.* Of course, my knowledge is limited to video games, so unless you can conjure up chain lightning, or you have a bundle of topaz gems lying around—"

"Miah..."

"Yep?"

"Just finish up."

I attempt a salute, but I just manage to crack the stapler into my forehead. It hurts, but it centers me a little bit. Leaning out a little farther, I place the stapler against the tarp, ready to pull the trigger.

But I stop.

I have a clear view of the empty street below. Of the house across the street and the neighbors still on the roof. And beyond them, the glowing horizon, as it billows up and out, racing toward us!

"Brace for impact!" I shout, like we're the crew of the *Enterprise*.

For a moment, the house is lit up the same as it is every morning when the rising sun hits it. Then it's too bright. A spiraling surge of energy roils through the wall, through my body, and then through my thoughts.

I feel myself fall.

But not hit the floor.

10

I wake on the floor, head propped up on something pliant, yet firm. Like a ham. I open my eyes to a view of the foyer window and the night sky beyond. Stars twinkle. The bright light is gone.

Maybe it's all over?

Nah. If it were, the Sun would be out. Unless I've been unconscious all day. Without sitting up, I dig into my pocket, pull out my phone, and tap the power button.

Nothing.

It's dead.

For a moment, I think I must have been lying here long enough for the battery to drain. But without me actually using it, that should have taken days. And...I'm still high. And in pain from the fall. If my head had landed on the floor instead of whatever is beneath me, I'd probably still be unconscious.

The cushion beneath me shifts.

Rich groans. "The hell happened?"

I sit up and turn around. Eyes already adjusted to the starlit dark, I'm able to make out Rich's sprawled form behind me.

"Were you lying on my ass?" he asks.

"Your cushy glutes might have saved my life," I say.

"Wonderful." He pushes himself up. "Laci, you okay?"

When my mother doesn't reply, I stumble to my feet and follow Rich to the kitchen, keeping a hand on the wall for stability. Farther away from the starlit foyer, I can't see a thing. "Mom?"

"Laci!" Rich shout-whispers.

I cup a hand to my mouth, but I'm not sure why. It's not going to amplify my whisper—or mute it. "Allie?"

My sister grunts. "Miah?"

I stumble toward her voice. Each step is pensive, leg searching like a blind man's cane. I don't want to step on her. "Where are you?"

"Hallway," she says, sounding more like herself. "What happened?"

"Bright light," I say.

"So descriptive."

"Only thing I saw, Sis." My foot thumps against her. "Reach your hand up."

I reach down blindly, waving my hand through the air until it thumps against hers. It takes a few more seconds of searching, but then we grasp hold of each other, and I pull her up.

"You find Mom?" I call back to the kitchen.

"She's on the floor," Rich says. Sounds worried. Maybe even choked up.

I don't bother asking for more information. I don't think Rich is knowledgeable enough or in the right headspace to give me an accurate report on Mom's well-being. There's panic in his voice, and it wounds me. Not out of worry, but because I've resented him for so long, I never really paid attention to how much he loves her.

And she him.

I kneel down beside my mother. She's on her back between the kitchen island and the sink. I find her arm with my hands, following it up to her face. Give her a few pats. "Mom. Wake up."

No response. I check her pulse, ignoring the buried battlefield memories trying to rise to the surface. Her pulse is steady and strong. "She's okay," I declare. "Just taking longer to—"

Mom gasps awake fast enough to send me sprawling back in surprise.

"Rich!" she shouts.

"I'm here," he says, cooing. "I'm here."

"We're all here," I say. "All okay."

"What happened?" she asks.

I shrug like they can see it. "The question without an answer persists ad infinitum."

"I don't know what that means, Miah," she says. "Speak plain English for once."

"We don't know what happened," Allie says.

"But the light on the horizon is out," I say. "And I'm pretty sure other sources of artificial light no longer work."

I can hear them all digging out their phones.

"Shit," Rich says.

"Damnit." Allie slaps her phone down on the counter, abandoning the device like it has betrayed her. Then there is a flicking sound, coupled with a faint burst of light.

A *lighter,* I think, and then Allie's face emerges in the darkness.

"No!" Rich shouts. He reaches out for the lighter, but he falls far short. The light extinguishes like he smothered it in a meaty hand. "Not until the windows are covered."

I hate to say it, but I do, "He's right."

"Miah..." Allie sounds concerned. She should be, and not just because the last of this household's skeptics is now on board with the whole Three Days of Darkness malarky. So far, everything that's happened has been covered by that prophecy. I'm still holding out hope for an innocuous scientific explanation, but I think we should prepare for the worst...

Hell on Earth.

And that means sealing this place up.

"Allie, get back to the windows," I say. "Mom, are you okay to help?"

"Fine," she says, standing with a little help from Rich. Mom isn't the kind of person that lets people see fragility. She's more likely to rip you a new one than show you she's hurt. And we all know to let it be, lest we summon her emotional wrath.

"Just...everyone take it slow and easy." I'm uncomfortable giving orders still, but they're listening, so I don't stop. "No lights, and no looking out the windows, right?"

"That's right," Rich says. "What about the foyer?"

I sigh. The big-ass foyer window.

"Same as before. You hold, I'll climb. Just keep that safety ass ready in case I fall again."

Mom takes hold of my arm. "You fell from the ladder? Are you hurt?"

"Everything hurts a little," I say. "But I'm okay."

Everything always hurts a little. Sometimes a lot. And I'm far from fine, but we need to get the job done, ASAP.

"C'mon. Let's do this."

Allie huffs a laugh. "You know how corny that was, right?"

"Indeed," I say, and we shuffle back to work in the darkness.

What should have been a nerve-wracking, but quick job of tacking a tarp over a window, becomes an hour-long ordeal. Climbing and descending a ladder in the dark, holding a staple gun, is not as hard as it sounds. It's *harder*. For me at least. At first, it helped that I couldn't see the floor.

Then my imagination kicked in. I started hearing sounds that weren't there. Seeing demons in the shadows. On one occasion, Rich's throaty breathing convinced me that he'd become a zombie. Then he cleared his throat.

Despite my request that no one look out the windows, I break the guideline every time I ascend and descend. I don't see anything noteworthy aside from darkness. The house across the street is a vague shape drowning in the dark forest, itself just a silhouette against the starry sky. If the neighbors are still on the roof, I can't see them.

Maybe they're stuck. Unable to climb down in the pitch black.

Not my problem, I decide, and I punch the final staple into the wall, fully sealing off the massive window. It's darker than ever inside the foyer now. I climb down the ladder like a traumatized sloth, hooking my arms around each rung, carefully placing my feet before lowering myself.

"Done!" Allie proclaims from some distant part of the second floor. A moment later, she's coming down the steps, one at a time, hand squeaking over the railing as she holds on tight. "Every damn window in the house is covered. It's going to get hot and stinky up in this joint."

Her energy makes me smile. Hell, the whole family is pulling through this with mostly positive attitudes. Despite the whole demons-roaming-free thing, the past few hours have been somewhat groundbreaking.

"I have candles." Mom's in the kitchen, rummaging through drawers. Her footsteps head for the dining room, where a few heavy objects are placed on the table, followed by the whisk of a match being struck.

Mom lights a candle. Tall and white.

"Sure you want to do that?" Rich asks, entering the dining room. He uses the meager light source to inspect the recently trash-bagged windows. "Pretty sure those aren't blessed or beeswax."

Mom waves him off and motions to the seven other white candles and two red ones lying on the table. "They're advent candles. For Christmas and Jesus and all that. Linda Harper gave them to me. I don't remember why, but I figure this is close as we're going to get to blessed candles. And I'll be damned if I'm going to sit in a pitch-black house for the next three odd days. Plus—" She motions to the windows. "How would anything outside know there's a candle lit?"

It's a solid point.

But it still makes me nervous.

"Just one, though," Allie says, sitting at the table with Mom. "Okay?"

"Fine," Mom says.

Rich takes a seat next to her. Puts his hand on hers. "We'll get through this. Whatever it is."

Wanting to be part of whatever familial bonding is happening here, I take a seat at the table's far end, close enough to absorb the good vibes, but distant enough to flee, should things take the all-too-familiar tangential path into an argument.

"Thank you, Miah," Mom says, sounding uncommonly and genuinely appreciative. "For…" Her eyes flick from mine to my forehead. That's when I notice Allie and Rich staring at me, too.

"What?" I ask. "Is there blood?" Did I bump my head when I fell? If so, the pot is working double time to dull the pain. All I feel is a weird kind of itch…on my forehead.

I rub the spot. Stings like a sunburn, but it isn't too bad.

The looks on their faces say otherwise. "What?" I ask. "What is it?"

Allie stands without a word and heads for the bathroom. She fumbles around in the dark for a moment and then returns, small mirror in hand. She moves the candle closer to me and hands over the mirror.

Face lit in flickering light, I lean down and inspect my forehead, eyes widening. "What. The fuck. Is that?"

11

"Did someone draw on me while I was knocked out?"

It's not a serious question, but Rich answers, "Hey, I was beneath you."

I lean closer to the mirror and get a good look at the symbol that appears to have been burned onto my skin at the center of my forehead. Two downward angled lines extend out of a central, vertical line. Looks a little bit like a crude spaceship, but it feels...evil.

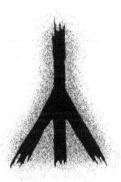

Vertigo effect again. Big time. I rub my finger over the mark, but it just hurts. I squish my forehead, wrinkling it, hoping that this is a sticker or a temporary tattoo that can be peeled off. Both are stupid ideas. Tattoos and stickers don't just spontaneously materialize on people. Then again, neither do weird burned-on symbols. Whatever it is, it's either there to stay, or it's going to take days to heal.

"When did it happen?" Mom asks, serious, like her heritage includes a Holmes or two rather than a series of nomadic fortune tellers.

"When I was on the ladder," I say. "Must have been."

"When the light outside got bright," Rich adds. "Right before we all hit the floor."

"The light hit you." It's not a question. Mom is declaring it. A logical deduction. She looks me in the eyes, abandons the Holmes routine, and dives headfirst into Romani superstition. "You've been marked."

"C'mon," I say. "What does that even mean?"

"You looked out the window," Mom says. Folds her fingers together. Waits for a reply.

"It was kind of hard not to," I say, starting to feel unsettled because superstition is supposed to not make sense. But I see where Mom is going with this, and I don't have a rebuttal.

Mom shakes her head, eyes tearing up.

A key portion of the prophecy flits back through my mind.

'He, who out of curiosity, opens his window to look out, or leaves his home, will fall dead on the spot.'

"Well, bright side, I'm still alive. The prophecy said I'd drop dead on the spot, but I'm still here, still breathing." I take a deep breath to prove it. "So, I think there's some wiggle room."

"Maybe it means you're as good as dead," Rich says.

I hang my head. "Thank you...Rich. Your contribution is spot on, as usual."

"What?" He's defensive now. "That's a thing. A mark of death. The black spot."

A laugh pops out, too loud given the current situation. "The black spot is Muppet Treasure Island. Don't get me wrong, it's a dandy of a movie, but that's about puppets, and this is reality."

"Miah..." Allie sounds apologetic. "He might be right."

"Really?" I ask.

"At least in some ways," she says. "It's a mark. A symbol. And it wasn't made by any of us. Also...I'm pretty sure it's an upside-down cross."

Rich leans forward, squinting at my forehead until his eyes open wide. "Ho-lee shit. You're right."

"It's not a cross," I say, studying the shape.

Allie retrieves a piece of paper and a pencil. Starts sketching. "We learned this in school last year. In a history class. The teacher was hung up on religion. Thought he would blow our minds by showing us that the Christian cross everyone uses is wrong." She turns the page around so I can see the crude drawing.

"This is what a Roman cross looked like. Kind of like a Y but with a line up the middle. I don't know. My teacher could have been full of shit, but this is what he showed us."

"It's an upside-down peace symbol," I say. "Without the circle. The irony..."

"But look." She spins the page around again, letting me see the upside-down cross. And she's right. That's exactly what's on my forehead.

"But it could also be a peace symbol..."

"Really?" Rich is dubious. "This is a Catholic prophecy. Demons let loose on Earth. And that just mysteriously appears on your head when you break one of the prophetic rules? Miah, that's not a peace symbol."

"It's not a cross, either." Mom's glare cuts through us all. "It's a rune."

"A rune," I say. "As in Thor and Asgard and all that? Oh, I like the Rainbow Bridge."

"A Nordic rune, yes." She takes the page and the pencil, filling in Allie's drawing. She holds it so we can see, the cross upright once more, fleshed out now.

"This is Algiz. The life rune. It is a blessing. Warriors would tattoo it on their bodies or have it emblazoned on their armor. For protection."

Rich looks confused. Downright suspicious. "Why do you know all this?"

Mom rolls her eyes. "I didn't raise my kids Romani. Doesn't mean I wasn't. When you roam all of Europe for generations, you pick up a few things along the way. Beliefs. Symbols. Myths. It becomes part of a collective whole."

Rich sighs. That he's uncomfortable with this means Mom has been hiding a part of herself from him. Her past. Her heritage. Her upbringing. But is that because she's ashamed, or because he wouldn't like it? Or understand it? Dad was Romani, but like me, he wasn't steeped in it. But he would have understood the history and the beliefs, judgement free. Rich...maybe not.

"This..." Mom turns the symbol upside-down again. "...is Yr. The opposite of Algiz."

"Death," I say.

Mom nods. "The entrance to the underworld."

We sit in silence, the dreadful information percolating. If this were a tattoo picked up at a mom-and-pop parlor downtown, I'd find the symbolism interesting, if not cool. Maybe not on my forehead, but I like that a symbol could mean life or death depending on its orientation.

But not now.

Not like this.

"So," I say, "I'll just stand on my head from now on."

It's a joke, but Mom doesn't see the humor.

"The rune is aligned with your body. Your head is up. Your feet are down. Doesn't matter how you position yourself."

Silence resumes. And then, an epiphany. I get up and take the candle with me, making a quick stop in the kitchen before heading for the bathroom.

"Hey," Rich says, just starting to object.

Mom stops him with a hand on his arm. "Give him a minute."

I stand in the bathroom, hands clutching the countertop, eyes closed. I slow my breathing, recite a calming mantra in my head, and let the marijuana in my system help even me out. I haven't lost my mind yet, so it must be working.

Or maybe I *have* lost my mind.

Maybe I'm in a padded cell somewhere, lost in a nightmare, crushed in a perpetual straitjacket hug.

Wouldn't that be wonderful?

Until I wake up in that blissful place, I'm stuck here, hell all around, and the symbol of death etched on my forehead.

"Not for long," I whisper, pulling the Sharpie cap and going to work. Five minutes later, I'm done. I've drawn a circle around the Yr, and outlined the symbol, transforming it into a modern-day peace symbol.

I leave the bathroom and guide myself through the house with the candle, imagining myself some ancient monk, moving through the catacombs. Then I'm back at the table, seated and facing the others.

Allie smirks.

Mom isn't impressed.

Rich...is mystified. "Do you think that will work? Maybe that could work?"

"Definitely won't work." Allie is all but laughing now, somehow finding the humor in my eventual demise.

I laugh with her, relieved that I didn't drop dead a la the prophecy. Which gives me a little bit of hope, because maybe Mom is wrong. Maybe this symbol means something totally different to whoever—or whatever—put it there?

"Hello?" The crackling voice booms louder than our hushed voices have been since we woke up. I flail back in fright, nerves firing every which way. My chair tips. I fall back, shouting, "Martha Stewart on a motor scooter!"

I slam to the floor, coughing the air from my lungs.

"Ohh," I groan. "I'm so done with falling over."

The others gather round, looking down at me, not one of them concerned for my well-being.

"What was that voice?" Rich asks. "It came from you. Hello?" Great, and now Rich is speaking to the mysterious voice. "Can you hear me?"

Mom silences Rich with a swat.

"Miah, are you there?" The voice crackles again, but this time it's recognizable—

Rich gasps. "*It knows his name.*"

—to some of us.

I dig into my pocket and pull out the walkie talkie. Looks dead, but I think the viewscreen light just isn't working. I hold the transmit button. "Jen! Jen. I'm here. Are you okay?"

She comes back a moment later, clearer, but somehow still distorted. "I'm here..."

Not distorted. She's crying.

"Jen, are you okay?" I ask again.

"I think..." She sniffs. Clears her throat. "I think Dad is dead."

12

"Where are you?" I ask Jen.

The radio crackles. "I-in my room."

"Who else is in the house?"

"Mom," she says. "And Emma."

"Jen," my voice is unintentionally deadly serious. "Have you covered your windows?"

"Covered the windows?"

She doesn't know about the prophecy. "This is going to sound stupid. It's going to sound completely crazy. But you need to cover your windows with anything you can find. Draw the shades and curtains, and then cover it all with blankets. Trash bags. Whatever. Every single window. And...don't look outside."

"Dad's outside," she says.

I hold the radio for a moment, unsure how to handle this. Then I ask, "Why did he go outside?"

"We heard something. Moaning. Like someone was hurt. In the woods. Dad went to check. A few minutes later, we heard him shout. Like in pain. Nothing since. I think he's—"

"You don't know anything for sure, though." I lock eyes with Mom at the table's far end. She looks as grim as I feel. We definitely drank from the apocalyptic prophecy punch bowl.

Allie places her hand on my arm. "If you tell her the truth, she'll freak."

"She's *already* freaking," I say. "Already thinks her dad is dead."

Allie speaks through gritted teeth. "Because he probably is."

I consider her point-of-view and find it lacking. Mercy in this situation will just hurt more in the long run. "If I don't tell her, they could *all* die."

Allie withdraws her hand from my arm, shrugging away her responsibility should anything happen as a result.

"Are you there?" Jen asks.

"I'm here. Just...do what I told you. And don't open your door for anyone that isn't your dad."

"Why? How do you know what to do?"

"I'll explain it when you're done," I say. "The longer you wait, the more danger you and your family are in. I know it sounds nuts, but I wouldn't bullshit you about this. Our house is already sealed up."

"O-okay. I guess." Her voice fades as she shouts something to her mother about covering the windows. There's an indiscernible back and forth and then she returns. "We're going to do that now. Miah..."

"Yeah..."

"If you see or hear my father..."

"I'll do everything I can," I say, and I mean it. Realistically, I might not be able to do much for anyone outside this house without risking the lives of everyone in it. But if Mr. Gearhart turns up at my door, I won't send him away. "Let me know when you're done, okay? The radio is on."

I don't remember turning it on. Must have already been on when I put in the batteries. Had I known, I would have made contact sooner.

She sniffs back tears. I wish I could be with her. Comfort her. We only spent a few hours together, but the connection is real. "I will."

Static.

I put the radio down. It weighs a ton.

How many people don't know what's going on? Out there, roaming the streets, looking at the sky, making fart jokes about the smell? They have no idea what's happening. What's coming.

Rich stands up from the table. "Be right back."

Mom leans back to watch him walk down the hall. "What are you doing, Hun?"

The hallway is illuminated by a flickering orange light. Rich has a lighter. Probably the 'aim and flame' he uses for grilling. "Just give me a minute."

The garage door opens and closes. I don't know why, but the garage feels unsafe. With no power, the doors are as good as locked, but the flimsy metal sheets seem more vulnerable than actual doors. Which is a sideways banana way of thinking because actual windows are easy to get through. I think I've accidentally broken a dozen in my life. A basketball here, a baseball there. When I was sixteen, my parents thought it would be a good idea for me to babysit an eleven-year-old, until I put *him* through a window during a wrestling match.

He survived. My babysitting career was terminated like its last name was Conner.

Doors and windows might not even matter to demonic forces. They're intangible. Maybe. But...I think they can't enter a home unless they're invited, for some silly reason I can't remember. Or maybe that's vampires? Maybe demons see open windows as an invitation. I imagine they're rude like that.

Something clatters in the garage.

The whole dining room and everyone in it goes still until—

—from the garage we hear, "I'm okay!"

Mom leans back again. "Keep it down! You're making a racket!"

"Well, now you're yelling!" Rich shouts back.

The tension is finally getting to them, reverting them back to their pre-apocalyptic modus operandi—arguing. And apparently sex. Ugh.

"Mom," I say with enough dire warning to get her attention. When she looks at me, I subtly tilt my head toward Allie, who's doing her best to hide the fact that she's shaking.

Mom deflates. "Sorry."

Rich returns triumphant, holding a radio. The face is black plastic, lodged in a brown, wooden shell. It's some kind of holdover from the 70s, when he was a strapping young man. I feel rather smug about his age until I see the stickers plastered on the side.

The Doors. Kiss. Queen.

Holy shit on a speeding toboggan, Rich and I have the same taste in music?

Used to, anyway. Unless...

Outside of my and Allie's rooms, Mom controls the audio inside the house, and in the car. I always assumed Mom and Rich liked the same music, but this ancient relic is revealing the truth, like some unearthed tomb of some Egyptian Pharaoh.

Rich tears open a package of D batteries and loads them into the radio. He turns it around and carefully turns the volume knob, which apparently also controls the power. Static fills the air.

He twists the frequency knob, taking us on a slow journey between various hisses of increasing density. When he reaches the former home of Kiss 108, rounded up from 107.9, he stops. Static all the way. No one is broadcasting because A) they're dead, B) they have better things to do, or C) no one knows they can broadcast because the power is on, but the lights are out. Good news for our food situation—it won't be melting—but bad news for the world's DJs.

"Stellar idea," I say, "but alas…"

Rich shuts the radio off with an angry twist. "Now what are we supposed to do?"

The question carries so much conviction, I'm fairly certain Rich believed it would propel us in a new direction. Give us purpose. A connection to the outside world. Maybe a little hope. But the airwaves are flaccid, and that shame has carried over to—

Good Lord, I am still high.

"Well," I say, "I vote we go our separate ways. Chill out in private. Maybe play a few rounds of solitaire. Catch up on a novel. Is anyone here reading a novel? Do people still *read* novels? Or is it all audiobooks and pretentious narrators? Whatever. Point is…I need to clear my thoughts."

"Need to take more weed is more like it," Rich says, sounding more than a little bitter.

Wait. Was Rich also a pot head back in the day?

Was that envy I heard in his voice?

"Rich," Mom says, scolding. "You know why he needs it."

Rich crosses his arms. "I know why he *says* he needs it."

"If it makes you feel better, I'll be out before three days are up. Hell awaits, either way." With that, I bid them adieu and head for my room.

Mom and Rich are in a whispered argument as I enter my room, and I realize I left without a light source. Doesn't matter, I'm not actually going to do anything but lie in bed and hopefully fall asleep.

The door thumps against something as I close it.

"I'm staying with you." Allie's voice startles me, sending tingles down my legs. "Sorry," she says, noticing my discomfort in the diffused light reaching us from the dining room table.

"C'mon." I stand aside and let her in. Rapid fire scratching on the kitchen floor announces Sanchez's approach. He's been lying in his bed this whole time. I feel bad for not remembering him until now, but I doubt he minds. Allie and I fumble through the dark and eventually flop down on my queen-sized bed, side by side. Sanchez leaps onto the bed and curls up between our heads, sighing.

After a quiet moment, she says, "Rich is a dick."

"He's afraid."

"Still. He didn't need to say that."

I shrug, but she doesn't see it. "I'm a twenty-seven-year-old with mental issues, living in my mother's house, under the same roof as my mother's boyfriend. That he allows me to be here at all says something good about him."

"Is this forgiveness shit what they taught you in the Army?" she asks.

"Quite the opposite, I'm afraid. I'm just trying to embrace a new path, Sis."

She snuggles close, head on the crook of my arm. "It's good."

"Better than I used to be, right?"

"Much," she says. "You...feel more like Dad now."

Smiling and crying at the same time feels funny. Probably looks even funnier. Glad she can't see me. I manage to get out a, "Thanks," without my voice cracking.

We settle into a quiet, rhythmic breathing. I can't see anything beyond the psychedelic purple blobs in my vision that have nothing to do with pot, and everything to do with phosphenes. Outside, the trees hiss in the wind.

It's pleasant.

My thoughts drift to Jen, and then to nothing at all.

"Miah!" Allie whispers.

My body jerks.

I was asleep.

"Uhnn." I stretch. "Yeah?" Allie is no longer lying on my arm. She could be anywhere in the room, but she sounded close.

"I heard something." She's sitting beside me on the bed.

"Probably Rich taking a shit."

"I heard something *outside*," she says, obliviating my bathroom worries.

And then I hear it, too. A kind of low, sad moaning. Mewling like a calf. Something hurt in the woods. Maybe Mr. Gearhart.

Or...whatever killed him.

13

"What should we do?" Allie whispers. Sanchez is whimpering the way he does when someone is at the door...right before he starts ferociously yipping.

"Probably exactly what we're doing," I tell her. "But with less talking." To Sanchez, I say, "Goes for you, too. No bark."

Sanchez snorts his irritation, but he stops whimpering.

"Isn't there like some kind of Army guidelines for something like this? I mean, not demons obviously, but being behind enemy lines?"

"Yes," I whisper, "And the first one is *shut the hell up.*"

She listens this time, not because me being stern makes a difference, but because the thing outside is moaning again.

It sounds almost pitiful. Like a kid who's just dropped his ice cream.

Or like a demon who's been locked in a lake of fire for a few thousand years and is sad that it hasn't found a person to munch on yet.

It knows we're in here. It must.

But I think it wants us to come out.

Any other night—or day for that matter—I'd have gone right outside to inspect the odd sound. Just like Mr. Gearhart. But now? Hell no. Whatever it is can fuck right off.

Allie takes hold of my hand. Squeezes, as the thing outside mewls again, a wounded baby cow.

Give me a break, I think. Demons are melodramatic little queens. I'm almost annoyed enough to shout it. But the next time it cries out, it's farther away.

I want to peek. Want to see what it looks like. Curiosity draws my eyes to the window. How would it know if I just peeled back the trash bag and lifted the shade's corner?

It wouldn't, I decide. *Unless they're psychic. Or they have literal eyes in the back of their heads.*

"Do demons have heads?" I whisper.

"*What?* How should I know?"

"I mean, in movies they're mostly black smokey blobs—"

"Or possessing someone," she adds.

"Right. And the devil's a big red guy with horns. Buuut, the devil is just a demon, too. But like their king."

"You realize that neither of us actually knows anything about any of this."

"Is there even a Bible in the house?" I ask.

"I think Mom has one. Also a gift from Linda. And Rich must have one of those old timey versions somewhere, right?"

"King James," I say.

"Yeah, that."

"I guess, but both options require leaving this room and communicating with adults."

"*You're* an adult, Miah."

"Sadly." I sigh, listening for a moment. "I think it's gone."

We sit in silence long enough for me to mentally hum halfway through *Rock and Roll All Nite* by Kiss.

Allie releases my hand. "I think you're right."

After a long silence, I say, "So. How's life?"

Allie huffs. "Fine. I'll get the Bible." She slides off the bed, standing still in the darkness. Then her lighter flicks to life, and she exits the room, on a mission that I'd actually already forgotten about.

Because if God is real, and he was going to unleash demons on Earth for three days and nights, wouldn't he include it in The Book? There's a whole section of the Bible dedicated to stuff like that. Why include something like this as a sidenote revealed to some lady that no one has ever heard of? Why make it obscure? If the point is to catch people off guard, why reveal it at all?

Granted, God is probably like some genius chess player who can see a gazillion moves ahead. I can't really imagine what it's like to be infinitely smart—and not just because I'm buzzing and terrified. But there's not a trace of logic in any of this. Despite everything that's happening, the prophecy still *feels* like a crock of shit.

Don't get me wrong, I'm on board. I believe it's all real. But it feels more like an interactive theater experience I'll be able to walk out of at the end.

"Got it!"

Allie's triumphal return makes me flinch. "Gadzukes, Al. Wooh."

She smiles at me, lit by a candle now. "You'll live." She places the candle on my dresser.

She's right. Hear that, limbic system? Chill out. We're fine. The world might be ending, but right now, we can be as chill as a toilet seat in an igloo.

"Hey, do igloos have toilet seats?" I ask.

Allie plops down on the bed. "Oh, my god. Miah, seriously?"

"It would be good to know before visiting the Great White North, don't you think?"

"Sounds like I'm doing the thinking for both of us." She places a dense, red book between us. It's heavy enough to dent the mattress.

"Did the Bible get longer?" I ask.

"It's a..." She looks at the cover. "A study Bible."

"Bonus info?"

"Something like that."

"Ooh. Index?"

She opens the book and flips to the end, where lo and behold— an index. "Look up Three Days of Night."

She turns a few pages. Scrolls down the comprehensive list. "Not exactly."

"But something?"

"Three days and three nights," she says and starts turning large chunks of pages. Then she stops and reads a bit. "Jonah."

"The fish dude? That's not right. Anything else?"

She takes another tour of the Bible, back to the index and then to another book. Or verse. Or whatever they're called.

"Jesus," she says. "That's how long he was dead for. Three days and three nights."

"Until he rose again." I flail my arms like a money-grubbing televangelist. "Praise the Lord!"

"Miah," Allie scolds. "Knock it off. If any of this is real, you probably shouldn't be mocking God, you know?"

"Pretty sure God has a sense of humor. Have you been to Walmart lately?" My bad joke doesn't turn her frown upside down. And I suppose she's not wrong. Why taunt the man behind the curtain? I clear my throat. "Fine. Look for demons. Or the devil. Or whatever he's called in there."

I lie on my back, listening to Allie turn pages.

Twenty minutes later, she says, "You awake?"

I lift my hand and offer an upturned thumb.

"The devil was an angel, which means he probably looks like an angel. But here's the thing, there were different kinds of angels. Some kind of looked like people, some made themselves *look* like people, and others were complete freakshows with eyes everywhere and wings and different kinds of heads."

"Sounds like a metaphor to me."

"Whatever that is. The point, Miah, is that if demons used to be angels, they could probably look like whatever, or whoever they want." She looks me in the eyes. "Including Mr. Gearhart."

"C'mon..." I say, not wanting anything to do with this new nightmare of a twist.

"You should probably warn Jen."

"And tell her what? 'Hey Jen, if your dad comes back, don't let him in?' I can't do that, and she'd never listen if I did."

"You can't not tell her because she might not like you anymore."

"That's not...okay, that might have something to do with it, but we have no proof. And if we're wrong, it might end up being our fault that he dies. Until we have more than a paranoid, Bible-fueled conspiracy theory, we need to be careful with what we tell people. That includes the parental figures, okay?"

She nods, but she looks unsure.

I press for a more substantive response. "*Okay?*"

"Okay. Fine. Geez."

Somewhere in the house... A *thump*.

It's followed by the clatter of something falling on the floor and Mom's voice. She sounds concerned, but not panicked.

Allie and I share a look, and then are up on our feet, candle in hand, heading for the door.

When we reach the kitchen, Mom's voice becomes clear. "Rich, I don't think it's a good idea. We're not even supposed to look outside."

I try to rush, but the candle nearly goes out.

I want to shout, but I'm afraid to alert whatever is stalking around outside.

"Mom!" I hiss. "Don't let him open the door!"

But my whisper is drowned out by Rich's elevating voice. "It sounds like Larry from across the street. We can't just leave him out there. He sounds hurt. Hell, maybe this is the test. The Bible says to do unto others. Maybe God wants to see who will still obey, right?"

A low mewl outside the front door that sounds like a man now, sends a zing of pain up my spine, radiating out through my shoulder blades like growing fractal tree branches.

I enter the foyer just in time to see a candle-lit Rich, yank the front door open. A rosary around his hand and wrist rattles, little Jesus on the crucifix staring at me.

A flash of confusion comes and goes over Rich, before it's replaced by abject terror.

He never gets a chance to scream.

Something long and dark crashes through the screen door, wraps around Rich's shoulders and yanks him outside.

14

Rich and the entire screen door disappear into the night.

We stand before the open doorway, a portal to another world. Death awaits on the far side, but we're unable to look away or to take cover.

Beside me, Allie's quivering voice. "Close the door... Close the door..."

I hear the words, but I don't process them. My mind is still playing catch up with what happened to Rich.

I saw it.

Saw...something.

Arms maybe. It was dark. And fast. Strong enough to pluck Rich off the floor and carry him out of the house, taking the screen door with him, tearing screws from wood.

Rich didn't stand a chance.

None of us do.

"Mom." Allie raises her voice. "Close the goddamn door!"

The shout snaps Mom out of her shock and sends her headlong into trauma fast enough to break her mind. Logic and self-preservation take a backseat. Mom steps up to the open door, grasps the frame, and screams out into the living darkness. "Rich!"

I reel away from Mom's voice. "What are you doing? Mom!"

It takes a moment, but concern for my mother's life overcomes my panic, and I reverse course, heading for the door. "Mom! You need to get away from the—"

"Hueych."

That's the sound that comes from my mother's mouth when she's ripped out of the doorway and yanked into the darkness.

I stagger to a stop, whispering, "Mom..?" Then I take her place in the doorway, screaming into the night with wild, terror-fueled abandon. "Mom!"

I'm tackled.

A scream tears from my lungs as I flail.

Then a voice cuts through. "Miah! MIAH! Stop it!"

Allie's on top of me, hands pressed against my mouth, her small body struggling to contain the flopping fish panic of her older brother.

My struggle winds down like my batteries have been pulled. I lie flat on my back, eyes turned toward the unseeable ceiling high above.

My mother is gone.

Taken.

Probably dead.

I've felt this kind of sudden loss before. The only way to get past it, in the moment, is to turn the emotion into something other than despair, and then deal with the long-term mental effects when life goes back to 'normal.'

So that's what I do.

"I'm okay," I say. "I'm okay."

I shuffle out from beneath Allie, who's finally going into shock, her body shaking. Back on my feet, I pick her up and kick the door shut. It's not locked, but at least nothing can just reach in and pluck us like apples from a tree.

The candle on the dining room table lights the path back to my bedroom. It's not necessarily any safer than any other room, but it feels like it to me. So that's where we go. Lost in darkness again, memory guides me to the bed, where Sanchez is still curled up, his little body quivering. I help Allie onto the mattress and then I step toward the dresser, where I left the AK-47. Had I known any of this was possible, I'd never have let it go.

I heft the weapon and flick off the safety.

"What *was* that?" Allie asks. Her teeth are chattering. Over the next few minutes, she's going to experience a lot of uncomfortable things, as adrenaline wears off, the shock numbing her fades, and reality sinks in.

Rich and Mom are gone.

Probably dead.

And I've left her...

"I need to try..."

"Try what?" she asks, but the sob that follows says she knows exactly what I'm doing.

I pick up a spare magazine, attempt to slide it into a pocket, and realize that I am still wearing the damn skirt. "Crap," I mutter, and I leave it behind. The AK has a thirty round magazine full of 7.62 ammunition powerful enough to take down any living thing on Earth.

Problem is, I don't know if demons are living.

Or material enough to shoot.

They were physical enough to grab Rich and Mom. Stands to reason, I should be able to shoot them.

"Stay here," I say, and I follow the flickering candlelight back out to the dining room and to the front door. I pause, clutching the handle, steeling myself for what comes next.

I've been here before. Full of pain and rage. Ready to throw myself into harm's way, saying it's righteous, but knowing it's vengeance.

Three quick breaths, and then I yank open the door, step out into the night, and close it behind me. I'm tense. Locked in place. Expecting to be yanked off my feet and pulled away. I just need a chance to pull the trigger. Put a few holes in the asshole who took Mom.

But nothing happens.

Weapon shouldered, I start down the steps, sweeping back and forth.

The air still reeks. Stronger now. Repulsive as a skunk's unwashed anus. Stings my nose a little bit, too.

Starlight guides me through the yard. Still hard to see, but I can see better than inside without a candle. There's no signs of struggle. They were taken without a fight.

But taken where?

I swivel in place, heart pounding, ready to shoot at anything moving. But I'm alone.

And alive.

Why am I still alive? I'm breaking the rules. I'm outside.

My sight snaps to an aberration. A white rectangle in the street. I move through the yard, searching for targets, but on course for the street.

I stop on the sidewalk. It's the screen door, bent and discarded and covered with a spritz of blood.

Rich's blood.

I hope. Which is horrible. But honestly better than Mom's.

Not that it matters. They're both gone.

My vision blurs. Despair sinks its claws into me.

"No," I say, and I start across the street. "*No.*"

I'm headed toward Larry's yard before I've thought about what comes next. I'm just following the trajectory of the door from the house, hoping that whatever took Mom likes to walk in straight lines. I'm jogging by the time I reach his lawn, heading up the incline.

That's when I spot the open front door.

Maybe they're inside? Maybe demons take a house and set up shop? Like a lion's den, full of its victims' bones.

The windows are all closed, but the shades are up. Good ol' Larry didn't know what was coming. Didn't seal himself or his family inside. One of the windows is covered in blood.

I look from the house to the woods behind it. Mom could be in either direction, and choosing the wrong one could...

Doesn't matter, I think. *She's dead.*

In my heart, I know it's true. Hell isn't merciful. I don't see why Hell on Earth would be any different.

"No," I say, like it's my one-word mantra, and I head for the house. Failing to catch up doesn't feel as bad as walking right past. It's unlikely I'll find anything in the dark woods. But if they're in the house...

I start up the stairs, pausing to listen.

Screams in the distance.

Even farther away, the *pop, pop, pop* of gunfire. People are putting up a fight. I'm not sure how much it will matter.

Suppose I'm about to find out.

I charge up the steps, weapon raised.

My memory flashes back to another time, another doorway, another home. Lost in that ancient moment, I miss a step, trip, and sprawl to the porch. The AK falls beneath me. I land on my hands and knees above it. Anyone watching might think I'm bowing in supplication to the home's new resident.

Fueled by embarrassment, I pick myself up. Then I'm inside the house, looking for someone or something upon which to vent my righteous anger. To my surprise, I can see. The long foyer is lit by a candle. There's a dozen more beside it, lying down and unlit. The flickering light dances over a pool of blood, giving it the illusion of movement.

I step over it, stuff as many of the extra candles as I can fit into the skirt's narrow pockets and move into the living room. Can't see shit.

"Mom?" I call. The house absorbs my voice, and nothing comes back. "Mom!"

I take a few steps into the darkness, but instinct stops me. I nearly squeeze off a round. The single burst would give me a quick snapshot of the room.

Might also blow out my eardrums.

"Slow down," I tell myself. "Breathe. Think."

A soldier's worst enemy is impatience. Rushing into a combat situation, without preparation, is a quick way to get dead. So said my Army captain. He was a philistine and a philanderer, but his advice held true—until it didn't. Hard to prepare for rockets raining down in the middle of the night.

I don't think I'll ever be prepared for whatever took Mom and Rich, but I can at least find a way to see and maybe avoid stumbling onto my enemy's sword.

I need the candle.

I turn around toward the foyer, eyes on the open door. The night sky beyond looks strange.

Incomplete.

Like something is blocking...

15

Muscle memory brings the AK-47 up to my shoulder before I've fully come to the conclusion that something is in the doorway.

Finger around the trigger, heart pounding, I hold my fire.

It's dark. I can't really see what it is. Could be an animal. Hell, maybe Allie followed me. I don't want to kill my sister, or a neighbor, or even a freaked-out black bear.

"Who's there?" The quiver in my voice is embarrassing.

I stagger forward a step, attempting to compensate, to project strength. I narrow my eyes, clench my jaw, and bare my teeth. I'm a predator. A killer. Not to mention a charlatan and a fool.

If I can't see whoever or whatever is outside in the starlight, they probably can't see me either, concealed in the lightless living room. The only benefit derived from my ruse is that I feel a little braver. Part of my PTSD recovery—the cringe-worthy laughter yoga—operates under the premise that if you laugh and smile even when you have no reason to, even if your life is a complete disaster, your brain responds to the input as though it were genuine. Dopamine, serotonin, oxytocin, and endorphins are the reward, shifting the brain's state from faux happiness to genuine happiness.

Basically, fake it till you make it.

Apparently, it works with other emotions, too.

I inch my way closer to the flickering foyer. I need the candle's light. Need to confirm my enemy's presence before opening fire. Need to look into the eyes of whatever is about to take my life.

Outside, clacking on the wooden porch. Slowly backing away.

If it's a person, it's a woman in heels.

Or a dude in heels. But that's unlikely in this neighborhood.

Then again, I'm still wearing a skirt.

"If you're a person, tell me now," I say, entering the foyer, trying to keep up the tough guy act. My legs are shaking. My trigger finger is twitching so much I have to pull it outside the trigger guard.

Nothing.

I stop by the candle. Look down at the small table. While I pilfered a handful of candles earlier, there are still several lying unused. Beside them, a pen, notepad, keys, and a roll of scotch tape.

Time to get tactical.

Moving as fast as I can, hoping whatever is outside isn't in a rush, I pick up three of the long candles and quickly tape them to the rifle's muzzle—one on the bottom, two on the sides. Takes just ten seconds, but I feel death's inevitable breath on my neck as I finish. With a gasp, I lift the weapon and aim it at the door again.

The rectangle leading outside is empty. The clacking fades, moving down the stairs.

"Where the hell are you going?" I ask, fear shifting to anger, to some kind of brazen mania. I hold the three candles to the one that's already lit, setting them ablaze and creating a portable light source. Then I'm heading for the door, keeping my pace slow and steady to accommodate the fledgling flames. If I move fast, they'll go out.

Not perfect, but it will hopefully keep me from shooting someone's pet.

The candles slip through the front door first, flickering in a gentle breeze that smells strongly of sulfur. I stop in place, waiting for the flames to stabilize. Then I push forward into the familiar unknown once more, looking over the rifle's muzzle.

A warbling orb of orange light surrounds me, illuminating every-thing in a ten-foot radius. Right now, that's just the porch, the steps, and a few feet of brick walkway and grass.

"Last chance. If you are a human being and understand what I'm saying, tell me now or I am definitely going to shoot you to shit. *Comprende?*"

I can hear it, shifting through the short grass.

Just out of sight.

What are the odds that a non-English speaking foreign tourist got lost in the backwoods of New Hampshire and just happened to stumble into this yard during the middle of a supernatural, end times, freak show?

Slim to none.

My finger slips around the trigger.

I brace for recoil.

What are the odds that Rich, or Mom, or Larry have been hurt? That they're unable to speak? Jaw broken. Maybe concussed and confused. That they're backing away because I'm pointing a rifle at them?

Much higher.

"Damnit." I glance to my right. An Adirondack chair offers a solution. A homemade knit pillow rests in the seat, both comfortable and flammable. The pillow lights from the gun mounted candles like it was made to burn. I barely have time to frisbee it away into the yard. It spins through the air like a UFO and then crashes in the front yard Roswell, coughing embers as it touches down.

During that brief moment of impact...

...I see it.

Not Mom, or Rich, or Allie. Not Larry or a bear.

It's...I don't know.

It's illuminated for just a moment. A blink. But it's enough to make me backstep.

The figure, at its core, is human—two arms, two legs, and a head. But all of that is hard to make out, because surrounding it is a flowing torrent of darkness, like living smoke. Churning. Agitated. A storm of its very own. And within the storm, frantic tendrils, like a squid...but chaotic. Four of them. I think. It's hard to tell. It's never not in motion.

I catch just a glimpse of the thing's face. Two black eyes surrounded by twisted, gnarled flesh—like an extreme burn victim whose skin has been molded to reflect malice, hatred, and seething rage.

The sight of it triggers some long dormant part of my brain, that understands what this creature is, that knows it isn't here just to kill me, it's here to undo me, to tear me apart, body and soul, and take great pleasure in doing so.

This is my enemy.

And has been for a very long time.

This...is a demon.

It's all true.

"In the name of Jesus," I shout, "Get behind me, Satan!"

Honestly, I don't know what that's supposed to achieve, but it's what priests say in movies, when someone is demon possessed. Or maybe it's the Pentecostals, shouting at their own congregation as they writhe around on the floor? Benny Hinn maybe? I don't know. I saw it somewhere. I'm not sure why referring to a common demon as Satan himself is useful. Wouldn't the demon be like, 'Hey, I'm Azimuth!' or something?

Doesn't really matter, because it doesn't work. Probably have to actually believe for it to work, and I've only had a few seconds to process all this. If there's a hotline to the J-man, I don't have the number, and even if I did, it's probably overloaded at the moment.

The monster moves at the light's fringe, wisps of its churning body slipping into the candle's flicker. It's circling me. Preparing to strike.

So, I decide to introduce it to the US of A's true god, and I pull the trigger.

Mr. Gearhart might be a former Marine with an arsenal in his house, but he's also a law-abiding citizen. While I'm prepped for a full auto spray, the AK-47 kicks off a single round.

The bright flash reveals the demon, five feet to the right of where I fired.

It's on the move, dashing on hands and feet, storm swirling around it like the fires of hell are still cooking its body, tendrils waggling behind it.

Compared to this...thing, I am insignificant. I feel that truth in my marrow. It's inescapable.

But that doesn't stop me from pulling the trigger again and again, quick as I can, spinning in an arc. The strobe lit demon lunges to the side, and then...

Up.

I follow the vertical leap with my rifle.

The rapid movement extinguishes the three candles. I lose sight of the demon, but I keep pulling the trigger, hoping to spot it again in the gunfire's light.

But there's nothing.

In a single leap, it rose thirty feet off the ground, climbed onto the roof, and disappeared.

The AK clicks empty. I pull the trigger five more times before I realize it.

Darkness settles around me.

"Shit..." I step back from the house, looking up at its silhouetted roof, framed by more stars in the sky than I've ever seen—day *or* night. The Milky Way distracts me for a moment, and I understand why our ancestors came up with the notion of God or gods. The night sky, sans light pollution, is stunning.

A fluid shadow moves through the field of stars, tapping its way across the rooftop. *Maybe demons really do have cloven feet?* I wonder. Doesn't sound like hands, paws, or even claws.

I can feel it glaring down at me. I might not be able to see it. Not really. But I get the sense it has no trouble seeing me.

And then, it mewls. Pitiful. Like a widow in mourning.

For a moment, I feel bad for it.

Then I remember that this thing, or something like it, took my family. Is taking other people's families.

I glance back at my house. It's hard to see, but my eyes are adjusting. The front door is closed.

You left Allie alone, my inner voice says.

I take a step back, knowing that if I run and it chases, I won't even make it to the street. The demon is faster than I can track, strong enough to pluck Rich from the house, along with the door, and it can jump like a mountain lion on the Moon.

I back away, slow, and steady.

The mewling rises, tearing into my nervous system, standing hairs on end.

I'm so distracted by the sudden shift, that I miss the transition from yard to street. The drop is just a few inches, but it throws me off balance. I topple back onto my ass, dropping the rifle against my shins.

Pain fuels a tirade, tears and rage spilling out all at once. "Fuck you, you fucking fuck!"

The mewling stops suddenly, as though my words have actually stung it.

And then...

...then it laughs.

16

I've been laughed at more than a few times in my life, most of it in the time between leaving the military and this moment, on my ass in the street, the recipient of a new kind of malicious laughter. Sounds more like a hyena. A hyperactive cackle that transmits and instills supernatural loathing.

I feel defeated. Degraded. Worse than at boot camp. Worse than when I picked up the wrong order at McDonald's in North Carolina, didn't notice until I was halfway through, and tried to bring it back for an exchange. Lady behind the counter was like, 'Would ya look at this Crackah? Bringing back a half-eaten Biggy and looking for seconds? Sorry, hoss, we don't accept white privilege here.' Just about every employee and customer gathered round to laugh and point at me.

They didn't know it, but after retreating from the restaurant, I curled up behind my car's steering wheel and wept—because I was humiliated, and because there I was, a broken Army vet with PTSD, and all I needed to make my day seem worth living was a damn double cheeseburger with double Mac sauce and extra pickles.

That was a low point in my life.

This feels worse.

Because push comes to shove, if any of those people in the McDonald's had seen me crying, they probably would have stopped laughing. Probably would have realized I wasn't okay. Probably would have apologized.

Probably.

Some people are just assholes. Would laugh at me for being emotionally vulnerable.

But this thing...

It feels like all the world's assholes and bullies run through a meat grinder, hand-shaped into a monstrous form and then charbroiled over a lake of fire for a millennium or two.

Hell, that might even be an accurate description.

But if that's all true, and this thing is a man-eating demon from the 13th level of Dante's Inferno, why is it laughing at me? Why isn't it attacking? Hauling me away? Noshing on my brain? Possessing my corporeal form?

Isn't that what demons do?

I shuffle over the pavement, scuttling across the street like a crab with four legs plucked out. Too afraid to get up. To turn my back and run.

Its hyena laugh cuts short, replaced by a deep, throaty roar, approaching from my right.

Is there a second demon? This doesn't sound like the first. Are there more than one kind?

Pop culture says yes. That demons come in many shapes and forms. The Bible apparently says they can look like whatever the hell they want. Standing next to a bush? Could be a demon. That seagull eating your fries? Demon. The porcelain doll sitting in your mother's craft room that slowly chimes out Beethoven's Für Elise every damn time you bump into it? Definitely a demon.

But the thing roaring downhill toward me sounds familiar.

Like…a truck.

Holy shit, it's a truck!

With no headlights!

The driver can't see me. Probably can barely make out the road.

I attempt to lunge, to scramble, to do anything other than wait to be just another roadkill in New Hampshire, guts popped out, limbs extended in perpetual surprise. But my legs aren't working like they should. I'm undone. Useless. For the second time in my life.

I feel the truck's pressure wave against my cheek.

I've got a second to act.

Foot planted, I extend my leg as hard as I can and just slip.

I fall onto my side, the pain just a mild harbinger of what is to come.

And then...

The engine's roar mixes with the sound of tire treads humming over pavement. The Doppler wave builds, intense and foreboding, and then—it passes.

The truck tears through the space between my head and the far curb, driving on the wrong side of the street.

If I hadn't slipped...

The demon cackles again, mocking my fortune, as though having my life snuffed out in an instant would have been a mercy. Then it leaps away from the roof. For a moment, I think it's coming toward me, but then its hard feet hit the street and clack their way downhill in pursuit of the vehicle.

Tires squeal. Just for a moment. The boom that follows is sudden and solid, mixed with the crunch of metal. I don't need to see to know that old truck, careening down the hill, came face-to-face with an even older pine tree—the kind you can't wrap your arms around, with bark armor and an old-fashioned New England sense of stick-to-itiveness.

If the driver isn't dead...I think he will be soon.

Probably without the demon's help.

A fresh laugh cuts through the air. Downhill. From the scene of the crash...which I can now see.

The truck's front end is on fire.

Silhouetted through the rear window, the driver sits up.

Eyes widening, I suddenly fear for the man's safety. "Get out! Run! It's coming!"

I don't know if the man heard me, or if he's reacting to the fire, but he starts frantically tugging on his seatbelt.

On my feet—I don't remember standing, but here I am—I take two steps toward the truck again, my instinct to help, if possible.

For a moment. A third step is all I manage before stopping again.

The demon is there, climbing into the truck bed, outlined by fire. It's indistinct, the storm concealing its true form, but the creature appears to have both a physical form, and a supernatural form—revealing its chaotic, powerful nature.

I don't bother shouting again.

I just watch.

With a suddenness I can't fathom, the demon tears the back window away, reaches inside, grasps the man, and then plucks him free with the same ease it—or something like it—did my mother and Rich.

Then it leaps away from the fire, slipping into the forest with its prize.

And for some reason...that prize is *not* me.

For a moment, all I can hear is the rush of blood behind my ears. Then my pounding heartbeat. The outside world starts to seep in.

Screams.

Gunshots.

A chainsaw.

The world is at war.

With Hell.

I stagger across the street, overwhelmed by it all, but carried forward by concern for Allie.

I shouldn't have left.

Shouldn't have come out here.

I could have died.

But I didn't.

Why didn't I die? Why didn't it take me?

The steps stumble me. I drop the AK and have to climb back down to retrieve it. When I do, the front door opens. "Miah?"

"Keep it closed!" I hiss, but Allie ignores me.

"Did you find Mom?" Her voice is a squeak. A frightened mouse.

I try to run up the stairs, but I'm clumsy about it. "Get away from the door!"

My foot snags on the top step. I topple forward, past Allie, through the open door, spilling into the foyer and dropping the spent weapon. Out of breath, I lie on my back, heaving air, looking up at Allie's back as she looks out into the dark neighborhood.

"Allie...please!" I'm having trouble breathing, and it's not just from being winded.

This is panic.

"Close the god-damn door!"

It's the angriest I've ever spoken to Allie, but I've seen how fast they are. One second she'll be standing in the doorway and the next she'll be gone, carried off into the forest. My volume gets the job done.

Allie slams the door, then locks the deadbolt, the knob lock, and the security slider.

She kneels beside me, her candle lit face streaked with tears. "Mom?"

"She's gone," I say, and a sob escapes my lips. "They're both gone."

Allie's face screws up.

She lies down beside me, face on my chest, tears wetting my shirt.

Unable to contain our despair, but afraid to make too much noise, we sob in silence, squelching the worst of it, grasping onto each other, our insides torn out and on display.

Ten minutes later, I'm spent, but Allie is still going. I wrap my arms around her, holding her tight, feeling a new kind of energy.

This is my sister.

This is all the family I have left.

And I will pierce the depths of Hell and fight my way back before I let anything happen to her.

17

"Miah?"

"Yeah?"

"Do you think they're dead? Mom and Rich?"

"Yeah."

"Me too."

We're in the living room, lit by a single candle. Allie is sitting in Mom's chair. I'm sitting in Rich's with Sanchez. I've never sat in this recliner before. It's not like Rich claimed the chair as his own. He just always sat here, guffawing at reality shows with Mom. It belonged to him. Was his turf. One of the only things in the house I saw as truly belonging to him. That and his car.

I don't believe in cooties—the imaginary kind shared between boys and girls, not lice. Haven't since third grade. But Rich's chair had a kind of inverse gravitational force that kept me from sitting in it, or even thinking about sitting in it.

But now...

The lifeforce keeping me at bay is gone.

That's why I'm sure Rich is dead. And if he is, Mom must be, too.

"This is too much, Miah," Allie says. Despite expressing the pain in her heart, Allie's face remains placid. Numb. We're both emotionally spent, but still trying to process the new paradigm. Demons on Earth was bad. But facing it without Mom...and even Rich...feels unreal.

"Way too much," I say.

"How did you deal with it before?" she asks. "In Afghanistan?"

I want to be honest. Want to tell her that I didn't deal with it. I let that monkey jump on my back, dig its talons into the meat of my shoulders, bite its vampiric teeth into my jugular, and come along for the ride. It's still there now, getting its jollies from my discomfort, growing heavier by the moment.

"Laughter yoga," I say.

Her eyes flick to me, expressionless, yet somehow transmitting the message, 'Bullshit.'

I shrug. "That's part of it."

She shifts in her chair, turning her body toward me. "The hell is laughter yoga? Is it like stretching and shit? Is it like goat yoga? Wait, you don't do yoga with Sanchez, right? That'd be like, I don't know, animal abuse."

"Laughter yoga feels like abuse," I say.

"How does it work?"

I sink a little deeper into Rich's chair. "Please don't make me."

"I don't have Insta or Tik Tok to distract me." Her slight smile wins me over. "So, it has to be you."

I sit up. "Screw it. Okay...here goes." I take a deep breath.

"Wait, you can do yoga in the chair?"

"It's not actual yoga. I'm not sure why it's even called that. You're just tricking your brain into feeling better."

"Hhhow?"

"Laughing. Sort of. Like this." I let out a forced and totally fake, "Ha, ha, ha," and follow it up with a "He, he, he!" The smile on my face is broad, but not genuine. "Ha, ha, ha! He, he, he!"

I wave my hands at Allie, motioning for her to join in.

Allie is a great sister, but she's also a teenage girl. There are some things she would never be caught dead doing for fear of being shamed relentlessly by other teenage girls equally afraid of being shamed. It's like a shame cyclone that everyone is afraid to step out of, for fear of being swept up in it. It's all about control, and Laughter Yoga... It's like stepping into the eye of the storm, shouting, 'I don't give a shit.' And laughing. Lots of fake laughing. So, it's a big surprise when Allie chimes in, almost shouting her 'ha, ha, ha' and 'he, he, he.'

Halfway through Allie's third run-through, her smile becomes genuine. Which influences me, sapping strength from the shoulder monkey.

On the fourth run-through, her forced laugh transforms into something magical, like a caterpillar that's been thrown off a skyscraper only to form a chrysalis on the way down, tearing its way out and unfurling colorful wings just before hitting the ground.

It's inspirational.

And I join in.

Laughter fills the house. Rolling through the dark, empty rooms and hallways. Laughter over nothing. For laughter's sake. Carrying away our pain and our worry and our sorrow better and faster than tears ever could. Even Sanchez joins in, tilting his head toward the ceiling and letting out little laugh-like yips.

We probably shouldn't be doing this. Making noise. Probably should be boarded up in a closet for the next three days, living on power bars and bottled water, shitting in a bucket.

But that's too...familiar. And it's no way to die, if that is what's going to happen. Better to go out comfortable and laughing. There's no avoiding death, so might as well enjoy life right up until the end. Easier said than done. Pain has a way of killing joy, but I think Rich and Mom went out quick. I hope so, anyway.

The laughter fades.

We settle into our chairs a little deeper.

"I'm still sad," Allie says, when things are quieter. "But...I feel better. Laughter yoga. Who knew?"

"Yep. It's a thing."

Sanchez stretches. Licks his lips. Looks me in the eyes. Doesn't need to say a word. We speak the same language, and it doesn't require words.

I raise my eyebrows at him. He tilts his head. I smile. His tail wags. When I nod toward the pantry, he leaps down off my lap and skitters toward the door.

I move to stand up and notice Allie staring at me. "What?"

"How do you do that? Talk to him?"

I shrug.

"He's a dog. With a tiny little peanut brain. But I've seen you two do that thing, like you're both psychic, knowing what the other is thinking."

The pantry is stocked with dry goods and dog food. Which is good, I guess. We're not going to starve. I listen to the fridge, still humming. Definitely not going to starve. And neither is Sanchez. I pop open his food container, take a half-cup scoop and dump it in his bowl. He attacks the food with tiny ferocious gulps. If he weighed more than my hand, he might be scary.

"We're not reading each other's thoughts," I say. "It's about body language and facial expressions. Also, routine. We've had the food conversation a few hundred times before. Same with playing. Needing water. Wanting to go out. Dogs aren't complicated. Like babies. There's a very limited number of things they're interested in. If you pay attention to them, you'll eventually see the subtle differences between, 'I need to go out and pee,' and 'I need to go out and shit.' And when you respond to those requests in the same way, over time, he knows that you know...and it looks like a conversation."

"Huh. Does it work on people?"

"If they're being honest. But most of the time, people are hiding what they really think and feel. Like when you see someone and say, 'How's it going?' and they say, 'Good,' or, 'Dandy,' or whatever the hell people say. It's bullshit."

"Why is it bullshit?"

"Because life sucks. And not just for sensitive vets with PTSD. Everyone's got something weighing on them. They just don't want to talk about it or think about it. So, they lie."

"Try it on me," she says. "I won't lie."

"Not sure it works like that."

"You have something better to do?" she asks. "We could always go back to yoga."

I groan.

"You liked it," she says. "I think we should try again, right n—"

"Fine... Fine. I'll Dr. Doolittle you."

She twists around in her chair and stares at me.

All I can see is Mom's face and dark brown eyes. Never realized how alike they look until right now.

I clear my throat and focus, playing Allie's game.

After just a few moments of facial expressions, eyebrow twitches, and body language, I say, "Okay, got it."

"Wait, I didn't even start yet."

"It's not really the kind of thing you can start or stop. It's happening all the time. The difference was that I was paying attention." I smile and head for the fridge. Dig into the back, find my recent purchases, and haul them out onto the island.

"I've got just the thing. You'll feel like a blue jay in a birdbath in no time."

"The hell does that mean?"

I think on it, and say, "Satisfied. Isn't that the emotion all the kids are after these days?" I dole out the bread, slather on the mayo, and do an impression of every current American teenager. "Oooh, the Play-Doh being squashed by a hydraulic press. So satisfying. Look at that! The pressure washer cleans the porch so evenly. So smooth. Ahh, so satisfying."

"Yeah, I guess."

I slap on the faux deli meat, the non-dairy cheese, a layer of lettuce, a slice of tomato, and a sprinkle of salt, and then the second piece of bread, holding it all together with a toothpick. I carry the sandwiches over to Allie and present hers like a royal chef in Buckingham Palace. "Madam, your grub is served."

She smiles at me. "How did you know? Really?"

I return to Rich's seat. Sanchez hops up on my lap. He's just eaten, but that won't stop him from chowing down again.

"How did I know you were hungry?" I ask.

She nods.

"Because *I'm* starving." I take a bite and enjoy it.

Allie follows suit, but she's as unprepared for the fake meat and cheese as I was at my first rectal exam. She winces and speaks through a full mouth. "Ugh! Wash ish shish?"

I have a laugh at her expense, and I'm about to explain, when a high-pitched wail tears through the house.

From behind the closed front door.

18

I swallow my food without fully chewing it. Gluten free razor blades scratch my throat. "The hell was that?"

Allie shrugs, but offers, "One of those things? A demon?"

"Sounded different."

"Pretty sure if they can look like anything, they can sound like anything."

It's a solid point. But instead of falling silent and hunkering down, I stand and face the door. There was something about the sound...

"What are you doing?" Allie asks.

"I need to make sure."

I'm halfway to the door when Allie grabs my arm. She's surprisingly strong. Fear can do that. "That's the way they operate. They woo you outside."

"Like a siren."

"I don't know what that is, but yeah. Sure. That's how they get you. Like it's a game. They're screwing with us, Miah. Don't play their game. Just...don't do anything."

She's right. *The hell am I thinking?*

I sling the AK-47 from my back to my hands. "Better?"

Allie moves in front, blocking my path. "I'll fight you if I have to."

That gets my attention. Opens my eyes a little bit. Allie burns with emotions. Her fingers are hooked, ready to claw me to bits if I push her. After what happened to Mom and Rich, who can blame her? She's hurting. Devastated. And my curiosity is making it worse.

"Shit." I let the rifle hang. "I'm sorry. I just—"

The wail outside the door repeats, high and loud, this time followed by a hiccupped sob.

Allie turns toward the door. "The hell is it?"

"A kid," I say. "I think. Maybe. Or something pretending to be a kid."

"A little kid." She faces the foyer, looking at the front door. "Like really little."

"Are there any little kids in the neighborhood?"

She looks at me like I'm high, which I am. A bit. "Have you not seen them?"

"I tend to notice older..." How can I say this? "...more refined residents."

"Tits," Allie says. "And ass. That's what you notice. Way to objectify—"

"Hello?" The voice, muffled by the front door, is young and desperate. "H-hello?" Barely audible tears follow. If this is a demonic ruse, it deserves whatever Academy Award exists for underworld minions.

"Allie..." I put my hand on her shoulder. "We couldn't save Mom, but maybe—"

She deflates. "Fine."

I step around her, AK in hand once more, creeping toward the door. "Hello?"

"Hello?" The voice outside sounds hopeful.

"What's your name?" I ask.

"Bree," she says. "Can I come in?"

I turn toward Allie. She gives a nod and says, "Three doors down on the left."

"Bree, where are your parents?" I ask.

"They got taken," she says. "I think maybe... I think..." She starts crying.

Shit.

"You don't have to tell us," Allie says. "We just need to make sure you're you. Okay?"

"O-okay."

"Is your Uncle Ben with you?" Allie asks.

Bree goes quiet. Sniffing. And then, "He's with Mom and Dad, I think."

Allie and I share a glance.

"That's ominous as fuck," I whisper.

Allie nods. "But probably accurate, right? I mean, here we are, too."

"How did you get away?" I ask.

Allie backhands my shoulder hard enough to hurt. "Oww! What?"

"She's seven. We shouldn't—"

"They didn't like me," she says. "The smoke-men."

"Didn't *like* you?"

"I tried to fight them, but they ran away."

"With her family," Allie whispers and backhands me again. "Open the damn door."

"You open..." I lift the AK. "I'll be ready. Just in case."

Allie moves to the door, hand on the top lock. "Ready?"

I shoulder the rifle. Give a nod.

Allie moves through the three locks, undoing our feeble security measures. Then she yanks open the door without warning, revealing a nightmare.

A shriek tears into my nervous system, clawing and tearing me apart from the inside out. The creature outside the door is crouched, poised to pounce. Every inch of it is covered in chunky red, its long hair dangling in thick tendrils.

I pull the trigger.

Nothing happens.

Pull it again.

The same.

"Whoa, whoa, whoa!" Allie shouts and shoves the rifle's barrel to the side. "The hell, Miah?"

"I never loaded in a fresh magazine!" I step back to recover a fully loaded mag. That I'd forgotten to do so earlier is a total amateur move and evidence that I've been out of the military for a while now.

Allie grabs hold of my shirt. Pulls me to a stop. Points at the monster standing outside. "That's *Bree.*"

I look at the thing, still standing there, sobbing now.

If I use my imagination, I can see a little girl, but it's difficult. Until I realize why.

She's covered in blood. Head to toe. The only part of her body not coated in coagulating dark red are vertical streaks on her face, etched clean by tears.

The smell of it washes over me, churning my stomach, taking my mind back to places I don't want to revisit, but which might actually be pleasant compared to now, when all is said and done.

Pushing past her revolt and fear, Allie steps outside, takes a quick look around, and takes Bree's hand. Leads her inside the house and down the hall. She glances at me as she passes. "Woods are on fire."

Led by Allie's lighter, they enter the first-floor bathroom and close the door.

I turn to the view through the open door, once again breaking the cardinal rule of Three Days of Darkness. And once again, I don't drop dead. Instead, I step outside, onto the porch.

The air smells of sulfur still, but it's overshadowed by the pleasant scent of burning pine. A lot of it.

The street is lit in orange light.

I turn left, looking downhill, toward the earlier truck crash. The vehicle is a smoldering ruin. As are several trees around it. Just beyond, trees burn like giant candles. Despite the summertime heat and the dry conditions, the fire appears to be spreading slowly—and downhill, following the breeze.

Away from us, I think, feeling a modicum of relief.

But it's going to burn unchecked. Probably for a long time. Probably taking out a lot of houses as it goes. There're a hundred acres of dry forest behind the neighborhood. Plenty of fuel.

Right now, it makes the neighborhood easy to see. So, I have a look.

And see nothing.

No people.

No demons.

No fleeing deer, panicked bears, or bodies. Just dark houses with open front doors.

The sounds of distant gunfire have stopped. The night is quiet, save for the *shhh* of wind in the trees and the faint crackling of burning wood and pinecones.

Maybe the worst has passed?

Maybe we survived?

I tug the walkie talkie from my waist band. Jen hasn't checked in. And to be honest, I didn't remember her until just now. I don't feel bad about that. A lot happened. Been kind of...numb. But now that hope is creeping out of the darkness, I'm starting to wake up a little.

"Jen, this is Miah, you hear me?" I release the call button and wait ten seconds. "Hey, Jen, if you're hearing me, let me know."

I wait again, tension rising. She could be hiding. Could be in trouble. Could be my call is giving her hiding spot away. I whisper, "Jen...my walkie's on. If you can't talk right now, but need help, just click away on the talk button. I'll hear it on my end. Over."

Nothing comes through. She's silent. Maybe dead or taken, along with everyone else.

"Miah!" Allie hisses at me from the first-floor bathroom. "Close the damn door and get me a towel!"

I step back into the dark confines of the house, close and lock the door, and then stand there for a moment, radio in hand, feeling impotent. Even if Jen needed help, I'm not sure I could leave Allie alone and undefended with a seven-year-old.

I head up the steps, listening to the gentle hiss of the first-floor shower running, grateful that we still have running water, that my sister is alive, and that we're in a position to help the kid. *Bree.*

When demons invade the Earth, it's the little things that keep you sane.

That's when Allie screams.

19

The sound of Allie's terrified voice fills me with a conflagration of emotions I can't process well enough to identify. But the effect is instant.

I charge to the bathroom, weapon in hand—still unloaded—and kick in the bathroom door. Instinct guides my foot, planting it just beside the knob, shattering wood. The door flings open to a candle lit bathroom. Inside, Allie falls away from the door, shouting in fear again, this time at me.

"Miah! What the eff!"

I take a moment to survey the scene. No monsters. Just Allie, on the floor, and Bree standing naked in the shower, body trembling as the steamy water washes away layers of blood.

"Shit. Sorry." I divert my eyes from Bree, feeling like a perv, and I look to Allie for an explanation. "You screamed. Why?"

She takes a steadying breath. Sits up. Points to the tub's floor without saying a word. I follow her finger and nearly let out a yelp of my own.

Lying between Bree's trembling legs is an eyeball trailing a few inches of wiry gore, washed bloodless by the water. I turn to Allie asking a thousand questions with my eyes. She answers the most pressing. "It was in her hair."

I mouth the word, "Damn."

"I know, right?"

The eyeball must have come from the same person as all the blood, but it's hard to imagine—short of an explosive device hidden inside someone—how something like that could happen.

Don't imagine it, I tell myself.

When it comes to managing trauma, the imagination is a double-edged sword. You can escape into a blissful happy place, or you can be

tormented inside your own conjured hell of twisted memories and paranoid projection. Avoiding the latter sometimes means chastising yourself aloud.

"Don't go there. Just stop."

"Are...you talking to me?"

I shake my head. "Give me some TP."

Allie reaches over to the toilet paper roll and starts unraveling it.

"A lot."

She unrolls a massive wad and holds it out. Looks like a giant, white
rose. I take it, and turn to Bree, acknowledging her for the first time. "Hey
honey, I just need to grab something by your feet okay?"

The kid just stares back at me.

"Okay..." I lean over the tub, reach down, and plant the rose over the
eyeball, pressing down. The plan is to pinch it inside the papery mass,
creating a barrier between my skin and the gore, then run to a trashcan,
hopefully without puking. It's a good plan. Simple with attainable goals.

But...the plan falls apart along with the toilet paper. Bloody water
saturates the paper from above and below. When I squeeze my hand
over the eyeball, I can feel it. But it's too late to be grossed out. Too late to
stop. Last thing I want is for Bree to look down in the eye of her mother
or father and recognize what she's seeing. If she's not already broken for
life, she will be then.

So, I squeeze...to no avail. The slippery orb eludes capture. And
the toilet paper has dissolved into a stringy mass.

"Damnit." I hurl the now pink toilet paper away. It strikes the shower
wall and sticks. I barely notice. My gaze is locked onto the eyeball. The iris
is blue. Looks alive. I can feel it judging me for being a sucky rescuer.

"What is it?" Bree asks. I can sense her leaning over for a look.

Instinct guides me. I snatch the eyeball in my bare hand, and all
but throw myself from the bathroom.

Behind me, Allie says, "It was just a spider. He took care of it."

Ahead of me, the kitchen, lit by the feeble candlelight from the
dining room. As I pass the island, my stomach churns and my body
convulses. I lose control, pitching myself over the sink and vomiting
up the first two bites of my unfinished sandwich.

I'll never eat again, I think, leaning over the sink, bile and drool hanging from my lips. As I catch my breath, I glance toward my still clenched hand. It looks...empty. I slowly open my fingers, knowing that if I crushed the eyeball, I'll vomit again, probably harder and for a long time.

But my hand is empty. It's not even bloody.

What the hell?

I turn on the water, rinse off my hands, give my face a splash, and then rinse out my mouth. I'm curious about the eyeball's whereabouts, but I need to clear my mind and body of nasty.

I turn around and search in the dim light. Seeing nothing, I tiptoe into the dining room, testing each step to make sure I don't crush the eyeball underfoot. Candle in hand, I return to the kitchen, crouching low, scouring every nook and cranny. Finding nothing.

I was holding the eyeball until I reached the island. I'm sure about that. But when I got sick... I must have squeezed and popped the thing out of my hand. Which means it could have gone flying. It had some weight to it, though. Couldn't have gone far.

My search grid garners no results. The eyeball is gone. Like totally gone. I check countertops, under the stove and fridge, even on top of the fridge. Nothing.

Hands on the counter, I collect myself and think it through. My sprint from the bathroom to the kitchen was chaotic. Hard to remember. Were my arms drawn in close, or was I flailing like Kermit introducing a new act?

Candle in hand, I check the hallway between the kitchen and the bathroom. More nothing. I pause outside the once again closed door, listening to the shower running. Allie is singing a song. *You are My Sunshine.* Mom used to sing it to us. Allie sings it better.

But it doesn't help reveal the eyeball's whereabouts.

Returning to the kitchen feels a lot like driving in a convoy through enemy territory, scouring the landscape ahead, looking for aberrations that might reveal an IED's location. But the road ahead is clear.

"Damnit." I say, and I allow myself to chuckle. This is nuts. Who loses an eyeball in a kitchen? Dad would have said, 'Eyeballs don't just get up and walk away by themselves!' He'd say it about his keys, wallet, and glasses. He almost always found the item in question in a pocket or on his head.

I pat down the skirt's pockets, but I only feel the candles still wedged inside.

"What. The. Hell?" I want to give up, but I can't. For Bree's sake.

I clear my head again, trying to come up with ideas. How would Sherlock Holmes find a lost eyeball? 'It's elementary...' *What does that mean?* Deductive reasoning. I just need to ask the right questions and that will lead me to the answer.

What was I doing?

Running to the kitchen. I look at the path I took. Hallway to sink, no eyeball in sight.

Why was I running?

Because there was a damn eyeball in my hand.

What was in my hand?

The aforementioned motherfucking eyeball!

What is an eyeball?

I'm about to disregard the question. It popped into my head, unbidden and ridiculous. But then the answer appears from my subconscious.

Raw meat.

Shhhhhhhit.

"Sanchez," I call, trying to sound cutsey, like he's not in trouble, like I won't absolutely lose my mind if he walks into the room with an eyeball in his mouth. "C'mere, Chezzy. Mr. Chiquita Banana. Speedy Gonzales. Here, boy."

Sanchez has dozens of nicknames that he responds to as though they're his actual name. It's all about the tone, and right now, my faux-friendly voice is the same one I use when he needs to go to the vet.

He knows I'm full of shit.

The kitchen is definitely empty, so I move to the living room, checking his little bed on the way. Empty. As are all the seats in the living room. Sanchez doesn't eat standing up. He likes to lie down to feast, like a little quivering prince. Never eats in the dining room.

That leaves...

I lift the candle up, illuminating my bedroom door, open just enough for a tiny dog to waggle his way through.

"Shit," I say, pushing the door open with my foot. "Shit, shit, shit."

The room emerges from the dark, but the candle casts long, warbling shadows. "Sanchez..."

I pause by my chair. Empty. Thank goodness.

Maybe he's not in here?

A growl catches me off guard, but it doesn't affect me too much. Because I know it. Sanchez and I wrestle a lot—his whole body versus my hand. Him growling at me is nothing new, but this is the first time I think he means it.

I hold the candle up, illuminating my bed.

Sanchez is lying on my pillow, teeth bared, the remnants of an eyeball on my pillow, now saturated with chihuahua drool and eyeball fluid. He's got a tendril of meat clutched in his little jaws.

"You little asshole," I say.

Sanchez snaps to his feet, growl shifting toward menacing. Stops me in my tracks. *The hell?* On a normal day, you could reach down and take food from his mouth without complaint. This... Sanchez really might be part wolf.

"Geez, man. Chill."

Sanchez barks at me, the chunk of meat falling onto the bed. With a savage growl, he chases it, grasps it again, and places it on the pillow. Then he turns his attention back to me. The sides of his little jaws draw up on either side. His whole body is shaking, but not with fear.

It's rage.

Toward me.

"Hey, man." I raise my hands and take a step back. "Just eat it all, okay?"

It's a little disturbing that Chez has a hankering for human flesh, but his belly is as good a place as any to hide the wayward eyeball.

But he's not hearing me.

Or...is he still hungry?

Holy shit, his growl isn't protective, it's *aggressive.* I back away toward the door, watching Sanchez's little body lowering, ready to pounce.

"You're better than this, man. You don't need to—"

A series of savage barks tears through the air as Sanchez launches himself toward me. I leap back two steps into the living room and slam the door shut behind me. His little paws scrabble at the door, his muffled growls sending a chill up my spine.

"Everything...okay?" Allie asks.

She's standing in the kitchen with Bree, now dressed in Allie's too long tights and a T-shirt. Bree's long brown hair hangs in front of her face a bit, but she looks less like a walking murder scene and more like a kid again.

Sanchez huffs and moves away from the door, presumably to finish his meal.

"Just...don't go in there. I think Sanchez is broken."

Allie's about to reply when her face scrunches up. "What's that noise?"

I follow the sound, down to my waist. The walkie-talkie is clicking. Someone on the other end is tapping out a message in morse code.

- - - — — — - - -

Dot, dot, dot. Dash, dash, dash. Dot, dot, dot.
S.O.S.

20

When the brief S.O.S transmission stops, I lift the radio to my lips and—

"Don't," Allie says.

My finger hovers over the transmit button. I'm desperate to reach out. To make sure Jen is okay.

"If she could ask for help, she would, right? She's trying to be quiet. If you call back and whatever's out there hears your voice..."

I put the radio down. "Shit." I pace in the kitchen. "I could have gotten her killed."

"Take a breath, Miah," Allie says.

"I need to help her."

"Well, not right now."

I stop, look Allie in the eyes. "Why not?"

"You have problems of your own," she says, glancing at Bree, who's watching me out of one eye—the other side of her face covered by a sheet of hair. Kid needs a ponytail.

"You guys just need to hang tight and stay away from Sanchez. I'll run up the street, check on Jen, and bring her fam back if I can. Simple, right? We already know that going outside isn't *really* instant death. The ol' prophecy lied about that. If I'm sneaky—"

"You're not getting it," Allie says, leaning out to look at Bree's face. Sighs. She takes one of the many hair elastics she keeps around her wrist, turns Bree around, and starts pulling the girl's hair back into a ponytail. When she's done, Allie turns Bree around like an aggressive show pony breeder, thrusting her hands out at the girl's wide-eyed face.

For a moment, I'm lost in Bree's big brown eyes. She's too young to fully understand what's happening, but every moment of this day—including what I say and do next—will have an impact on her for the rest of her life, even if she can't remember it.

When she blinks, the spell is broken, and I see what Allie is really pointing out. At the center of Bree's forehead is a painfully familiar image.

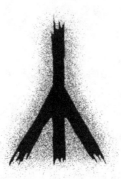

The upside down cross. The death rune. It matches mine. Same size. Same redness. Same screwed up message: You are marked for death. But on a little girl's head. On me, it almost seemed appropriate, I guess. Something I might have done to myself during my darkest days. Hell, I cut up my wrists, gave myself little star tattoos using a sewing needle taped to a pencil and ink from a Bic pen. Why not a brand?

But on Bree, an innocent seven-year-old?

"The hell?" I grumble.

"Should probably start watching our language," Allie says.

I want to point out that all our parents are dead. That most of the world is probably dead. And the social paradigm enforced by older generations, deeming certain words bad, offensive, or even sinful has likely died with them. But I don't want to crush any hope either of them might be holding on to, so I give a nod and say, "Sorry."

I take a knee in front of Bree, looking over the symbol. "Do you remember when this happened?"

"When the sky got bright," she says, with an earnestness that breaks my heart.

"Does it hurt?" I ask.

"Itches." She looks at my forehead. "Is yours itchy?"

"A bit," I say. I'd actually forgotten about it until Bree's mark was revealed.

"Can I draw on mine, too?"

"Of course," I say with a smile. "But let's try to understand them first, okay?"

She shrugs. "Okay."

The back of my mind is still focused on Jen, mapping out paths to approach her home—from the front, the back, and the side. Whether or not I should attempt driving in the dark. Or if I should break out my old ninja costume, and see if it fits. Go all incognito. But the front of my mind homes in on the death rune mystery.

I turn to Allie. "How old is the Three Days of Darkness prophecy?"

"Uhh. Seventeen hundreds, I think. And the second one in the early nineteen hundreds. Something like that. Why?"

"What about death runes?"

"They're like a Norse thing, right? Older than 1000 years. Sometime in the 900s, I think. I'm guessing, obviously."

"Better than I would," I say. "So, some of this is hundreds of years old, and some of it is thousands of years old."

"What's your point?"

"Maybe it happened before. Maybe it's less of a prophecy and more of a retelling, or at least a warning based on actual, not divinely inspired, evidence. Maybe the Norse didn't come up with this." I point to my forehead. "Maybe they came across it the same way we did."

Allie stares at me, either dumbfounded by my brilliance, or by my stupidity. I can't tell which. "That's a lot of maybes."

"Don't the Norse have an end of the world scenario?"

"Ragnarok," Allie says.

I snap my fingers. "That. Yes. What if Norse religion and concepts of life and death, and all that were inspired by the last time this happened? Hell on Earth. What if it was a localized event? Maybe a warmup to the real thing."

"A thousand plus years later?"

"I don't know. Isn't time different for supernatural entities or something? Maybe they were waiting for the right population density? Or the max damage it would do to God. Or who knows what. I don't think we can speculate on *why* they chose now."

"Right... What if it's localized again?" Allie asks. "What if it's just, like, New England or something? Uncle Silvanus would still be alive. He's in California. Maybe we'll still have family if we make it to the end?"

I take Allie's hand. "We still have family *now*." And just to be sure I don't further scar Bree, I take her hand, too. "And I'm not going to let anything happen to us. To any of us? Okay?"

"Okay." Bree wraps her little arms around my neck and leans her head against my shoulder.

The dam I didn't know existed, holding back my emotions, cracks a bit. I manage to hold back the sobs fighting to escape my chest, but my tears flow freely. Allie wipes her own tears from her cheeks, watching the little girl embrace me, both of us understanding that we can't crack up now—for Bree's sake.

This is what it feels like to be a parent, I realize.

How hard must it have been for Mom when I deployed? How hard when I came back broken?

How much sleep did she lose, wondering what I'd seen? What I'd been through? How much did she wish she could have saved me from it? How much did she wish that Dad never died?

Stow it, I think. I'm never going to stop crying if I allow my thoughts to go down that path. *Compartmentalize that shit and deal with it later.*

I pull back from Bree, quickly wiping my eyes and clearing my throat. "Back to the rune."

I spot my partially eaten sandwich on the counter. Grab a knife, cut it in half, and transplant the clean side to a fresh plate. The disk slides loudly over the granite island, stopping in front of the chair Bree is standing beside. "Here. Are you hungry?"

Bree climbs into the chair. I watch her take a bite. Doesn't even wince. She just nods to herself and chews. A pickle and mayo fan if there ever was one. I like this kid.

"What if we're thinking about it backwards?" Allie asks.

"About what?"

"The rune, stupid." Allie heads for the remnants of her own sandwich, hunger reawakened by seeing Bree nosh with abandon. "We assumed it was a bad thing, right?"

"Well, yeah, there's a death rune etched into my forehead. Hard to take it any other way."

"But what's the point of it? Who's going to see it and know what it means?"

She knows the answer. Just wants me to say it. "The de— The... I don't know what to call them."

"Hey, Bree," Allie says. "Do you know what demons are?"

Bree shakes her head. Takes another bite, and with a full mouth says, "Nope."

"Demons it is..." I take a bite of my own sandwich, and I swallow it fast. "The demons would see it."

"We thought you were marked, right? For death. But that's not what happened. They didn't take you. They took Mom. And Rich. Neither of them had the mark."

She's right.

"And you saw one of them, right? Outside. Did it see you?"

Memories of my supernatural encounter surface. The silhouette standing on the rooftop, staring down at me, cackling at me.

It could have eaten, killed, or taken me.

But it didn't.

It just watched.

"Holy shit..." I turn to Bree. "Sorry."

She shrugs and takes another bite.

Then to Allie I say, "The symbol is a *warning*. *To* the demons."

"Warning what?" Allie asks.

"*I* am death." I look at Bree's forehead. "*We* are death."

21

"Don't touch. No, no, no. It will make you sick. That's what Mom says about the blue bottle. Even though it does look yummy." Bree sighs and takes another bite. "Like, why do we have Blueberry Blast Coolers and yucky stuff that looks the same?" She rolls her eyes, big and dramatic. "It's stupid."

"Exactly," I say. "That. It's like a warning label."

"I guess," Allie says. "But if you're so bad that demons don't want you in hell, that can't be great either, right?"

"What if it means we're too good?" I ask.

A lone eyebrow makes a slow climb toward the peak of Allie's forehead.

"Point taken," I say. There's no way that Bree and I are on equal footing when it comes to goodness or purity. "So, what do I and this little cherub have in common?"

"What's your birthday?" Allie asks Bree.

"December 18th," Bree says. "But I wish it weren't. It's too close to Christmas."

"Well, that's not it," I say. I was an April baby.

I look to Allie, waiting for her inquisition to continue, but she stays quiet. "That's all you got?"

"I mean, what else could it be?" she says.

"Maybe it's not something good, or even neutral. It's got to be dramatic if the worst of the worst doesn't want us, right? We need to elementary the shit out of this." I turn to Bree. "Sorry."

She shrugs again. "Daddy says shit all the time. Fuck and bitch, too. Mommy tells him not to, but he doesn't listen. I think they're fun. 'Fucking bitch, clean up this shit!'" She tee-hees a laugh, leaving Allie and me to stare at her, dumbfounded.

Guess our house wasn't the only one on the block whose interior life wasn't accurately reflected by the pristine exterior. Neighborhoods are kind of like the original social network—flashy on the outside but screwed up on the inside.

"As I was saying..." I pry my eyes away from Bree, wondering if we have more in common than I previously assumed. "We need to ask the right questions."

"How do we know what the right question is?" Allie asks.

"When the answer makes sense," I say. "We're different ages, different sexes..." I look at Bree's face. Best guess, her heritage harkens back to England or France. "Different genetic pasts, and genes are already ruled out because they took Mom, and you didn't get this." I point to my forehead. "So, what's the right question?"

"Why?" Allie says.

"So we can deduce—"

"No, I mean 'why' *is* the question. Why are they taking people at all? What's the point? Is it for fun? Sport? A competition? Is it just to be dicks? To take people to Hell? Isn't that what happens when people die anyway? Why the extra effort now? And why not everyone? And what's with branding people?"

"That's a lot of questions rolled into..." My mind drifts. Back to a farm. Not much older than Bree, on my father's shoulder, looking over a roadside electric fence at a field full of cows, chewing the cud. I had a lot of questions then, too. Why they liked grass so much. Could I eat grass? Why they had marks on their hips. My father explained branding to me. That livestock was branded so people knew who the animals belonged to. In case they got lost.

But this brand is different. It's not identifying us as belonging to some demon. It's a warning. Like on a bottle of Windex. Consume this... and die.

"We're spoiled. Bad meat." I look Allie in the eyes. "They're here to eat us. Or take us and eat us later. I don't know."

"Tommy got eaten," Bree says.

We slow turn toward the girl of endless surprises. "Who...was Tommy?"

"My brother." She frowns. Puts the sandwich's remains down. "I don't want to eat meat anymore."

I blink. "It's not meat. It's fake meat. Pea protein or something. Veggies."

"Okay," she says, but she doesn't pick up the sandwich. "A demon ate Tommy. In our kitchen. Then they took Mommy and Daddy."

My heart breaks for the kid. That was her brother's eye in her hair, currently being scarfed down by my feral chihuahua. She's clearly in shock still. Going to have to deal with all this someday, but not right now.

I take Bree's hand. "They took our mommy and...daddy, too."

"Can we get them back?" she asks.

"I don't know..." I give her hand a squeeze. "I don't think so."

"I don't think so, either." A shiver runs through her body. A kind of emptiness fills her eyes. She picks up the sandwich and keeps eating.

We sit in silence for a moment, letting everything percolate.

"So..." Allie says. "You guys are what? Spoiled meat? Like, do you both have cancer or something, and we don't know?"

I shake my head. I see enough doctors to be fairly sure I don't have cancer yet. But I do have... "Lyme."

"I don't think that will go well with her sandwich," Allie says.

"Not a lime, lime, *the disease Lyme*. It's a bacterial infection. It's in my blood."

"So, the demons, from hell, are susceptible to bacterial diseases?"

I shrug. "I don't know, but why risk it, right? Would you eat infected meat?"

"I'm not an immortal demon," Allie says.

"Maybe demons aren't actually immortal." It feels like a stretch. Stands to reason that if demons are real, then so is everything else associated with them, including their angelic past. And everything I know about angels says that they, unlike the human race, don't face death the same way we do.

But they probably don't eat, either, except maybe for fun. And I guess feasting on humanity is a pretty gnarly thing to do. Demonic for sure.

"Maybe they're not demons?" Bree says, taking another bite.

"C'mon," I say. "That's just... I mean... The prophecy is..." My eyes drift to Allie's. "What if she's right? If something like this happened to the ancient Norse, they'd process it through their world view, right? Ragnarok and death runes. But what if that information was passed down through history, to people with a different world view, who viewed the information through a Catholic lens and then passed it down to us as a warning. But instead of Fenris and dire wolves or whatever the Norse were into, it became demons from hell, three days of darkness, God's judgement on the world. But what if this has nothing to do with God?"

"I have herpes," Bree says.

I reel back from the girl, reassessing my preconceived notions about what her life was like before now. I'm about to unleash a solid, 'What the fuck?' when Allie smacks my arm. "Not all herpes is that kind of herpes. It's common. And once you get it, you always have it."

"How do you know so much about herpes?" I ask.

Allie rolls her eyes. "My friend Orin. Orin Enloe. From school. His family likes to share drinks. Turns out his dad had herpes, also probably from childhood, and now they all have it. Probably all still do, with matching brands on their foreheads."

"How far away are they?"

"Rochester, why?"

"Just, if we could find them. It would confirm—"

Allie crosses her arms.

"Unless Jetpack is holding an end of the world sale, we're not going to Rochester."

"But...if we're right, it means I can leave."

"Also means that if we attract too much attention, I could become demon kibble."

"*If* they're demons. And if they're not..." I swing the AK around from my back and give it a pat. "Maybe this will help more than beeswax candles and rosary beads."

"Still, you can't leave, because I can't leave, and we're not separating. That's some stupid-ass horror-movie bullshit, and it's not happening." She finishes speaking, fists perched on her hips the same way Mom does. She's also making a good point, like Mom does.

"But...if they're not eating everyone right away... Maybe they're, I don't know, collecting them in like some kind of people pantry. Maybe they're still alive." I turn to Bree. "You walked all the way here, right? And nothing bothered you?"

"I heard them," she says. "In the woods. But nobody stopped me."

"Allie, if I can go outside, and those assholes don't want to eat me, maybe I can—"

"You are not going out there," she says. "Not without me."

"But *you* can't," I say. "You don't have the thingy. The death rune. You're like Grade A, prime beef, Sis. And probably so is Jen."

She squints at me. "Is that really what this is about? You getting your dipstick wet at the end of the world?"

"First," I say. "Who talks like that? Are you a forty-year-old New Yorker? Second, yeah, I'm worried about Jen. I know that boys come and go in your life. That you don't have trouble making or replacing friends. But she's the first person I've connected with since... Well, a really long time. I want to help her if I can. And help Mom. And Rich. But I can't do that from in here."

Bree throws her hands up. "We don't even have lights!"

"What? Okay. Thanks for the help, Chief, I got it."

"Would you calm down," Allie says. "I'm not saying you can't. I'm saying you can't without me."

"But the death rune..."

"I have an idea about that." She smiles, raises a victorious finger, and does an impression of me, "To the craft emporium!" She offers me my trademarked two fingered salute and then heads toward the foyer.

"Oh!" Bree says, hopping off the chair. "Crafts!"

Candle in hand, the pair clomp up the steps to the second floor together.

I look toward the ceiling and address God, who a moment ago I thought must definitely be real, yet whose existence has once again become debatable. "You know, I understand trial by fire and all that jazz, but two females under sixteen? This is getting out of hand. How about you cut me some slack? Maybe send an angel to tell me what to do? Burning bush the shit out of this?"

I wait a moment, listening to two sets of footsteps moving down the upstairs hall. The craft room door opens, and Bree lets out an, "Ooooooh."

I sigh. "Didn't think so."

22

It's been a long time since I set foot in Mom's craft room. Been a long time since I had a reason to visit the entire second floor. But the craft room... Once upon a time, this was my sacred space, where I would lie alone in bed, looking out the window, crying about Dad's death. It felt safe in that room, to be vulnerable.

Now...

I step inside the craft emporium, and I don't recognize a thing. Even the room's corners look different, viewed now through the eyes of an adult. I thought this would be hard, but I just feel indifferent. Maybe because Mom did a good job organizing. Despite the paints, brushes, and assumed glue sticks, everything has a place.

For a moment, it helps Bree forget that her brother was eaten, and her parents were taken. "Wooow," she says, wide eyes looking around the space, which is impressive, even in the feeble firelight.

Allie is already seated at a table, leaning down in front of a makeup mirror, smearing something on her forehead. A closer inspection reveals a horror effects kit, sporting photos of kids with their faces peeled open.

"Are you sure this is a good idea? That looks pretty hard to pull off."

"If you weren't blazed out of your mind last Halloween, locked in your room watching slasher films, you might know that I'm actually pretty good at this." She leans forward, painting red onto her forehead.

"We were trying to find the right dose," I say.

"Uh-huh."

"And I wasn't watching slasher films. Those are no bueno when you have PTSD from seeing such things in full 3D colorvision."

Allie pauses just long enough to roll her eyes. "Uh-huh."

"Seriously. I was watching 'It's the Great Pumpkin, Charlie Brown.' And even that felt like too much. Lying out there in the middle of the night? In a pumpkin patch? No thank you."

"You're kind of a chicken," Bree says, pretending to shoot a glue gun.

"He's not a chicken," Allie says, a hint of annoyance in her voice. "He's braver than we will ever be. He's just..."

"Broken," I say. "And that was almost a year ago. Right now, I'd take the Great Pumpkin out for drinks, if it meant being done with all this."

"Drinks and a little sumpin' sumpin' after." Allie laughs until I give her a playful shove. "Hey! You're going to make me mess up."

I wander the room trying to distract myself from feelings of impending doom—which is pretty impossible. Despair follows me around like a gremlin, just waiting to tear me apart. What happened to Mom... I don't think all the marijuana in the world is going to numb that pain. I'm doing okay right now. Allie, too. But we're just conjuring our Romani ancestors, swallowing hardship and despair while putting on a show.

Playing piggyback on the gremlin is my concern for Jen. She's new to my life, but I had high hopes. Unable to reply to her S.O.S, for fear of revealing her hiding place, I can't even let her know that we're working on it.

Best case scenario, she's okay and annoyed when we find her. Worst case scenario, she's an eyeball in someone's hair. Or taken. That seems to be the most likely scenario.

"Hey, Bro," Allie says, close to the mirror, tapping her finger against her forehead. "Do me a solid and put on some real clothes."

I look down. Still in the skirt. Still holding candles in its little pockets.

"If we're going to be traipsing around in the woods, it'd be great if you weren't flapping in the breeze, if you know what I mean."

"Traipsing?" I ask.

"Someone needs to fill Mom's shoes while she's...not."

"I like the skirt," Bree says. "It's pretty."

"It is, right?" I twist around, posing until Bree giggles.

Allie raises one hand to the side of her face, and the other in front of Bree. "God, Miah, if you spin any faster, you'll scar her for life."

"Copy that," I say, and I give my two fingered salute. "The asset is en route to the target area. One mike out. Over."

I'm in the hall when Allie says, "Who's the asset in this scenario?"

"Ass..." I say, flipping the back of my skirt up, flashing a full moon in her direction. "...set."

I laugh my way down the stairs, as Allie grumbles to herself, trying to hold back the tirade she'd normally unleash, which makes it even funnier. I'm still giggling when I reach my bedroom door on the first floor, but I stop the moment I remember that the darkness beyond is now guarded by a one-headed, petite Cerberus.

Maybe he's calmed down. I knock on the glass. "Sannnchez."

Furious barking and gnashing of canine teeth responds, his tiny feet scratching at the wood. He's incensed. Out of his little head. Is it just him? Or have all animals gone loco? And if so, are people next?

Future problems.

Right now, I need access to my clothing.

Sanchez isn't really a threat. I could lie still, and I'd starve before he was able to kill me. But I don't want to hurt him.

I smile when the idea comes to me, which is horrible, but also appropriate. I head for the first-floor bathroom, open the closet, dump out dirty clothing, and return with a laundry basket. Back at the door, hand on the knob, I take a steadying breath.

I shove the door open, leap back, and barely have time to prepare myself before Sanchez charges out, mouth frothing, eyes burning with rage, snarling and yipping.

I shout, "Mousetrap!" and slam the basket down toward him. But he's got plans of his own, leaping toward my face, tiny jaws open.

"Gah!" I shout, arms flailing up.

The basket's underside strikes Sanchez's body. It's like he struck a trampoline at high speed. His little body pinwheels through the air until he lands with a thud and slides to a stop ten feet down the hall.

In a little bit of shock, I turn around to find him lying on his side. "Chez? My man? You okay?"

The candlelight is faint, but I can see his chest rising and falling, rapid, like there's a little Pac-Man inside him, opening and closing its mouth. 'Wakawakawaka...' The imaginary Pac-Man must eat a power cookie, because Sanchez is suddenly back on his feet and charging again.

This time I crouch low, putting my dangling nards in the danger zone, but hoping Sanchez hasn't also become smart enough to change tactics.

He's not, and he doesn't. Once again, the little man's hunger for eyeballs leads him to jump at my face. I raise the basket like a baseball catcher. When Sanchez hits the back, I slam it—and by extension, him—on the floor. He yelps from the impact, but I think this is one of those parental 'hurts me more than it does you' scenarios, because he's nipping at my fingers a moment later, and I'm devastated for hurting him. I hurry to a nearby bookshelf, take a sampling of Mom's cookbooks—the biggest and heaviest of them—and put them on top of the laundry basket. Unless Sanchez has been exposed to gamma radiation, I don't think he'll be muscling his way out.

"Hell, dude," I say to my former BFF, "chill."

Doggy spittle flies against my shoes. He growls and barks and tries to gnaw at the little holes in the basket, but he makes no progress.

Disturbed by his savage display nearly as much as I was by the appearance of a legit demon, I slide back into my room, taking a candle with me. The moment I'm out of sight, Sanchez settles.

Definitely demons, I tell myself, rummaging through my drawers, looking for clothing I haven't worn or thought about wearing for a long time. There was a time when I was happy about being in the military. Before seeing any real action, when I felt strong and emboldened by the training, like I could do anything—including get over my father's death. I bought my own camo gear, nighttime grays for sneaking around in the woods, day or night. Really, it's just a step up from the old ninja costume. But more functional.

I take out the cargo pants and short sleeve T-shirt, both gray camo. I could go head to toe camouflage, but I decide against it because the girls don't have it. Wouldn't seem right, getting all gussied up for stealth but having nothing for them. And my black T-shirt is already dark enough, if you ignore the big 'KISS' on the front. So, instead, I throw on some boxers and cargo shorts, and tie my shoelaces tight. Next, I gear up with the AK's two remaining magazines, a handful of candles, a lighter, and a big ass KABAR knife—the kind used by King in those Delta novels I read while deployed. I should probably find a cross, too, but it didn't seem to help Rich. At all.

"I'm as ready as I'm gonna be," I tell myself.

"You ready?" Allie asks from the doorway, Sanchez growling at her from his prison cell. I jump at her voice. Hands on knees, I catch my breath. Then I slap in one of the two AK magazines, chamber a round, and say, "Ohh, hold on." I flick my lighter, set the three candles still mounted to the barrel ablaze, and raise the weapon to my shoulder. I give a confident smile, like Arnold Schwarzenegger in Terminator 2, when he finds the mini gun, and say—

"Moment's lost," Allie says. "Could have been cool, though."

"Damnit," I say, and I follow her out of the room and to the front door, where Bree is waiting.

We huddle up in front of the door.

"How did I do?" Allie points to her forehead. In the darkness of my room, I missed the death rune on her forehead, but here in the foyer, lit by multiple candles now, I see the symbol burned into her flesh.

I suck air through my teeth, wincing at the sight of it. "Youch, that looks painful."

She swats my hand away when I reach a finger out to see if it feels real, too. "Don't touch it, dufus."

"Well, it looks legit." I look down at Bree. "Ready to kick ass?"

Bree gives a brave nod, though her eyes look somewhat dead...like she's only half here. "Ready."

Allie and I share a look. Neither of us really want to do this. To risk Bree's life, or our own. But we're New Englanders. We might normally be distant and standoffish with neighbors, but when the shit goes down, we step up. Blizzards. Ice storms. The god damned Perfect Storm. Hell on Earth is just another reason for us to help our neighbors.

And that's what we're going to do.

I open the front door, see what's outside, gasp a breath, and freeze.

Beneath me, Bree says, "Fuck."

23

Outside. In the street. A living darkness moves. Lit by the occasional flare from the forest fire, now distant and moving away, the figure is mostly concealed by a churning storm of wispy smoke shifting around it like a separate being...or maybe many beings.

The souls of its victims, I think.

I don't speak the words aloud, mostly because I can't. Because I'm locked in place, eyes shifting from the demon to the person it's dragging across the pavement, trailing a streak of blood through the middle of the road, where there should be double yellow lines.

I don't recognize the victim. He's balding, probably in his fifties, and just shy of three hundred pounds. I can't tell much more about him because he's saturated in blood.

I think he's dead.

Please be dead.

I'm not ready for a fight. Not ready to deal with the guilt that will come from allowing someone to be dragged to their death, either. He's probably someone's father. Or husband.

The demon drags him along, almost casually, like the man's girth means nothing. The monster is taller than me, by maybe a few inches, but it's all lanky. What I can see of its musculature, past its dimly lit, rough skin, is tight and sinewy.

But if it's a demon, who can look like anything, muscle probably has nothing to do with its strength.

I watch the man's chest as he's dragged along. It doesn't rise or fall. And all that blood... He must be dead.

The demon stops, detecting us finally, or deciding it doesn't enjoy being watched. Black eyes inside a swirling storm turn toward us. Beneath them, a hint of teeth through a snarling mouth. Four wicked tendrils rise up from its back, emerging from the storm like snakes, tremoring with spastic fervor.

"I think it sees us," Allie says.

"Uh-huh." Bree takes Allie's hand.

I slowly lift the AK-47 to my shoulder. "If it charges, go inside and close the door."

The demon drops the dead man's arm and turns fully toward us, letting out a hyena yip.

Inside the house, Sanchez goes wild, barking and snarling. I'd like to think he's being protective, that his big dog display is meant to fend off danger, but I'm pretty sure the demon's presence is bringing out the pooch's dark side. If he were free of the basket, he'd probably help this thing tear us apart.

I can feel the demon's eyes on me, probing. Then on Bree and finally on Allie.

Braced for an attack, I'm a little caught off guard when the thing cackles like we're the funniest thing it's ever seen—or maybe the pain in our eyes is. Then its tendrils hoist the big man up and bind him to the demon's back. Two long strides and a leap is all it takes for the thing to disappear into the woods across the street.

Behind Larry's house.

"It worked." Allie motions to her forehead. "The death rune works. It didn't want anything to do with us."

Bree tugs on my shorts. "Was that a demon?"

"Pretty sure," I say, heart hammering.

"That's not what ate Tommy," she says.

"Great," I say, moving down the porch steps on shaky legs. "That's... that's just great."

"Miah," Allie says, sounding worried. She and Bree are on the porch, watching me. "Are you okay?"

"Fine," I say. It's a bald-faced lie, like the photos of pristine burgers on the McD's menu. "Hey, did you know that in Australia, McDonald's is called Maccas?"

Their brows furrow in unison.

I'm cracking up. They both see it.

"Miah..."

I whirl around. "How are you two just standing there? How are you not freaking out? There was just a *demon* in our street, with a dead dude Dora the Explorer backpack, leading the way to hell, which is apparently somewhere behind Larry's house. Yeah, I'm freaking out, and you should—"

"Miah!" Allie shouts. It's the first time I've heard her sound like Mom, and it shocks me into silence. "Can we lose our minds later, okay? Right now, I'm the only one out here whose death rune is fake. If they figure that out—"

My emotions are like a soda can that's been shaken and popped open, but moving in reverse, sucked back inside, and resealed inside its pressurized state. I suck in a breath and hold it like that can. Then I let it out slowly, centered again...as much as anyone can be, during an invasion from Hell. "I'm good. I'm good."

They stare at me, unsure.

"Seriously. I just... I didn't think I'd ever have to do anything like this again, you know?"

"Again..." Bree says.

"War is hell, kid. For some people on this planet, all of this craziness—the death, people being taken, attacks by powers beyond comprehension—is normal life, except the demons look a little more like..." I turn to Allie, stoic. "I'm fine. I just didn't like what I saw."

They move down the steps, following me through the front yard, toward the woods lining the sidewalk.

"What does that mean? We all saw the same thing, right? Swirling, demon-thing with a dead man, right?"

"Right," I say, stopping at the dark forest's fringe.

Allie takes my arm. Forces me to face her. "What did you see?"

My sister is persistent. She won't let this go until I answer her honestly. "A reflection."

"A reflection?"

"You saw yourself?" Bree asks. Kid's smart. She gets what I'm saying, but not the ramifications.

"Yeah," I say, tussling the girl's hair. "I did." Then I blow out the candles taped to the rifle and slip into the forest, headed uphill toward Jen's house. The lack of light is unnerving, but it also makes us hard to see. Demons have good night vision, I'm assuming, because, you know, they blotted out the sun and all that, but the candles in this darkness would be a beacon. A visual dinner bell—at least for Allie. And that's unacceptable.

Allie doesn't say another word. I know her curiosity is far from sated, but the darkness around us—hiding God knows what—sucks the conversation from our lungs.

Every few steps I pause to listen for the telltale rattle of feet moving through dead leaves coating the forest floor. Other than Allie and Bree behind me, I hear nothing. Smelling for danger is useless. Sulfur and smoke slides through the trees like stinky apparitions. I could be standing over a dead body and my nose would be none the wiser.

As we approach the first of many homes separating us from Jen's house, I chart a new course, deeper into the woods. This home belongs to the Jeantet family, I think. Dad is Adam. Sometimes talks to Rich. Man gossip that I can hear from my room's open windows, mostly about the neighbor across from Adam. Corey Simpson? No...that's the mailman. Susan Smith. Susan Lewis-Smith. They call her the 'hyphenator,' like she's extra tough for keeping her maiden name.

"Huh," the sound just kind of slips out.

"What?" Allie whispers. "Did you see something?"

"I just realized I know more of the neighbors' names than I thought."

"What?" Allie is flummoxed. "*That's* what you're thinking about? What, are you? ADHD, too?"

"Yeah," I say. "Kinda." The truth is, I'm pondering names and faces because I don't want to dwell on the open door, broken windows, and blood spatters decorating the backside of Adam's house.

How many kids did he have?

I push the answer from my mind and pick up the pace, no longer bothering to stop and listen. The sooner we're behind solid walls and locked doors, the better.

Halfway to Jen's house, I whisper, "Allie."

"What?"

"What's behind Larry's house?"

"Trees."

"Well, yeah, but how many?"

"Larry is funny," Bree says.

"You know Larry?" I ask.

"He's Zack's dad. I wonder if Zack got eaten..."

"I'm sure Zack is fine." I can almost feel my nose growing longer. The truth is, Zack is probably as screwed as Larry—and just about everyone else in the neighborhood, including Bree's family and mine. But I'm still fishing for a nugget of hope.

"Isn't there like a sanctuary or something?" I ask.

"That's right," Allie says. "Bellamy Preserve or something. Why?"

"And beyond that?"

Allie stops. "It's the river. And Great Bay."

I nod in the dark. "A dead end."

"So where are they taking them?" Allie says.

I'm about to say, 'That's what I want to find out,' when Bree tugs on my hand, and whispers, "There's Jen's and Emma's house."

Like Allie, the kid gets around. Or maybe it's the whole neighborhood? I spend a lot of time in my room, judging everyone here, but I'm starting to get the feeling that I'm the odd man out, and not just because I'm funny looking and behave strangely. Allie and Bree seem to know everyone and their houses, from the front and back. How many barbecues have I missed?

The back of Jen's house looks quiet and normal.

"Let's go," I whisper, pushing through a wall of ferns. I head for the home, thinking, *please be alive, please be alive, please be alive.*

24

The house seems empty from the outside. Some of the windows are covered by what look like blankets, but not all of them. They either skipped some rooms, opting to close doors instead of covering windows, or they were interrupted before they finished, which I guess wouldn't be surprising if Mr. Gearhart had already been taken...or eaten.

I head for the back door, weaving my way past a dope inground pool, a patio, and a barbecue big enough to cook half a pig. The back door is a slider. I give it a tug. I turn to Bree, standing behind me. "Know how to pick a lock?"

"Pick a lock?" Allie says. "These are wealthy white people in New Hampshire."

"They might not normally lock their doors," I say, "but they're definitely locked now."

"Obviously." Allie starts scouring the landscaping around the patio. She lights a candle and leans down, inspecting plants and bark mulch. Then she reaches down and picks up a hunk of granite.

"I'd normally be down for pitching a rock through a window. Sounds like fun, but I think it might be a little loud, given the dire circumstances."

Allie makes her patented, 'There has never been a bigger idiot in the history of world than you' face, and she gives the rock a shake. Something metal jingles inside. A key.

"Wait," I say, "Do we have one of those?"

She shrugs and smiles, a noncommittal yes.

"All the times I've been locked out, I could have just plucked a key from a rock like Excalibur from the stone and—"

Bree holds a finger up to her lips.

"Shhh. So loud."

"Sorry," I say, leaning down to her, hands on knees, while Allie opens the rock and recovers the key. I whisper, "It's just...have you ever been locked out of the house?"

"My parents left me in a Walmart parking lot for two hours," she replies. "They forgot I was with them."

"Geez." I purse my lips. "Okay, that's worse. Never mind."

"Hey," Allie says, inserting the key and giving it a twist. "We're in."

I light the three candles taped to the rifle. "I'll go first. Stay close. If anything goes south, we bolt."

"Penguins live in the south," Bree says. "In Antarctica."

"Yes," I say. "They do. You know, I was doubtful about having a seven-year-old tagging along, but I'm starting to understand the skills and knowledge that you bring to the table." I give her a smile and boop her nose. Then I step through the door and into a dining area separated from the kitchen by a countertop.

I do a slow scan of the space, working hard to see inside every shadow while attempting to avoid extinguishing my light source. No blood. No bodies. No...nothing.

Allie steps in beside me holding Bree's hand.

"This place is immaculate," I say.

"Mrs. Gearhart keeps a clean house," Allie says. "She's one of those non-career ladies who gives everything to their house and family."

"Sounds dreadful," I say.

"One hundo," Allie says, "but I think she kind of loves it."

"To each their own," I say, and I close the sliding door behind us. Somewhat muted to the outside world, I speak a little louder. "Jen!"

When I get no reply, I take out the walkie and give it a few clicks. I haven't seen evidence of anything in the house yet, no sight nor smell, but something could be lurking.

I step deeper into the home, knowing where I'm going, despite never having been inside the building. There are a few basic floor plans for McMansions, even big ones like those in this neighborhood, and all of them have second floor access in the foyer. Most of the first floor is open. If she's here...and alive...she'd have heard us. That leaves the second floor, or the basement. But who hides in a basement? They're scary enough on their own, even when they're finished, and they have a pool table, a wet bar, and an arcade...

Then I remember exactly whose house I'm in. There's probably an armory in the basement. But still, it's a basement. Upstairs first.

Bree shivers, clutching her goose-bumped arms. But not because she's afraid. The house is absolutely freezing. The AC is cranked, filling the house with a white noise buzz and frigid air.

"It's cold enough in here to cut glass," Bree says.

I can't help but snicker. The kid's running commentary is helping take the edge off. But she takes offense at my laugh. "What? Daddy says that when it's cold."

"Your dad has a way with words," I say. "It makes me happy."

Satisfied, she gives a nod and then falls back in line, following me into the foyer—

—where my stomach lurches. The front door, and most of the frame that had been holding it to the house, are missing. Looks like a wrecking ball slammed into the wall, from the inside headed out.

Lying in the grass outside, the door's remnants lie shattered. It's hard to see in the dim light, but the wood fragments are glistening. Wet. Probably blood. I don't bother checking.

I head up the single, wide staircase. It's carpeted in red, and it's well-constructed. No creaky boards here. Our ascent is silent. I pause at the top. "Where is Jen's room?"

Both girls point to the right.

We move down the hallway, inspecting each door we pass. The doors are all open, the windows covered. "Jen... Jen!"

"Next door on the right," Allie says.

We move in as a unit, fanning out inside the room. It's empty. Decorated with dark and surreal paintings. Jen's work. Lurking creatures. A lot of black and dark red. More than a few tentacles. "Definitely a freak," I whisper to myself. Then I check the closet.

Empty.

Two minutes later, we've confirmed that the entire second floor is empty. No one hiding. No signs of death. Whatever happened here, it was by the door and in the front yard.

Same as Mom and Rich.

"So," Allie says. We're all standing at the top of the stairs, looking down at the carnage outside the gaping hole in the home's front. "Basement."

I sigh. "Yeah."

"No one's allowed in the basement," Bree says.

"At your house?" I ask.

She shakes her head. "Here. Mr. Gearhart says it's dangerous."

Right. The armory.

After pausing to glance out the front door again—the night is calm and quiet for the moment—we stand at the closed basement door.

"Should we knock?" Allie asks.

"Do we really want to announce ourselves?" I ask.

"Pretty sure if there's anyone or anything in the house, they already know we're here."

"But not who or what we are."

"It's okay," Bree says.

We turn toward her small voice. The basement door is now wide open, the knob still in her little hand. I move to the doorway, aiming the rifle down. Nothing but steps and white walls. Definitely finished. At the bottom is a framed black and white photo of Muhammad Ali, all sweaty and punching another guy, whose name no one remembers. I read it like a street sign, 'Tough Guys Ahead.' Definitely Mr. Gearhart's world.

I descend the steps slowly, my aim locked on the doorway at the bottom, leading to the right. Halfway down, I say, "Hello? Anybody home?"

It feels like a stupid thing to say, but if anyone is down here, and armed, I want them to know I'm human and not a demon pretending to be. "It's Miah, from down the street. Jen's friend. I'm here with my sister Allie and, uh, Bree, also from down the street."

By the time I finish speaking, I'm at the bottom of the stairs, just outside the door. A nudge with my foot is all it takes to open the door. Beyond, another hallway, one door on the left, an open space beyond. More black and white sports photos line the walls. Moments that look historic, but I can't place them. So, I follow them, pausing for a moment to check the door on the left. Locked. Also, metal and solid.

I'll come back to it, I think, and I push onward, entering a large space. The man cave is different than how I'd pictured it. There's a wet bar, but it's pretty slick, fashioned from a single slab of tree. Probably something exotic or illegal like redwood. The kind that lots of money and privilege buys you. No sports memorabilia here. The walls are covered in animal heads, antlers, and mounted fish. It's a taxidermist's wet dream, and an actual nightmare. At least in the flickering candlelight. Everything looks alive, shifting about, glass eyes glinting.

"Yoo-hoo," I say, trying to hide my growing fear. "Hello?"

No response. I pick up the walkie again. Hold it to my face.

"What if they're hiding out in the woods?" Allie asks, stopping me. "That could still give them away."

I sigh and put it away. It's an annoying point, but a good one. "That leaves just one more room."

Back down the hallway, Allie and Bree beside me, we stand in front of the metal door. I raise my fist...and knock. Gently at first. Then I say, "Hello? Hello!" When I get no response, I pound. All of my worry and grief comes out all at once, positive that no one is inside, that Jen is gone, taken, or dead. I pound the door with my fist, and with a burst of anger I kick the door as hard as I can.

The door doesn't even shake. It was designed to take a hit.

But then the door takes another hit—this time from the inside.

We collectively step back from the door, eyes wide.

"Holy shit," Allie says. "They trapped one."

The door shakes, pounded from the inside. The collision sounds distant. The faint cackle of a hyena follows, muffled, hard to hear. I think it's an armory and a safe room, but it's been used in reverse.

"It's trapped," I say, "Demons aren't immaterial."

"But they totally are," Allie says. "Or can be. That's like supernatural being 101."

The door is struck again. This time harder, the metal bending outward a little bit. "Also, I don't think it will be trapped for long. Can we leave before it gets out? The death rune might mean we're spoiled meat or something, but that doesn't mean it won't see us later and be like, '*You!* and kill us out of spite."

Something cracks when the door is struck again, the demon inside shrieking louder, whipping itself into a frenzy. We bolt up the stairs, through the kitchen, out the back door, and straight into hot blazing death the likes of which haven't been seen since the Allies stormed Omaha Beach.

25

"Fuck! Shit! Cock!" I shout, dive tackling Allie and Bree to the patio behind the brick encased grill. Bullets thunder through the night, disintegrating the masonry and pummeling the barbecue. Feels like a familiar eternity, but it's over in seconds.

"Whoa! Whoa! Whoa!" I shout, feeling a bit like Dr. Peter Venkman after the Ghostbusters shot up an elegant dining room. "We're human!"

Debris rattles to the patio floor around us.

I wince as the scent of propane overwhelms the sulfur stench.

"Get up," I whisper to the girls. "We can't stay here!" Before Allie can argue, I pull oven the barbecue's lower doors, revealing a propane tank with a bullet hole, the gas hissing out. Happily, this isn't a video game. Propane tanks don't explode when you shoot them. But breathing in a tank full of gas could be just as deadly.

"We're coming out!" I shout. "Please don't shoot!"

I haul the girls up, raise my hands, and then lead them into the open, away from the toxic gas. "Don't shoot! Don't shoot!"

We stagger to a stop, exposed and vulnerable. My body is tense, waiting for the gunfire to resume and my life to be snuffed out. I could live with that. Me dying. But not Allie, and not Bree. So, I shove them behind me, making myself a meat shield, and hoping the shooters' bullets aren't powerful enough to punch straight through me and into my sister.

For a moment, I feel like I might vomit.

Then...

"Miah?"

I blink in surprise. "Jen?"

Two shadows move out of the woods. They're dressed in black, head to toe military garb, tactical vests, black hoods. If they weren't both shy of five foot four, I'd think Russian Spetsnaz had invaded. The taller of the two pulls her mask off, unfurling blonde hair and uncovering a face that is both familiar and a stranger.

Jen's smile doesn't reflect joy. Just relief. Her face is spattered in blood. Probably not her own. Since her father was already missing, and I'm assuming the short spec ops soldier by her side is Emma, the blood must belong to Mrs. Gearhart.

"Are you okay?" I ask, moving closer, still wary of the M4 clutched in her hands. It's angled toward the ground. She's been trained well. But her finger is still on the trigger.

Jen's eyes snap to mine. "We— We trapped one in the basement. We thought you were—"

"We're not one of them." I reach my hand out. "Ease up, Jen." She flinches when I rest my hand on the M4, making sure it can't come up. "Before you shoot your sister's foot."

Jen looks to her weapon's muzzle and then over to Emma's feet. Her hand jerks away from the trigger. I turn to Emma, and repeat my calm, but insistent order. "Ease up."

"Finger off the trigger," Jen says. "They're friendlies."

So strange to hear the neighborhood babe/artist speaking like an operator, but I suppose it shouldn't be surprising. Wouldn't be surprised if her dad took them hunting, or paintballing, or to the range—or all of those in one day.

"Emma?" Allie says.

Emma peels her mask off. Holds her arms out. The sisterly duo embraces like long lost friends. Bree joins in.

"I feel like we should be hugging, too," I say to Jen while my inner monologue cringes. *So lame!* But then Jen has her arms wrapped around me. I can feel her body shaking, even through the armor.

She whispers in my ear. "They took Mom."

"Mine, too," I say.

We squeeze each other a little tighter, releasing our sorrow in unison, comforted by the other, united in pain.

"We trapped one in the safe room," Emma announces.

"We noticed," Allie says.

Bree giggles. "It was annngry."

"It was after me," Jen says into my ear.

"Not Emma?"

She shakes her head. I lean out of the embrace and look Emma over. She's a bit frazzled, her sweaty blonde hair covering her forehead and part of her face.

I reach out for her hair, but she flinches away. "Hands off, creep."

"I just want to see," I say, and I motion to my forehead.

Emma's eyes widen upon seeing the symbol.

"We all have them," Bree says.

"Mine is fake," Allie confesses.

"I'll do it," Emma says, moving her hair out of her face with a shaking hand, revealing the death rune branded on her forehead. "Do you know what it means?"

"Bad meat," Bree says.

"Geez," I say, forcing a smile. "It's...not that simple. It means that you have something inside you that they don't like. Something that would be...bad for them to...you know what. 'Bad meat.' Means that you and me, and little Miss Straightforward here have something wrong with us that is potentially deadly to them."

"Like...*cancer?*" Emma is mortified.

"More like a disease, or a bacterial infection. Something chronic that doesn't go away. You might not even know about it, but they somehow do. So, you were marked, along with the rest of us when the sky got bright."

"But yours is fake?" Jen asks Allie.

"Did it myself," Allie says. "Probably should give you one, too."

"Why..?"

"They leave you alone," I say, "when they see the symbol. Demons are kind of germaphobes, or something."

"Demons?"

"Like the kind from hell?" Emma asks.

"Yeah. Sort of. Maybe, but probably definitely demons. Honestly, we don't know, but they're pretty supernatural."

"Except that I stabbed one in the back, and it definitely did not like it," Jen says.

"You *stabbed* one?" Allie asks, unable to contain a smile of respect. "That's frickin' awesome!"

All eyes turn down to Bree. She looks back, unblinking, a slight smile on her face.

"*Bree,*" Jen says, a little shocked. Then to me, she says, "Is this because of you?"

"One would suppose, but I think it's her father's influence...and she's processing a lot. There's a reason she's here. With us."

Jen sobers fast, trying not to react to the news that Bree's family is dead. She swallows, puts her hand on Bree's head, and says, "It *was* fricking awesome."

"But we don't want to revisit it," Allie says. "That door isn't going to hold forever. And we don't want to be here when that happens."

"Where can we go?" Emma asks.

"Our house," I say. "We still have a front door, not that it really matters. And Emma can give you one of these." I point to my death rune.

"What if it remembers?" Jen asks. "That I don't have a...whatever it's called."

"Death rune," I say. "And let's just...try not to be seen. I'll take point. Emma, you bring up the rear."

"Why am I in the back?" she asks. "Are you trying to get rid of me?"

"What? No." She's not buying it, so I elaborate. "Look, you've got a death rune on your forehead. Same as me. You also wield an M4 like your dad was John Rambo, and he kind of was—*is.* Since I'm not about to give Potty Mouth Petunia a weapon, you and I are going to sandwich the others between us. Because they're more vulnerable. Because we are badasses with rifles, right?"

Emma stares at me.

"Miah..." Jen's about to scold me. But then—

"Right," Emma says, she ejects her magazine and slaps in a fresh one. "Badasses."

"You just..." I point to her weapon. "You need to..."

Emma pulls back the charging handle and hits the bolt release, chambering a round.

I smile at her. "Badass. Now, everyone stay close. Slow and quiet." When I get four nods in return, I head for the woods, spurred onward by the repetitive boom emanating from the Gearhart basement.

26

Our journey through the woods isn't slow, or quiet. Thirty seconds into our stealthy hike, we all felt the cold claws of darkness poking into our backs like some ancient primal warning system that screams, 'There's scary shit in the dark, man!' And the moment we sped up, filling the woods with the sound of shuffling feet and crunching leaves, I started getting peppered with questions.

About demons.

About the prophecy.

About hell, and the sun, and every other tangential subject matter related to current events. By the time we reach my yard, I feel like we've covered the totality of human knowledge just short of tampon usage and toxic shock syndrome, which I—a single man—somehow know is a thing.

I stop at the tree line and crouch. The line of ladies sidles up next to me and lower themselves into the shadows—quiet once more.

"What are you doing?" Allie asks.

"Making sure the front door is still there," I say. It is. "And that no one is waiting inside."

"Looks dark," Emma says.

"That's because the windows are covered."

Allie gives me a look that screams, 'Dufus,' but she doesn't say it aloud.

"Right," I say. "I'll check it out before we head in." To Emma I say, "If something tries to get at our sisters, you get between it and them. Hold that trigger down until it's empty, or until the target stops moving."

When she nods, I find a new level of respect for her. The bratty little sister has guts.

"You," I say to Bree, "are in charge."

She gives me a wide-eyed smile, and I boop her nose again, saying, "Boop." It's totally corny, but I'm thinking about making it a thing. At least with the kid. Aside from Allie growing up, I haven't spent a lot of time— well, *any* time—with little kids. Booping them on the nose seems like an acceptable, but not a creepy way, to express affection for a child that isn't a blood relative, and who is mostly a stranger.

"Adorable," Allie groans. "Can we get this over with? I don't want to be out here anymore."

A nod and a dash later, I'm at the front steps. Feels like I'm at some- one else's home. Like I shouldn't be here. Like going back inside is a violation. I'm not sure why. I'm just unsettled.

Probably because I'm imagining a horde of demons on the door's far side.

But why would they go inside an empty house?

Ambush, I think. *Duh.*

But not for me. Putting a little too much faith in the power of the death rune, I head for the door, grab the handle, give it a turn, and—

—nothing.

"What are you doing?" Allie hisses from the woods.

"It's locked!" I whisper back.

"Seriously?! You locked the door?"

"*I* didn't lock it!"

Rustling leaves announce the girls' exit from the woods. Crouching low, Jen leads the way and Emma brings up the rear, both with guns up, sweeping for trouble. They look like an Oompa Loompa Spec Ops team.

I take a moment to smile—it's the little things—and then I try the door again.

Still locked.

Allie breaks ranks and heads for the bushes lining the porch, disappearing inside them for a moment before emerging with another fake rock, from which she plucks a key like it's Excalibur and wielding it makes her King. Which I suppose it does, because we all move out of her way and let her approach the door.

The key slides inside the deadbolt lock, but before Allie can turn it, my hand snaps out and grabs her wrist. For a moment, I'm confused about why I did it. While Allie turns her sisterly stink eye in my direction, instinct and logic have a momentary pow-wow.

"If you didn't lock the door," I say. "And *I* didn't lock the door..."

Her eyes widen with understanding. She moves to the side, hand still on the key. "I'll open, you...shoot."

I aim the AK-47 toward the closed door. Finger on the trigger, I give Allie a nod. She slowly turns the deadbolt lock until it snaps open, confirming my suspicions. The only way to lock the deadbolt from the outside is with a key, and neither of us did that.

Someone or something is waiting inside our home.

Allie moves the key to the knob lock. The moment she turns it, I'm going to kick the door open.

"This might be loud," I whisper to Bree.

She covers her ears. So does Emma. Jen looks ready to fight, M4 shouldered.

"Okay," I whisper to Allie. "Do it quick, and I'll give it a kick. Sorry. Accidental rhyme. That was horrible."

"Just..." Allie rolls her eyes. "Are you ready?"

I set my eyes on the closed door. My eyes have adjusted to the starlit environment enough to see the people around me. But the inside of the house is going to be pitch black. I won't know what I'm shooting at until it's dead and I've lit a candle.

Or until I'm sprawled in the grass, bleeding out, while a demon hyena laughs at me. One of the two.

"Do it," I say.

Allie twists the key and the doorhandle together. The door cracks open. As Allie releases the knob and steps back, I kick the door in, raise the rifle, and stare into the black.

For a moment, nothing.

Then a Doppler effect banshee scream races toward me.

My finger twitches, but I don't pull the trigger. A large part of gun training involves shooting the right target. We want to kill the enemy, not civilians, even when they're terrified and acting irrationally. So, I spin the rifle around and thrust the butt into the darkness, aiming for the sound.

The impact that follows cuts the scream short. It's followed by a thud.

I stand frozen for a moment. Turn to Allie. "I don't think that was a demon."

She shakes her head.

We flick our lighters to life at the same time, illuminating the foyer. Laid out on the floor, arms akimbo, legs folded over, the man looks like a crucifix adorned in Red Sox garb—T-shirt and hat. Beside him lies a baseball bat.

"It's Mr. Patton," Emma says, as the girls enter the Foyer.

Jen closes the door behind us, locking it again.

"From across the street," Allie says.

"I know who he is," I say, meaning I know his name and not much else.

Mr. Patton...aka, Danny, is the Bostonian. New to the neighborhood. A New Hampshire virgin. Probably not the best introduction to the area, but I sure as shit wouldn't want to be in a city right now.

After lighting a few candles, I crouch down over him. There's a lump emerging from his forehead where I whacked him, but no death rune. Which means he survived—outside—on his own.

Somehow.

He's from the city. Doesn't have a gun. Clearly didn't know about the prophecy. And yet, here he is, sprawled out on my floor, bedazzled in Red Sox gear. Maybe demons are Yankees fans? That would probably make sense to anyone from New England.

"Ungh." He's coming around.

I step over Danny and take his bat, just in case he returns to consciousness swinging. We stand around him like a cult, looking down at the helpless victim we're about to sacrifice.

"Oh my frickin' gahd..." He raises a hand to his head. "Jay. I swear to god, Jay. If this is anothah one of your—" His eyes blink. Sees that he's not where or when he thought, and that Jay, whoever that is, isn't here.

He looks from me to Allie and then around the circle, forehead furrowing when he lands on Bree. "Are you guys frickin' real?" He turns to me. "Guy, please tell me you are frickin' real."

"We're real," I tell him.

His eyes widen.

"You're the deah man, yeah? Almost got creamed by the stampede. Fuck me if we shouldn't a seen this coming. I mean, deah don't act like that, right?"

"You think that because...deer ran out of the woods...that we should have guessed hell was unleashed on Earth?" I ask.

"Is that what this is? Hell?"

"On Earth," Allie says. "Yeah."

"Shit. I thought it was frickin' aliens."

"He swears more than Daddy," Bree observers.

Danny turns to Bree. Seems to notice her age for the first time. "Oh, shit. Double shit. Sorry, uh, little one."

"Little one?" Jen says.

"Kid. Whatever. I'll, ahh, I'll try to clean it up, yeah?"

Bree shrugs. Like most people under thirty, she's indifferent to the dirty, filthy, crude words deemed inappropriate by older, stodgier generations.

"Sorry about the head," I tell him, and I mean it. If I'd known someone was inside, I'd have announced myself, and probably not kicked the door open.

He feels his forehead. Winces. "I don't remember what happened."

"You thought we were a demon," Bree says. "But we thought *you* were a demon. So, Miah hit you in the head."

Danny sits up. Groans, holding the sides of his head. "Couldn't have hit me a little less hard?"

"The plan *was* to shoot you," I tell him, patting the rifle. He seems to notice it for the first time, then the M4s carried by the Gearhart girls.

"Oh, sweet. Have you killed one yet?"

"Easier said than done," Jen says. "I stabbed one, and it just kind of seemed annoyed."

"I domed one with the bat," Danny says, mimicking the overhead swing and then he regrets the motion, squinting and groaning from head pain. "More than once, actually. If it was a human being, I'm pretty sure it'd be dead. Probably not if they're demons, yeah? Killing a demon takes like an angel or something. Spear of Destiny, right? And if these are demons, where are all the angels and shit? Why aren't they out heah protectin' us? Maybe gahdian angels are on strike or something. Are you sure they're demons? I was thinking more like aliens, you know? Like from—"

"Danny," I say.

He blinks to a stop. "Yeah, guy?"

"Slow down. Take a breath. I think you're in shock."

"And probably have a concussion," Jen adds. "You should lie down."

I offer my hand to him. "I'm Miah, by the way."

He doesn't take my hand. Doesn't seem to even see it. "Like Nehemiah. Or Jeremiah? Or—"

"The first," I say, and then I point to each of the girls. "Bree. Jen. Emma. This is my sister, Allie."

He looks us over. Looks uncomfortable. "What's with the...?" He motions to his forehead, but I understand that he's talking about the death rune adorning four of our five foreheads.

"Long story. I'll explain it once we're settled, along with everything else, okay?"

"Okay...yeah. Sure." He looks around the house like he'll see something he missed earlier. "Where are your families?" He motions to me. "I mean, I know you're like a grown man an' all, but you live with your family, right?"

"They're dead," Allie says, matter of fact.

"Or taken," I add. "We don't know which."

"But Tommy is definitely dead," Bree adds, breaking my heart.

"W-who was Tommy?" Danny asks.

"My brother," Bree says. "They ate him."

Jen puts her hands on Bree's shoulders, saying, "Let's see what's in the kitchen," and she leads her away from a stunned Danny.

"Is there ice cream?" Bree asks.

Jen and Bree slide out of sight. "Let's find out."

I offer my hand to Danny. He takes it, and I pull him up to his feet, steadying him while he holds his head. "Got any pain ki—"

A tremor rolls through the house.

Everyone goes still.

"What was that?" Danny whispers.

I hold a finger to my lips.

The tremor repeats. On a normal day, I'd miss it completely. Assume it was a heavy truck rumbling past, or construction somewhere, or something in the house. Anything. But today...

The shaking repeats. Again. And again. Louder. From the side of the house, and then past it.

Something large is walking past, I realize. I frantically hold my finger to my lips again, making sure Danny, Allie, and Emma all see it. When they're nodding, I blow out the candles. Then I sneak to the door, feeling around in the pitch black until I find the knob and the deadbolt. I unlock the door slowly, avoiding making any sound, and then I give the knob a turn.

The door opens. Just a crack. Just enough for me to get a single eyeball's view of the street.

I look for just a second, because it's all I can stand.

Panic swells over me. I close the door, a little too fast, thumping it. But I barely notice. I'm breathing hard. Heart pounding. Throat closing up. I went from curious to panic after just a moment.

"What is it?" Jen asks, shuffling through the darkness. "What's happening?"

"It's Miah," Allie says. "He looked outside. I think he's having a panic attack."

I flinch when a pair of hands finds me in the dark, but I calm when they slide around me, and Jen whispers in my ear. "Just breathe. Slow down. I have you. Breathe in....and out. Breathe in...and out."

I follow her instructions, which has a double benefit—I'm breathing in a way that calms the nervous system, but I'm also distracted from my panic—which is just as much a product of the mind as it is emotion.

When I slow down to normal—faster than I'm able to even with drugs, Jen leans back. I can't see her, but I imagine she's smiling. "You okay?"

"Am now. Thanks."

"Can you tell us what you saw?"

A lighter flicks to life, the light expanding as Allie lights a candle. No one is smiling. Not even Jen. She looks terrified.

For a moment, I pay attention to my senses, confirming that I no longer hear the thing outside. No longer feel the tremble of its weight through the earth.

I swallow. Take in one more deep breath. Let it out slowly. Then I look her straight in the eyes, so she knows, without a shadow of a doubt, that I'm not screwing around.

"The Devil."

27

"Like...the literal Devil?" Allie asks. "Capital D?

The scene outside replays in my mind. It was just a few seconds, but it was enough to take a mental snapshot that will never fade. And yet, it's difficult to fully comprehend.

This creature crossing the street, heading for Larry's house stood a lot taller than the demons we've seen before. Thirty feet hunched over, the same swirling storm surrounded its body, as broad as it was tall, concealing most of the details behind chaotic gray wisps. The same flailing tendrils. But its skin...was red. And on its head...horns. I didn't see a tail, or a pitchfork, or even cloven hooves, but all that's bullshit anyway. Right?

"Right?" I say aloud.

"Right, what?" Allie asks.

"It's bullshit? The Devil. With the horns and the redness. That's like a construct of modern...or medieval...or whatever artists. A fabricated look. To scare kids or something. It's not in the Bible or anything else."

"No," Jen says with some authority. "It's not."

"But we already established that demons can look like anything," Allie says.

"We did?" Danny says. Looks like he's about to lose his mind. "They're shapeshiftahs?"

"They're supernatural." Allie shakes her head, unimpressed by Danny's cognitive abilities. "They can take any shape because they don't really have a shape at all."

"That...might be accurate," Jen says.

"So, they could look like any of us," Danny says. "They could look like you." Turns to Bree in the hallway. "Or her!"

"We're not demons," Emma says.

"No one here is a demon," I say, trying to sound confident, even though I am most definitely not. What I saw outside was just as far outside the sanity wheelhouse as demons impersonating people. "If it chose that form, it was to scare people. To make us do exactly what we're doing now."

"Freaking out," Bree says.

"Yeah," I say. "That. When the enemy is panicked, they don't get organized, and if they're not organized, they don't fight back and generally don't survive."

"There's another possibility," Jen says. "The death rune is old, right?"

I explained all this on the journey between our homes. "Yeah. It's from the Norse."

"Like Thor?" Danny says, perking up a little. "The rainbow bridge and lightning hammer and all that? Love those movies."

"But not...you know what, yes, like the movies."

Danny nods with enthusiasm, on board with team Scared Shitless once more. "Wicked awesome."

He strikes me as a good guy at heart, but his emotions are fluid, shifting back and forth like a weeping willow in the breeze.

"So, like a thousand years ago," Jen says. "And if you're right about the Norse, that their mythology is based on this kind of thing happening before, then maybe it's happened in other locations, too. What if the medieval depiction of the devil wasn't conjured from someone's imagination? What if it was real?"

I nod. Makes sense. At least to me, having seen it with my own eyes.

A detail snaps to the forefront of my thoughts. I hadn't paid much attention to it, because, you know, the Devil. But what had been lost in my periphery is starting to come into focus.

The Devil was carrying something. Over its shoulder. Dragging something behind it.

It was a sack.

A living, pulsating sack, the size of a Prius, covered in purple and white veins—like a placenta.

And it was full.

My mind's eye focuses on the memory of its surface, bending and undulating as something inside was fighting to get out. I see hands stretching against the fleshy wall. Limbs. Faces.

There were people inside.

Living people.

The memory of it staggers me.

They're collecting people. Taking them. But where?

Behind Larry's house. Into the preserve. But probably not past the river.

"Are you okay?" Jen asks.

"They're not killing them," I say. "Not everyone. The Devil...it was carrying people. And we've seen the demons take people into the woods."

"Where?" Jen asks.

"Behind Larry's house," Allie says. "To the preserve."

I nod.

"Are my parents still alive?" Bree asks.

I kneel in front of her. "It's possible, but babe, you know I can't promise that, right?"

"Do you promise to get them back?" she asks, blinking wet anime eyes impossible to deny.

I look at the others, judging the strength of their convictions, their bravery, their fortitude. "I can promise we'll try."

Jen nods. Then Allie and Emma.

When I look at Danny, he takes a step back. Raises his hands like I've got a gun pointed at his junk. "Hey, don't look at me. I'm not going up against the frickin' Devil, guy. My cousin, Franky, from Reveah, he got in a fight once. Dude was twice his size. Cracked his skull into a bubblah. Can't walk a straight line now. Cops always think he's drunk, like he spends half his life at the packy or some shit. Point is, no frickin' way."

"But you already fought one," Jen says.

Danny huffs. "Catching a dipshit demon off guard and going Ted Williams on its skull ain't the same as going to pound town with the Devil."

Allie raises her hand. "I don't think you know what 'pound town,' means."

"Whatever," Danny says. "Whole neighborhood is empty now, yeah? I'll take my chances in another house. You all can wage your little war without me."

"Coward," Emma grumbles, putting off some of that serious little sister resting bitch-face vibe that used to be reserved for me.

"Better a cowid and alive, then a freak'n moron who doesn't know when to not pick a fight. *And* dead." He backs away toward the door. Picks up his bat on the way.

When he puts his hand on the doorknob, I say, "I wouldn't go out there..."

"You can stay in one of our rooms," Allie adds. "You don't need to be a part of what we're doing."

"You want to bring hell down on yourselves, I'm not gonna sit in your My Little Pony bedroom waiting to get ass-fu..." His eyes flick to Bree. "I ain't gonna be here for it."

He unlocks the deadbolt. Is definitely leaving. I turn to Jen. "Get away from the door." To Allie, I say, "Both of you."

They get it. The death rune on Allie's head is fake, and Jen still doesn't have one. They shuffle Bree into the dark dining room, out of sight from anything that might be lurking outside. Jen waves for Emma to follow, but the girl shakes her head, stands by my side, and readies her M4.

I give her a nod of recognition, fortifying our solidarity, at least in this moment, and she gives it right back.

"You guys ahh Andy Warhol bananas, you know that, right?"

I give him a smile. "You weren't even here when I was wearing a skirt."

He doesn't know what to make of that, so he turns the doorknob, opens the door, and backsteps onto the porch.

"Ten houses down on the right," Emma says.

Danny pauses. "What about it?"

"Don't go there," she says. "We locked one in the basement."

His face screws up. "You locked one in the ba—"

A shadow falls over Danny and then wraps around him like a red-tinged specter. I'm seeing it, and even I'm not sure what I'm seeing, in part because it's out of focus, or concealed, but also because it happens so fast. One second, he's standing there, the living embodiment of a middle-aged Bostonian, and the next—*crunch*. The sound his compressing ribs make is like breaking a handful of spaghetti, but louder, and coupled—for a moment—with a sickening scream that's suddenly silenced.

Candlelight spills out of the front door, lighting the scene.

Danny, now very dead, is lifted up in a large red hand with black nails. A chaotic storm of what might actually be smoke, or brimstone, or whatever counts as breathable air in hell, conceals most of the body, but I can see the shape of it through an opening here, a gap there, as everything moves about.

The Devil has come back. Behind it, across the street, the dark shadows of several demons drag the organ-sack into the woods.

Neither Emma nor I react. We're locked in place, staring into Medusa's eyes, momentarily numb.

The Devil lifts Danny over its head, grasping him in both hands. Tendrils snap up, coiling around his body. Frenetic constrictors.

Look away, my subconscious begs. But the best I can manage is to lift my right hand in front of Emma's face.

The sound that follows is...revolting. I don't just hear it, I feel it. Wet, stretching tears. A slurping suction, and then the weight of insides falling out...

...into what I imagine is the Devil's open mouth.

28

"God..." I say, stumbling back a step, placing my hand against Emma's trembling face. She doesn't flinch. Just lets me cover her eyes. She can hear it—and now she can smell it.

That's bad enough.

Seeing this will scar me for life, far beyond anything I've endured.

And yet...that part of me I felt crack, what feels like a lifetime ago, is now different.

Because this isn't over.

Because there is still a chance Mom and Rich are alive.

And if that's true, maybe...*maybe* we can get them back. Given the monstrosity standing on the lawn, that seems incredibly unlikely.

The Devil glugs Danny's insides, its throat pulsating as it swallows his slippery organs down like a beakless pelican. It's mostly just a shape inside the storm, but the color of its skin shines through, as do the two horns curling up and out of its forehead.

Finished with its gory meal, the Devil tosses the two halves of Danny's body over its shoulders, casual, like an asshole with truck nuts would do with a crushed beer can.

The swirling mist parts, revealing a face.

A human face, if you ignore the horns, the size, and its red-snapper hot dog skin. It sneers at me, eyes flicking to my forehead for a moment. Disdain and contempt roil from it. It doesn't just see me as a spoiled snack. Tearing me apart would be orgasmic for this thing.

But it can't.

And that...for better or worse...emboldens me.

I step outside, onto the porch, ignoring the chorus of whispers behind me, urging me to return.

The Devil's eyes widen. It's just a touch, but enough to know I've caught it off guard.

I should be crying. Begging for mercy. Pissing myself dry.

"Pray tell, good sir, do you speak English?" I ask.

The surprise fades. I've offended it. Viscous rage washes over me but has no effect. I should be crippled by nerve pain, but aside from feeling a bit sick to my stomach, and having a pounding heart, my nerves are settled.

I'm not even high anymore.

The Devil lowers itself onto all fours, the storm around it churning fast, throwing its sulfur stink far and wide. Inside the chaos, the tendrils whip and crack.

It's a threat display, I think. I hope. Because if it's not, I'm basically killing myself.

"Stop it," I say. "You're embarrassing yourself."

The storm continues its frenzy, but the beast inside is hidden— and unmoving.

"Really," I say, "we both know that I'm off limits, yeah? And I'm just really interested. I guess you could say I'm a fan. I mean, look at me." I motion to my KISS T-shirt. "These guys must be heroes where you're from, right? What music do you listen to in hell? AC/DC? Ozzy? Or is it like actual torture music, like Yanni or Kenny G?"

The whispering behind me stops. They're as curious as I am. How far can I push this? Does the death rune make me unfit for consumption, or am I actually untouchable, like a leper outside some ancient city gate?

A low, rumbling growl emanates from the storm.

"Not working," I say, and it's really not. Every second I'm not eviscerated, my confidence builds. I feel like I'm going through some kind of metamorphosis, becoming the man I wish I'd been years ago. Maybe because I'm defending my sister, my crush, her sister, and a little girl. I'm not sure. But I'm starting to feel less like the Cowardly Lion and more like John Wick, minus the mad skills. "Way I see it, you have three choices. Kill me, because we both know you're not going to eat me. Or sit down and have a chat. Fill me in on what's going on. Maybe have a beer. We can be like those guys in Strange Brew, ehh? Or, you can stop the alpha-male bullshit and GTFO."

Turns out there is a fourth option.

It laughs. Each exhalation is deep. Rumbles through my chest.

All at once, I realize that I am nothing in its eyes. An ant doing a jig—surprising sure, but nothing more than pitifully amusing.

It makes me so angry, that I answer the question whispered from the doorway, with, "Yes, fucking, please."

Emma steps out on the porch beside me, M4 in hand.

This is stupid.

This is insane.

This is a really, *really* bad idea.

But I don't care, and neither does Emma.

From inside the house, I hear Jen's voice. "Cover your ears!"

Then I raise the AK-47 and pull the trigger. Beside me, Emma does the same. Neither weapon is fully automatic, so the bullets only fly as fast as our fingers can twitch, but there're two of us, and Emma's trigger finger is a blur. How long has Mr. Gearhart been taking them to the range? And why wasn't I invited? Kid sister has a faster fire rate than this former Army grunt, and probably better aim.

Inside the storm—sparks.

Some of the bullets are whipped aside by the storm, flinging off to strike distant trees and windows. But others sneak past, pinging away after striking something solid. Hopefully not the Devil's skin. That would be discouraging. But I don't think that's the case, mostly because Jen stabbed a demon, and Danny beat one over the head with a bat. We might not be able to kill it, but maybe we can injure it enough in this form that it goes away.

Yeah, I think. *Sure.* All this time, the human race has been terrified of the Devil, but it's not crucifixes or holy water or Jesus who defeats him, it's an AK-47? Not likely, but I'm pouring all my anxiety and anger into each bullet, and I'll be damned if it doesn't feel good.

The laughing snaps to a stop and is replaced by a grunt.

Two grunts!

"Keep firing!" I shout, stepping closer while pulling the trigger.

Emma advances beside me.

And the Devil—the most ancient of evils—falls back!

With just a few rounds left, I focus on my aim. The smoke swirling around its head is steady, right to left. I shift the muzzle to the right and pull the trigger five times, emptying the magazine. The last bullet I fire sounds strange, like the cartridge's boom is coupled with a loud crack.

I hit something.

But I never get the chance to see what. The storm around the creature bursts with the energy of a cyclone. The Devil is airborne and then out of sight, sliding up into the dark sky. Stars shimmer as its silhouette moves through the sky. A moment later, a distant thud, off behind Larry's house.

The Devil retreated.

"Holy shit," I whisper, smiling.

"Yeah," Emma says, also smiling. She looks up at me, newfound respect in her eyes. "I guess you're okay. For my sister."

"Thanks," I say, raising a fist.

She pounds it out, and just like that, we're good. Comrades. And not just because she likes me now. We fought side-by-side, each relying on the other for life and limb. When you do that with someone, the bond is fast and stronger than super glue.

Emma and I are separated as a small body shoves its way between us.

"Get back here!" Allie calls, as Bree heads down the steps. I want to grab her, but I'm loading my last magazine. Also, I'm not really worried about her.

Like me, she's been marked. I just humiliated Satan, and he did nothing about it.

But that doesn't mean he won't seek revenge. That seems like a guarantee.

"We can't stay here," I say into the open door.

"What?" Allie says. "You want to leave? We just got here."

"I don't know a single person on this planet, who's prone to violence, and who would let what I just did stand. We can't be here when whatever comes for me arrives."

I head down the steps.

Emma follows.

The three of us move together, drawn toward the front lawn.

The grass, where the beast had stood, is matted and discolored. I flick my lighter and ignite my three gun-mounted candles, illuminating the scene.

Bree moves a little bit farther out, closer to the street, crouching down over something.

"Is that blood?" Emma points to a spatter of black fluid. The spray pattern is chaotic, churned by the storm.

I'm not about to touch it, or taste it, so I say, "Could be."

"You think we hurt it?" she asks.

Before I can answer, Bree says, "You hurt it, all right." She stands up and turns around, holding a god damned horn in her hands. She lifts the horn up and places it against the death rune on her forehead. She smiles and double taps her eyebrows. I'm unnerved by it for a moment, and then she says, "I'm a unicorn!"

29

"Give it to me," I say, waving Bree over.

"But it's mine," she says. "I found it."

"Just..." How do I tell a seven-year-old she's holding Satan's horn in her hand and that he might come back for it? *Screw it,* I think, and I say, "That's not your horn, or mine, and the big stormy red guy to whom it belongs might come back for it. And if he does, I don't want you to be holding it."

"Because he might eat me?" she asks.

"No," I say. "You, and me, and Jason Statham over here—" I hitch my thumb toward Emma. "—won't be eaten. But our sisters, Allie and Jen, who are your friends, might be. And even though they don't want to eat us, or take us, or generally touch us, that doesn't mean they won't find a way to kill us."

"They could knock over a tree and crush us. Splat. Guts everywhere." Emma says.

"Thank you for that creative and vivid depiction of our demise," I say.

"What?" Emma shrugs. "It could happen. They're demons, right? Isn't that like their whole thing? Deceiving people, catching us off guard, making us think something is good, or just totally normal, and then *whack*, a tree falls on you, or you find your boyfriend..." She looks Bree in the eyes, like the next bit is just for her. "...Corey Simpson, at Frank Green's birthday party, instead of at baseball practice like he said, making out in a closet with Stefanie Maubach."

"That doesn't sound good," Bree says.

Emma nods. "Worst day of my life."

"That...can't possibly be true."

I motion to the scene around us, cringing when I notice Danny's two halves lying nearby. How did I miss them before? How have the girls not seen him yet? Are we already that numb to carnage? If so, it's probably a bad sign for our psyches, if not our souls, which might actually be a thing.

"Second worst day," she says.

"So, in this scenario, Corey and Stefanie are…"

"Demons," she says. "Obviously. I should have killed them both."

"Whoa. Geez."

Emma is still seeing red.

"I'm down with killing literal demons, but killing people for *any* reason…" I shake my head. "It's no good. Bad for the mojo. Okay?"

"What if they're murderers?" she asks.

"Doesn't matter what they've done," I say. "If *you* kill them, it will change you forever, and not in a good way."

Emma shrugs and heads back to the house.

Bree mimics her shrug and follows her newfound role model, pausing for a moment to hand me the horn.

I stand in the yard, by myself. Above me, the sky looks normal. Still dark, but there's no big black curtain blocking out the sun. Because it's actually night. The sun is on the far side of the planet. The Moon is nowhere to be seen, though.

Around me, the neighborhood is quiet. If anyone is left alive or untaken, they're doing a good job staying quiet.

I don't know why, but I take a deep breath through the nose, mentally expecting the scent of pine, which is the neighborhood's natural fragrance. Instead, I get sulfur and blood.

Danny's body lies just at the fringe of my rifle candles' light. On either side of me. I don't bother inspecting him more closely. He's definitely dead. And a reminder of what could happen to Jen and Allie.

I look down at the horn in my hand, seething. I'm both revolted by the thing, and curious. If demons and/or devils are supernatural, how can part of them be shot off? It was material at the time, but if it became immaterial again, wouldn't the horn as well? None of it makes sense. But the supernatural, by definition, is beyond understanding, like Tofurkey.

The horn looks like it could have come from a bull, black and curv-ed, coming to a deadly point. But it also doesn't look organic. While much of it is shiny black, it's covered in a pattern of etched lines. Precise, like it was created by a computer guided laser. And the way it's broken... The edges feel sharp and crystalline, like the inside of a quartz geode.

I drop the horn by my feet, happy to be rid of it, and not just because it's demonic. Something about it intrigues me. Honestly, I want to keep it. Maybe as a trophy. I don't know why. When it strikes the ground, glints of light leap up from the grass.

The grass feels nice on my fingers as I slide my hand over it, search-ing for one of the little discs. I frown when I find one. It confirms what I was afraid of. The devil is bullet proof. I pick up the pancaked round and look it over. When a bullet strikes flesh, it fragments and causes all kinds of internal damage. To look like this means it struck something solid—like steel—and it compressed.

I glance at the horn. Not all of the creature was bullet proof, and it certainly didn't like being shot in the head. But why would some of it be impervious to harm, and not all of it?

Getting tired of all the questions without answers.

The woods beyond Larry's house tug at my attention.

That's where they're going.

That's where they're taking people.

And it's where I feel myself drawn. I need to go there.

Need to save Mom. Or at least try.

But I can't do that with Allie or Jen. They need a place to hide. And I...need more ammunition.

Mind made up, I head back to the house, no longer fearing what might be lurking in the shadows.

Back inside, I'm greeted by a chorus of desperate, whispering voices.

"Close the door!" Allie says.

"Is it gone?" Jen asks. "Is it coming back?"

"It's afraid of us," Emma says, feeling bolstered by our encounter. Feels weird coming from a teenage girl, but I'm right there with her.

"It's gone," I say, no longer whispering.

I light a few standing candles and then blow out the three now fused to my rifle's barrel, melting during my *Scarface* reenactment with Emma. "But, we can't stay here."

"We *just* got here," Allie complains.

"And now," I say, "there are two halves of a body on the lawn, and the Devil's horn."

"The Devil's what now?" Allie says.

"Horn," Emma says. "We shot it off."

Jen puts her hands to her temples.

I know an impending panic attack when I see it. "You need support?"

"Support?" she asks, almost offended by the question.

"'Support' is code," Allie says. "He means pot."

"I don't think that's a good idea," she says, sucking in a deep breath.

"I'd rather you chill than freaking out." I dig the bottle out of my cargo shorts pocket. Give it a shake. "Even just a half, or a quarter gummie might even you out."

She looks unsure, and I don't blame her. Being high right now wouldn't be helpful, either, but people who lose control in a combat situation tend to get other people killed.

"Don't you need it?" she asks.

"Yeah," Allie says. "What's with the Mr. Confident routine?" She leans in close, looking at my eyes. "You're not even a little bit buzzed right now. Shouldn't you be, like, fetal in a closet or something?"

"I should be." I smile. "But I'm not. I'm actually...okay."

Allie smiles at that, genuinely happy for my turn around.

"I'm okay, too," Jen says. "I just...need a minute."

"A minute is all we have," I say. "Then...we're going back to your house."

"What?" Jen's panic rises anew. "Why?"

"To kill a demon," I say, and I give Emma a nod, which she returns. "To get more bullets. And to lock you two—" I point to Jen and Allie. "—inside."

"That's a stupid idea," Allie says.

"We need to see if we can kill one." I'm not looking forward to the attempt, but until we know if the enemy is immortal, our options are limited.

"The door might be broken already," Allie says. "The demon could be gone. Then you can't kill anything. Or it could be waiting to ambush us."

"Or it could be hunting us right now," Jen says.

"Point is, it'd be stupid to go back." Allie gives my shoulder a poke, like it's going to drive home her point. "Even if there're enough guns and bullets for an army."

"Mr. Neiman has lots of guns," Bree says from the kitchen, where she's wandering around inspecting things.

"Where does Mr. Neiman live?" I ask.

"Two doors downhill from Bree's house," Allie says, confirmed by Jen and Emma both nodding.

"Then that's where we're going," I say. "We'll arm up there, and we'll find a place for the unmarked to hide."

"What the hell are *you* going to do?" Allie asks.

"Get our parents back," I say.

"Not with my sister, you're not." Jen is adamant, but I don't have to say a word. Don't need to. Emma has that covered.

"I just fought the literal Devil. And I've got this thing on my head that makes it so they don't fight back. Dad would call that a tactical advantage, *and* he'd call anyone not willing to utilize that advantage a fool...or probably something worse, if Mom wasn't around. And *when* we get him back...he can tell you all that himself." Emma crosses her arms. "I'm sixteen. You can't stop me."

Jen turns to me, teary eyed, imploring.

"I can't stop her, either." And I don't want to, though I keep that to myself. "We can argue about it later. Right now, we need to move. If it comes back, with friends, you two can't be here."

That takes the fight out of them.

"Allie," I say, "how fast can you get a death rune on Jen's forehead?"

"Harder doing it to myself. Won't take long." She takes a candle and heads for the stairs. Turns to Jen. "C'mon."

Jen looks at me like I've betrayed her and then storms up the stairs after Allie. I sag a little bit, watching them go, realizing that any hope I had at a future with Jen has just been dashed.

Emma pats my arms. "Other fish in the sea and all that."

"How's that working for you and Corey Simpson?"

She purses her lips. "Screw you."

I smile, but it disappears when Bree says, "Oh, look, a puppy!" from the kitchen and lifts the laundry basket, freeing feral Sanchez.

30

"Bree! Wait!" I shout, but I'm too late. The basket is already lifted, and the pint-sized predator contained within set loose. Sanchez's little claws click over the floor, scrambling to grip like some old cartoon character, running in place before springing forward.

My mind fills with images of Sanchez biting Bree's face. It's not overly gory or deadly in any fashion, but the little man's transformation into pint-sized serial killer has me worried about his future. Biting a little girl might help seal his fate. Then again, given the circumstances and the state of the world, I doubt animal control will be a thing.

Sanchez leaps, headed straight for Bree's face, as she leans forward, arms open, squealing with joy.

Then he's wrapped in her arms, squirming, and licking, little tail twitching madly.

Bree stands, beaming and giggling. "I think he likes me."

"Yeah," I say, a little surprised. I approach the pooch, hand outstretched, as I have a thousand times before. This time, I'm a little nervous. But it turns out to be for nothing. Sanchez welcomes me back into his wolf pack with a few apologetic licks. I pet his head and feel something odd.

"What's that, buddy?" I lean in close with a candle. There's a patch of hair missing on his forehead, between the eyes.

"No way," Emma says, seeing it at the same time I do. "He's one of us."

I rub my thumb over his little forehead, brushing away loose fur, confirming it for myself. Tiny little Sanchez has a teeny little death rune on his head, same as me. "One of us..." I say the words to myself, but they feel accurate. And wrong.

"All set," Allie says, entering the dining room with Jen. "What are you guys do—"

She sees Sanchez, happy and held. "Aww, Chezy is feeling better?" Allie approaches, reaching for the pooch.

His lips peel up, revealing needle teeth. A high-pitched, guttural growl rises from his tiny chest, like a motor scooter on its last legs. Allie stops. Yanks her hand back, aware that Sanchez was about to give her a half dozen itsy bitsy puncture wounds.

"Hey!" I snap my fingers at Sanchez, and he reacts as he should, ears folding down, body pressing against Bree. "Knock it off." But he doesn't take his predatory gaze off Allie until she backs up a few steps.

My sister looks wounded. Sanchez's unexplainable angst toward Allie pushes her toward complete overwhelm. Her resolve and fortitude have been admirable, but everyone has a breaking point. I wrap my arm around her back and give her a vigorous rub. "He's just out of sorts still. Give him time."

"Whatever," she says. "He's just a dog. Are we going?"

"Can I bring him?" Bree asks, holding Sanchez up.

It's probably a bad idea, but I suspect we won't be back any time soon. Maybe ever. And the idea of abandoning Sanchez doesn't sit well. I get his leash and crouch down in front of Bree. "He's your responsibility now, okay. Don't let go of him, no matter what."

She gives an earnest nod and takes the leash handle while I clip the other end to Sanchez's collar. "You listen to Bree, okay?" I give him a kiss on the forehead, and then to Bree I say, "Thank you for taking care of him."

And then for some reason beyond me, the great Buddha, Socrates, and every other enlightened and/or wise man that's ever lived, I give Bree a kiss on the head, too.

When I turn around, Allie looks weirded out, but Jen is smiling slightly, which would normally feel good, but the death rune expertly painted on her forehead reminds me of what comes next.

"Let's go," I say, and we head for the door.

Five minutes later, we're crouched in the woods, looking at a foreign landscape. The forest beyond is scorched. The ground is ash. The black trees are sticks, their pine needles and most branches burned away. The scent of sulfur is hard to detect here, because it smells so strongly of smoke...like when Mom burns a candle and blows it out in the bathroom, claiming that smoke masks foul odors. Rich's mostly.

Maybe there is something to it.

Bree is to my left, doing a good job keeping track of Sanchez, who seems happy to stay by her side. The only real issue was when he nipped at Jen's feet as she walked past. Otherwise, he's been the model pup. Emma, Jen, and I are armed and as ready as we can be. Our ammo is limited, but we still have enough to take down a herd of elephants...and hopefully a demon or two, if it comes to that. Allie doesn't have a gun, but she carries a backpack full of food and water, just in case we're forced to hide in the woods long term.

"Okay, stay close," I say, and I step into the burned-out forest. It's brighter under the starry sky, which makes moving easier. But I feel exposed. Bree follows close behind with Sanchez. Behind her, out of necessity, is Emma, followed by Allie and Jen, who can't get too close to the pooch without him giving our position away.

Ash floats around us like snow, kicked up by the now distant fire, drifting on the breeze. The ash beneath our feet absorbs our footsteps. Other than the sound of our breathing, we walk in silence, a hundred feet in from the backs of several homes, some of which have burned down.

Bree tugs on my shirt. Points to a swing set on the backside of a charred home. "My swing set is still there!"

It's hard to tell in the darkness, but the swing set does indeed seem whole, probably because it stands at the center of a large lawn with no trees nearby. Her house, on the other hand, looks like it was struck by a fiery meteorite. She says nothing about it, so I don't bring it up. "How much farther?"

"Two more houses," she says, and we carry on through the husk of a forest.

It's actually three houses, but who's counting? Aside from me, I guess. The home is untouched by the fire, and I actually recognize it. The neighborhood's dirty little secret. While most of the homes here are just ten years old, Mr. Neiman's home was on the property back when cows grazed the land. The farmhouse is a hundred and fifty years old—ish. And it looks like it. Needs paint. Some of the wooden siding has fallen away. The shingles are curled up and cracking.

The house is an eyesore on its own, but it's the yard that really offends. Dilapidated vehicles line the dusty clearing, along with various appliances— refrigerators, washers, and dryers—more than this house could have required in the past century. Stacks of tires rise like ancient burial mounds. This is the yard of a hoarder, collecting every side-of-the-road piece of junk that even has a whiff of being useful.

And all of this is plainly visible, because there are a dozen tiki torches, stabbed into the ground, lighting the scene and tempting fate.

Wildfire missed your home? Why not start another and see what happens?

I approach carefully in the long warbling shadow of a tire pile. Folks like this tend to have 'No Trespassing' warnings—like someone might steal their shit—and the means to enforce them.

"Stop," Emma says, pointing to the ground at my feet.

Case in point. A bear trap. It's rusted and stained. I wouldn't have been its first victim. It's nearly perfectly blended in with the leaf litter. How the hell did she see it?

Watching the ground more closely, I forge a path around the tires, between two cars, over a trip wire, and into the yard...which isn't a yard at all. It's a firing range. We're surrounded by targets—the round paper variety, cans and bottles, metal sheets, and a few mannequins, all of them dressed as women, which is a little disconcerting. Mr. Neiman might be a hoarder and a philistine.

It feels wrong, but I hope he's been taken already.

Closer to the house, I suspect we'll find Mr. Neiman at home.

The windows are all covered, but not in plastic or blankets. It's...piles of junk. Boxes. Books. Who knows what. Stacks of it, covering every single window.

The back porch sways and creaks as I climb the steps, pausing halfway up to hold out my hand. "Stay there. This doesn't feel safe."

"Neither does being outside," Allie says.

I swear the rotted porch is going to give way under my weight, but I make it to the top without it collapsing or me plummeting into a booby trap. I pause at the back door. Its window *is* covered, by taped-on, brown paper bags.

I knock, gentle and friendly. A little tap, tap-tap, followed by a, "Hello? Mr. Neiman? I'm your neighbor from down the street."

"If he's sleeping or something," Emma says, "he's not going to hear that."

She's right, of course, the house is quadruple insulated with walls of stuff. He probably can't hear children playing or cars driving past. And maybe that's the point, walled off from the outside world. I suspect he's not going to be happy about visitors in the middle of the night-day.

"Are you sure your father was friends with Mr. Neiman?" I ask.

Emma nods, but Jen doesn't look so sure now. Everything she's seen is telling her the same thing it's telling me: her father didn't spend time here because he and Mr. Neiman were peas in a pod. He was here to make sure Mr. Neiman wasn't a threat.

I lean close to the glass and peek through a gap in the paper bags. Beyond the door is a maze of garbage—boxed, bagged, and loose. There's barely enough room to walk, one foot in front of the other. A low burning candle perched atop a stack of paper lights the scene. If Mr. Neiman is asleep, he's going to have a rude awakening.

"What are you doing?" Jen asks, when I reach for the door handle. I ignore the question and try turning it. Locked.

"There's a candle burning inside," I say. "I think he's alive."

"You're damn right I'm alive," says a gruff voice from the darkness behind us. "But you all are five licks of a dog's balls away from repainting the back of my house in red." The threat is followed by a vigorous shotgun pump.

31

Five licks of a dog's balls?

What the hell kind of backwoods New Hampshire hick am I dealing with here? I raise my hands, letting the AK hang from its strap. "Sir, we're all neighbors."

"Don't give a rat's ass if you're Mother Teresa selling Girl Scout Cookies," he says. "Now turn around, one at a time, starting with you."

"Me, sir?" I ask.

"You been the one I'm talking to. Shit. You kids are stupider than a turtle turd in the Sahara Desert. Staring at your phones. Getting thumb cramps."

I turn around to find him shaking his head, and even though I'm just seeing him now for the first time, I feel like I already knew exactly what he looked like. Bushy whiteish-yellow beard. A worn-out Navy ballcap hiding his eyes in shadow. Dirty jeans and a soiled white T-shirt.

Why do dirty people always wear white?

"Okay," he says, "now the rest of you, one at a time from left to right."

Jen turns first. Then Allie, Emma, and finally Bree, holding Sanchez in her arms.

"You four..." He motions to the line of girls. "Step inna light. Let me get a look at ya."

I start lowering my hands, but his shotgun swivels toward my gut. "You stay right the hell where you are. And I don't think I need to say it, but I will. The first one of you who touches a weapon, is gonna be the first to get shot and die knowing you got all your friends killed."

"Geez," Emma says. "Hard core much?"

Jen tilts her head toward Bree. "She's only seven, Mr. N—"

"Step. Inna. Light."

"Do what he says." I try to sound confident, like we've got nothing to fear from Mr. Neiman. Truth is, I'm mentally rehearsing the steps it will take to raise my rifle and shoot him down. Had I known the old coot was off his meds, I wouldn't have come looking for help at his doorstep. In my experience some people are just as bad as demons. Some of them are worse.

Mr. Neiman looks at each girl in turn, saying, "Uh-huh, uh-huh," as he moves down the line, finishing with, "Huh..." when he looks at Sanchez, who's actually wagging his tail.

"I know you and you." He points at Jen and Emma. Then he stabs a finger at Bree. "And I've seen you around." He turns his attention to Allie. "I ain't sure about you." And then he turns his shaded eyes toward me. "And I sure as shit don't know your druggy ass."

"I'm as sober as the day I was born," I say, trying to smile.

"Bet you are," he says. "Come to see what I got?"

"Huh? What? No. We're not looking for drugs."

"Can't tell me a man walking around with a harem isn't up to no good."

Before I can refute his claims, Allie says, "Gross! He's my *brother*. And she's seven." She thrusts a hand out at Bree. "Quit being an old perv and stop threatening to kill a bunch of kids."

The old man's shotgun rises from my chest to my head. "He ain't a kid."

"Mr. Neiman," Jen says. "You know my father, right? That's how you know who we are?"

Neiman gives a nod. "Seen your photos. Your dad's a good shot. Better'n me."

"I'm probably better than you," Emma grumbles, and I don't doubt it.

Neiman smiles for the first time. "Might be."

"Mr. Neiman, we need your help." She has his full attention now. Doesn't waste it. "Our neighborhood... There's something bad going on."

He nods. "Heard the gunshots."

"People are being taken from their homes," she says.

The old man huffs. "Only a fool would come here."

"Or five of them," I mumble, and I nearly get myself shot. I raise my hands a little higher. "Sorry."

"Mr. Neiman, please," Jen says. "The first person they took...was my father. Mom's gone now, too."

"And our parents," Allie adds, motioning to me, and then Bree. "Her parents, too."

"They ate my brother," Bree says, matter of fact, no trace of emotion. Kid's going to be more broken than me for a lot longer. Right now, shock has numbed her, but that's eventually going to wear off. If she's lucky, all of this will be suppressed, and she won't remember a damn thing.

"Is it the Puerto Ricans?" Neiman asks.

"The *what?*" I say, lowering my hands in frustration. "Seriously?"

"Mexicans? They've been storming across the border, some of them from Canada, if you can believe it. Planning something, you know. Something big. Heard rumors that they were cannibals."

"I...don't know where to even start," I say.

But Jen does. And it's not with the truth. Mr Neiman clearly has no idea what's going on. Hasn't left his home or his backyard. He's just hunkered down and walled in, waiting for the storm to pass. If we started claiming demons had taken our families...

"Cubans," she says. "With Russian support. Coming in from the coast. Taking kids' parents. Breaking up families. They think they're making us weak, but we're aiming to show them wrong."

Neiman lowers the shotgun and his head. Paces back and forth, muttering to himself. I'm tempted to drop him where he stands. Would be easy now. But Allie and Jen would never look at me the same again. Also, it would be wrong, and hell on Earth or not, that still counts for something.

I'm surprised when Emma lifts her rifle. She has the same idea as me, and she's about to expedite the shit out of our backyard rendezvous. Jen catches the rifle's muzzle, shakes her head at Emma, and shoves the weapon back toward the dirt without Neiman noticing. The two sisters have a silent argument with their eyes, but they quickly stop when the old man turns around.

"Can't say I'm surprised," Neiman says. "Cubans...Puerto Ricans... Mexicans. All them equatorials are the same. Speaking Spanish. Sacrificing kids to Quetzagonads." He laughs at his own horrible joke. Then he takes off his hat to rub his head. The top of his gleaming dome is hairless, the sides covered in long, yellowed hair, like wings. Normally, I'd fixate on the sight, imagining a bald eagle rising from his head and soaring away, screeching, 'America!' but my attention is locked on his forehead, where a death rune has been etched.

Neiman might not know about what's happening in the world, but he's been affected by it just the same. Explains why he's able to move about the yard without being taken. Then again, not even a demon would want the old man for a snack. Probably tastes of alcohol and tobacco. I can smell both from here.

"Well," he says. "What can I do you for?"

"Guns," Emma says, eager.

"Mostly ammo." Jen pats her M4. "5-5-6 and 7-6-2 if you have them."

"Spare magazines would be appreciated, too," I add. More bullets would be great, but without magazines to put them in, we'll have to spend a lot of time restacking our spent mags, and I doubt the lords of hell will give us the chance.

"You all are fighting back, huh?" He heads for the home's bulkhead. "Good on you. My fighting days are over. Can't do much more than hobble round the yard, but if I see any of them Cubans wandering the neighborhood, I'll pop 'em for you."

I try to calculate the odds of someone Hispanic wandering into this neighborhood, post apocalypse, in a state that's 98% white. *Pretty slim,* I decide, but I'm still uncomfortable with his proclamation. "There is a U.S. born Cuban resistance, sir. They're fighting for us. You can tell the difference because...the ahhh, the actual Cubans are..."

Jen helps flesh out the lie. "...wearing red and yellow tiger striped bandanas on their sleeves."

"Ugh," Neiman says, shaking his head in disgust. "Commie colors and a do rag. Sounds 'bout right. Thank you much for the intel." He yanks the bulkhead door open. Steps inside. Looks back. "You all coming, or what?"

He disappears into the dark void. A moment later, orange light flickers from within.

"I'll guard the entrance," Emma says.

"Me, too," Bree adds. "I bet it's stinky down there."

"It's stinky out here," Allie says.

Bree shrugs. Must be getting accustomed to the sulfur stench. Then again, I must be, too, because I'm barely noticing it.

"Works for me," I say.

"What?" Jen is aghast with us all. "We can't leave two kids outside to—"

"I am sixteen." Emma levels a glare at Jen that had previously been reserved for me.

"Also," I say. "They're safe out here. You two—" I motion to Jen and Allie. "—are not."

"And the whole yard is surrounded by traps," Emma points out.

It's a solid argument.

Jen sighs. "Anything goes wrong, fire off a single round."

Emma gives a sarcastic salute.

The vibe coming off Jen is intense. She's being pushed past the limit. Sooner or later, she's going to crack. Allie, too. They both just seem... done. Emma and Bree are different. Maybe just numb. Or psychologyically scarred. But somehow ready to go. A little bit fearless.

"Let's get this over with," Jen says, and she steps into the bulkhead. Allie follows, and I bring up the rear.

Before climbing inside, I pause and look back at our three diminutive security guards. I point at each one of them, smile, and say, "Be good."

This time, Bree salutes, and I head down the stairs into a new kind of hell on Earth.

32

The basement is filled with an array of wall to wall, quasi organized junk. Used peanut butter jars line shelves, filled with screws, nails, bottle caps, and coins that are separated by denomination. Every household knick-knack you can imagine is here. It's kind of impressive. At first.

Then I notice stacks of electronics, most of it unrecognizable and torn apart, like he's been pillaging the spoils of some war that took place in the 80s, using parts to fix whatever is working upstairs. Or he's selling the parts. But who, other than Mr. Neiman, would have use for bits and pieces of these relics?

"What you're looking for is back here," Neiman says. He rounds a corner and disappears in the maze.

It's then that I notice the dirt floor, which appears to be covered in some kind of small, black gravel that crunches underfoot. The path we're walking on is mostly powder though.

Because it's not gravel.

It's rat shit.

Layers of it.

I scan the space with fresh eyes, spotting several mounds of rags, hollowed out boxes, and torn up pillows. This place is an ecosystem for rodents...all of which are currently hidden. Smells like it, too. I thought the sulfur stench outside was bad news, but the air in here is toxic, and not just because of the rats. The fetid scent of small mammals mingles with the smell of human waste. Feels like I'm standing in an outhouse, over an open pit of shit and piss. I try to breathe through my mouth, but I stop when I can actually taste the air.

Ahead of me, Allie puts a hand to her mouth. Glances back, disgusted and nervous. And she ought to be. Neiman could have a body rotting

in here and you'd never know from the smell. Hell, the rats would probably pick it clean. For all we know, the pellets coating the floor used to
be people.

Slow down, I tell myself. Neiman is an ally. You have nothing to fear
from him.

And I believe it. No idea why, but I feel a strange sort of kinship with
him.

Allie pauses to look at an old photo of a uniformed man standing on
the deck of an aircraft carrier. I assume it's Mr. Neiman, but he's unrecognizable.

All of this is a little disturbing, to tell the truth. Is this my future?
A broken man, destined to live alone, surrounded by junk, rats, and
maybe dead bodies?

I slide around my curious sister, reach out, and take Jen's hand.

Not if I can help it.

I'm a little surprised when she doesn't pull away, and even more
surprised when she grips on tight and pulls me closer. Whatever camaraderie I'm feeling with the old codger, she is not.

"How come he didn't say anything?" Jen whispers.

"About what?"

She points to my forehead. "About that!"

I shrug. "He has one, too. Maybe he just figured we all had them."

"He lives here by himself," she says, "and he doesn't strike me as the
kind of guy to spend much time in front of a mirror. Probably doesn't
have one that isn't covered."

She's right. I didn't know about my death rune until it was pointed
out to me. He should have noticed our foreheads, but he seems blind to
them.

"What's taking you so long?" Neiman calls out. "Better not be going
through my shit!"

"Just admiring," I say, hurrying Jen along and snapping my fingers
at Allie, pulling her away from her snoopery. We round the corner and
squeeze through a doorframe congested by a pillar of toasters on one
side, and a stack of microwaves on the other side.

The space beyond is...clean.

Relatively. The floor is still crunchy, but the bits and pieces, boxes, and jars in this corner of the Minotaur's maze have a united theme—guns. The armory has a Unabomber vibe to it. A workbench is covered in electronics and a stack of what might be pipe bombs, or at least the makings of them.

This is why Mr. Gearhart was keeping tabs on Neiman. To make sure all this was just a hobby and not a threat.

Neiman turns around with a gleam in his eye and a smile that reveals teeth like weathered piano keys, both yellow and black. He extends his arms, toward boxes of ammo and wall-mounted weapons. "Whadaya need?"

I can't speak. I'm awed by the one-man war contained in this basement, waiting for an enemy.

"Here," he says, opening a drawer. "M4 magazines for the young lady outside. Pre-loaded. Never can be too sure."

Too sure of what? A home invasion? A rodent uprising? Hell on Earth? He's prepared for all of that and then some.

Neiman opens a metal cabinet, a magician showing his assistant in a one-piece. Ta-da! Three AK-47s hang inside. He pulls out the drawer beneath them. Magazines up the wazoo, taped together in groups of four.

He sees my attention on the magazines. Smiles. "You ever rocked an AK jungle style?"

"Can't say that I have," I admit, though I'm familiar with the term and the practice. 'Jungle style' means multiple magazines have been taped together. Serious operators might tape two together. Still portable, but doubles the amount of rounds carried by the gun. When the first magazine runs dry, you can yank it out, spin it around, and slap in the other side. Saves a few seconds. Weekend cowboys go a little bonkers with the practice, as they do with most things. I once saw a soldier—on leave, off base, and at a range—firing an AR 15 with sixteen jungle style mags. It was impossibly heavy, but it got a laugh. Would take the brawn of a man like Bishop to be of any use, but he's a fictional character in a movie franchise.

Luckily, Neiman's jungle mags aren't in groups of sixteen, but they are in stacks of four. The curved AK magazines are taped together at the ends. They're reminiscent of a fluid swastika, or the Glaive—the crazy throwing weapon from Krull, a weird 80s movie that people from my generation only watch if they're deployed and have no other options. The jungle mags are going to be heavy. Will make it harder to sustain fire for a long period of time. But it also means I can carry a shit-ton of ammunition.

The M4 mags are jungle style as well, but only in stacks of two, which is optimal. The AK mags will boost my total number of rounds, but they'll make reloading awkward.

Neiman holds an AK jungle mag out to me. I take hold and test the weight. Not too bad. I swap out my lone magazine, pocketing it, and then replace it with the jungle mag, testing the weapon's weight. The jungle mag almost doubles the weight, but at eighteen pounds total, it's like holding a baby...that shoots bullets instead of milk-turds.

"Once you have it in there like that, pop the mag into your hand like this." He holds his hand out, palm up.

I follow his instructions, ejecting the heavy quad-mag into my hand.

"Then give it a quick flip." He motions how to throw the mag.

I'm careful about it, hefting the mag a few times before tossing it up with a spin. The next mag in line lands in my hand and I jam it back into the rifle. Wasn't too hard. I perform the task again, and again, each time a little faster. Might actually be something to this.

"You got it," Neiman says, like a proud father, whose son has just scored his first soccer goal. "You're a natural."

Allie inspects the work desk, attention on what I think are pipe bombs. They must not be primed or armed or whatever you do to pipe bombs to make them explode, because Neiman doesn't offer a warning or even pay much attention. Instead, he's watching Jen with suspicious eyes.

"Eh, eh!" he says when Jen reaches for a jungle style M4 mag. "Not for you."

"What?" Jen says. "You said these were the M4 magazines, right? They look like M4 magazines."

"What I said..." Neiman chews on his lip. He's agitated about something. "...was that the M4 magazines were for the young lady outside."

"Emma?" Jen says. "I don't understand. Why can my sister—"

"Because *she* is one of *us.*" Neiman looks at me, pulling me into 'us.' "And you... Well, I don't know what *you*, or *her*—" He nods toward Allie. "—are."

"I'm your friend's daughter," Jen says. "Remember my father? The big muscly Marine, who was captured or maybe killed by...fricking ...*whatever.*"

"Cubans," I say.

"Fricking Cubans!" Jen throws her hands up in the air.

The sudden motion triggers Neiman. He lifts his shotgun toward Jen. At this range, indoors, it would carve her in half and blow out all our eardrums. "Don't you move!"

"Whoa, whoa, whoa!" I hold my hands out, trying to ease him back from the edge. "What gives, brother? I thought we were comrades? Fighting the commies. Side by side. Millbarge and Fitz-Hume."

The obscure reference isn't lost on him. "*We* are. But not them." He motions to Jen and Allie, who are standing together now.

"Why...not?" I ask.

"Because they're different. You can feel it, too. I know you can. We can't trust them."

"You can't kill them, either," I say.

Allie frowns at me, probably noticing that I didn't refute Neiman's claims.

Because I can't.

Because he's right.

There is something off about Jen and Allie, and I'm not sure what it is. But I also know I care about both of them, and I would kill this old man before letting him hurt them.

"It would make a mess," Neiman says. "You're right. We can do it outside."

I take a moment to think through my options, and then say, "You heard the man. Outside. Both of you. Now."

33

My father and I used to play hide and go seek inside the house, on snow days when we were both stuck at home and Mom was annoyed with us. Inside a house, there are a limited number of places to hide. Closets. Under tables. Behind sofas. It's just a matter of time before you're found.

Unless you're creative. The one time my father gave up was when I crawled inside the dryer. Normally, all he really had to do was wait. Because when I get nervous, I have to piss. I nearly filled that dryer with a half-gallon of urine, because anticipation wrings out my bladder like a sponge.

Like right now.

Problem is, I can't relieve myself. No way in hell I'm going to use Neiman's bathroom, if it's even functional. And I'm sure as shit not going to go off behind a tree or a booby-trapped tire pile, leaving Jen and Allie with the old kook, certainly not when he's intending to shoot them.

I think. I need to be sure.

At the back of the line, headed for the open bulkhead, I'm doing the pee pee dance instinctually known by all children around the world, thinking, *What am I going to do? What am I going to do? What am I going to do?* Vacillating between my two conundrums—where and when to relieve myself, and how to stop Neiman.

They're not of equal importance, but they're taking up the same mental headspace.

"Up," Neiman commands, pointing his shotgun at Jen and Allie. Jen is still armed, but smart enough to not reach for the weapon hanging over her shoulder. Fast as she might be, she wouldn't be able to grasp the weapon, haul it around, take aim, and squeeze off a single round before she was torn apart by the 12 gauge.

Jen lets Allie go first, and I see a subtle exchange between the two, a conversation with their eyes, Jen imploring, Allie resisting—and then giving in. A plan has been hatched. And Neiman is none the wiser.

Allie moves up the steps quickly. Jen takes her time.

She's giving Allie time to run, I realize, sacrificing herself to save my sister. I'm not sure I could like her more without falling in love.

I stick close to Neiman on the way up the stairs, which is awkward because the steps are steep, and it puts my face level with the old man's ass. The second I realize it, Neiman makes me regret it. There's a faint hiss, like a tire releasing air. The scent of decomposed two-day old Quaker oats stumbles me. Makes me gag. "Wilford Brimley on roller skates, that is foul!"

Neiman chuckles. He definitely meant to.

We emerge into the warmer humid air of summer at night. Eventually, the perpetual darkness should lower the temperature, but so far, it's still hot and muggy. Maybe a side effect of hell visiting? Heat rising from the boiling lake. Something like that.

"Where'd she go?" Neiman asks, before I reach the top. Sounds angry. "Where's the smaller one?"

I exit the bulkhead to find Jen standing at the end of a shotgun barrel, hands raised. Allie is nowhere in sight.

Wherever you are, Allie, stay hidden.

I'm more than a little pissed when both Emma and Bree, neither of whom seem surprised by Jen's situation, point in unison to a nearby refrigerator. It's hard to see with all the bullet holes in its antique white surface, but the outline of a woman is painted on it.

Neiman is...horrible. Plain and simple horrible. Racist. Misogynistic. And willing to kill people just because they're different, like Jen and Allie.

Why are they different? I don't know.

But they are...in a way I don't trust. But I can't allow them to be killed. Same as Rich. Much as I disliked him for being a cheap knock-off of my father, he's still family, and I'll save him if I can. But Allie isn't Rich. She's...like my other half, a connection to Dad and Mom. She's blood. To Romani people that's everything...but I can feel that connection crumbling. At least emotionally. The knowledge of it hasn't faded.

"C'mon out, or I kill this one now," Neiman says, and he pokes the shotgun barrel into Jen's gut hard enough to make her wince, and scare Allie out of hiding.

Allie steps out from behind the fridge, but she's not looking at Jen or Neiman. She's looking at me, trying to figure out what the hell is going on, and I wish I had an answer for her. She must sense the same strange distance that I do. It's reminiscent of when I was deployed, separated not just physically from my family, but also emotionally. At times it was like they no longer existed. Like all my past, and everything that once mattered to me was a bland movie about which I didn't really have an opinion. It followed me when I left the Middle East. Flew with me on the plane. Stayed with me when I came home to Mom and Rich. But it shattered and fled when I saw Allie again, and she said the same thing she says, now, "Hey, big Bro..." like she sees me, but is also asking if I'm there.

I hugged her then. Wept into her shoulder like a wounded child.

Now...now I just hold all that in and focus on Neiman.

I don't think I can disarm him without getting Jen killed. Even putting a bullet in the back of his head might make his finger twitch enough to pull the trigger.

"Can I do it?" I ask.

Neiman looks back at me, shotgun unwavering.

"Think you're up to it?"

Not sure if he senses my apprehension, or if he understands what Jen and Allie mean to me.

"I brought them here. To your doorstep. And I shouldn't have. This should have been taken care of before we came to you. My mistake. My responsibility. Let me clean it up."

He looks me in the eyes. I try to reflect the manic paranoia vibe he's putting off, putting a twitch in my right eye, licking my lips like I've got a taste for blood.

He gives a nod, believing the ruse, possibly because I didn't need to try very hard to sell it. I feel...vampiric. Hungry for violence. Thirsty for blood. And suspicious of people I know I shouldn't be.

Something is wrong. And it's not just me. Gone is the overprotective sister. Emma looks almost eager for the carnage to start. Bree just watches, a slight smile on her face, holding a quivering Sanchez who looks ready to scarf up the scraps.

I step up beside Neiman, AK in hand, already feeling its doubled weight. "Before I do it," I say, "a question..."

"Shoot," he says, and I'm not sure if he's actually telling me to shoot.

"Ask away, kid," he says, impatience boiling over. "We got shit to do."

"We do?"

"You haven't been listening," he says.

I've heard and dissected every word he has said, so I'm not sure what—

He cocks his head to the side, eyes glazed for a moment, like he's hearing something.

He's cuckoo for Cocoa Puffs, I think. Probably was before all this. Stocking up for a war. Hearing voices. I'm not going to get any answers out of him. But I need to try.

"Why do you want to kill them?"

His forehead furrows. "Kill who?"

I motion one hand toward Jen. I think maybe he's forgotten about All-ie, who is inching her way back toward the fridge, so I don't point her out.

"I...don't want to kill anyone," he says. "I just... We don't have a choice, right? It's why we're here. Why we're alive. You, me, and those two." He motions to Emma and Bree. "We've been chosen."

He's talking about the death runes. Nothing else makes sense. He might not know about the mark on his head, but it has marked his soul. And mind. All at once, I can feel it, a corruption moving through me, tiny roots expanding out through my mind and body.

Changing me.

"You need to open yourself up to it," he says. "It'll be easier that way."

"What will be easier?" I ask.

"Doing what needs doing." With that, he turns toward Jen, and I know he's going to do it.

My arms fly into motion before I've had a chance to process my options. The butt of my rifle strikes the shotgun to the side, just as it fires. Buckshot tears past Jen's abdomen and decimates a mannequin in a skimpy dress. The thunderous boom is like a slap in the face, but I ignore it.

Neiman has pumped another shell.

This time, I take hold of the shotgun and shove it to the ground. He fires again, this time into the dirt, nearly shooting his own foot.

I look him in the eyes, glaring. "You don't need to listen to the voices, or whatever these are doing to us." I point to the death rune on my forehead. "We are still in control. Still human. Just like Jen and Allie."

"We...need...to..."

"What war did you fight in?" I ask.

"Korea."

"I was in Afghanistan."

He looks at me with new eyes, realizing that we are united in other ways beyond the brands on our flesh and a newfound craving for blood.

"You heard of psy-ops?" I ask.

He gives a slow nod.

"That's what's being done to us," I say, and then I look at Emma. "To all of us. They're getting in our heads. Turning us against the people we love." I point at Jen. "She is not the enemy. My sister is not the enemy."

"Then...who is?"

Hyena cackling rises up from the far side of Neiman's house. A demon coming this way, no doubt drawn by the shotgun blasts.

"*That* is," I say. "Now...are you with us? With all of us? Or are you with them?" Motion at the top of Neiman's roof draws my eyes. He tracks my glance and sees the shadowy figure cloaked in its own personal storm for the first time. He stumbles back a step and then answers my question by pumping the shotgun again, lifting it toward the rooftop, and shouting, "You're not gonna take my house, you sons-a-bitches!"

Then he fires a shell into the swirling storm.

34

The demon barely flinches. The buckshot can't penetrate the whipping wind surrounding the creature. A warm breeze swirls, tickling my ears, as though the demon's storm is radiating around us. Neiman pumps his shotgun again, but he's smart enough to not pull the trigger a second time. At this range, the weapon is ineffective.

The AK-47 on the other hand... It's like Samuel L. Jackson once said, 'When you absolutely have to—'

"Wait!" Bree scurries between us and the house, Sanchez in her arms. "Don't shoot it!"

"Why the hell not?" Allie asks.

Bree taking a stand on behalf of a demon is surprising, but the absolute menace in Sanchez's bulging eyes is disconcerting, like hearing Mötley Crüe live for the first time. His whole body shakes with manic agitation, teeth bared, a high-pitched growl rumbling in time with his quivering muscles.

"It's not here to kill us," Bree says.

"How do you know that?" Jen asks.

"Because I can hear him," she says, and she turns to me. "Can't you?"

I'm about to deny it when I hear the faint sound for myself. In the wind, gathering strength around us. It's a voice. Just a whisper, but powerful and demanding, like a compulsion.

Do it.

You want it. You've never wanted anything more in your life.

Problem is, I don't know what it is, and I'm not sure Bree does either. But she recognizes the voice's source—the demon.

The creature climbs over the rooftop, chuckling as it moves toward the gutter. Inside the storm, a black body moves in agitated fits and spurts, limbs and tendrils snapping about, like it's incapable of smooth motions, or even standing still.

Like it's uncomfortable.

"I...I hear it," Neiman says.

I take his arm. "Don't listen to it, Neiman. Remember, psy-ops. It's getting in our heads." I point at Emma, issuing an order. "Do *not* listen to it."

"But it's just coming for a sniff," Bree says.

Bree is facing me, but she's backing away toward the house. Toward the demon. Shifting allegiances and taking Sanchez with her. By the look of him, Sanchez has already been recruited.

Whatever this is, it's affecting the simpler minds among us first, and Jen and Allie not at all. *It's the mark,* I realize. The death runes. We're not just tainted meat, we're...what?

Like-minded?

Simple-minded?

Broken?

Corrupted?

Maybe all of the above, or one of the above. I don't think we'll ever know how or why some of us were selected for the brand and whatever comes along with it, but I'm sure now that it's a little more complicated than having Lyme disease.

We're predisposed to violence.

The thought just pops into my mind, unbidden and unwelcome. I get Neiman. Even myself. I might be ashamed of my past, and scarred by it, but when push comes to shove, I know who I am, even when drowning in pot. But Emma... No, I can see it. She's definitely a 'shoot first, ask questions later' kind of person. And Bree... She's got the 'innocence of youth' thing going on, but she's dealing with her parents' disappearance and her brother's consumption rather well.

Looking at her with this new thought, she's kind of frightening.

Like a future serial killer or something, now that the darkness in her has been unlocked.

As for Sanchez, the dog has savagely eaten raw meat his whole life, and while he was always kind to me, he violently defended our house from newcomers. I was in his pack before, but now he's found a new pack...

And I'm not sure I want any part of it.

It's tempting. Dark desires tug at me, prodding.

But I resist, because I am *not* my predispositions. I am a brother. A son. A loyal friend. A kindhearted, god-damned freak who frightens people until they get to know me.

The demon leaps to the ground without effort. The storm buoys the creature in the air, softening its landing. Dust from the grassless firing range whips up, concealing the beast within. There are hints of its flailing tendrils, but little else.

"What does she mean, it's going to *sniff* us?" Allie whispers to me. The question is packed, and not just the words. Allie's tone says she knows exactly what it's doing and why.

It's seeing six death runes, but the demon senses at least some of them are not legitimate. So, it's coming to inspect, apparently by smelling us.

"Stay behind me," I whisper, and then to Jen, I say, "Both of you."

Displaying that she is, at least for now, still herself, Emma stands beside me, eyes on the beast. "I don't want to do this," she admits.

I nod. I don't want to, either. Whatever change is taking place in us, it includes a sense of...kinship with denizens of the underworld. Fighting it feels like a betrayal. The idea of killing it—if that's even possible—is revolting. But no more so than allowing it to kill people that I love. The demon is the aggressor here. Not Jen. Not Allie.

Though I'm not sure how much longer I'll feel that way.

Bree smiles as the demon looms over her. Sanchez wags his tail. When he looks up into the chaotic storm, instead of yelping and running away to hide under something, Sanchez wriggles free, leaps to the ground, and runs into the storm.

Even Bree looks a little surprised.

Sanchez has been...absorbed.

Might be alive in there.

Might be dead. Probably is a snack.

I want to cry for my little pal, but I've got nothing left for despair...or perhaps I'm simply not able to feel it anymore.

The storm closes in on Bree. She doesn't move. Just closes her eyes, takes a deep breath, and waits. I should be worried for her, but I'm not.

The demon isn't here to eat her, and I already know what it's going to find—Bree is one of their chosen. A newly willing disciple of darkness.

A shape emerges from the storm. A hand. Long black fingers, blackened nails, and charred skin. Flakes of flesh are torn away by the churning air, revealing bright red wounds that heal, dry, and peel away again. Over and over. The churning dust surrounding the creature is composed of its own husked skin. It looks…like torture.

Mobilized torment.

The black fingers wrap around Bree's arm. They gently take hold. The demon means her no harm. She's guided back to the storm's fringe.

A face emerges, both human and inhuman. Two eyes, a mouth, and nose that are in a constant state of destruction and reformation. The storm tears away sheets of dried skin, which regrow moments later. Just like the hand. The snarling face emanates evil, but also pain. It's in a constant state of agony.

Is that why demons are such pricks?

I'm both revolted and filled with pity for the thing.

The peeling face leans down beside Bree. Whispers in her ear. I can hear the swishing sound, like wind through trees, but I can't make out the words.

Bree giggles and nods. "Okay."

Then she's released. Scurries to the side.

The demon's face slides back inside the storm, like a retracting turtle shell, and I wonder if it's for the same purpose—protection.

"Why is Bree smiling like she just found out that demon was Santa Claus?" Allie whispers, her voice shaking.

"More like Satan Claws," I say, smiling at her. "Am I right?"

Her faces screws up. "None of this is funny, Miah. It's going to kill us."

The tears in her eyes snap me back to myself. I need to stay vigilant about what I'm feeling and thinking. This is one of the assholes that killed or will kill my mother. And if we can't stop it here and now, it's going to kill my sister. "Sorry."

"What did it tell you?" Neiman asks Bree.

The tone of his voice has changed.

He's eager. Less afraid.

"Ask Giggles yourself," Bree says, motioning to the demon, whom she has apparently named Giggles.

"Neiman..." I say. "Don't."

"Maybe we should?" Emma asks. "Just to find out.

"*Emma.*" Jen is in shock.

"Well, how else are we going to know?" Emma says.

Jen gives Emma her best big sister stare. "Know *what?*"

Emma turns to her older sister and without mincing words, or showing emotion, she says, "What it wants us to do with you."

35

Emma stands there for a moment, staring at her sister. Then her own words sink in. Her face scrunches up. "Sorry. I..." She turns to face the demon as Neiman zombie walks toward it.

The old man drops the shotgun, in complete submission now, his mind closer to that of the seven-year-old in our midst than to Emma or to me. But how long until we're right there with him? How long until I can no longer resist the voices flowing past my ears, whispering honey-suckle, and promising unending happiness?

"It's a lie," I say to Neiman, but it's too late. He takes off his hat, drops to his knees, and supplicates at the demon's unseen feet.

The hand emerges anew, resting on Neiman's yellowed hair. It's reverent and gentle. Almost affectionate. And...disturbing. A perversion.

"When it comes out," Emma says, and once again I find myself in synch with her.

I tighten my grip on the AK and give a nod. It's only then that I wonder if the demon has good hearing and can understand English. Then its face emerges, leaning down toward Neiman.

Its face comes apart, whisked away by the storm. Then quickly heals and comes apart again. It's contorted in pain. In a constant state of dying.

A burst of wind shears off half of its face, shattering it to dust. A fit of hyena laughs cuts through the air. In this new context, I understand the sound for what it is—a stuttering scream of raw agony. Giggles isn't laughing.

Giggles is despairing. Wailing.

And when his red eyes meet mine, I don't see hatred or anger or loathing.

I see desperation.

He's begging...to die.

"Now," I whisper, and I raise the AK.

Emma follows suit and we both open fire.

The demon doesn't try to retreat inside its protective maelstrom. Doesn't attempt to run, or attack. If anything, it looks like it's trying to hold its ground. To make itself vulnerable, even as the storm becomes frantic, shredding its face, and probably the rest of it, like a well-cooked roast.

The demon howls in pain as bullets buzz through the air, some of them punching through the storm, some deflected away, and at least one finding the creature's forehead.

The blackened face snaps back from the impact, but the wound heals anew.

I run out of ammo before Emma, but I have my new jungle-style mag flipped around and slapped in place just as she runs out. The barrage continues, but I think it's hopeless—until a spark lights up the storm's interior. I hit something, and the whisper in my ear becomes an inhuman shout. "Yes! YES!"

My aim shifts toward the spark, unleashing the last of this magazine's rounds. Sparks fill the storm like fireworks in a cloud. And then— something bursts.

The storm disappears with a final gust that scatters dust to the ground and to the top of Neiman's head.

The demon is revealed.

And it's not a demon at all.

It's...a man.

Or it used to be. He stands on all fours, lanky and emaciated. But his body is recognizably human, and I don't think it's because a demon chose this form. Why would anything choose this?

He's charred from top to bottom. His blackened skin cracks with every movement, no matter how subtle.

"His forehead," Jen says, and I see it. At the center of his flaking head, just above his red eyes, is a death rune.

This...is what we are becoming.

We're not spoiled meat... We're recruits.

That's why they don't want to hurt us. Sooner or later, those of us with the death rune will be just like this monstrous man. A slave. Tortured. Dying forever, yet forbidden death's mercy.

My eyes follow the jagged contours of his body, stopping at a black strap. There's one around his waist and two around his shoulders. When he hunches forward, growing weak, he reveals a device on his back. It doesn't look like a product of hell, but of advanced technology.

Advanced technology that's been shot to shit.

This is what made the storm.

The man wheezes, unable to breathe. He's growing weaker by the second.

The swirling winds weren't just a defensive barrier.

They were an atmosphere.

That's why the air smells of sulfur.

These things breathe it, and they don't seem to have much need for oxygen.

With a raspy voice, the man whispers what sounds like, "Takk," and then he collapses. A hiss slides from his lungs, deflating his body.

We all move in for a closer look, but I flinch away when his back comes to life. Tendrils rise up, writhing and reaching.

"Everyone stay back," I say.

"It's in pain," Bree says. "We have to help it."

I suspect the 'it' might be the real enemy. A hijacker embedded in the tortured man's back. "It's a parasite," I say.

"No!" Bree shouts, as I raise my weapon anew. She runs for the flailing appendages as they reach out for her, looking for a new home. But there's no saving it. Not without an atmosphere. So, I put a handful of bullets in it, stopping Bree in her tracks and shredding the now unprotected tendrils.

The black limbs flop to the ground.

I move closer, alone this time. The tendrils emerge from the small of the man's back, below the futuristic device that I now see is fused to his body.

"It used to be a person," I say. "Then they took it over. Used it like a robot."

"That doesn't look very demonic," Jen says. I'm about to argue with her until I realize she's talking about the portable atmosphere generator. The man, and the tentacles emerging from his back encapsulate my vision of hell. It actually reminds me a bit of her art, as if the knowledge of these things is stored in our DNA, fueling the imaginations of artists and writers like Jen, or inspiring prophecies in the minds of the religious.

But it's not from hell.

"It's not a demon," I say.

"Then what is it?" Allie asks.

"Giggles," Bree says, sniffing back tears. "He wanted to be my friend."

The voice of Giggles, whispering sweet nothings in our ears, didn't come from the man. He was just a vessel. Giggles was the parasite. And as hellish as it is, I don't think it's from hell.

"I'm not sure," I admit. "Best guess, aliens."

Emma crouches down. Pokes the end of her gun muzzle into the man's shoulder. It crumbles to dust. The body is completely dried out, like dead wood rot. "Is that really any better?"

Giggles's lower back bulges and cracks. I take a step back. Something within is emerging.

The dried flesh rises like a newly forming volcano, bits and pieces rolling away as a small black snout emerges.

I take aim, about to shoot, when its head emerges.

"Sanchez," I say, relieved.

I move in to help the little guy when he snaps and snarls at me, his little lungs huffing up a frenzy as he claws his way free. Then he bounds from the corpse, lets loose a barrage of not very intimidating barks, and scurries away around Neiman's house. Headed for the street. No doubt to the woods beyond.

"We can't stay here," I say, and then I turn to Emma. "You good?"

The whispered voices propelling me toward violence have faded, but they aren't completely gone.

"Better," she says, and then she nods her head toward Bree. The kid looks out of it. Confused. Giggles has lost its grasp on her, but it left her...vacant. She's just standing still, blinking at the body.

Then, all of a sudden, she cocks her head to the side and smiles at us. "I'm okay!"

"That might be creepier than the demon-dude," Allie says, trying to sound casual despite her whole-body jittering. Jen has her arm around my sister, looking at me with new eyes...eyes that say, *I know who you are now, and I don't trust you.*

And she's right not to. She can't trust any of us. Not completely. Especially when one of these things is around.

"You girls should find someplace to hide," Neiman says. "Whatever it is they want you for, it ain't good. But it's better'n what they got in store for us."

The old man looks me in the eyes.

"Not a fight you can win, son. Best you can do is get these two someplace safe, take care of the other two, and then yourself."

I'm not exactly sure what he's getting at, until he picks up his shotgun, places the barrel under his chin, and says, "Don't go upstairs..."

—and then he pulls the trigger.

36

"No!" I scream, but the sound of my voice is drowned out by the boom of a shotgun and the liquid crunch of buckshot shattering a human skull from the inside out.

I lunge away from the human geyser, wrap one hand around Bree's eyes and the other around her waist, twisting her away from the sight.

"Let me see," she says, trying to squirm free, but I lock her down, holding her in place until the last thump of brain matter hits the ground.

"Oh my god," Allie says. "Oh my god. Oh my god."

"Basement," I say. "Everyone. Now."

I pick up Bree and carry her toward the open bulkhead. She kicks and flails like a spoiled child being dragged away from a Dairy Queen because she wanted gummy bears in her ice cream, instead of gummy worms. But it's no use. I haul her down the steps and into Neiman's fantastical maze of shit.

The sudden shift in scenery takes the fight out of her. Instead of raging, she's curious.

"Close the door," I say to Jen, as she descends the steps behind Allie and Emma. The bulkhead creaks to a close and then clangs as Jen locks it.

"S-smells horrible down here," Allie says.

Emma shrugs, looking around. "I don't mind it."

Allie stands still behind her, arms reaching out, shaking. "C-can we light a candle or something?"

"Why?" Emma asks. "I can see fine."

"Look at this!" Bree says, picking up a snow globe with a Navy Destroyer inside it.

They can both see as well as I can.

In the dark.

Allie comes to the same realization. "You three can see."

"Yeah," I say, taking a candle from my pocket and lighting it. The room flares brighter—almost too bright. I hold the lit candle out to my sister. "Be careful with it. Pretty sure everything in here is flammable, including the floor."

"What's on the—" Allie looks down. Winces. "Gross."

Bree is totally distracted by the junk lasagna filling the basement, so I slide past Emma and wrap my arms around Allie. "You okay?"

"Not at all," she says. "I'm not sure how much more of this I can take before I crack up."

"That's good," I say.

She looks up at me. "How is that good?"

"Means you're still human. Means you're not like us." I glance at Bree and Emma.

"Don't say that." Jen has her arms crossed and tears in her eyes. "You are not going to become like...like that thing."

"Giggles," Bree says. Like me, her hearing is more acute now, too.

Jen clenches her fists, holding in her anger.

"I don't know how it works," I say, "but I can see in the dark. I can hear better than I used to. I don't feel afraid, or panicky, or even very disturbed about all of this."

"It feels good," Emma says from the other end of a basement, where she's inspecting an old magazine.

"But it won't for long," Jen says. "If you end up like—"

"Giggles," Bree inserts.

"If you end up like Giggles, you won't feel good. At all."

I nod.

I know she's right in my head, but I don't feel as concerned as I should.

I don't know when, but sooner or later, our skin is going to dry and blacken. We'll be faster and stronger, but every movement will cause us unceasing agony, and our lungs will be acclimated to a different atmosphere. On the plus side, we'll suffocate to death. On the downside, I suspect by the time that happens, we'll be drawn toward our new devil overlords and subjugated by demonic parasites.

If Emma, Bree, and I can be saved, I don't know how. Until that becomes clear, I have a two-fold mission: keep Jen and Allie safe, and rescue our families. In that order.

For now, those of us with legitimate death runes on our foreheads are the walking damned. Since we're now on day two of a three-day prophecy, I don't think we have a lot of time.

"We need to find someplace safe for the two of you," I say to Jen and Allie. When neither of them argue, I know they understand the situation the same way I do. Outside, for them, is death. One way or another, they won't be able to escape it. Best case scenario is that they follow the prophecy's guidelines and make it through the cull. But the rest of us...we can go where we want. And that means there is a chance—albeit a small one—that we can find our families.

"What's wrong with here?" Bree asks.

"Aside from smelling like piss and shit?" Allie says. "This place is a bacterial infection waiting to happen."

"I think the smell is a good thing, actually," I say.

Jen raises an eyebrow at me, waiting for an explanation.

"Because I can't smell you," I say.

"Can you...normally?" she asks.

"Not before today." I look toward the closed bulkhead. "But outside... Yeah."

"Me too," Bree says. "It's like a nice smell that isn't pretty."

"Like steak," Emma says, revealing a detail I had hoped to keep to myself.

Jen's expression falls. "We smell like *food?*"

"Tasty," Bree says, and licks her lips. I definitely need to get her away from anyone without a death rune. She's toned down a bit since Giggles bit the dust, but we're all still changing.

"You and Allie kind of stand out." My attempt at saying it diplomatically comes a little too late.

"Okay," Allie says, "so we hole up in this shithole for how long?"

"Day and a half," I guess. "But definitely until the sun is out again."

Allie sags against a pile of books. "Great." The books topple over, thumping against the floor, kicking up a cloud of rancid, black dust. Waving our hands and coughing, we file deeper into the basement maze. "I'm definitely not staying down here, though. I think I'd rather be dead than spend two days in this basement."

"I think that's an option." Bree grins and her sidelong glance is unnerving.

"No. It is not." Then I remember Neiman's last words.

Don't go upstairs.

I turn my head toward the ceiling. Was he just being protective of his shit? Would he feel embarrassed if we saw how he really lived? Or is something up there dangerous? He's dead, so I really don't care about any personal reasons he might have had for the warning. The old dude erased the fledgling amount of respect I had for him when he blew his brains out in front of a bunch of kids.

But if the warning was legit...

"I'll sweep the upper floors first," I say.

"Alone?" Jen asks.

"Anyone else here have experience sweeping a house for danger? No? I'll go by myself." I try to smile at her, to lighten the mood, but it's hard. My sense of humor is fading along with what I think might be my humanity. "But first..."

I move into Neiman's armory and quickly find what I'm looking for—a drawer full of handguns, laid out nicely, each one cleaner and more well-kept than the rest of the house. I pick out a familiar favorite—the Colt 1911. Standard issue for Marines and frequently used by the U.S. Army as well. Optimal for close quarters combat—unlike a jungle style magazine AK—and it packs enough punch to drop anything with a heartbeat ...or a personal atmosphere generator.

"Oh, this is sweet," Emma says, entering the armory. "He's got even more than Dad. And look at these bombs!"

"Eh, eh," I say to Emma, as she approaches the pipe bombs. "We don't know if they're armed. House won't be much good if you blow it up." She's disappointed until I say, "But see if you can find something else with a little extra punch."

I eject the handgun mag, make sure it's loaded, and then head for the door.

"Stay here," I say to Allie, and then to Jen, I say, "Arm up, and teach her what you know." I tilt my head toward my sister. "If the kid...acts up... I'm sure Neiman's got some zip-ties around."

That gets a genuine smile from Jen, which in turn tugs a little joy out of the depths and puts a smile on my face, too. I head for the staircase dividing the two sides of the basement. The majority of each step is covered in layers of household detritus, stacked several feet up. The only path is along the left railing. Just enough room for a single foot on each stair. "Be right back." Then I lean into the far side of the basement where Bree continues her exploration. "Hey Magellan, I'm going to clear the upstairs. Listen to the others, okay?"

She ignores me, focused on discovering her new continent of filth.

I start up the stairs, one hand on the railing, the other holding the gun. Moving up the narrow pathway is awkward and slow going. Just slow enough to allow my mind to drift. It's just for a moment, but my thoughts land on Sanchez. My little man. He's gone. No longer himself. Essentially dead. Maybe worse—a two-pound lord of the underworld.

In a way, it's the role he was born to play.

But he was also kind of my best friend.

When I reach the top stair, I pause to wipe a tear from my eye, sad about Sanchez, but hopeful because I can still feel something.

Then I turn the doorknob, push open the door, and reveal a strange new tropical hell.

37

Neiman must have a humidifier running. The air is thick with moisture, like Florida before a storm. Or Korea in the summer. Lush potted plants grow in every available area, hanging from ceiling hooks, standing atop piles of books, boxes, magazines, and random hoarded mounds of who-knows-what.

There are lamps mounted on the walls. Probably daylight lamps to keep things growing, because the windows are walled up with heaps of crap. Neiman was unintentionally prepared for the Three Days of Darkness.

I lead with my gun, moving through the thin line of available floor space. It doesn't take much imagination to be transported back in time, to a battlefield, surrounded by enemies.

Who could live like this?

Someone who never left the war. At least in his head.

When I came home, what I had seen and done pursued me across the ocean and haunted my thoughts. But I never embraced it. Never welcomed it. Or attempted to recreate what I experienced.

I guess everyone deals with trauma in their own way. Some people do laughter yoga, others turn their home into North Korean enemy territory...complete with buzzing flies.

They're everywhere, feasting on grime and probably on shit. I wave my hand in front of my face, shooing them away, trying to keep my gun raised and ready. A high-pitched whine grows louder by my ear. I swat the side of my head.

"Mosquitos," I complain. "Seriously?"

A jar full of water, sitting on the kitchen counter, twitches with mosquito larvae.

This place is overwhelming. Claustrophobic. I felt safer outside than I do in here. Neiman must have lived in a constant state of near panic. Always afraid. Always on the lookout for the enemy. Always uncomfortable—smelly, itchy, and irritated.

The various rooms are difficult to tell apart, each one filled with crap and transformed into a jungle. The kitchen is only recognizable because the fridge has a clearing in front of it and the blackened microwave door isn't blocked. Stacks of scraped-clean paper plates, tied in bundles of a hundred, line the walls like sandbags.

I kick open a door with my foot. A wave of hot, fetid stench rolls out, and tackles me away. The bathroom. I'm not even going to look. Pursued by the stench, I follow the trail to the second-floor stairs.

I don't know why I'm bothering at this point. Unless they're prepared to hunker down in the basement, Jen and Allie can't stay here. On the off chance they do decide to stay, I push onward and upward, through the narrow path leading up the stairs. Stacks of magazines line the sides of the stairs. Toward the bottom, National Geographics. Their bright yellow borders like a landing strip, guiding me up instead of down. Halfway up the staircase is a mix of People, Time, and Life, followed by several stacks of Guns & Ammo. Near the top, things take a turn. Playboy. Penthouse. And some lesser-known nudie mags I've never heard of. But he's censored them, using a Sharpie to draw clothing over their exposed bodies.

"Okay..." I say, feeling more unnerved. I knew Neiman was... different, but I hadn't imagined an indoor jungle combat scenario and pseudo-sadomasochistic entertainment. The disturbing sights are made worse by the increasing heat and humidity that comes with elevation.

The top of the stairs opens into a landing that most people would have used for a reading nook. But not Neiman. He's created a kind of bunker, using bricks made of elastic-band bound magazines. It looks like a military check point, like anyone desiring to pass would need to stop and show their papers.

But there's no gate.

Still, I stop by the window, where I imagine a gate should be, and I lean in for a look. "Gah!" I shout in surprise. A female mannequin dressed in an old-school military uniform sits in a folding metal chair, her frozen expression accentuated by a bright red, painted-on smile.

I take a moment to catch my breath and collect my thoughts. Whatever changes are happening to my mind and body, it wasn't enough to prepare me for that. Hands on my knees, I shake my head, wondering what else I'm going to find.

That's when I see it.

The gate.

The thing that will keep unwanted eyes from seeing what lies beyond.

Only, it's not a gate. It's a tight fishing line stretched across the hallway between the banister and the bunker. I follow it to a grenade, the pin just a slight tug away from popping free. It looks old, but Neiman wasn't an amateur.

I crouch down, mumbling to myself. "Damn, old coot..." I pinch the fishing line in one hand and grasp the grenade in the other, keeping the pin locked in place. "Freaking mouse poop basement, jungle-ass house, and pervy stairs."

With a quick tug, the fishing line snaps free of the banister.

I slap the back of my neck. My hand comes away smeared with the corpse of a mosquito and my own blood. "Sunuvabitch mosquitos. How the hell did you sleep, Neiman?"

After making sure the pin is secure, I slip the ordinance into my pocket, raise my gun anew, and move down the hallway toward the three doors. The first is open, the next two are closed.

My desire to leave this place and never come back is at war with raw curiosity. This deadly gate was here for a reason. Everything before this point could be boiled down to an unusual, perhaps mentally disturbed, lifestyle. Beyond it...that's where the secrets lie.

I don't need to know, I think, and that's true. But I *want* to know.

Something is drawing me down the hall. I feel...something.

Like a presence.

Neiman's ghost probably, ready to jump out shouting, 'Git off my land!'

I slide up beside the open door, gun at the ready. I dip my head in. It's just for a moment, but long enough to take in the jungle's worth of plants, walls of garbage formed like rough terrain, wall-mounted sun lamps, and a mosquito net-covered hammock.

Neiman's bedroom.

Is this what the grenade was protecting? The time a soldier is most vulnerable is when he's asleep. Was the grenade meant to protect him from an imagined enemy?

I shake my head. That's not it. The grenade was protecting something else.

Neiman's secret.

I move past the bedroom without entering and slide up next to the closed door on the opposite side of the hallway. The door appears to be free of traps, but who knows what's lurking on the other side. Could be Bozo the Clown dressed in S&M leathers, wielding a katana. That wouldn't even be surprising at this point.

The handle turns smoothly. I hold onto it until the door starts moving. Then I let go, stand back, and nudge the door open with my foot. As the room is slowly revealed, like a Star Wars wipe, I track the space with the gun.

Then I wince. Where the rest of the house is full of junk that's been piled, sorted, and in some cases bound into building materials, this bedroom is basically a dump. A rotting pile of compost, food scraps, and who knows what else. A layer of white wriggles over everything.

Maggots.

Clenching my mouth shut and holding my breath, I reach out for the door and slowly pull it closed. Once it's shut, I take a deep breath and wince. I'd grown somewhat accustomed to the home's stench, but now... my sensitive nose is picking up on a thousand different wretched odors.

Including one that stands out.

And it's not coming from either of the two bedrooms I've already explored. It's coming from the doorway at the end of the hall.

And I can't place it. It's rotten, but not like spoiled food. Offensive, but not because I recognize the odor. I don't. Because...it's not really an odor. Not in the way I'm used to thinking about them.

It's...fear.

I'm not alone.

"Hello?" I say, creeping toward the door. "Who's there?"

The floorboards beneath my feet creak, and I experience the closest thing I have to panic since getting branded. But it's over before it begins—and it doesn't belong to me.

I'm not smelling the person on the other side of that door.

I'm sensing them. Sensing...her. I can feel a feminine presence. Her fear and anxiety. Her raw, abject horror at my approach.

She thinks I'm him.

"It's okay," I call out. "I'm not going to hurt you. Neiman is dead."

A wave of relief rolls out of the room, and it's at that moment I realize that whoever is in there is a prisoner. Before I can rush to the door, a voice stops me. "He told you not to come up here."

It's Bree.

Standing behind me. Fists clenched by her sides. Eyes staring out from under a furrowed brow. She's giving me a pugilistic stare down, daring me to turn my back and see what happens.

The darkness claiming her might have slowed down, but it's still affecting her faster than Emma or me.

"But he didn't tell me." She smiles wide. "I can go in there if you want."

"I don't want," I say. "Go back downstairs."

"You're not my mother," she says.

"But I'm in charge."

"Says who?" She crosses her arms. "I don't think I want to listen to you anymore. You always tell me 'no,' and 'you can't,' and 'do this.' Well, I'm going to—"

"Stop!" I shout, but the sound comes out deep and rumbly. Pain lances through my body, little lightning streaks, like I've been sliced up by a razor blade for just a moment.

Bree shrinks back, her borderline tantrum defused.

"That was ugly," she says, and she stomps her way back down the stairs.

Below, I hear Jen enter the first floor.

"Where did she go? Bree?"

And then she shouts in revolt before quickly vomiting. She must have reached the bathroom.

"I'm coming, I'm coming," Bree complains, and I turn my attention back to the closed door while wondering why Bree called me ugly. I touch a hand to my face. Feels normal, but for a moment there, I didn't feel like me at all.

Hand on the doorknob, I raise my gun and open it a crack, wary of another trip wire. Seeing none, I put my hand against the door and push, unable to fully comprehend what I find on the other side.

38

It's a kid's bedroom, decorated mostly in shades of pink. Pristine. It's like Neiman raided a furniture store and took a bedroom display. The walls have Hello Kitty wallpaper. A basket of stuffed animals catches my attention. There's a blue and white penguin with a yellow hat and round, orange glasses. An orange fox with big red ears. And what I think is a frog wearing a blue jumpsuit. They have a vaguely Asian vibe to them, but not Japanese. Then I spot the group again, in a poster over a dresser, atop which sits a vase full of fresh flowers. It's a kid's show, apparently. The logo reads: Pororo.

"Huh..." I lower my gun a bit, not wanting to frighten whoever's hiding in the bedroom. "Hello? I'm here to help."

I nearly pull the trigger when I spot a woman standing beside a makeup table. Well, half a woman. The mannequin nearly takes a bullet to the forehead. She's done up in make-up. A lot of it. Pale skin and red lips. A vacant stare. Short black hair and green eyes. I can feel the good intentions of whoever painted her up, but they've accidentally created a monster. And it's not the first one.

This is why Neiman had the mannequins in the shooting range. It wasn't repressed sadomasochistic rage, he simply found them so repulsive that he couldn't bear to keep them in the house. I might have done the same if I had a collection of nightmare women glaring at me. The dude was clearly disturbed already. The blank staring feminine faces probably made him feel haunted...by more than his memories.

"Hellooo," I say in a singsong voice. "I'm going to come in. Real slow, okay?"

I lower the gun to my side and extend my free hand, palm out, a gesture of peace. I hope. The rest of the room slowly comes into view.

A queen size canopy bed with decorative netting around it, probably in case mosquitos get in. A lot of toys. A bean bag. A desk with a lamp and a laptop. All things considered, this is an ideal room for a modern child.

But Neiman didn't have kids.

"If you tell me where you are, I can help."

Nothing.

But there is someone here. I can feel her presence, tickling my senses. Her agitation fills the space, almost audible.

The room's two windows have the shades drawn, but they're not covered. One is facing the backyard.

She saw.

Knows that Neiman is dead, and that he took his own life.

"You're okay now," I say. "No one is going to hurt y—"

The gunshot nearly takes off my ankle. Punches a hole in Pororo instead.

Instinct guides my hands to my ears. One side is covered, the other is smacked by my handgun. When my senses return, I hear crying. From a girl. She fired that gun from under the bed.

Pulling a trigger in an enclosed space is never a good idea without ear protection. Best case scenario, it'll hurt like hell. Worst case scenario, your ear drums will rupture, and you'll go deaf or call tinnitus a friend for the rest of your life. The bed's porous surface might have diffused some of the sound, maybe enough to avoid the worst effects, but the kid was definitely not prepared for the painful report.

I throw myself into motion before she has a chance to recover and maybe pull that trigger again. She'll think twice about it for sure, but she's still deathly afraid, even though she knows I'm not Neiman.

It occurs to me then that if she saw the old man blow off his own head, she's known from the get go that I wasn't him.

She's not afraid of him. She's afraid of me. And maybe with good reason.

I leap across the room, rolling over the comforter-padded mattress and back onto my feet. Below, her Converse Chuck Taylor adorned feet extend out from under the bed. I take hold, yank her out, and put a foot on her small 9mm pistol.

She wriggles like a caught fish.

"Stop," I say, bending down and prying the gun from her small hand. She fights me the whole way. "Stop!"

She shouts in despair, as I take her weapon, but she stops when I let go of her and step away. "I'm not going to hurt you."

She cowers in the corner, terrified of me, staring at the death rune on my forehead. Did she see the same thing on Neiman's head? Does she understand what it means?

She looks a little younger than Allie. Twelve. Maybe thirteen. She's dressed in jeans and a pink T-shirt.

"I'm Miah," I tell her. She's either out of her head bonkers, or she doesn't understand. I do my best impression of a Hollywood actor, playing a role, meeting a caveman or a primitive for the first time, patting my chest and saying, "Miah."

And holy shit on a burger bun, I think she gets it. She places her shaking hand against her chest and says, "Sung."

"Sung... I like it." It's also Korean, I think.

My stomach turns. Has Neiman been fulfilling his delusional Korean war fantasies by kidnapping Korean girls and holding them hostage for God knows what? Or did he buy her? There's probably a black market for that kind of thing.

I pat myself again. "Friend." I point toward the window facing up hill, toward my house. "Neighbor."

She nods and says, "Friend." At least she understands that. She motions to her gun in my hand. "So-rry."

English is not her first language. It's barely her second language. I don't know how long she's been in the country or living in Neiman's house, but she was clearly born and raised in Korea.

Then she points to the window looking out over the backyard. "Hal-abeoji."

I frown. She knows more English than I do Korean.

She scrunches up her face, frustrated by the language barrier. Then she thrusts her arms out toward the window, tears in her eyes and shouts, "Hal-abeoji!"

The girl's sorrow over Neiman's death clicks everything into place.

I step toward the window, looking down, imagining the backyard through the shade and Neiman's corpse. I motion to where his body lies. "Hal-abeoji..."

She nods.

I repeat the motion, and this time, say, "Grandfather."

Her eyes widen. "Yes. Grand...father."

Whatever darkness is transmogrifying my mind and body into something else is overcome by empathy for this poor kid. I put both guns down on her dresser and with tears already filling my eyes, I open my arms and say, "I'm sorry."

She rushes into my embrace, sobbing, unleashing the kind of pain that I've never experienced. Best guess, she lost her family. Father, mother, grandparents, and any aunts, uncles, or siblings she might have had. Korea is big on family, so she was sent to live with her only remaining blood relative—the American who knocked up grandma during his time in Korea. And Neiman, for all his vast faults, was trying to do right by the girl.

He had a long way to go, but who knows how long she's been here. Might have been a year, might have just been the last month.

And now I understand what his death means to her—she is alone. Without family. In a scary foreign country, in a messed-up house, and now with hell loosed upon the Earth.

I lean back and look down into her sad brown eyes. Then I put a hand to my chest and say, "Hal-abeoji?"

Her little eyebrows turn up in the middle. I can't tell if she's moved by the idea, or horrified. My intention was to let her know that I'm taking responsibility for her. By inserting myself in a familial role, using the only Korean word I know. Her bottom lip quivers and she manages to say, "Abeoji."

Grandfather without the grand. *Father.*

I hug her close again, wondering if I just agreed to become the father of a girl who can't even speak English.

"Miah?" It's Jen. Downstairs and very distressed.

"Up here!" I shout. "Bring everyone up. It's safe. And I think I know where you guys can hide."

The bedroom isn't ideal, but it's clean, it doesn't smell, it's hidden behind a firewall of filth even a demon might avoid, and it's two sets of stairs away from an armory.

Four sets of disgusted voices rise from below. They're all coughing, and swearing, and dry heaving. Together, they sound like some kind of mythical creature being birthed from the depths. When I hear them coming up the second flight of stairs, I say, "End of the hall," and I stand in the doorway, waving them on.

They all but sprint down the hall, entering the bedroom one after another. Bree sees the pretty room and lights up.

"Oh my god, that was nasty," Allie says. "I swear, if I have to—"

Jen nudges Allie. The girls have just noticed Sung, and they are staring at her with the same kind of confusion I felt upon first discovering this tween oasis in a house of paranoid, pack-rat filth.

"Guys," I say, stepping toward the bed, where Sung waits, eyes wide and nervous. I put my hand on her back. "This is Sung. She was Mr. Neiman's granddaughter. From Korea. She doesn't speak much English. She's scared shitless and confused. Oh, and I'm kind of her dad now."

39

Silence is not what I expected. My gaggle of gals just stares at me, suddenly immune to the kaleidoscope of horrors outside this door, and the knowledge of what is happening to the world. I envy them.

Jen is the first to snap out of it. She smiles at Sung and says, "I'm Jen."

Allie moves next, closing the door, sealing out the smells and insects. The moment the door clicks into place, this oasis room becomes our only reality. The house around us feels normal, like everything leading to this point was a delusion.

"Jen," Sung says, nodding in understanding.

"Tell her your names," Jen says to the other girls.

"Allie," my sister says, rounding Emma and Bree, forcing a genuine looking grin. "I like your room."

Emma and Bree don't seem very interested in Sung, or her room. Instead, they're drawn toward the window, trying to peek around the drawn shade, more interested in what new denizen of Hades might be lurking outside.

Jen points at each of them. "Emma. Bree."

"Hey," Emma says, giving a casual wave.

"Whatever," Bree says. Kid's agitated. I need to get her out of here soon.

"Okay…" I clap my hands and rub them together. "Here's the plan. Everyone with a death rune is bugging out. We'll see about getting our families back. Everyone *without* a death rune is staying here."

Allie winces. "In *this* house?"

"In this room," I say.

"But what about a bathroom?" Allie asks. "I have to pee!"

"Bath-room." Sung scoots to a door I took for a closet and opens it to reveal a spacious, clean bathroom, a candle already lit inside.

Allie steps into the bathroom, gives it a once over and then returns. "What about food? We don't know how long you'll be gone, or—"

"I'm coming back," I say. "I promise."

Allie frowns. "You can't promise that, and you know it."

I extend my little finger. "Pinkie-promise."

Her eyes grow wet as she fights back tears. "Fine." We link our pinkies.

"I'm coming back," I say. I turn to Jen. "I promise."

Sung gently claps her hands together. She might not understand English, but apparently the power of a pinkie promise is universal.

"Ugh," Bree says. "Can we go now?"

I turn to Jen, "If I don't come back in the next few minutes, it means there is food in the kitchen."

"And if there's not?" she asks.

"We'll hump that donkey when we get to it."

"Ugh," Allie says. "Gross."

"I mean, jump that hurdle," I say. "Sorry. Forget the other thing. Something we used to say in the Army."

"Soldiers are gross," Allie says.

"You have no idea." I muss up her head the way Dad used to...and then I do the same to Sung. Leaves both of them smiling. Then I turn to Jen and find myself on the receiving end of a kiss. Right on the lips. For a moment, it pushes the growing darkness within me back. Then she leans back and says, "Just in case."

Sung is all smiles. Claps again.

She knows things are bad. Knows that her grandfather is dead of a self-inflicted shotgun blast, and she possibly saw the demon in the back yard. But she doesn't know the true gravity of what's happening. Hell on Earth and all that. I envy her.

"If you have to leave the house," I say. "Use the bulkhead."

"Why?" she asks.

I take the grenade from my pocket. "I'm going to booby trap the rest." I show the grenade to Emma. "You find any more?"

She nods. "Handful in the basement."

I take the jungle style AK from my shoulder and hand it to Jen. Coupled with her M4 and the two handguns, it should be enough to repel a small army...of people. "Only use it if you have no other choice. My ears are still ringing from that single 9 mil round Sung fired. This..." I pat the AK. "This will hurt. A lot."

"Are we good?" Emma asks. She and Bree are standing by the door. "Can we go now?"

"Hey," Jen says to Emma. "Not even going to say goodbye?"

Emma twists her lips. "Nope."

Jen is wounded, but she doesn't say anything. She just packs that pain away with the rest.

Bree opens the door. "Byeeee." She heads out into the humid stink without wincing or crinkling her nose.

Emma follows, turning around briefly to address me with, "Make it snappy."

"I'll try to get them back, too," I say.

Jen puts her hands on my cheeks. "Try not to lose yourself while you're doing it."

I huff. "Been doing that for years." I head for the door and pause to address Allie. "Catch you on the flipside, Sis." She smiles, and I leave the room, close the door behind me, and do my best to keep a stiff upper lip. The stifling humidity and an assault by a mosquito squadron hurries me away from sorrow, to the steps, and down to the first floor. I pause in the kitchen long enough to confirm there is packaged food in the cabinets and fridge. Enough to hold them for a week or more.

If they need more than two days' worth, we're probably all screwed.

Back in the basement, I find my pint-sized Lady Jaye and Scarlett armed and ready to go. Bree is holding a small, chewing gum-pink concealed carry pistol. Looks brand new. Probably a gift meant for Sung. At first glance, it's kind of adorable. Then I remember that Bree is a somewhat unstable seven-year-old packing a 9mm pistol capable of killing a human being.

"Nice," I say to the kid, and I check out Emma's personal arsenal. She's still carrying her father's M4, and now she has non-jungle style magazines stuffed into an old SWAT assault vest. I give her a nod of approval.

She turns around, revealing an olive drab backpack. "Grenades are in here. Some of them."

I turn my attention to the array of weapons from which I can choose. I reach for an AK—feels familiar now—but Emma stops me. "Take an M4. We should be carrying the same ammo. In case we need to share. Also, I dig the jungle style, but it's going to slow us down, and make you tired." She points to the wall where a second combat vest is hung. "Load that up and we'll be good to go."

My smile offends her. "What's funny?"

"Just thinking your father would be proud," I say.

Her tough façade cracks a little. Jen was the creative free spirit. Emma was daddy's girl. My family is centering me, keeping me on task, despite growing...distractions. Reminding Emma of her father might do the same for her.

Bree is the wild card.

With a gun.

I slip into the combat vest and cinch it tight. Emma hands me magazines and I load them up. Six in all.

Bree waits for us in the doorway, aiming her pink pistol at imaginary targets. "Pew, pew."

Emma smiles at her. "Most of the last day has been ratchet, but seeing in the dark is pretty dope, right?"

"Is ratchet bad?" I pick up two loose grenades and pocket them.

She looks at me like I'm crazy.

"I know I've got a young vibe and all, but I'm twenty-seven, bro."

She smiles. "Ratchet is bad."

I find a big knife and strap it to my belt.

"Do you think we can do this?" Emma asks. "Get our families back? Really?"

"How honest are we being right now?" I ask.

"More honest than you were upstairs," she says. "Because I know you feel it, too. What's happening to us. And right now, yeah, it's kind of cool if you ignore the violent urges, but..." She glances at Bree and lowers her voice. "I don't want to be one of those things. If we start to change? Like really change? Mr. Neiman had the right idea."

Emma's words are like a sucker punch to the nuts. I want to curl up and pretend the world doesn't exist. But she's also not wrong.

"If that happens... If I lose control? If I can't breathe normal air? If I try to hurt someone? Or if my skin starts coming apart?" She snaps her fingers in my face, forcing eye contact between us. "I want you to take care of me, and then her." She tilts her head toward Bree. "But since we're being honest, she's going to go first, and I don't think I can do that. At least not yet."

"I'll do it," I whisper. Then I clear my throat and repeat it with a little more conviction. "I'll do it. But I'm going to do my absolute fucking best to avoid it."

"We all will," Emma says. "Right, Bree?"

"I'm going to do my absolute fucking worst," the kid says, and then she offers a lopsided grin. "To the monsters."

"Great," I say, laughing a little. "That's great." I chamber a round, then say, "We are so screwed." Both girls have a laugh, while I head back upstairs, grenades and fishing line in hand. Two minutes later, the first-floor doors leading outside are rigged to blow.

Back in the basement, Emma and Bree wait by the bulkhead, like a rebooted A-Team kids show.

"We're going to figure out what the hell is going on, find our families, get them home safe, and kill every asshole that gets in our way. You both ready for this?"

They nod, and I believe them. I extend my fist. "Pound it out, and let's get this done."

Both girls punch my fist with theirs, driving home how much smaller they are than me. Everything about this is crazy.

Emma moves up the stairs, shoves the bulkhead open, and exits into the night. I follow Bree out and then close the bulkhead behind me. No way to lock it from the outside, but it's loud. Jen and the others should be able to hear it open if someone, or something, decides to inspect.

Bree chambers a round on her little gun and smiles. "Okay, let's go hump this donkey."

40

"Feels good." Emma stands in the middle of the road, looking relaxed.

"Good how?" I ask, standing beside her.

"To be outside and not worried. About Jen. And Allie. About my own life. We're outside and safe. It's only been what, two days? Feels like longer. Like I spent my whole life being afraid."

"Might want to keep an eye on that feeling," I say.

She looks at me beneath the kind of raised sarcastic eyebrows only a teenage girl has the power to wield. "Why?"

"Because you *should* be afraid." I turn my gaze to Bree. She's in the road too, skipping in a circle, humming a kid's ditty, one hand still clutching the Rainbow Bright pistol.

A loud yipping laugh tears through the night. I twist toward the sound, but I stop short of raising my rifle. Hostility is not the vibe we're going for. We're incognito. Fresh troops for hell, ready to serve our dark overlords. It's a ruse, for me. I think Emma is on the fence, but she's clinging tight.

Bree, on the other hand, catapulted over the fence and is free falling toward the far side.

"Hello!" she shouts into the darkness of the woods ahead of us. "Can you play with me?"

Leaves crunch beneath the heavy feet of something unseen. The cackle identifies it as a demon. And it's getting closer.

"Hi." Bree crouches and reaches a hand out, like she's speaking to a dog.

Maybe it's Sanchez?

I feel hopeful for a moment.

And then it steps out of the dark forest.

The beast is concealed by its personal atmosphere, but the churning, gray eddies are subdued, swirling in a gentle breeze. The demon is calm... Among friends.

It stops at the side of the road, watching us, perhaps judging our intent. I feel its gaze land on me, scrutinizing. Its attention rakes through my insides, violating my brain, and something clicks. A wellspring of rage rises within me, long buried but still potent. It nearly overwhelms me. Focusing on my family helps me maintain control.

The demon chortles at me, sensing my resistance, but like a Borg, knowing it's futile.

"Get out of my head," I growl, tightening my grip on the M4.

"Hi," Bree says again, standing just inches from the demon, and she's managed to sneak up on it. The monster flinches to the side at the sound of her voice, the gentle breeze surrounding it whipping into a frenzy, tendrils flailing and vibrating in agitation.

Bree isn't intimidated. "Be nice to my friend." She glares at the thing. For one heartbreaking moment, the girl's pupils expand, her eyes going solid black. "Or I won't be nice to you."

I'm disconnected from the demon, its presence reduced to its physical form. Did Bree just tell it what to do? And did it obey?

In the distance, a gun pops.

The demon churns, its attention shifting to the sound of combat. With a high-pitched yip, it lunges back into the forest and charges toward the sound. I'm caught off guard when several more hidden demons call out from the darkness and pound through the woods.

How many were here?

They must have been drawn by the sound of gunfire earlier, seeking out the sound's source. Perhaps searching for their missing comrade, though I can't imagine parasite demons caring about each other. They had been closing in on Neiman's house. Whoever is out there, fighting for their life, might have just saved the others. I look back to Neiman's house. It looks abandoned and empty.

"They don't like you very much," Bree says.

"I don't like them either," I say.

"You should probably try to," she says.

"Like them?"

"And be like them," she says. "It's nice. It's easier."

"You'll change your mind when you've got a parasite in your back and fillets of skin are peeling off your body."

Bree crosses her arms. "I don't know what a fillet is."

"Chunks of skin, peeling off your body, over and over again, forever."

"You're not being nice." Bree stomps her foot.

"Since when do I need to be—"

Emma grabs hold of my arm, hard enough to hurt. "Miah."

I blink out of my rage, only now realizing that I'd been shouting—really shouting—into a seven-year old's face. Not that Bree was fazed by my sudden shift into anger. But it's a sign that I might be a little more far gone than I'd like to think.

"Thanks," I say to Emma.

"We can't do this without you," she says. "And I don't think we have much time." She motions to Bree, who is back to skipping. "Me and her. I can feel it, you know. Creeping up on me. It's like a craving for ice cream ...but evil."

I nod and say, "Let's go." I head for the woods and turn to Bree. "Both of you."

Bree rolls her eyes, but she falls in line.

A moment later, we're enshrouded in shadow, in the darkness of night, and I can see. It's different than daylight. The colors are muted. Like an old Polaroid photo. We push through a stand of ferns and slowly traverse the rough terrain, covered in fallen trees, tangles of low hanging branches, and granite rocks that pepper the entire state.

Ten minutes pass without Bree or Emma saying a single word. Feels strange. That either of them has nothing to say, given the circumstances, is hard to imagine. Then again, I'm not speaking either. My grandmother once described me as having the 'gift of gab,' which is a polite way of saying, 'This kid never shuts up.'

She wasn't wrong. I talk a lot, even when I'm alone.

I just don't have any words now.

Mostly, I have a confusing mash of feelings, some of them mine, some of them invaders from the past, or maybe from hell.

And then I feel something new.

A presence.

Some kind of weird instinct tells me it's not a demon or a devil. It's a person. Like us. Branded and changing.

"You guys feel that?" I ask, looking back.

Both girls nod, searching the forest around us.

"Hello?" I call out. "Show yourself!

"Show yourself?" Emma says. "Are you like an old-fashion-y knight or something?"

"Shush," I grumble. "He's getting closer."

"Feels like he's right here with us," Emma says. "But I don't see him. Maybe he's invisible?"

I shake my head. We've seen the denizens of the underworld do some pretty messed up things, but invisibility isn't one of them. Though I suppose we wouldn't be able to see them in that case.

"He is with us, silly." Bree points to the starry sky. "Up there."

A shadow plummets toward us. Emma and I leap back and raise our weapons. I hold my fire, caught off guard, but sensing no real danger.

Because he's one of us.

In fact, he's *more* than one of us.

The man stands from a crouch, but he remains hunched, his body being pulled to a four-legged posture. He's naked, but somehow not indecent, probably because his skin has begun to char—and nightmare of all nightmares, it appears his genitals have fallen away. His skin has begun to crack, revealing red wounds, but he doesn't seem to mind it.

Yet.

There's a kind of euphoria that comes with the change. When he's infected by a parasite and sucking on a fart cloud for the rest of his life, I think his positive outlook will shift. Giggles the suicidal demon-man-thing certainly didn't have a jolly view of his life.

The man bares his teeth and hisses at us. Then his savage expression falls flat. "Damn." His voice is raspy and deep. "I didn't know you were a changeling."

"A...changeling?" Emma says.

The man shrugs. "I think it fits."

"Because...we're changing," Emma says, clearly displeased with the title.

The man nods. "Right."

"I like it," Bree announces.

"You have a name?" I ask.

"I used to be Michael Crawford," he says, like we should know who he is. "I'm a Minecraft streamer. Screen name is Silver."

"Sorry, dude," I say. "I don't watch YouTube."

"Twitch, more likely," Emma says. "But...sorry, I don't know you either."

"Doesn't matter," he says. "That's not who I am anymore."

"Who...are you now?" I ask.

"I'm not sure yet," he says. "I'm not done changing, you know? I think my new name will come to me when the time is right."

"I don't think you'll have a name at all," Emma says.

Michael's brow furrows, cracking the skin around the death rune on his forehead. "Why not?"

"Because the people not like us—"

"Maelstroms," he says. "The bad asses that walk in living storms." He's enamored with the idea.

"—because Maelstroms are slaves to parasitical demons, in constant pain, longing for death."

Michael sneers at the idea. "That's not right."

"It's the truth." Bree is the last person I expected to speak out against the change. She seems to have embraced it, but she also understands the truth. "Giggles told us."

"Giggles?"

"A Maelstrom," I say.

"He wanted to die," Emma adds.

"You *spoke* to one of them?" His flicker of concern is replaced by awe. "How cool was that?"

"Not cool," I say, and I don't bother explaining that we didn't actually have a conversation. It was more of a feeling, of knowing without being told. "He's dead now, and happy about it. That's what being a Maelstrom means."

"Pfft." He waves our concern away. "You'll see. Just give it time. Everything about it feels good. Wait until you bring someone to the gate for the first time. That's—"

"Gate?" I ask.

"Yeah," he says. "To where they're from."

I hold up an index finger. "There's a gate...out here in the woods...to *hell?*"

Michael smiles, his wide eyes pitch black. "Yeah." His smile widens into a sinister Cheshire Cat grin. "Want to see it?"

41

I said, "Yes," and I have been regretting it since.

Who willingly walks to hell?

The damned, that's who. Michael's 'changeling' name has a ring to it. Kind of cutesy. But it doesn't convey the gravity of who and what we are. The Damned. Capital D.

Thing is, we were already headed to the gate. At first, I thought logic was guiding me, following the path of all those demons heading into the woods past Larry's house. But I can sense it guiding me, drawing me deeper into the forest. Feels like when I came home from my last deployment. Like I'm headed home.

"This is exciting, right?" Emma's trepidation has steadily dissolved.

"Totes," I say, oozing sarcasm. "How much farther?"

"Half mile." Michael has devolved in the past few minutes, no longer walking upright. He's all hands and feet now, but it's awkward—like that girl online who trots around like a horse. He bounds forward, galloping fifty feet and then squatting while we catch up. "You already knew that, though. You can feel it."

Shut-up, I think, and I nonchalantly shrug like, 'You caught me.'

"You know, you don't need those anymore." He motions to my M4. "Whatever that can do, you can do with your hands."

"Force of habit." I pat the M4.

Emma holds her rifle closer. "This belonged to my Dad. I'm going to keep it."

"Pfff. Your dad? I bet he's gone, right? Off to the grinder. Not like us." Michael leaps ahead, this time landing sideways on a tree. His fingers and toes wrap around the pine's rugged bark.

The grinder... That doesn't sound good.

"I think mine is pretty." Bree gives her little pistol a kiss.

"Won't be long until you're thinking differently." Bark peels away from the tree, dropping Michael to the ground. He doesn't flinch or complain. He just gets up again, free of any embarrassment, and leaps onto another tree, practicing his craft. "I was like you, not too long ago."

"How...long ago?" I ask.

"About an hour. Maybe two. Hard to say. Time's a little funny right now. But I was like, 'Oh Hun, don't worry, nothing will separate us. Just stay quiet and they won't find us.'" He pauses for effect, grinning. "Well, they did find us. But *they* wasn't *them*, they was *me*. Does that make sense?"

"You changed," Emma says. "And betrayed someone you love."

"Yes!" Michael says. "You should have seen her face when I dragged her outside. She screamed so loud. Sooo long. Even worse when she saw the gate. Stopped on the other side, but that might be because it's hard to breathe there. For them. Not for us."

"How did you do it?" Bree asks, and I cringe inwardly. If I have an hour, maybe two, before I transform into the Devil's limbed turd, how long does she have? Thirty minutes? Less?

Before I can request a faster pace, Michael answers. "At first it was hard. I felt a little bad about it, too. A *little* bad. I held her around the waist, and she was kicking and screaming. Clawed at my face a lot. That...hurt. Not anymore, though. Right now, nothing hurts. Then I threw her to the ground and dragged her by an ankle. She squirmed a lot. I think I broke her ankle. And there was blood behind her after we crossed the road."

Michael drifts, lost in the memory, his face falling flat.

Is that remorse?

Is there a trace of humanity in him?

"Who was she?" Bree asks.

Michaels stares into space for a moment, and then blinks out of it. "My wife." He leaps away, clinging to one tree and then jumping to another, running from his past.

"Dark," Emma says to me. "You're going to do it, right? Not let me get like that?"

I nod without hesitation. "Even if you change your mind."

"Good," she says, and she follows after Bree, who's skipping up to Michael. He's stopped again, body rigid, focused on a singular direction, like a hunting dog. He's even got one hand lifted up. If he had a tail—thank God he doesn't—I'm sure it would be extended straight out.

"You guys smell that?" Michael asks.

I'm about to say I don't, but that's a lie.

A scent floats in the air. Something fruity. *Deodorant,* I think.

"Someone is out here," Bree says. "One of them."

Michael nods. "They must be scared shitless. They're headed straight toward the gate." He turns to Bree. "You wanna help get them through?"

Her eyes light up. She bites her bottom lip and gives a gleeful nod.

"Hold on." I have no idea what to say next. While I share their desire to chase down our newfound prey, I still know it's wrong. What I don't know is if I can say that. Is there a point where Michael will lose his patience and turn on me? Or turn me in, to the devil squad? Is it even possible to resist, or is it just a matter of time?

The latter, I decide.

Damnation is inevitable. For me. And Emma. And Bree. I just need to make sure death claims us first.

"What?" Michael says.

I hold my hand out to Bree. "You shouldn't run with a loaded gun."

"That's a good point," Michael says. Apparently, concern for each other is still acceptable.

Bree scrunches her nose and squishes out her lips. It'd be kind of adorable if her eyes hadn't turned solid black. "Fine." She hands the gun to me. "Can we go now?"

"Have at it."

I don't know what I was expecting to happen, but it wasn't Michael letting out a cackling laugh and bounding away, or Bree racing after him, at first like a regular ol' human being, and then on all fours.

I tuck the pink pistol into my back pocket, safety on, so as not to shoot a hole in my ass.

"Be honest," I say to Emma. "What do my eyes look like?"

"Like you," she says. "Still human. What about mine?"

I look into her jet-black eyes and say, "The same."

Then I head after the others before she can see the guilt in my expression. At first, keeping up with Michael and Bree is a challenge. Despite not being built for running on all fours, they're fast, and they're able to avoid all of the low hanging branches whipping my face.

What I'd like to call a second wind suddenly fuels me. Pain and exhaustion fade. My muscles are energized. My mind is focused. I can see the smell in the air, follow our prey's path through the forest. Without trying, I'm hauling ass like an Olympic sprinter, ducking and weaving obstacles, and leaping from rocks, somehow being transformed into both a predator and a kid again.

Reveling in dragging someone to hell isn't the same as reveling in nature as a young man, though. When I start leaning toward the ground, the shift in equilibrium snaps me out of the hunt long enough to realize that I was about to run on all fours. I think the only thing that stopped me was the rifle in my hands.

Emma lied to me, too.

Ahead, a young man screams, his voice cracking.

Michael scoops the boy up, black arm around his waist. Knocks the air, and a scream, out of him. Then Michael slams him against a sapling, steps around it, and pulls both of the boy's arms back. Without missing a beat, Bree leaps at the poor kid, turning her body into a cannonball. She collides with his stomach, knocking the last of his air from his lungs.

The kid's legs go wobbly. He falls to his knees, tears streaming down his face. Can't be more than fourteen. Might even go to school with Emma. He's dressed like every other boy in New Hampshire—cargo shorts and a T-shirt sporting cartoon characters—in this case Rick and Morty. His mop of hair clings to his sweaty forehead. The rest of him is caked with mud. He's been out here for a while, hiding from the denizens of hell...and finally caught, by us.

Bree gets back to her feet, snarling. She raises a hand and strikes the kid's face.

My heart breaks for both of them. This is...this is messed up.

Righteous anger pushes back my looming darkness. When Bree raises her hand again, this time in a fist, I take hold of her wrist.

She tugs against me. "Let me go!" Her voice is raspy now. The skin around her black eyes is darkening. Won't be long until her humanity has been erased.

With a roar, Bree swipes her hand at my midsection, raking her hooked fingers across my combat vest. Newfound instinct guides me. With a quick yank, I toss Bree away. She rolls to her feet and coils to pounce... but she doesn't. Savage or not, she doesn't stand a chance against me.

"Miah," Emma scolds.

"I know," I say, just as disturbed by every aspect of what's happening.

"What are you doing?" Michael asks. "How are we supposed to get him to the gate if he's wailing and kicking and shit?"

"We'll ask him," I say.

Michael's face screws up. "*Why?*"

"If you had an apple fresh from the tree, or one that was dropped and bruised, which one would you eat?" His expression tells me he'd never eat an apple now. "Try to remember. From your life before."

He nods slowly. "I get it, but...I'm not sure it will matter."

I'm about to ask why, but then I remember 'the grinder,' and I decide I'd rather not know. "Matters to me," I say, and I crouch down in front of the kid. "Sorry about the eyes," I say. "Wasn't always this handsome."

My joke gets nowhere. How could it?

"What's your name?" I ask.

"D-David Burchell..."

"Well, Dave... Didn't really need your full name, but whatever. I'll be honest. This is going to suck, but if you'll trust me, I'll have your back, okay?" I give him a wink. "Promise."

He stares at me through his tears, judging me, and for some reason I'll never understand, he decides to trust me. His subtle nod means a lot. I just hope I can follow through on this promise, and all the others I've made.

42

Dave is either very trusting or very stupid. He's the perfect hostage. Goes where I tell him. Doesn't speak unless he's asked a question. I wonder if he thinks good behavior will change his fate. If anything, it will solidify it. Demons probably think ground-up goodness, broken down and masticated, tastes good. A dash of mercy here. A sprinkle of granulated humility there. Nom, nom, nom.

Up ahead, Michael proclaims, "Almost there! Just over the hill."

The ground ahead rises up. It's steep, but not very high. An ominous red glow cuts through the trees at the hill's crest.

Dave's pace falters.

He stumbles to a stop. Looks back at me. "I don't want to go out like a punk."

"What?" I ask. "A punk? How does a punk go out?"

"I don't know. Like stupid, I guess. Embarrassing."

"I feel like that'd be going out like a little bitch," Emma says.

"I guess," Dave says. "B-both, then. I just. I don't want it to hurt."

"We're not there yet," I tell him. "Don't give up hope, okay."

"I'm trying," he says, and his earnestness is like a Satanic ritual blade in my still beating heart. "But...I couldn't really see your face before. Because it's so dark. But now..." He looks up at me, cast in red light, trying to hide his revulsion. I'm still changing.

Please don't let my nuts fall off...

"If it makes you feel better," he says, and he motions to Emma, "she's a little scarier. And neither of you are like them." He looks ahead to Michael and Bree, whose skin is withering and turning black. How long until her hair falls out? How long until she sheds her clothing and fully embraces her new, savage self? They scrabble up the hill. Michael leaps from tree to rock, and back again. Bree follows him as best she can, a baby chimp imitating its mother, learning fast.

"Whatever happens," I say, "don't worry about dying like a punk. All things considered, you're probably the bravest person in these woods."

He shakes his head, face twisted in disgust and shame. "I shit my pants."

"Oh...okay. That's...uh..."

"You can't smell it?" he asks.

At first, no, but then I do, and I quickly realize why my mind never gave it much thought.

It smells...good.

Which in turn, is revolting.

"Just, don't sweat it, okay? With all that's going on, no one is going to notice, and no one from here on out is going to care. Just stay by my side and on your feet. Once we crest this hill, you belong to me, get it?"

"Kind of ominous," Emma says.

"I don't want to belong to anyone," Dave adds.

I shrug. "We don't know how this works, or even if I can claim you as my...property. If I can't, we'll probably be separated and there won't be anything I can do for you."

"What if I *am* taken?"

"Choice is yours," I tell him. "You can play nice, like you have been, and maybe you'll get by long enough for me to figure out something. Or... maybe something else. Speculation only makes people worry about what scares them."

"Right now, that's everything," Dave admits.

Wish I could say I was right there with him. I am in spirit, but I've never felt so self-assured. My emotional scars have been smoothed over. Probably means Dave should make a break for it now, but like a ball rolling past a cat, the Damned among him would pounce. Myself included.

"So, let's stop thinking about it," I say with a smile that makes him wince. "And maybe stop looking at our faces."

He looks away and nods.

"We should go before Bree and Michael lose their patience and drag him up." Emma motions to the pair, now at the top of the hill, crouched in branches, looking back down at us like a couple of hungry barn owls.

I motion for Dave to go first, because Emma is holding onto my wrist. He starts up the hill without us, struggling to stay upright, unable to see the obstacles. Bree and Michael have a laugh at his expense, sounding more and more like hyenas.

"Yeah?" I ask.

"I'm not sure how much longer I'll be me," she says.

"Same," I admit.

She shakes her head. "Seriously. The only reason I'm still me at all is because of you. You're...inspiring. And if you tell Jen that I said that I'll deny it."

"Just keep thinking about your family," I say. "About Jen waiting for us, and your parents, somewhere on the other side of this hill. We are their only hope. You and me. Okay?"

She sighs. "We better pick up the pace then."

"Double time," I say, and then we head up the hill. As I pass Dave, I take hold of his belt and lift him off the ground. "Running out of time, buddy. Sorry about the wedgie."

He doesn't complain. Being hauled up the hill like a suitcase is probably easier than scrabbling in the dark, scraping bloodied fingers over bark and rocks.

Bree and Michael climb down from the trees as we approach.

"Ready to have your mind blown?" Michael says.

"Sure," I say.

"Can we not?" Dave says, doing his best to keep a stiff upper lip.

Bree eradicates it with, "I wonder if pieces of you will get in my hair, too."

I make a 'What can you do?' face at Dave and then crest the hill with the others, staggering to a stop. Ahead, the trees are all knocked down and charred, creating a thousand-foot-wide clearing that looks a lot like an impact crater. The clearing ends at a peninsula, around which wraps the Bellamy River, a wide swath of water fueled mostly by Great Bay's tidal surges, rather than water flowing downstream.

Emma points at the peninsula. "That's Clements Point. Used to be."

"How do you know that?" Michael asks.

"I hunted these woods, with my father." She looks at me. "Still do."

"Look, there's somebody down there," Bree says, pointing to the maze of tree husks.

A lone demon bounds through the rubble, dragging along an unconscious man, letting him slap and thump against every obstacle.

"You see," Michael says. "Bruises don't matter."

"Matter to me," I say, looking him dead in the eyes. We're both changing, but I don't yet see these things as family, and I sure as shit won't have a problem putting a bullet in Michael. He's too far gone for redemption. Death would be a favor.

Before we can argue more, Bree gasps, drawing my eyes back out to the view.

As the demon nears the peninsula's end, a shimmering red light stretches to life between what I thought were two limbless, burned trees. I see them now for what they are—two pillars. They're rough, black, and covered from top to bottom in strange symbology reminiscent of Viking runes...or actual Viking runes. I'd never know the difference.

The pillars stand fifty feet tall and thirty feet apart. The space between them shimmers with energy, a crackling wall of red light. A network of octagonal light cuts through it all, giving it a futuristic look.

I'm not looking at some kind of arcane spell, or Diablo-esque portal to the underworld. This is technology. Modern and sophisticated. Like something out of Star Trek, invented by Klingons.

Hold on...

I turn my eyes to the sky, replaying the events of the past few days. The stars are still shining, but it's daytime again. I can tell because a large portion of the sky is blotted out. Is this day two? Or day three? Time feels funny without a sun. *Doesn't matter,* I decide, looking at where the missing sun should be with new eyes.

So far, every aspect of what makes hell's armies supernatural has turned out to be technological, like the personal atmosphere, or explainable, like parasites making humans their hosts. Maybe the sun is being blotted out through technology instead of demonic magic? And this thing down below...if it is a portal, it might not be to hell after all.

"Holy shit," I say, getting everyone's attention. "I don't think they're demons."

"Demons?" Michael said. "What made you think that?"

"Three Days of Darkness," I reply.

His face screws up and cracks, seeping blood. "Don't believe everything you read. I've seen what's on the other side of the gate, and it's not hell."

"Then what is it?" Emma asks.

I answer before Michael can, all the pieces falling into place. "Another planet."

43

"Another what?" Bree says.

"Planet, dingus." Emma shakes her head and rolls her eyes.

"She's seven," I say, in defense of the tiny human-hunter.

"Even seven-year-olds know about planets." Emma turns to Dave. "Right?"

David directs his gaze away from her. "Don't look at me."

"You're here, aren't you?" Emma crosses her arms, unleashing some of that teenage angst that used to be reserved for the likes of me. "Why not have an opinion?"

"I think," I say, "he means literally don't look at him. Because, you know." I wave my hand in front of my face, which if it looks anything like hers, ain't pretty.

"Oh..." Emma's head hangs low.

David mumbles something.

Sounds like sarcasm.

"What?" Emma says, lifting him by his shirt so he has no choice but to look her in her demonic eyes. "What did you say?"

"I-I said...t-that's not true."

Emma lowers Dave back to his feet. "How am I anything other than hideous right now? I know what I look like. What I feel like inside."

"Because I know who you are, Emma," he says.

"You know who I am?"

"We've been in the same grade for like, all of our lives. I mostly sit behind you. In the back. By myself. You...you still have really nice hair." Dave smiles at her.

I hold my hands over my heart and force a swooning smile. "Morrison was right. Love *does* hide in the strangest places."

"Ugh," Emma says, stepping around Dave and stomping down the hill, into the clearing of flattened trees. She's feigning annoyance, but I suspect ol' Dave here just buoyed her hope a little.

Michael and Bree start down the hill after her, fixated on the interplanetary gate.

"This is your chance," I say to Dave.

"W-what?"

"We're all too distracted by the gate to notice you scurrying off," I say.

"But...you're talking to me right now."

I pinch the bridge of my nose. "Seriously... You know the old farmhouse back there?"

"Where the old guy lives? Who shoots a lot of guns?"

"That's the one. If you can make it there, it might be a safe place to hide. But you need to enter through the bulkhead. Do *not* use any other door."

"Why?"

"Because they'll explode." I pluck a grenade from my pocket. "Booby traps." I hand the grenade to him. Then I take the pink pistol from my back pocket and place it in his trembling hand. "Just in case. You know how to shoot a gun?"

"I have Pistol Whip for VR," he says. "And Super Hot."

"Is that like a porn game?"

"What? No. It's shooting. Like with guns. I have a lot of them."

"Okay, just..." I reach down and switch the pistol's safety off. "Point and shoot. But you only have ten rounds. Use them as a distraction, and let that do the rest." I motion to the grenade. "You good?"

"Not at all," he says, looking at the weapons like he wants to drop them on the ground.

"Now," I say, "entering that house is going to probably be worse than walking through the demon gate. It's full of junk and shit... It's just nasty. Like, really nasty. But there's a safe room on the second floor. A bedroom. Just...announce yourself first. The people hiding there will shoot you if you don't, okay? Tell them Miah sent you."

"That's your name? Miah?"

I nod, keeping an eye on Bree and Michael. Neither of them has turned around. They're on target, pulled toward the gate. I feel it, too, like we're in the parking lot at Disney World. "Last thing, Dave. The people in that bedroom mean everything to me, so if you use that—" I motion to the pistol. "—on them... I'll give in to this darkness, and hunt you to the ends of the Earth." I smile at him. "'K?"

He nods. "Thanks."

"Just go," I say, "before I pounce on you myself." Letting him go is a lot harder than I'm making it look. Now that I've seen the gate, I'm craving it, and it wants me to bring Dave. Wants me to bring as many people as I can. "Go now."

When Dave hustles back into the dark woods, I nearly tackle him. My muscles tense. My mouth salivates. I want to take him down. Bite the back of his neck. Thrash him around.

Let him go, I tell myself. *Let. Him. Go.*

When he slides out of view, the feeling fades and I'm drawn back toward the gate. I hurry down the hill, gaining on Michael and Bree, hoping they don't hear me and turn around. If they realize Dave is missing now, they'll hunt him.

I slow when I can hear them talking. Bree is peppering Michael with questions about what's on the other side of the gate. His answers are mostly made-up guesses. He's seen a lot of things he doesn't understand, and his seven-year-old audience doesn't yet have a bullshit detector.

Emma pauses, squatting atop a fallen tree, bearing her weight on her hands and feet like it's natural. Her eyes are on the gate, but she's waiting on me. After Michael and Bree pass her, she glances my way and then up the hill from whence we came.

"You let him go?"

"Don't go after him."

"I'm glad," she says. "He was nice. And I swear to God if you make a deal out of that—"

I raise my hands. "Not a word. He's a good kid. I hope he makes it."

"Where'd he go?" she asks.

"Probably better if I don't tell you, you know, in case..." I bare my teeth and growl.

"Right." She turns back to the gate. Its red surface, divided by orange polygons, is nearly translucent. There are hints of things on the other side, but they're still hidden from view. "So...aliens."

"Yeah."

"You sure?"

I shrug. "Makes more sense than demons from hell."

"Yeah," she says, imitating me.

"I don't know if that increases or decreases our odds of success. I mean, there's a chance we'll be able to figure out some technological solution. You are a Gen-Z after all. Most of your time is spent interfacing with tech. And we know they're not invincible. At the same time, this being hell on Earth gave me a little hope of some divine intervention, you know?"

"Aliens are cooler, though," she says.

"Absolutely," I say. Bree and Michael near the gate. "We should catch up. I don't want to lose sight of her."

"Should we kill him?" she asks.

"Michael?"

She nods. "Before we go through."

It's not the worst idea. Michael's life will soon be one of perpetual torture. Killing him would be a mercy, and being able to move freely on the far side could be beneficial. But we don't want to tip our hand. "Not yet."

We leap over the maze of fallen trees, catching up to the pair as they approach the gate.

"Wait for us," Emma calls out, and they do.

We stand there, the four of us, looking up at the towering gate like Dorothy and crew seeing the Emerald City for the first time. The sheet of red hums with energy. All along the bottom, twisting wisps of yellow fog roll past our feet—the alien atmosphere seeping through. This is what's making everything smell like sulfur. This and others. While I haven't seen any other gates, I know they're out there.

"Well," I say. "We're off to see the Wizard."

"Lame," Bree says, and she takes a step toward the gate. But she stops short when the sheet of energy crackles, shedding sparks of orange as something massive moves through from the other side.

We scatter, leaping back, giving the newcomer room. The ground trembles beneath its heavy black feet, causing plumes of dust with each step.

I look up at the powerful red body and have no trouble recognizing the beast.

The Devil.

Satan himself.

Missing horn and all.

44

"The Devil is…a robot?" I ask no one in particular. Confusion roots me in place, and I'm nearly squashed for it. One of four heavy limbs avoids me by a few inches, moving past, crushing a tree to dust beneath what looks like a bona fide cloven hoof. But it's actually a broad, black metallic foot. The great machine stands thirty feet tall, rising to a crown of ten horns—one of them broken by me. Its body is built like a tank, great sheets of layered red metal forming an armadillo-like carapace. Two arms extend from the sides, hydraulic and powerful, tipped with black hands. Hanging from its underside is a cage—empty, but soon to be filled with victims.

"I am so screwed," I say, looking up at the broken horn.

The devil robot stops in place like it heard me, its insides whirring and grinding.

"Whoa!" Bree says, enamored.

"Cool, right?" Michael says. "And this is nothing."

"There's more?" Bree asks.

Michael gives her a slow, over dramatic nod and a smile that splits his cheeks open and has the vibe of a pedo ice cream man on the lookout for gullible kids. "More and bigger. A vast army."

His words take my lingering confidence behind a metaphorical shed and put a bullet in its head. What can we do against a vast army, aside from join them, when our transformations are complete? One adult, one teenage girl, and a diminutive sociopath who might already be a lost cause.

Inside the monstrosity, something churns to life. It sounds like… breathing. Deep and heavy, becoming rapid. Fervent. Vents along its back snap open. Yellow-gray atmosphere coughs out, forming long tendrils that begin to wrap around the great beast. Caught in a wind, the source of which I can't fathom, the mist begins swirling around the machine, cloaking its true form.

Before it's fully concealed, a hatch opens. A humanoid figure, dressed in armor that matches the robot's—layers of shiny red—rises from inside, seated on what looks like a throne. The creature's face is concealed by a mask and a helmet with glowing yellow eyes, reminiscent of Iron Man, but with a ring of horns around its head—as though mocking the Catholic depiction of a crucified Christ. The devil controlling the devil.

I now have little doubt that these assholes have visited Earth before, and that those visits have inspired tales of hell, and demons, the devil, and prophecies of visits to come. How long have they been pilfering our planet? From the beginning, I suspect.

The devil robot's pilot is humanoid, meaning two arms, two legs, a head, and hands in normal proportions, though I suspect he'd stand closer to eight feet tall. Is this another corrupted human being controlled by a parasite, or is this one of *them*—whoever or whatever they are?

I'm not about to ask, so I just watch as the storm kicks into full gear, concealing the devil, protecting it from attack and enabling the Controller to breathe.

The ground shakes as it moves on, sliding up the hillside, looking once again, like the actual Devil.

The Controller either didn't recognize me, or he's not the same dude. The robo-devil is just a mech. One of many. The pilots might rotate. Then again, I'm not the same person who shot the horn off the beast, and he probably knows that. If he doesn't sense it, he can look at me and see something no longer totally human.

So maybe he didn't recognize me. I don't know. Whatever.

I let out a long breath, and I realize I was holding it. When I breathe in again, the air doesn't satiate me like it used to. Won't be long before I need a personal atmosphere of my own—at least on this planet.

I turn to the gate. Its luminous red energy calls to me, beckoning me home.

"Definitely aliens," Emma says, watching the devil shove a tree aside and enter the forest, heading back toward our neighborhood—and our sisters.

Run, Dave, run, I think, and I say to Emma, "Let's get this done."

She gives a nod, and we walk toward the gate, M4s in hand, grenades in pockets, ready to throw down with alien invaders.

I'm a little surprised and moved when Emma takes hold of my hand. Her grip is tight enough for me to feel her rapid pulse. Or is that mine?

When Bree and Michael stand beside us, I ask, "So how do we do this?"

"You just...walk right through," Michael says, and he strides forward. The sheet of energy crackles around him, envelops him in light, and then ...he's gone.

"Just like a town portal," I tell myself. "I just need to Timmy the Great the shit out of this."

"Timmy the who?" Bree asks.

"The Great," I say. "It's from a game. Diablo. I would lure people through a portal like this, pretending to be a helpless noob running for my life in the catacombs beneath the church in Tristram."

Bree looks at me like I'm still high, but unlike the first time I recently conjured the name of Timmy the Great, I'm stone cold sober now.

"Anywho, people would walk through my portal thinking they were coming to rescue a kid, but they'd end up in the depths of hell, surrounded by a horde of succubi. They'd die, I'd take their armor, wait for them to come back for it, kill them again, and collect their ears."

Bree smiles like it's the best children's story she's ever heard. I cringe when she doesn't notice the skin on her face cracking open.

"Great story," Emma says.

I shrug. "It was a thing. Fun at the time. This..." I look up at the towering portal. "...is different."

"Is it?" Emma says. "Because I think Timmy just went through and is waiting for us on the other side."

I frown...but I don't see any other options. Staying here means giving in. Means changing into a demon without a fight. Means succumbing, and that's just as deadly as succubi. At least succubi are sexy.

"Ugh," Bree says. "You two talk sooo much. Byeeee."

She steps forward before I can stop her, and she slides through the wall of energy. I can see her shadow on the other side, but it fades as she walks away. And I'm grateful both she and Michael seem to have forgotten about Dave entirely.

"Find our families," Emma says. "Set them free. Bring them back. Right?"

"And if there's a way to undo this—" I wave my hand in front of my face. "—we make it happen. Otherwise..."

"Bullet to the head," Emma says. "Like Rage Against the Machine."

I smile at her. "Why haven't we been friends before now?"

"Sometimes it takes a demonic alien invasion to bring people together."

I sigh. "We should probably stop killing time."

"Not much of it left."

"On three," I say. "One...two...*three*."

I've never been good at jumping into pools. I could count to three a dozen times and still not work up the courage. That timidity changed while I was in the Army and came roaring back with a vengeance after I got out. Now...

We step into the wall of energy together. My mouth fills with the zing and flavor of a 9-volt battery pressed against my tongue. For a moment, my vision is a wall of red, seen through my closed eyes. My skin tickles. My muscles relax. Nothing about being shunted to another place in the universe is unpleasant. It's like walking through a door made of bliss.

I stumble out of the gate, dazed by how good it felt. It's like an Olympic team of tall, blonde Swedish masseuses have worked me over in record time. I lean forward, hands on knees, eyes on what looks like volcanic rock. A laugh escapes, and then I breathe in deep.

In my mind, I know I'm smelling—even tasting—raw sulfur, but it is exquisite. My lungs absorb the stench, leaving me feeling strong and bold. Everything about this place feels heavenly. Transformative.

But it's a ruse, says a voice from deep inside my conscious mind.

"Wow," Emma says, chuckling. "This is—"

"A lie," I say, looking over at her. "Don't forget that."

"Whatever," she says. Her eyes aren't on me. She's looking into the distance, seeing what I have yet to.

I lift my head and stand up straight, seeing an alien landscape for the first time. "Huh..."

"Hell, right?" she says.

"Uhh, yeah. Kinda. If you ignore the sky." I turn my head upward. Unfamiliar stars litter the sky, but the object commanding the view is a planet—crystalline blue and green. Looks like a nicer place to live than Earth. The planet is either very close or very large because it fills up a quarter of the sky. I stare at it until I feel like I'm falling toward it. Then my gaze drops to the planet upon which I'm standing.

The background looks like something out of Middle Earth. Mount Doom spewing lava, filling the horizon sky with gloomy soot, and setting the barren mountains surrounding it ablaze in orange light. The foreground is...I don't know. A city? An alien forward operating base?

The terrain is unforgiving and jagged, carved up by glowing rivers of magma, over which bridges have been built. The base, like the land around us, is black—what I can see of it, anyway. The walls are imposing, standing thirty feet tall, peppered with lookout towers and massive turrets, sporting cannons the likes of which I've only seen on battleships.

Everything has a vibe of future technology, but it's dark and brutal, decorated with spikes. Glowing orange runes line the pillars connecting each segment of wall, lit from the inside by flowing lava.

If hell was ever imagined as a technological place, rather than primitive, this...this would be it.

Someone escaped, I realize. Maybe more than one someone. They got out of this place and back to Earth. Not fully understanding what they'd seen, they told the stories that became our modern vision of hell. Fire and brimstone. The lake of fire. Demons and Devils. All of it is right here...but instead of an underworld lurking beneath our feet, it's another world, somewhere far out in the cosmos, plundering Earth not for its mineral or liquid resources, but for its people.

For its meat.

I try not to dwell on the realization, and I keep my attention on soaking in this new world.

The massive base is surrounded by another wall, this one composed of gates. Hundreds of them. Maybe thousands, each one of them leading to a location on Earth...or maybe other planets, like the one above us. To my left and right, the gates stretch out into the distance, wrapping around the base. Through them, the vile denizens of this world come and go. Those on their way out are empty-handed. Those returning are flush with captives, their screams filling the air like...a pleasant song.

45

"Exquisite," I say, closing my eyes and listening to the sounds of horror.

"What?" Emma asks, pulling me away from my corrupted reverie.

"Their screaming," I say.

Emma nods. "Like music."

I'm not the only one feeling it.

Our senses and morality are being auto-tuned by the transformation. Taking something that I *know* is abhorrent, changing it into something by which I feel pleasantly moved.

Like art.

Or movies. But mostly music.

The demons on this world are...happy. Reveling in a newfound carnal bliss. What once was disgusting now triggers dopamine floods, keeping the once human parasite hosts placated. But when they go back... When the effects of this place lose just a little of their grip—the torture commences, heaped upon with layers of guilt over what they've done.

That's why they're mewling as they skulk through the woods and around houses. It's not a ruse. It's genuine despair.

"We need to fight it," I say. "No matter how good or right all of this feels, it's not."

"I'll try," she says, fixated on a nearby devil, its belly cage filled with writhing, screaming victims. It holds my attention, too, until my gaze lands on Bree. She's perched atop Michael's shoulders, marveling at Hell, singing a song and being whisked away.

Despite the strange kinship felt between those of us with death runes, Michael is a stranger, and I have committed to caring for Bree. I can't let him just wander off with her. "C'mon." I give Emma's shoulder a slap and chase after Michael.

The ground is solid beneath our feet, but the path through the black, volcanic spires has been worn to dust. They've been doing this for a long time. Thousands of years, at least.

Ahead, Michael and Bree step to the path's edge, allowing me to catch up just in time to join them against a jagged stone wall, giving a devil just enough space to pass by. Its four heavy limbs shake the ground. My eyes drift down from its red body to the cage on its underside. This close, I can see dangling bits of flesh and clothing. The black beams glisten with fresh blood and are coated with layers of old blood.

Those captured by the...whatever they're called...begin their torture long before ever reaching Hell. I have no trouble imagining them, crammed together in that tight space, struggling to breathe, desperate to escape, pulling and clawing, screaming for help. The thought makes me smile—until my mother's face emerges in my mind's eye, hand reaching out, begging me to help.

I blink the disturbing image away and turn to Michael. "Do they have a name? The things in charge? The parasites?"

"Tenebris," he says. "But it basically means, the Dark."

The Dark...

Emma scrunches her now transformed face. "How do you know that?"

"You can talk to them," he says. "On this side, at least. Not the big ones."

"Devils," I say. "The little ones are demons."

"Huh," he says. "That actually works."

For a reason, dumbass, I think, but I keep it to myself.

"Demons, then. What we'll be soon. They all used to be like us. Most of them don't speak English, but some do. Not that they like talking, but some will."

The devil passes, and is followed by two rows of demons—eight in all. They were clearly once human, but their bone structure has adapted to walking on all fours. Their faces have been charred to the point of being featureless. Hair and genitals have fallen away from their uniformly emaciated bodies. Their nails are long, sharp, and black. They're expressionless, eyes on the devil leading them. The tendrils emerging from their lower backs lazily flap about, resembling something closer to black starfish limbs now. Each and every one of them wears the contraption that will generate an atmosphere for them on the other side.

"Hey," Emma says in greeting as they pass.

She's ignored, but she persists. "Hey. Hello. Hey."

The last in line sneers at her.

"Hi," she says with a wave.

"Fuck off," comes the deep, resonating reply. A ripple of irritation flows through the creature's stringy muscles. Then his black eyes snap to me, and the M4 in my hands. "Better hurry. You don't have much time."

The parasite on his back spasms. The demon winces and walks past, eyes forward.

Did he just see through my plan?

Maybe I'm not the first person to waltz into Hell, weapon in hand, in search of their loved one? Maybe all these evil bastards realize what I'm up to, but they know that it's futile. Know that in a few hours, or maybe minutes, I'll be one of them.

"Let's go," I say, and we follow the path toward the looming base. There are several gates surrounding the structure, all of them open, all of them active with devils and demons either coming or going, moving in and out unfettered. There appear to be guards in the towers, but not on the ground—probably because the place is a beehive, full of activity and monsters that have a sense of who each other are. An intruder would be easily detected.

Hoping I've changed enough to pass the Hades litmus test, I fall in line behind another devil, this one weighed down by captives. Faces and outstretched hands beg for help. A woman with a bloody face spots me. Sees me as different and cries out for help.

It breaks what's left of my heart to ignore her, but I manage it. There are thousands of people here. Hundreds of thousands. I can hear their choral voices rising up from inside the base, crying out in unison. I can't help all of them, and I can't help her.

So, I look away, turning my gaze up to the turrets mounted on the walls. They're bigger up close. I don't know what they fire, but they look powerful enough to cut down a skyscraper in a single shot.

"You thinking what I'm thinking?" Emma asks. She's looking up at the turrets, too. I wait for her to finish the thought. "People, or demons, or aliens, or whatever with big guns, tend to have big enemies. And those...are really big guns."

She's got a point, I think, but, "A good number of Americans have a lot of guns..." I pat my M4. "...and never have to use them."

"Case in point," she says, mocking me, "We're in Hell. Or is it *on* Hell?"

"The planet, Hell." I nod. "Sounds right."

We pass through the gates and into the sprawling base. It has two competing vibes. First—a military complex, complete with barracks, which are essentially caves leading into the ground. Demons lurk around them, sometimes entering or exiting—none of them wearing atmosphere generators.

Off duty, I think. There's a repair yard full of devils and other machines I haven't seen in action. They're being tended to by humanoid figures wearing metal suits similar to those of the devil pilots.

I wonder, for a moment, if the parasitical Dark might also have gates to other worlds, collecting, corrupting, and enslaving other species of life. A few days ago, that concept would be laughably impossible. Today, looking around a forward operating base on another planet, it seems... likely.

Beyond the military complex is what looks like an industrial plant. There's a large central structure, fifty feet tall, black, and domed. In place of windows are glowing orange holes, from which slip tendrils of smoke. A dozen smaller structures surround the central one, connected by large pipes, big enough for a rhinoceros to lumber through. They're also domed, and they're covered with large circular openings. But there is no orange light emerging, or smoke.

Only screams.

The devil we'd been following breaks left, heading for a receiving area, where other devils are unloading their catches, which are dumped onto the ground in a pile and shoved into holding pens like crabs caught at sea.

"Awesome," Michael says. "Right? I told you. It's just—" His shoulder spasms, knocking Bree off his back. She falls with a shout, but I catch her.

"Got you," I say, and I plant her on her feet.

She gives me a subtle smile, but that's it.

Michael pitches forward, landing on hands and knees. He grunts in pain, teeth gnashing. He plants his feet on the ground, spreads his legs wide and presses himself down into a deep squat. A scream tears from his mouth, both human and not. The sound doesn't get a second glance from any of the creatures around us. It just blends in with the audible backdrop of terror.

Two wet pops announce the dislocation of Michael's hips, or rather, the relocation of them. He sighs in relief. "So much better."

Michael walks on all fours, strutting his stuff for a moment, like a prince decked out in new finery.

Bree giggles. "You look like a pink-butt monkey."

"A what?" Michael asks.

Emma translates. "A baboon."

"Sans the actual pink badonkadonk."

Michael smiles. "Cool."

Not cool, I think. *Not cool at all.* His transformation is nearly complete. He looks and moves like the other demons. But he's thinking and talking like a human being still.

He's missing the parasite. That's the final step.

"Okay," Michael says, a little pep in his step now, despite his skin cracking and oozing with every movement. "Over here. You need to check this out."

He heads for the nearest of the smaller, factory domes.

As we approach the arched entryway, I ask, "What is this?"

"One of the grinders. Remember?" He pauses by the door, looking back to smile and double tap his eyebrows. "This is where they take people from our side."

46

"Hold on," I say, taking Bree's hand and crouching in front of her. She barely looks like a child anymore. The innocence is gone from her eyes, and not just because she's one of the damned. She's experienced enough messed up shit in the last day to ruin any human being on the planet.

The only reason any of us aren't catatonic with panic right now is because the part of our minds that processes things like compassion, empathy, and love is either catatonic, dying, or already dead.

But I promised to protect her, and that includes from whatever mind-numbing horrors await inside. "You don't need to go in."

"Why would I not?" she asks. "I want to see."

"C'mon, man," Michael says. "This is who we are now. Embrace it."

The edge in Michael's voice rubs me the wrong way. I nearly put a bullet in his head right then and there.

Inside, a chorus of screams rises, emitting palpable dread. Horror hangs in the air like a mist.

This is what it was like in Nazi-controlled Europe, I think, imagining we're in a World War II concentration camp. Anger churns inside me, but it's different than the darkness overtaking my soul. This is righteous anger. Remembrance that my ancestors once rotted in a camp like this. In addition to the millions of Jews slaughtered by the Nazis, 500,000 Romani were tortured and killed by a regime seeking ethnic cleansing. Stories told to me by my father rise to the surface. My great grandfather and two of his sons were taken to Auschwitz in 1943. They were beaten, forced to perform horrible acts on other prisoners, and lived in wooden shacks meant to house 300, but which held upwards of 1200. They were marked—*like me,* I realize, placing an absent-minded hand on the death rune—with tattoos on their wrists and a black triangle attached to their clothing.

Only one of the sons survived the ordeal. My grandfather.

The Romani called it Porajmos. The Devouring. And it's happening again.

This time to my mother.

"Let me see," Bree says. She's on her tippy toes, stretching to look past me, into the darkness beyond.

I look back into the gate. Even with my newfound ability to see in the dark, I see nothing but shadow. But I can hear the screams, the clunking metal, and something...wet and crunchy. I can smell the blood, piss, and shit. It's worse than any warzone.

"Fine." I stand up and turn to Michael. "Lead the way."

"Let's go," he whispers excitedly to Bree. They slip into the darkness beyond the gate, like they're about to get on a roller coaster at a theme park. I share a concerned look with Emma and then follow them.

Inside, the space is lit by streaks of orange—lava flowing through clear tubes, forming ancient runes up and down the building's arches. Holding pens frame the circular, arena-like interior wall. They're overflowing with people, most of whom stare vacantly at nothing, their will to live sapped. They languish in the jaws of a predator, waiting, perhaps hoping, for death. Some look dead already.

There are no demons here. No armored workers. No devils thumping around. Everything is automated, like a factory farm.

I want to call out for my mother, but I hold my tongue. I'm not sure she'd hear me over the screaming, the moaning, and the hum of machinery. Besides, stealth is our only advantage at the moment.

A large machine with a cylindrical opening at the top, like a massive metal drinking glass rimmed in blood and gore, stands at the center of the chamber.

It's a blender.

For people.

The term 'grinder' wasn't creative or exaggerated.

As we approach a large metal staircase leading to a network of elevated catwalks, something to my left gurgles. It's a pipe, large enough to stroll through. One of four leading from the grinder to the wall. On the side of each segment is a large porthole window. Something inside is moving.

Curiosity draws me closer. On the other side of the curved glass, a kid presses his face against the surface, squishing his expression around and around.

I smile and whisper, "What the hell?"

I'm about to point it out to Emma, when one of the kid's eyeballs sinks away.

The face is squashed about farther than anyone could do without screaming in agony.

And then, all at once, I understand what's happening. I'd been so focused on the face that I'd missed the mash of ground up body parts and blood filling the tube. The face is just one of many lumps of recognizable flesh.

The packed-in gore pulsates back and forth inside the tube, juices gurgling with each surge. Somewhere farther down the line, a clog is being cleared. A slurp rolls through the pipe from the building's exterior. When it reaches my porthole of doom, the ground-up meat is sucked away. Layers of human strata whisk past until the tube is empty, save for dripping blood and stubborn chunks of viscera.

"What is tha—"

I turn to Emma, holding out my hand. "Don't look."

"Are you okay?"

I want to cry. I should be devastated. My mother and Rich could have been inside that pipe. Could have been unrecognizable amidst the mash. But mostly what I feel is numb.

"This is the way we go upstairs," Bree sings, ascending the stairs on all fours, maybe because she's finishing her transformation, or because all kids charge up stairs on their hands and feet. I did, until I was a teenager. "Go upstairs, go upstairs. This is the way we go upstairs to see all the dead bodies."

I sigh, shake my head, and follow them up to the catwalks, making a conscious effort to resist walking like a dog.

A klaxon sounds briefly, and all at once, the massive space comes to life. The clog has been fixed and the factory is back in action. Hatches around the edges open up, letting in ambient red light and cascades of new people, screaming as they topple into empty cages—or some that are already full. A large crane with thick metal claws at the end swings to life, dropping down atop an overfull cage. It clamps onto the top, and it lifts the whole thing away.

The people inside know what's about to happen. They've seen it. Some, still resigned to their fate, just track the grinder's opening as they're lifted toward it. Others scream in desperation. A few of them reach out toward me, perhaps recognizing my lingering humanity. Or maybe it's just because I'm still dressed and clutching a weapon.

A young man catches my eye. Over the din of screams, I hear him shouting, "Shoot me! Please, shoot me!"

Death is coming for him. He knows it. But being ground up, alive... it's too much to bear. He'd rather a bullet to the head. So would I.

And honestly, it's almost time for that.

I want to help the man. To end his suffering. But it would expose me and sound the alarm. I search the sea of faces as the cage spins around, looking for someone familiar. The man cusses me out as he rotates away.

We stroll down the catwalk like we're getting a tour at a brewery, casually taking in the grinder up close. We stand ten feet above the hopper, holding onto a railing, looking down at the interlocking, thick metal blades, slowly, inexorably, rotating. The metal walls are covered in layers of dried blood and ground up meat. A long, winding intestine encircles everything, like a whirlpool leading down into jaws—all that's left of the grinder's previous victims. Looks like it hasn't been cleaned in an awfully long time.

"Bree," I say.

"Leave me alone," she says, shaking her head at me. A clump of her long hair falls out and lands on the catwalk. Michael gives me a disapproving stare and puts his arm around her shoulder.

It's at that moment Michael seals his fate.

I'm going to kill him.

When the time is right.

Above, the cage, which is about the size of a double-wide trailer, comes to a stop, swinging back and forth. Below, the grinder spins faster, eager for a fresh meal.

"Emma..." I say.

"My eyes are closed," she whispers, still fighting the darkness twisting our minds and bodies.

Before I can join her in silent protest, refusing to watch the scene play out, the bottom of the cage parts, disgorging the mass of people into the grinder. The first man to reach the spinning blades has it easy. He disappears in a puff of pink, sucked down inside, killed instantly.

Then the rest of them land. While those below are ground up, the few still fighting to survive atop the mass, scratch and claw at the sides, trying to climb out. But the walls are too smooth, and the people below, trying to pull themselves out, drag those on top down. At the center of it all is a woman, resigned to her fate, bouncing up and down as the people below her are pre-chewed for the Dark. She catches my eye. Looks up at me, not in anger or judgment, but in pity.

In her eyes, I've got it worse.

And she's not wrong.

Then, above the rising cries, the cracking of bones, and the slurp of blood, I hear a voice—

—shouting my name—

—from above.

I turn my eyes up and see her hanging from the cage's side, beside a dozen other people with fight left in them. "Mom?"

47

She's hard to recognize—covered in blood and grime, but it's definitely Mom, arm wrapped around one of the cage's bars, clinging tight. She looks at me with a mixture of revulsion and sorrow.

I'm surprised she even recognized me, but mothers see more than our faces. She knows my posture. The shape of my body. My taste in clothing. Maybe my voice.

We lock eyes for a moment, both of us caught off guard by the moment. Me: a monster, her: dangling over a meat grinder.

The crane shakes back and forth. Inside the cage, stragglers are slapped around. Half of them fall free from the first whack, screaming as they fall into the now empty grinder, disappearing with slick pops.

"Mom!" I prepare to leap. It's an impossible distance—for a human. Before I can lunge up to the shaking cage, Michael stands in my path.

"She's not your mother anymore," he says. "Let her fall. It will be—hck!"

My fist punches through the front of Michael's neck and emerges out the back, his spine clutched in my hand. Gurgling, he stares at me through wide, black, very surprised eyes. Then I twist, severing his spine and ending his life. I kick him free and send his body toppling over the railing. He falls onto the hopper's wall, precariously perched on the edge, teetering between falling in, or falling to the floor.

Obstacle removed, I shout, "Hold on!" and I leap for the cage, ten feet out and fifteen feet up.

I sail through the air, faster and farther than I expected. I'm stronger and more agile than I used to be, but it's more than that. The gravity on this world is less than on Earth. Feels like I've entered a reality-bending cheat code. I collide with the cage's exterior. I grip the bars and hold myself in place opposite my mother. I reach through and wrap a hand around her back, helping to hold her in place.

"Got you," I say. "I got you."

"What happened to you?" she asks, more worried about me than her own precarious situation.

"Death rune," I say, knowing she'll understand the reference. "It changes people...into them."

"Demons..."

"Aliens...but yeah. Demon aliens, I guess." This *is* Hell after all, it's just a planet instead of a supernatural realm.

"Why are you here?" she asks. "Are you..."

"With them? Screw that. I'm here for you and Rich."

Her eyes tear up.

Rich is dead. She doesn't need to say it. *Shit.*

She sniffs and sets her jaw. "Allie?"

"Safe," I say, hoping it's the truth. "She's with Jen."

Mom nods her head toward Emma. "That's her sister?"

"Yeah," I say. "And Bree, a kid from down the—"

"I know who she is," Mom says, hand to her mouth, combating rising tears.

The cage's shaking grows frantic. There must be sensors detecting the three remaining stragglers. It's attempting to shake them free. And it's going to succeed, even with me.

"In case I don't get a chance to tell you later on," I say, "you did a good job. After Dad. Thank you. And...I love you."

She can't reply. Overcome with emotion and struggling to hold on, speaking is impossible. But I can feel her appreciation and reflected love. It's enough to fight back the growing darkness and propel me to action.

"I'm going to let go. Hold on tight. Just a few seconds. Can you do that?"

Mom's arms python-grip the bars. She grits her teeth and nods.

I release her and drop down, catching the cage's base, dangling twenty feet above the grinder, chewing up the last bits of some poor soul. A Doppler effect scream rolls past me as a man falls. A sound like a watermelon being torn open silences the man. I hang in place, looking up at

Mom. She and another woman are all that's left of the hundred-odd people that were stuffed into this cage. I don't give the stranger much attention until the cage spins, suddenly dislodging her in my direction.

"Got you," I shout, reaching out and catching the woman's arm. I swing her toward Emma. "Catch!"

The woman Tarzan-swings on my arm, and I toss her out. After flailing through the air like a penguin that's only now realized it's flightless, her mid-section strikes the catwalk's railing. Wind knocked out of her, the woman nearly topples back, but Emma grabs hold and yanks her over the railing. The woman slams down onto her back. It's not gentle, but she's alive. Beside them, Bree hops around and claps, entertained by the action and not at all upset about Michael's fate.

"Miah!" Mom shouts, her grip failing.

The cage starts spinning, gaining speed. Centrifugal force holds me against the bars as I climb.

I scrabble up behind Mom, holding onto the bars with one hand, the other wrapped around her midsection. "We need to get to the bottom. From there I'm going to throw you."

She nods. Too afraid to speak.

"But you're going to have to let go," I say. Mom's hands come away from the bars, and I barely feel her weight, not because I'm strong or the gravity is reduced, but because the cage has become a carnival tilt-o-whirl, pinning us in place, until—

It stops.

All at once.

Hulk Hogan in his Andre the Giant-lifting prime couldn't resist the sudden force. We're flung around the cage, I manage to hold onto Mom, wrapping my arms and legs around her, taking the brunt of several impacts before toppling downward.

I reach out, catch hold of the cage's dangling door, and pinch my fingers down like a vice. We swing together, and this time, I launch my passenger up and over the railing.

But there is nothing I can do for myself.

At the top of my swing's arc, the cage starts spinning in the opposite direction. It's enough to wrench the door from my hand.

I fall through the air, silently resigned to my fate. Above, it's Bree who screams my name, "Miah!"

Instinct guides my hands, stretching out, looking for something—anything to grasp onto.

I slam into the sharply angled hopper wall, just below the lip. Lubricated by blood and gore, I slide toward the churning grinder. My fingers wrap around the edge, clinging, arresting my descent. But it's a momentary reprieve. The sludge beneath my fingers prevents me from maintaining my grip. I have seconds.

"Find something to lower down!" Emma shouts from above, on the catwalk, desperately searching, but finding nothing. Bree watches me, crouched down, hands clutching the railing. Mom is trying to push herself up, desperate to help but exhausted. Beside her, the stranger I saved looks on in horror.

"Hey," Bree says. "How high can you jump?"

My brow furrows. I feel it crack. "High enough...if the grinder wasn't running. You know how to shut it off?"

She shakes her head slowly.

"Can you jump high with me?" she asks.

"Probably," I say, slipping an inch, hanging by my fingertips.

"Get ready," she says, and she steps over the edge.

"Wait!" I shout. "Stop!"

But I'm too late. Bree leaps down to the hopper and lands on Michael's body, teetering on the edge. Clutching on to his back like Spider-Man about to spring away, she says, "Slide down behind him. Jump off his body before he's juiced."

"That's...that's fucking insane!" I shout.

She smiles and nods. "Go!" She tilts to the side, her weight pulling Michael's body into the hopper. As his body falls, Bree jumps to me. My hands lift away from the lip. I spin around, catching the girl and slide down the hopper wall, aiming my feet toward Michael's corpse. I might get a second to push off before he's consumed.

Michael hits the spinning grinder feet first. It sucks him in like a piece of paper in a shredder, forcing him upright as it pulls him downward.

A buzzer screams through the chamber.

The grinder slows, chewing Michael up, like it's savoring him. His upright body flails back and forth, his limp arms waggling, like he's doing the floss dance. I plant my feet on his shoulders. He's too wobbly to push off, but it keeps us hovering over the blades as they slow to a stop.

Apparently, the denizens of Hell don't like eating corrupted people. The moment Michael's flesh was chewed up, sensors detected the mistake and stopped production. It saved our lives, but it means someone or something will be en route to clear out the problem—probably the same person who unblocked the clogged pipe.

I stand on the now motionless grinder, lean down, and lock my fingers together. "You ever do ten fingers?"

Bree lifts her foot and puts it in my finger cradle. "Go."

"Hey," I say. "Thanks."

She shrugs. "We're on the same team, right?"

"Yes," I say. "Yes, we are." I lift as Bree shoves off, tossing her into the air. She soars up and over the railing, landing with the grace of a cat.

I bend down, take aim, and spring up and out of the hopper, catching hold of the railing and hoisting myself over, landing beside my mother. "Hey, Mom."

She puts her hand on my charred cheek. Rubs her thumb over my skin. I barely feel it.

She smiles up at me. "You've got some schmutz on you."

I embrace her tightly. Feeling overcome with gratitude, I offer up a prayer to whoever or whatever might be listening.

Help me get her home.

That's it. No deals. No offers of servitude. No begging to save my own life. Just help me get Mom home.

If God is real, I'm not sure he's listening, or maybe he's overwhelmed by the sheer number of requests flowing through the supernatural switchboard. Down below, between us and the exit, is an armored man, hands on hips, head cocked to the side in a clear sign of irritation.

Behind him, is a devil.

48

I crouch in front of the woman I rescued. She's middle aged, dressed in white shorts and a pink polo shirt, ready for a day on the tennis court, or maybe the golf course. If not for the blood and grime covering her from head to toe, she'd probably look successful and capable of taking on the world. But now...

She shuffles away from me until she bumps into Bree's feet and looks up into her demon eyes. Sensing a scream on the way, I hold out my hand. "Whoa, whoa, whoa, you're okay. I know we look gnarly, but I just saved you, remember?"

I give that a second to sink in. "We look like them, but we're not. Not yet, anyway. Ugh. Forget I said that. What I'm trying to say is, I'm Miah. This..." I motion to Mom. "...is my mother. I'm here to save her. To get her home. If you want to tag along—"

She nods frantically, pushing herself up.

"Got a name?" I ask her.

"C-Christina Randal," she says.

"Okay, Christy..." I wave my mother over. "Mom. You guys know we're still ourselves, but the angry robot dude down there doesn't."

An angry, garbled voice in a language I don't know rises from below. The armored man is headed for the steps. The devil is motionless. For now.

"Just...I apologize in advance okay?"

"What?" Christy says. "Why?"

I bounce my head back and forth, debating how to say it. "I...might need to rough you up a little."

Before she can complain, I pick her up and throw her over my shoulder. She punches my back, shouting.

It's not an act, but that's good. It'll look real.

I turn to my mother, whose gaze freezes me in place. She's taking stock of me again, looking for any trace of her son. Then she nods and turns her back to me. I grasp the back of her shirt, bunch it up, and shove her forward.

Emma leads the way down the catwalk stairs. I carry and shove our 'prisoners.' Bree brings up the rear, humming the *Dora the Explorer* theme song. I glance back at her and say, "Keep it down back there, Boots."

"Okay, Swiper." She giggles, and then she shifts gears so hard I nearly stumble. "Can we kill him? The robot man?"

I shake my head. "We're just going to walk out and keep on walking." I'm pretty sure I remember which gate leads back to our neighborhood, but I'm also pretty sure anywhere is better than here.

She makes a sour lemon face that somehow manages to be cute, despite her looking like the child of a gargoyle and a charcoal briquette.

The armored man waits a few feet away from the bottom of the stairs. No idea what he's thinking. The metal face with glowing eyes hides his real expression—and species. His body language transmits annoyance, but his armor—covered in gore, bits of it dangling from his arms—radiates dread...until I remember how he got like that.

This man—or whatever he is—isn't blood soaked from the battlefield. He's been cleaning pipes, and he's about to unclog a half-chewed demon from a grinder. This is Hell's janitor.

I grunt and wave a hand back at the grinder, then I raise a hand in what I hope is a universal gesture of annoyance. Then I give Mom a shove. She falls past the armored man, who is taller than he looked from above. He's at least a foot taller than me, and I'm a solid six feet. His head tilts to the side, glowing gaze shifting from me, to Emma, to Mom, to Christy, and finally to Bree.

Mom shouts in honest pain, as I grasp her arm and yank her up, moving past the man. But he's not the only one we need to convince. The devil has a pilot—another armored figure, but this one can't be more than four feet tall. Is it a child? A little person? A small adult?

A snort stops me in place, somehow conveying the command to stop. I have no choice but to comply.

The janitor taps the back of his hand. His mask splits down the middle and opens, revealing a twisted face, black and charred like ours—but not human. Never human. He has sharp cheeks, sharp brows, sharp everything, including teeth. His black eyes probe. His nose twitches, sniffing.

"What?" Bree grumbles, approaching the janitor. "What do you want?" She gets in his face, baring her teeth and letting out an authentic, low growl. He leans down, looking into her eyes.

His expression relaxes.

We're clear, I think. He thinks we're one of them.

And then... "Bree?"

Bree's dark eyes shift to the side, looking at a nearby cage, full of desperate people waiting for their lives to end after the clog is cleared. Pressed against the bars is a blonde woman I vaguely remember seeing around the neighborhood, but she's instantly familiar to Bree.

"Mom?" Bree leans back from the janitor, turning fully toward her mother. "Mom!"

The janitor's face screws up. He knows this isn't normal.

Bree breaks away, sprinting toward her mother, all at once looking more like a little girl again. "Mom!"

Her mother wraps her arms around her, holding her against the bars, despite Bree's new appearance. They weep together. I can feel their hearts breaking.

And it fills me with rage.

"Hey," I say, getting the janitor's attention. He turns toward me, showing a flash of surprise when he finds the business end of an M4 leveled between his eyes. "You understand English?"

He sneers at me, but he gives a slow nod. These alien bastards might be the inspiration for hell, but they still value their own lives, even if they are spent unclogging human sausage meat from oversized pipes.

"How do I open the cages?" I ask.

His faces twitches, trying to remain stalwart in the face of his own fear. But there's a reason he's a janitor and not on the front lines, operating a devil, collecting people for the grinder. He tilts his head toward the entrance. Lining the wall is a line of levers, each with a glowing orange rune above it. I can't read them, but there's one lever for every cage.

He must need to clean them out on occasion, dislodging any bodies that couldn't be shaken loose.

"Thanks," I say, and I pull the trigger.

The gunshot is the catalyst for a string of reactions.

The bullet enters the janitor's forehead at an angle and strikes the inside of the helmet, sliding around the curved wall and exiting his forehead following a different trajectory. The round punches a hole in the clear material holding back the lava in the wall runes. A stream of glowing orange bubbles out, steaming as it hits the bars of a cage, the people inside screaming in horror as beads of magma scorch their outstretched hands.

Christy screams in my ears, clutching her head, kicking her legs. She's shell shocked already, but I got bad news for her—things are about to get a whole lot more nuts. I'm not sure what kind of nuts, but probably something between a sweeping Steven Spielberg World War II battle sequence and a balls-to-the-wall, explosive Michael Bay car chase.

Mom stumbles at the rifle's report. She falls to her hands and knees, but she turns around in time to see the janitor fall back like he's doing a trust fall.

"Miah!" Emma shouts, and before I can turn toward her, I'm not just tackled, I'm lifted off the ground, Christy still over my shoulder, and launched. I sprawl through the air, twisting around to see Emma beneath me and the devil's powerful arm sweeping through the air where I'd been standing a moment before.

The pint-sized pilot might not be battlefield material, but he's got a bad case of short-alien syndrome, and he's finally found an outlet for all that pent up aggression—me.

I roll to my feet the way I used to when I was a kid pretending to be a ninja. Emma springs away, clinging to the underside of the catwalk. I yank Christy to her feet, shove her toward Mom, who's already falling back away from the devil, and I shout, "Run!"

A scream pulls my attention back to Bree. She's trying to lift the cage by herself, the last of her humanity fueling the effort. Strong as she might be now, there's no way she's picking up a metal cage the size of a double-wide trailer, full of people. It must weigh tons. But then something shifts.

The bar she's holding onto bends. A little farther and the people inside might be able to squeeze out.

But there's a better way.

"Mom!" She looks back, and I point to the levers. "Open the cages!"

She makes a beeline for the levers.

The devil grinds as it turns to face me, its pincer arms reaching out.

"You ready for this?" I ask Emma, upside down above me.

She nods.

"Time to make daddy proud," I say, raising my rifle. "Yours," I add. "Not mine."

Emma drops down beside me, raising her rifle. "No duh."

We pull our triggers together, unleashing nearly sixty rounds in three seconds. Sparks fly. Bullets ricochet. When the bullets run out, Emma and I swap out our magazines, but hold our fire. The bullets had no effect on the giant machine or its armored pilot.

"Any ideas?" I ask Emma. She's two steps ahead of me. She lifts a grenade, gives me a lopsided grin, shouts, "Yeet!" and lobs the explosive toward the devil.

49

The devil pilot might not be a warrior, but he's been around long enough to recognize a grenade as a threat. The mech rotates, swinging its arms out hard, striking the grenade like a baseball, and sending it toward the nose bleeds. The explosive bounces off one of the large pipes, falls between two of them, and detonates.

The pressurized pipes burst. A geyser of carnage rises and slaps back down, coating everything in a twenty-foot radius, slowly oozing out toward us.

I'm so distracted by the body part Old Faithful that I miss the devil's spin snap to a stop and rotate the other direction. A metal hand open-palm swats me. I lose and gain consciousness as I careen through the air, waking up just in time to experience rolling across the concrete floor and coming to stop against a catwalk support beam.

Emma attempts to hurl another grenade, but she—and the grenade—are struck next. She slides to a stop in the growing puddle of mashed people. The grenade follows a higher arc, landing inside the grinder, clattering around its inner surface, and then exploding. The boom is amplified by the hopper, bouncing off the hard, domed ceiling and slapping my ears. Everyone in the chamber, who's not dead or unconscious, shouts in pain, hands to ears.

Except for the pilot. And Bree.

With an angry shout, Bree pries the bars of her mother's cage wider. She stops, steps back, and shouts, "C'mon!" Her mother squeezes through the bars. It's a tight fit, but Bree is pulling her through. One way or another, her mom is getting out of that cage.

I want to cheer when her mother falls out and lands atop her night-mare of a daughter, hugging and kissing the girl like she hasn't changed at all. She's a good mother...even if Bree can be a little psycho. And Bree's mother is on the ball, climbing to her feet and dashing to join Mom at the levers. They embrace, both of them weeping. Know each other, apparently, like everyone in the neighborhood...excluding myself. Together, they start yanking the levers down.

On the far side of the massive arena-like chamber, the front end of a cage snaps open and starts rising. Before it's even a foot off the ground, people are scrabbling out, desperate for freedom. One after another, cages begin opening, unleashing a wave of humanity already running toward the gate—behind the devil.

I push myself up.

They're going to get slaughtered. Worse, Mom now has the devil's undivided attention. It turns toward the pair of wom-en, reaching with hands powerful enough to crush them.

"Hey!" I shout, firing off a few rounds. The bullets ping off the pilot's helmet, but he doesn't even glance in my direction. He's compartmentalizing. His eventual discipline for allowing an insurrection will probably be worse than a few dings in his armor.

I sprint toward the pilot, trying to conjure a plan. Bullets don't work. Grenades would be more likely to blow up the people who are just now getting a taste of hope. I don't have a plan, but it doesn't matter. I won't get there in time. Emma is closer, but she's slipping in gore, trying to escape it without falling again.

The massive metal hands reach out.

"No!" I shout. "Stop!"

For the first time since the darkness started changing me, I feel completely helpless.

Bree's mother sees the devil coming first. Screams in fear. Flinches back. But her cry is drowned out by a roar.

Bree lunges through the air, landing on the devil's arm and springing away. Hands outstretched, fingers hooked, she lands on the pilot. With a banshee shriek, she takes hold of the pilot's helmet. For a moment, I think she's trying to wrench it free, but she doesn't just lift the helmet, she yanks the pilot out of his seat and tosses him away. The short pilot pinwheels through the air, landing hard on his back. The impact must be jarring, even with the armor, but the diminutive alien sits up a moment after landing, only to be tackled by Bree.

She's gone savage, punching, clawing, and howling. Wolverine in a berserker rage. The short dude doesn't stand a chance. If not for his armor, he'd look like pulled pork by now. And he still might.

Bits of metal shed away from his body. Sheets of armor follow. And then Bree is back on the helmet, screaming as she yanks at it, over and over. The lease on her humanity is up. Hair falls from her head in clumps. The pilot is at her mercy, and she's got none left.

The helmet slurps away from the pilot's head, revealing a shimmering sheet of mottled brown, Jell-O mold flesh with two round black eyes. The head—if you can call it that—jiggles around, expressionless and inhuman, like a snail. Definitely not the same species as the janitor. Hell is populated by a coalition of alien species, but how many are here willingly?

Bree flinches back in surprise, but she recovers quickly. Claws rend slimy flesh as she swipes both hands out, striking the flaccid face like a living guillotine, severing the pilot's nub of a head. It hits the floor and bounces a moment before the creature's little body collapses, lifeless.

Bree's tiny form heaves with rage, her teeth bared, looking for another target.

Over by the levers, her mother watches on in horror, hands raised over her mouth, just now realizing how far-gone Bree might be. Mom finishes the job, yanking down the last of the levers. Hundreds of people have been freed, but they've stopped short of the fight, recognizing Emma, Bree, and I as a threat, but confused by our confrontation with the janitor and the devil's pilot.

"It's okay!" I shout. "We're with you."

For now.

"We need to go, all at once. Safety in numbers. Like a herd of Zebra."

Slick, Miah, I think. *Why don't you remind them they're prey, while you're at it?*

Then I decide to run with the metaphor. Because it's the truth. "I'm not going to bullshit you. Anyone not absofuckinglutely running for their lives is not going to make it home. But this is not every man for himself.

You see someone in trouble, you help. That's how we get through this. That's how you get home. We clear?"

A few people nod. Most just look overwhelmed.

The devil rises up, under control once again. I spin around, ready to throw down with a new pilot, but the person in control of the satanic mech is all smiles.

"Clear," Emma says. She looks down at the controls, moving hands and feet to operate the machine. It stumbles back a few steps, but she gets it under control, and gives a thumbs up.

"Mom!" I whisper. "Bree's mom!" I wave them over, and when they arrive beside me, in the devil's shadow, I wave a hand toward the exit. "Let's go!"

While the mass of humanity floods toward the exit, I pull the two mothers close. "Hi," I say to Bree's mom. "I'm Miah."

"This is your boy?" she asks my mother.

My Mom nods, like she's proud of who I've become.

"She always said you were brave."

I sigh. "How many neighborhood barbecues have I missed?"

I'm surprised when she offers me her hand and says, "Stephanie."

I shake her hand. "All right, Steph. I'm calling you Steph, okay? Never mind. Look. I need you two to stay with the devil." I hitch a thumb toward the mech. "That's the devil. As long as it's moving, and we're still us..." I look up to Emma. She's standing in her seat, looking out over the sea of humanity flowing past. "...this is the safest place."

Both mothers nod.

"See them?" I call up to Emma.

She shakes her head. "I don't see them."

Normally, I'd question her ability to pick faces out of a crowd of dirty people, but our newfound sight and instincts make it easy.

"Have either of you seen mom or dad Gearhart? Are they here?" I look from Steph to Mom and back again. They're searching their memories, but they're shaking their heads before Mom says, "No."

"They're not here," I tell Emma. "Could be a good thing."

She looks at the broken pipes, oozing human remains. She doesn't have to say anything. I understand her meaning. *Could be a bad thing.*

"Time to go," I say, and she gives a begrudging nod.

The devil lumbers to life, a little shaky at first, but it doesn't take Emma long to get the hang of the simple controls.

"Bree," I say, turning to where she'd been standing. All that remains is the headless pilot corpse and a clump of hair—maybe all her hair. It takes just a moment to locate her, but I might be a moment too late.

"Hey!" I shout like I'm scolding Sanchez. "Bree!"

She doesn't hear me. She's focused on her prey, slowly crawling along the catwalk's underside, approaching the panicked herd, ready to pounce. I break into a run, "Bree!"

She leaps, claws extended, mouth open wide, ready to kill.

I lunge and tackle her out of the air. We land in a heap, but she's already moving. Springs to her feet, coils to jump. I catch her in time, lifting her up by her shirt. "Stop!"

"Nooo!" She hollers, her voice no longer her own. "I'm hungry!"

"Your mother is watching," I growl, but it doesn't get through. Her eyes flick toward her mother, but it's brief and followed by a roar. She swipes at her clothing, shredding it and falling from my grip. She lands on her feet, and she tries to pounce again.

This time I catch her by the neck, every fiber of my being telling me to crush her throat. Squeeze the life out of her. "They're almost home. Almost free. We just need to hang on a little longer."

"I...can't." Her raspy, choked out voice is weak, but it hits me like a tsumani. She glances down at the rifle still hanging from my neck. Doesn't need to say another word. It's time.

"No." I shove Bree's head back, slamming her into a support beam and knocking her unconscious.

I carry her to the devil. "Sorry," I tell Steph. "She's...we're all struggling."

She nods through her tears, and watches as I open the cage beneath the devil and place Bree inside, closing it behind her. Then I join Mom and Steph beside the mech and head out through the gate. The flow of humanity outside is like rapids, carrying us along. Beyond the exit, hundreds of freed people fan out into the courtyard, charging for the still open main gates.

And it's nothing like I imagined.

Nothing like Zebra. Or wildebeest. Or gazelle.

The Dark flow into the courtyard, outnumbered, but making up for it in speed, strength, and unbridled savagery. Still, it's our only chance. Live or die, we need to take it. "Go! Go!" I shout. "Don't slow down! Go!"

Ahead, two devils stand between the mob of escapees, arms open wide as though to embrace. All around, demons flow out of the base's nooks and crannies, flowing out of the underworld barracks, pouncing on everything that moves. It's a slaughter...and I charge headlong into it.

50

Screams rise into the night sky and I wonder if I haven't just accelerated the timeline of all these people's collective demise. The Dark aren't trying to recollect or subdue their fleeing prey, they're cutting people down, flowing through the crowd of terrified people like a murder hornet through a beehive, severing heads and limbs with wild abandon.

But there's no turning back. Death awaits in either direction. Forward holds the only possibility for salvation.

Plus, I'm mostly here for Mom. It's selfish, I know, but—

No buts... It's just selfish, and that's not who I am, demon or not.

"Be right back," I say to Mom, and then I leap onto the devil beside Emma. "You should go."

"I am going!" she says, focusing on controlling the big robot.

"I mean, you should go look for your parents while you can. There's a lot of other places they could be."

She looks at me for a moment, torn between commitments.

"I got this," I assure her.

She relinquishes control and climbs out of the pilot's chair. The devil staggers to a stop, but the flow of humanity around us continues charging toward the gate. Mom and Steph are among them, exposed and in danger. Mom looks back, catching my eye. I give her a thumbs up, and I take the controls.

"Works like how you'd imagine," Emma says. "Pedals for the feet, joysticks for the arms."

"Go," I tell her. "Go fast."

She nods and leaps away, soaring over the crowd. She lands amidst the throng, disappearing a moment later, headed for the nearest grind house.

"Just like I'd imagine..." I look over the controls, finding the sticks and pedals. There're a lot of other buttons and levers, but I ignore them, taking hold of the sticks and trying out the pedals. It's slow going at first. I don't want to step on anyone. But then I'm on the move, pounding the pavement toward Mom. People scatter out of the way, clearing a path. No idea if they see me as friend or foe, but it doesn't really matter. I'd run them over, either way.

"Mom!" I shout. She doesn't hear me over the sounds of carnage. "MOM!"

She looks back. Sees me coming. Takes hold of Steph's arm and stops, confident that I won't run them down.

The devil comes to a slow stop. I lower the arms and shout, "Get on!"

Mom and Steph climb onto the arms, and I lift them the rest of the way, letting them climb onto the carapace. "Hold on!" I start the devil moving again, forcing them to hold on to the ring of horns above my head, like an unholy crown. All of us on board, I push the devil as fast as I can.

Ahead, the two devils blocking the gate look like a pair of giant crabs playing *Hungry Hungry Hippos*, their arms snapping out, clubbing, crushing, and severing every person who attempts to get past. The bodies are starting to pile around them like sandbag bunkers. As long as those devils are around, none of these people are going to make it past the gate.

A man screams as he arcs over my head, trailing blood from his two severed legs.

Most of them won't make it to the gate at all.

The man sees me, judges me in slow motion as he sails past, his eyes screaming, 'You did this.'

A growl rises from my throat, and I push the devil faster.

A path clears.

My devil's arms extend, rising up just over the heads of the people on either side. "Faster," I will the machine. "Faster!" I pump my feet, controlling the devil's pace, building into a sprint. "Hang on!"

The pilots don't recognize me as a threat until it's too late. My devil charges between them, arms outstretched, crushing both pilots with a robotic clothesline. The impact tears my devil's arms away, but it disables my two targets. We flow toward the gate, trailing a line of humanity, all of us charging for the portal that will take us home.

Problem is, the returning Dark have formed a wall between us and escape. More devils now wait patiently. Demons pace and twitch, eager for the fight.

But there's not going to be a fight. The mass of escapees slows to a stop, all of them exhausted, wheezing, lungs desperate for air that has more oxygen than whatever gases are floating around in this stank-ass atmosphere. It's breathable enough to keep people alive, but with oxygen levels closer to a mountaintop.

Not that I'm feeling it. My modified body thrives on this air. Feels good in my lungs.

But the air is the least of our problems. The waiting army ahead of us is advancing now, calmly stalking toward us. I want to tell everyone to stand their ground, but I don't think it would make a difference. To stand is to die. They all know it, so they start backing away, herded back to the slaughterhouse…but only for a moment.

A torrent of shouting rises behind us, emerging from the base. A tsunami of sound. I lean to the side and look back to find a sea of humanity flowing out of the grindhouses, numerous enough to overwhelm the demons laying into them.

Emma.

She set everyone free!

Buoyed by the increased numbers, the hundred people with me stand their ground, waiting for the swarm of humanity to reach us.

I want to shout something inspirational, like Gerard Butler at the hot gates in *300*, but the sea of humanity roars as one and charges forward. I shout with them, and push the armless devil into action, racing out toward what I still think is certain death.

Aiming for a line of demons, my plan is to plow through and keep on going. If I can crush a few, maybe some of these people will make it through. "Red Rover, Red Rover, send devil Miah right over!"

Before I reach the line, an enemy devil fills the gap behind the demons, blocking our exit.

"Damnit, shit, damnit."

Before I can come up with an alternate plan, one of the enemy devil's legs explodes. The machine falls to the side, twitching as the pilot hangs limp, its armor shredded.

What the hell?

The devil collapses, giving me a view of the gate behind it, where a second army of heavily armed humanity flows into hell. The man leading them, grenade launcher in hand, is Mr. Gearhart. He's shirtless, bloody, and dirty, like some kind of 80s action hero. And he's not alone. Jen, Allie, Sung, and Dave are all there, arsenal in hands, unleashing a torrent of bullets. And the people keep on coming. Survivors from the neighborhood and beyond. I see uniforms among them. Police. National Guard. Army.

Demons race toward the newcomers. Devils wait for the wave of escapees to reach them. The odds are still against us, but not quite as severely.

"Miah!" It's Mom, shouting in my ear. She points behind us, terrified. I lean around and have a look. My devil stumbles to a stop as my eyes widen. The base's big turrets are turning toward the crowd.

That's why the devils are waiting. In a moment, the sea of humanity will resemble a chunky beef stew.

My mind races for a solution. I can't think of anything that will spare the majority of people here. But maybe I can save Mom and Steph. Throwing them in the cage beneath the devil will give them some cover, but they'll be stuck with Bree, who may or may not be conscious now.

And if the big guns target us...

I climb out of the cockpit, ready to pick Mom up and jump below. That's when I see a turret gun stop, its barrel pointed straight at us.

At least it will be quick, I think.

And then...

The turrets all adjust their aim, rising up over us, over the people fighting off waves of demons by the gate, until the guns are all pointed toward the sky.

What are they—

The big guns fire. Hot, blue plasma launches into the sky. All around the base, the cannons unleash a barrage. I follow the blue streaks into the starry sky and nearly fall over when I see a hovering fleet.

Of spaceships.

They're sleek and modern, shaped like giant footballs. They're glowing white with streaks of blue, a contrast to the orange lines permeating the Dark's technology. Hundreds of smaller ships detach from the outer hulls, falling through the atmosphere, zipping down past the rising cannon fire.

A large oval that looks a little like a classic UFO drops down over us and swoops over the battlefield. Armored soldiers drop from holes in the bottom. As they fall to the ground, glowing blue beams of energy jut from their bodies, forming swords extending from their forearms. Glowing wings extend from their backs, buzzing and cutting through the air.

"They're...angels," Mom says, a smile spreading wide.

The alien race we believe are angels, I think, but I keep the cynical thought to myself. My feelings about the aliens are mixed. On the surface, I feel awe. But just beneath, and down to my twisted core, I feel rage. The darkness in me sees them as the enemy, to be destroyed, hated, and laid to waste.

Then one of them drops toward my devil, its wings flaring wide, slowing its descent. It lands in front of my devil, facing me, totally focused, ignoring the battle around us. Waiting. For me.

I want to attack. To rip its head off. But I fight the urge to the point of physical pain and force myself to abandon the devil and the threat it presents. I drop down still holding Mom, putting myself between the newcomer and her.

The angel's armor resembles that of the Dark's, hinting at some common past, but it's bright white with gold trim and electric blue lines. The buzzing wings, some kind of solid energy, retract. The swords extending from its arms slide back.

"Uh," I say, "Hello?"

It steps toward me. I stumble back into my mother's arms. She holds me, whispering, "It's okay, Miah. I think they're on our side."

Behind the angel, its kin engage the Dark. Demon, devil, and angel duke it out in a line of practiced, poetic action. Both sides are merciless, exacting a serious toll on the other. But the angels are unflinching, their resolve and confidence never wavering, even when injured.

"Al tifached," the angel says, and it reaches a hand out toward my face.

"Miah!" It's Emma, off to the side, standing beside her rescued mother, terrified for me. She leaps through the air, clawed hands outstretched toward the angel's face.

Moving with liquid grace, the angel catches Emma by her throat. She claws with her hands and feet, a frenzied human-sized cat, but she only manages to scratch his armor. Behind her, Emma's mother shouts for her release, desperate to help her child, despite her transformation. I've been judging my neighborhood for years, feeling smug and better than everyone else, but I'm starting to understand that behind the gaudy flaws are parents who love their children unconditionally.

The angel turns Emma left and right, inspecting her face, her eyes, and the hair still clinging to the top of her head.

"Al tifached," it says again, followed by, "Hachoshech lo yikaf otanu." It places the thumb of its free hand against her forehead. Blue light flares from the digit, drawing a primal scream from Emma's lungs, growing in pitch as the thumb swipes across her skin, tearing away the dry char— and the death rune with it.

51

Emma goes limp in the angel's grasp. *She's dead,* I think, stepping toward her hanging body. The background chaos fades to a blur. Emotions that feel ancient erupt inside me, quieted by the Dark, but not yet snuffed out. I feel despair for my fallen friend, sorrow for her mother, who's watching with tears in her eyes, and remorse that I couldn't do more to avoid this ending.

I want to feel angry at the angel. Want to unleash hell's fury on it. But that wouldn't change anything. Death is my fate, too. Perhaps the angel's method is more merciful than a bullet?

Didn't sound like it.

Emma's final scream was full of anguish, as though her soul was being torn from her cells.

One of the angels' fighters zooms past overhead, firing at the base's turrets and kicking up a hard wind. Layers of dry black peel away from Emma's body. *She's turning to dust.* I watch in horror, as ash that used to be Emma floats away, twisting in the breeze.

Then I see a flash of white. Is that...bone? Is she being reduced to a skeleton? When the char flakes away from her face and falls away in a sheet, I understand the truth.

Emma has been purified. The effects of the death rune have been negated. The symbol has been erased. Emma—the real Emma—is being reborn in the alien's grasp.

The angel crouches and holds Emma out to Mrs. Gearhart, who collects the unconscious and fully healed teenager in her arms.

"Thank you," I say, voice trembling.

The angel turns toward me, reaching out again, even as explosions, screams, and gunfire tear through the battlefield.

Believing I'm too far gone to save, I step forward to meet my fate: death or damnation.

The angel places its cold, metal thumb against the death rune on my forehead. For a moment, nothing, then I'm consumed by white hot torment. It radiates from my forehead, out through my torso and limbs, transporting me to a realm of exquisite pain—

· —and then into the past.

"Two doors down," Carter whispers, double tapping his fingers toward a crumbling, bullet-ridden building on the left side of the debris-strewn street. The remnants of cars and trucks, shot to shit and crushed by a tank or two, provide cover as we move down closer to our target.

It's hard to hear him. My ears are still ringing from the previous day's rocket attack, which claimed the lives of twenty soldiers, including my friends. And Carter's.

Yesterday, we were defeated.

This morning, we sent the dead home on a Chinook helicopter.

Today, sun scorching our army combat uniforms, we're performing recon, in search of those responsible for the attack. Revenge, U.S. Military style, usually comes from above in the form of a laser guided bomb, or a few Hellfire missiles launched from an MQ-9 Reaper UAV. But this is personal.

Having identified a group of men we believe took part in the previous day's assault, Carter decided to forgo calling it in, and to collect his pound of flesh in person.

No one disagreed. Ten soldiers. All of us complicit in carrying out an attack on people who look like the enemy. We're not doing anything wrong. The Brass will forgive us—if we all survive the encounter. We could call it in right now, and death would fall out of the sky. But we want to see their eyes, and I want them to see us.

It's primal. Territorial. You kill ours; we kill yours. Let it be a message to anyone else thinking of joining the Taliban.

We slide up to the building's entrance, a loosely hanging door full of holes.

I frown. How many times has the U.S. Military delivered a message to these people? And yet, they persist.

Realization sours my stomach. Nothing we do here today is going to make a positive difference. If anything, we'll push the families of those we kill into the conflict. They'll hit back at us, we'll drop more bombs, their outrage will grow, and the cycle will continue.

But I'm committed, I'm here, and this is the only thing holding me together. When we stop—when the fight is over—I'll have to face what I saw yesterday. I'll have to remember the eyes of my dying friend going glassy as I attempted to pinch his artery closed.

Fuck these guys, I think, and I blink back to the present, as Carter points at me, and then toward the ground. He wants me outside. A sentry, guarding their backs. It's a necessary job. A smart move. But none of the ten soldiers here wants it.

I argue with my eyes, demanding inclusion, but he's made up his mind. Maybe sees something in my eyes. Maybe he knows I have doubts.

I contain my litany of curses, for not being able to take part, for being perceived as weak or broken, or whatever the hell Carter believes. I owe my fallen comrades more, but I'm also a good soldier. An order is an order, even if it's regarding an unsanctioned assault. I give a nod and stand aside, training my eyes on the ruined buildings around us, any one of which could hide the enemy.

Soldiers line up by the door. Count to three. The door is yanked open, flash bangs tossed inside. A burst of sound and light act as the gunshot at the beginning of a sprint, soldiers charging in. There's no announcement. No chance for surrender. They just open fire.

Heads bob up and down in windows and doorways lining the streets. I shift my aim from one to the next, all of them ducking away in fright.

Screams rise through the dusty air, a swirling storm of anguish that takes me back to the previous day's events. But the voices are different. Wounded and dying soldiers weep, and curse, and cry out. But they're not confused. The people inside have no idea what's going on. And they're not all men. I hear women.

And children.

"Carter," I say into my comms. "Carter! What the hell is—"

The gunfire ceases.

The street goes quiet.

One by one, the soldiers file out of the building, unharmed and stoic. Carter is out last, closing the door behind him. "What did you do?" I ask him. When he doesn't respond, I grasp his sleeve and shout, "What did you do?!"

He looks me in the eyes, unflinching, and says, "What we do." Then he shrugs out of my grip and walks away.

I shouldn't look.

Ignorance is bliss.

But I played a part in this. I need to know. Need to see what we did. The door squeaks open. I step inside and make it just a few steps before being shocked to a stop. Men, women, and children lie in pools of their own blood. All of them dead. This was a family. I step into the next room. More than one family. Unarmed. Just trying to survive in a war-torn country.

Tears spill from my eyes.

This is wrong.

But they can't be saved.

And...I can't change anything.

I wipe my face, bury my shame, exit the building, and wade through the sea of judgmental eyes, back to the waiting Humvee that might as well be a hearse carrying away my dead-inside, shell of a self.

I return to the present, a scream tearing from my mouth. Feels like the angel's thumb is burrowing through my skull. It leans into me, its glowing blue visor flaring with energy. I try to see the being within, but it's just light. Contained energy. And it's flowing through me, severing and remaking every cell in my body one by one.

"Al tifached. Hachoshech lo yikaf otanu." I have no idea what it's saying, but I feel reassured. The angel knows what it's doing. It looked into my soul and saw something worth saving. I try to rest in that confidence. That I'm not a lost cause. That my mind, body, and past can be redeemed.

The angel's thumb moves over my forehead, but it doesn't wipe across my skin like it did to Emma. Doesn't erase the death rune. Instead, the scorching digit rotates a hundred and eighty degrees.

I thought I was in pain before, that I could feel my cells being made whole again, but I don't think that's what's happening. I go from feeling a sinister kind of power, to almost normal, and then to feeling torn apart once more, burning with sunlight and energy. Just as I feel consciousness fading, I'm released.

"Miah," Mom says, looking at me with wide eyes.

I lift my arms, watching as the darkness is peeled away by the wind, flitting off in the air like embers. Beneath the cracking exterior, blue light seeps through, flaring brightly. All at once, the remaining exterior bursts away in a surge of light that drops me to my hands and knees. Beneath my clothes, my old self turns to powder and sifts through the gaps, pouring out of me like hourglass sand.

Beneath me, my hands look normal again.

I'm healed. Myself.

I look up at the angel, as it turns its head toward the battle being waged by the Dark, angelic forces, and an armed neighborhood. It's going to leave.

"Wait!" I shout, turning. Beneath the mech, the cage containing Bree... is empty. "No... Where is she?" I scour the battlefield, seeing no sign of her.

Without thinking, I leap up onto the crown of horns, twenty feet off the ground. High on my perch, I have no trouble spotting her, running on all fours, carving a path through a sea of humanity all charging toward and through the gates. "That's her," I shout, pointing to Bree. "You can save her, too."

I turn to the angel, hoping for an answer I can understand. But it doesn't speak. It just points at me, as though to say, 'You.' Electric blue wings flare from its back, extending wide and lifting it away.

"No!' I shout, but it's gone, flying ahead to join the fray. I watch it for a moment, landing amidst a throng of demons, extending glowing blue swords from its forearms, and then attacking with blades and wings, carving a path toward the gate for our people.

I look down at Mom. "You need to go."

"I'm not going to leave you here," she says.

"Allie's up there." I tilt my head toward the gate, where Allie and Jen stand beside Mr. Gearhart, laying down suppressing fire in support of the angels. "She still needs you." I give her a genuine smile, and I'm relieved when my skin doesn't crack open. "I'm good. For the first time in a long time." I look back toward the base. "I can't look away while innocent people die. Not again."

When I turn back to Mom, there are tears in her eyes. I never told her what happened in Afghanistan, but I think she just figured it out. She nods, and says, "Go. Just...go quick."

"That's the plan," I say, and I leap away from the devil, landing thirty feet away and sprinting back into the depths of Hell.

52

Fleeing people see me coming and make way, opening like a zipper, fear turning to confusion, then to hope.

The hell is everyone looking at? I wonder, but I don't stop to ask.

I pass through the gates, back inside the now smoldering base. Stragglers and the dead are all that remain of the captives. The Dark are all outside the walls, or on the walls, fending off the angelic attack. I wish I knew what they really were. All of them. Calling them devils, demons, and angels feels...*off.* They're all advanced, spacefaring alien species who've been trafficking in human beings for thousands of years. For all we know, one of these species might be responsible for the human race's existence.

And if that's true, maybe angels and demons really are the best names. Until I know better.

I scour the grisly courtyard and spot a flash of movement, low to the ground, dashing toward one of the open demon dens. "Bree!"

She either doesn't hear me or ignores my shout, disappearing into the depths.

Damnit.

I look back through the gates, gauging how long I have before everyone has escaped, the angels destroy the gates, or the forces of evil push them back and regain control. Right now, the outcome is up in the air.

Five minutes, I tell myself. In and out. No muss no fuss. Knock her the shit out, take her to an angel, get her fixed up, and then return home to make a big-ass sandwich with a god damned pound of pickles and mayo.

Plan solidified, I step up to the glowing orange tunnel and look into the depths. The tunnel is round and smooth like obsidian. The floor is scratched up into a walkable surface—marred by years of demons passing through.

Runes have been etched into the tunnel's side, glowing orange with a thin trail of flowing magma.

I've been in a cave just once before. When I was a kid. When Dad was still alive. He took me to Polar Caves up by Pinckney, New Hampshire, just past Refuge. One of the most distinct memories was the temperature difference. Stepping from summer heat, into the earth was like walking into air conditioning.

This is different. The cave is hot. Sweltering. The deeper I go, the hotter it gets. The tunnel twists downward, following a random path.

It's a lava tube, I realize, formed long ago, and converted into a tunnel by the Dark. Urgency and the downward slope push and pull me into a run. Just a few steps in, I'm running faster than I ever have before. For a moment, it's invigorating. Then the tunnel opens and the terrain levels out before I'm ready. I fall forward, roll a few times, and slide to a stop.

Scorching heat, like I've placed my skin against a red-hot stove burner, sizzles my arm. I flinch back and climb to my feet, finding myself on the black, crystalline shoreline of an actual lake of fire. Gas rises from within, farting from the magma with twenty-foot-tall plumes of fire.

"You've got to be kidding me." I glance down at my arm. Looks okay, but I don't spend long thinking about it. I'm in a massive cavern, the size of a half dozen superdomes, merged into one. It's a natural wonder on the scale of the Grand Canyon, but it's been marred by construction. Several large pipes descend through the ceiling, branching off into a network of smaller piping that bends and twists around the chamber, each line coming to an end at a downward facing spigot, positioned over a crater into the solid floor.

Curious, I head for the nearest crater.

My stomach turns when I see what's inside. A bulbous larva the size of a football bobbles about. Its mouth is like four beaks working in unison. It gnaws on lumps of flesh slurping from the baseball-sized spigot. The grinders are providing nourishment for a nursery.

But for what?

I move through the field of craters, looking for Bree, but I'm distracted by the nests. There are thousands of them, spread out around the massive space, warmed by the lake of fire, and by an occasional stream of lava flowing from the wall, slithering across the landscape. The air dances with rising waves of heat. It must be more than a hundred degrees in here, but I'm not feeling it. Not like I should.

"Bree!" I call out, my voice echoing and amplified. No way she didn't hear me.

But she's not the only one here.

A slippery flopping sound rises into the hot air. My mind's eye fills in a picture for the sound—oversized shelled snails wrestling in some kind of mating ritual, slathered in olive oil, just waiting to be discovered by a French chef. An unbidden smile manages to find its way onto my face, but it quickly fades when I see the sound's true source.

A coiling black shape twists at the bottom of a crater, surrounded by rotting meat and the remains of a molted larvae carapace.

A parasite.

I look out over the field. They're *all* parasites, suckling on human remains and eventually taking control of a host—human or otherwise. And I'm surrounded by them.

"Bree!" I call out again, my desperation reflecting off the hard ceiling, the walls, and the floor.

Black limbs stretch out from the parasite, spreading wide and pulling itself toward me. I backstep away from it. "I don't think so, you slimy piece of—"

A slurp spins me around. Another parasite, coiled inside a crater, springs out at me like Coily, the purple spring-shaped snake from *Q-Bert*. I let out an uncensored, "Fuck!" and reach out, catching the mind-controlling alien in my hand.

It wraps around my arm, pulling its slick body from my grasp. "No!" I shout, trying to tighten my grip. I'm filled with a new kind of revulsion, powerful and righteous. It fuels me, supercharging my grip.

Something inside me changes. Like nitrous for the soul.

The parasite begins twitching. Then writhing, as though it's being electrocuted. I'm confused about why until I see my hand, glowing with white-hot, blue energy. The parasite goes rigid, its body calcifying and then crumbling to dust in my grip.

"Holy shit..." I look at my hands, normal once more, but somehow different.

Remade.

Capable of who knows what.

The angel didn't just heal me like it did Emma, it remade me into something else. Something more than human. Maybe a little bit...angelic.

Not sure how I feel about that as an overarching concept. It's not that different than how the Dark makes demons, but I'm still me, and very much not an angel. My thoughts are my own. My feelings, too. My transformation into a demon broke down who I was, drowned out my moral compass, and made me embrace the kind of sinister deeds and thoughts I'd been tortured by for so long. This is different. I'm not being controlled, or divinely inspired. I've just been given a gift. How I use it is up to me. And honestly, if my winged friend could speak English and had asked, I would have said yes.

Hell yes.

It's then that I realize how far I jumped earlier. I was so used to being enhanced by my demon self that I didn't notice. *Let's see what I can do,* I think, and I leap into the air just as another parasite lunges. I sail in an arc through the cavern, rising twenty feet in the air and covering twice that distance. At the pinnacle of my jump, I spot Bree, sprinting through the cavern, chasing after something smaller.

She's focused. Locked on her target. Oblivious to the parasites emerging from the nests as she passes, squirming after her, desperate for a host, perhaps aware of the fight above and the knowledge that hosts will be less common.

I land with ease, between a handful of nests. The moment I touch down, the parasites within reach for me. But I'm gone just as quickly as I arrived, adjusting course, and going airborne a second time.

"Bree!" I shout, as I cruise overhead. "Behind you!"

This time, she hears me. Doesn't see me, but follows my warning, craning her head around until she sees the swarm of parasites climbing over each other to reach her. She doesn't flinch. Doesn't panic. She just faces forward, closing in on her target, which I'm unable to see as I land again.

I overshot her by thirty feet. Jumping is fast, but there's not enough control. Thing is, I'm not about to run through the throng of parasites. I might not be a demon, primed for control, but I don't think that would stop them from planting a demonic flag in my lower back and claiming it as their own.

Adjusting my aim again, I leap, trying to get ahead of Bree.

But Bree isn't moving in a straight line, and I'm off target again. I growl in frustration, wishing I had a way to control my path through the air. "C'mon," I shout, and I flex my back.

I'm not sure why.

It's like an instinct. Muscle memory from childhood.

And somehow, my flight path changes. My confusion lasts just a second, which is the exact amount of time it takes me to notice an electric buzzing behind me. I turn my head to the side, see a pair of laser wings emerging from my back, shout, "Holy shit!" and then fall to the ground, crashing before a small, black creature, teeth bared, body shaking.

I smile at the pint-sized savage beast. "Chezy!"

Then he attacks, teeth sinking into my outstretched hand.

53

Sanchez is latched on like a hungry calf on a momma cow's teat. He's not letting go, so I reel him in toward me. He snarls and shakes his head back and forth, claws scraping over the cave floor.

I don't care if he's gone full-on, Thundaar the Barbarian demon dog, Sanchez is my pooch, and he's coming with me. Something that Bree, even in her transformed state understood.

Sanchez thrashes harder when I reach out for him, and he yelps as my hand wraps around the scruff of his neck. Dry, black skin and hair flake off under my hand, creating lines of open, seeping wounds. But the small dog doesn't flinch until my thumb comes to a rest on his forehead.

Light flares from Sanchez's forehead, spilling out around my thumb the same way the angel's had when it healed Emma. *How much did it change me?* I wonder, and I put it to the test, drawing my thumb across Sanchez's forehead. He thrashes and wails like he's being torn apart. Having experienced it myself, that's exactly what it feels like, right down to the bones. It's like death. And then...

Charred flesh falls away from Sanchez. Stick tail wagging, he slowly opens his mouth and gives my finger an apologetic lick.

"Don't sweat it, dude," I tell him, and I lean my forehead against his. "Good to have you back."

A low growl draws my eyes up. Bree is there, low to the ground, stalking toward me, ready to pounce.

"Bree," I say. "It's me. It's Miah."

She creeps closer, black eyes locked onto mine, just waiting for me to flinch, blink, or glance away, which is really hard not to do. In my periphery, a wall of parasites closes in, vying for position, hoping to claim a host.

Bree is primed and ready.

Would probably welcome it.

Might be too far gone to save, but of course, I'm going to try. "It's the hand or a bullet," I tell her, but she's not hearing me. Even if she did, I'm not sure she'd get it. That made as much sense as firm dog shit after a rainstorm. Mostly because I seem to have lost my gun. Killing her would be... personal. A gun provides some mental separation from the act. Breaking her neck with my own hands, not so much.

I tuck Sanchez behind me without taking my eyes off Bree. He sits between my ankles, shaking like a humorless Tickle Me Elmo.

Then, I look away, giving Bree the window of opportunity she's waiting for.

I use the second it takes her to pounce to evaluate the situation. We have maybe ten seconds before the parasites reach us. And they're coming from all sides now.

Bree leaps, sailing toward me, arms outstretched, clawed fingers hooked. She'd fillet me if I let her.

Wasting no time, I catch Bree by the wrists and use momentum to flip her onto the solid cave floor. I cross her arms over her chest and then sit on them. I place one hand behind her head, say, "Sorry," and press my thumb against the indented death rune.

Whatever this power is, it requires no thought from me. It's automatic, flaring to life on contact with the rune. Bree's furious roar transforms into an anguished, high-pitched squeal. Unlike Sanchez, I'm awash in images of Bree's life, from before the Three Days of Darkness until this moment. I feel the dichotomy of who she once was, and who she's been turned into. I also get a sense for who she will become. And it is...absolutely bad ass.

My thumb slides across her forehead.

Her small body convulses, ash falling away, revealing human skin and a mostly bald head. Pain lances up through my hand and arm, forcing me to yank back.

And just in time.

The most ambitious parasite is upon us, lunging toward my face. I swipe out with my fist, intending to back hand the living black loogie away. Instead, I sever it in half with the luminous blue sword—*extending from my wrist.*

"Holy shit," I say, and then I correct myself. "Holy sword!"

I focus on my other arm, willing a second sword into existence. I feel a kind of tickling energy and then this supernatural light extends from the top of my forearm. I don't know what the hell this is, but I like it. Just before the wave of parasites reach me, I flex my back like I did when I was in flight, unfurling my buzzing energy wings.

The ravenous parasites are undaunted by the sight of me. It's a mistake.

I swing with both arms, and both wings, cleaving dozens of parasites at a time, sending the rent bodies sprawling over the cavern floor. I spin and swing, becoming a flowing blur of blue light.

And then...they stop coming.

Sizzling remains of a hundred parasites lie around me. All across the cavern the nests are quiet. The remaining parasites and larvae are lying low and holding still. The enemy is in their midst, and the demon primed to be a host has been purified.

Mostly.

I crouch over Bree, swords fizzling out of existence, wings furling down from whence they came. "Hey."

Her eyes are open a crack. She smiles. "You're an angel."

"Or something," I say, not remotely interested in being an official representative of what that label stands for. I don't have any answers about what I am or who the angelic beings are.

"I saw your wings," she says, like that is all the evidence she needs.

"Cool, right?"

She nods, and her eyes drift to the ceiling. Her brow furrows. "Where are we?"

"What's the last thing you remember?" I ask.

"You...hit my head." She lifts a hand to her forehead, rubbing it, but mostly inspecting the death rune, which is mostly faded, but still present—like a scar.

"Sorry about that."

She shrugs. "I was going to hurt someone. I'm glad you stopped me."

"Well, where we are now is someplace we don't want to stay. Can you get up?"

Bree attempts to sit up, but she doesn't make it far before collapsing back. "It's okay," I tell her. "Just relax. I got you."

"I know you do, silly."

I scoop her up, cradling her in one arm, and I bend down to pick up Sanchez with my free hand. "I got you too, buddy." That's when I notice a scar on his forehead, too. The angel did a better job with Emma, fully restoring her and erasing the evidence. Might mean that I need practice. Might also mean that it was the best that could be done for them.

"Hang on to my neck," I say, and I tuck Sanchez in like a football. I brace myself to leap across the cavern, but I freeze when a shadow flows into the cavern and settles down between us and the distant exit.

It's a new species, twice the size of a human being, demonic wings sprouted from its back. Its blackened, charred, batlike body is both emaciated and powerful, twitching with nervous energy. Coin-sized, dark gray pill bugs scurry all over its body. *Larvae,* I realize, before they're big enough to suckle on human slurry. A sheet of dark skin peels away from the demon's shoulder. The larvae nearby wriggle toward it, consuming the flaking flesh. Whatever this is, it's protecting the nursery, and feeding the young with its own body.

A collection of eyes covers the top of its head. All of them black and unblinking, capable of seeing all around. Literal eyes in the back of its head. Mandibles twitch around a small mouth. Eager and agitated.

"It's like a bat and a spider had a baby," Bree says, and that's pretty accurate.

I nod and hold Sanchez out to her. "Hold on to Chezy, okay?"

She takes him, wraps him in her arms, and nods. He licks her arm furiously, happy for the attention, or maybe just thankful that she came back for him.

I focus on the demon standing in my way. It opens its wings wide, spreads its arms, and splays its three-fingered, claw-tipped hands, ready to throw down. A four-armed parasite rises from the small of its back, writhing and hungry. Standing twice my height, the thing is intimidating. If I wasn't on the tail end of an all you can eat nightmare, I'd probably have pissed myself. But I'm kind of numb to horrible things now, and I'm not exactly defenseless.

"Going to give you one chance," I tell it. "Get the hell out of my way…" A hot blue sword slips out of my free arm. From my back, electric wings extend, illuminating the field of dead around me. "Or…"

Pretty sure the round eyes are incapable of expression. They're black and unmoving. Hollow. But the creature's body language shifts. It stands back and tall, its broad wings wrapping around its torso, protecting the larvae. I stop short of thinking about this new demon as a mother. That role might belong to the parasite on its back. The winged creature is more likely another unwilling species recruited to fulfill the role of parasite day care worker.

I keep my sword pointed at the creature as I work my way around it through the cavern. When it's no longer in my way, I retract the sword into my arm. What it does next will bother me forever.

It nods.

Like we've come to an agreement. An understanding. I'm leaving it alive to carry on its nefarious ways, and it's allowing me to walk away with Bree and Sanchez.

This isn't like Afghanistan, I think. These aren't innocent bystanders. These are monsters, feeding on the flesh of human beings.

They're also babies, born into a life they didn't ask for.

So, I nod in return and leap away, soaring across the chamber on the wings of a futuristic, laser-winged eagle. I hit the cavern floor, running, and not growing weary. Then I haul ass up the tunnel, emerging from the fiery depths, walking amidst a field of carnage, and not growing faint. I've gone into the bowels of hell and come out feeling renewed.

Then I see what's left of the forces of good and evil, fighting over the gates, and I realize we're nearly out of time. "Hold on," I say, and I leap into the sky.

54

I hang in the air for a moment, Bree and Sanchez clutched in my arms, buzzing wings holding us aloft in a hot updraft that rises from the fortress walls. I see the battlefield like a landscape painting, everything frozen in place for a moment.

The neighborhood fighters have fallen back to the gate, fending off the few remaining demons while the last of the humans escape. Mom is with them now, standing beside Allie, who's got a cut on her cheek, but she's still on her feet, still armed, and still firing. Next to Allie is—if I'm a man of my word—my new daughter, Sung. She's dropped her rifle and is firing a handgun. Dave is behind them, handing out magazines from a satchel. Emma is there, too, back on her feet, held up by Steph and Jen. Neither are armed or fighting, but I suspect Emma doesn't want to leave her sister and father again.

Along with a dozen other people I don't recognize, they form a wall of bullets that the demons can't penetrate, but they've got to be nearly out of ammo. There's only a dozen stragglers still running toward the gate, navigating a battlefield full of angels and demons and devils, all attacking mercilessly. The angels are better equipped, more mobile, and trained fighters. But the Dark's forces are vast, savage, and fearless. Right now, I'm not sure who's going to win the fight, but I suspect this isn't about winning. It's about setting the people free—a small attack in a larger war—designed to cut off vital supplies. Human meat.

When people imagine intergalactic war and our place in it, in movies or books or comics, we're commonly underdogs, but central to victory. Star Wars. Star Trek. Battlestar Galactica. Independence Day. The universe would be lost without us.

Reality is a little starker.

We're chicken nuggets.

Sure, some of the chickens are putting up a fight, but without the galactic federation of PETA angels doing most of the work, our neighborhood—our planet—would be easily overrun. Again. As it has been who knows how many times in the past.

How embarrassing would that be for humanity? Saved by the universe's anti-meat movement, thought of throughout the cosmos as nourishment for more refined alien species. Hubris keeps us from considering the possibility.

The only evidence I see against it right now is me.

Even PETA wouldn't give chickens laser wings. Because chickens are mindless. Because they'd kill each other and every living thing that ever got close to them.

Which begs the question, how am I different from a laser chicken?

Below me, one of the remaining turrets turns away from its target in the atmosphere—a great starship, now smoldering and retreating. The big gun rotates toward the battlefield, taking aim at both angel and demon, willing to kill their own to take out the enemy.

"You okay for a little more excitement?" I ask Bree.

She nods. "I'm feeling...better." Kid's not a demon anymore, but she's still fearless. "What are you going to do?"

I smile down at her. "Be better than a laser chicken."

Before she can ask what the fart-stanky hell I'm talking about, I furl my wings back and dive, aiming for the two cannons about to fire.

"Yeah!" Bree shouts as we plummet. Sanchez yips along with her.

I let out a, "Whooo!" and I extend my new wings as I drop between the guns.

There's a gentle tug on my back. Nothing painful. Almost imperceptible. But the effect is exactly what I'd hoped it would be. I turn back for a look, as I swoop low and out over the battlefield, watching the two cannons fall away. A damaged turret explodes, crumbling a portion of the wall.

Bree, Sanchez, and I soar toward the gate. Mom sees us coming and waves us down, not in a 'Hey, it's great to see you,' kind of way, but more in a 'Get the hell down here, shit's going sideways,' kind of way. Shit's been going sideways for a few days, so whatever Mom has to say must be important.

I flare my wings wide, slowing my descent. I touch down gently, placing Bree on her feet, and holding Sanchez out to Mom.

She puts a hand on my cheek, "Your father would be proud."

"Both of them," I add, bringing tears to Mom's eyes. She nods, hand over her mouth.

"Miah..." I turn to find a wide-eyed Allie stepping toward me, gaze flicking from my eyes to my wings and back again.

"Sorry," I say, retracting the wings with a thought. "It's me. I'm good."

Allie throws her arms around me, squeezing me tight, oblivious to the guns, the shouting, and the explosions for a moment. Before she releases me, a second voice shouts, "Father!" Sung wraps her arms around my waist. I'm thrown for a moment, but then I put one of my arms around her, the other still around Allie.

Mom leans down, making eye contact. She mouths, "Father?"

"I made a pinkie promise."

I raise a hand to say, 'What can you do,' and then extend my pinkie to Sung. "Made a promise."

Sung links her little finger with mine and says, "Pinkie promise."

"This is sweet and all," Mr. Gearhart says. He's like a real live action hero, the blood, the ash, and the regrets of his enemies covering his military body armor, his gun smoldering along with his thick bearded face. "The gates are being shut down."

"That's what I wanted to tell you," Mom says.

"Shut down or destroyed?" I ask.

"Same difference," Jen says, putting her hand on my shoulder. "Good to see you, Miah." Her smile just about kills me, and it is so casual I'm positive she and her father didn't see my new winged self.

Mr. Gearhart points to the gate and says, to me. "Time to go. Get them through."

"Actually, sir," I say, giving Jen a smile and a wink. "You get them through, I'll cover you."

"Son, we don't have time to measure—"

I unfurl my blue laser wings.

Those who hadn't seen them during the chaos take a step back, feeling some good ol' U.S. Military style shock and awe. Then I extend the swords from my arms. Mr. Gearhart has seen enough angels in action to understand the firepower I'm packing.

"Okay," he says, "You cover us." He steps toward the gate and stops. Gives me a wry smile and offers his hand. When I shake it, he pulls me in close. "Make it home, and I might let you see my daughter again." He gives me a wink and releases my hand.

"Yes, sir," I say, and I turn to Mom and Allie. "Love you guys."

"Love you, too!" Sung says, beaming with pride over her winged pinkie promise dad.

"We all do," Emma adds, tugging at my heartstrings. She's weak, but she's recovering, hanging on to Steph, who stays silent, but who's moved by the moment. I thought I didn't have a community, that I was alone after my friends in Afghanistan were killed. But I've never been alone. I had all these people, family, and friends, around me all this time.

"Oh geez," Allie says. "He's gonna cry." Then to Mr. Gearhart, she says, "He's a crier."

"The strongest men are," Mr. Gearhart says, and then he barks out a, "Let's move!" and he heads for the gate.

"Miah," Bree says, and then she gets a fiendish look in her eyes. "Go kick their asses."

I give her a two fingered salute. When she returns it, I leap into the air and soar just a few feet before folding my wings back and dropping to the ground. While the neighborhood caught up, two demons snuck past the angelic wall. They're racing toward me, frothing at the mouth, tendrils going wild. They're frenzied. Impossible to predict.

So, I wait, wings curled forward, arm blades extended.

One demon breaks left, the other right—order amidst their chaos. They leap at me from opposite sides, but I'm ready for it, swiping out with wings and arms.

Black dust poofs into the air, followed by two corpses falling in opposite directions. One has been cut in half and the other is missing a head. The blazing weaponry extending from my body didn't just cut through flesh just as easily as it did metal, it also cauterized the wounds, keeping me from looking like Carrie after the prom. The demons are definitely dead, but the parasites on their backs fight to reach me, either supremely dedicated to killing their prey or hoping to claim a still living host.

"Not going to happ—"

I'm struck from behind and sent sprawling. Before I hit the ground, I'm caught, my thigh searing with pain. I scream out and look up into the beady black eyes of the winged nursery demon. Our understanding has come to an end now that the young are safe, and it's here for vengeance. It's two-toed feet are wrapped around my leg, talons buried into my flesh.

My first thought is, *It's going to drop me*, but then remember I can fly, and I swipe up with a wing. With a flick of its leg, the demon tosses me away. My strike misses, and the momentum keeps me from breaking my fall. I spin around, facing forward, about to unfurl my wings when I collide with a wall of red light and slide right through.

Disoriented by my passage through the portal, I fail to stop my fall and collide with the ground, rolling to a stop atop what feels like a comfortable, but damp bed.

"Why did it throw me home?" I wonder, eyeing the portal, waiting for it to follow me through. But the demon never comes.

Was it just trying to get rid of me?

Water seeps around my feet, drawing my eyes down to the ground. A puddle has formed around me, drawn out of the ground by my weight.

The purple ground.

It looks like a sponge.

What...

Realization sets my heart pounding. A quick look around confirms my fear.

The landscape is mostly barren—endless purple sponge pocked by large swirling pools of water.

This...isn't Earth.

I'm on another planet.

Some of the gates might lead home, but not all of them.

Hell is an interdimensional hub, through which the parasitical Dark claim and enslave their victims.

Before I can ruminate on the mind-boggling revelation, the portal's red wall starts flickering.

It's closing!

I lunge forward, slipping over the soggy terrain until I push off with my wings, pulsing up into the air and through the portal just as it snaps shut.

Hell greets me with its stink and heat. I fall to the ground and roll to a stop on the much less forgiving volcanic rock.

Just as I open my eyes to see a smoldering starship falling from the night sky, the winged demon fills my vision, descending from above with an ungodly shriek, ready to rend me to pieces. I shout in surprise and react out of fear, raising my palms over my face like it will help.

Blue light blossoms from my hands and launches skyward, striking the creature's chest, flaring out around its body. The demon's fall slows and then...stops, as the creature turns to ash and floats away.

"Seriously..." I say, looking at my dimming hands. "What the hell?"

I sit up and find the angel who gave me these powers looking at me. I sense surprise in its expressionless, helmeted face. Then it raises a hand and points to the portal leading home.

All around the battlefield, portals are winking out.

Message received.

I get to my feet, sprint toward the portal, and throw myself into the air. While my wings function like you'd expect, providing lift to keep me aloft, they're also a source of propulsion. I accelerate at the speed of my imagination, launching toward the gate home as it starts to flicker.

And then winks out.

55

TWO MONTHS LATER

"Just ketchup," I say, "thanks."

Steph squirts a line of red along the top of my hotdog, cooked by Mr. Gearhart. "Beans? Potato salad? Corn on the cob?"

"Just the dog for now," I say, and I accept the paper plate holding a hot dog that's almost twice the length of the bun. It's a 'man's man' hot dog, bought and cooked by Mr. Gearhart, who decided to throw the first neighborhood get-together since the Three Days of Darkness. The event claimed half of the neighborhood's residents, including Bree's father, Dave's family, Mrs. Gearhart, and Rich. Collectively grieving has been helpful. I now know everyone on the street, in part because I'm making an effort, but also because many of them saw what I did in Hell.

The wings.

The swords.

All that crazy shit.

Emma, Bree, and I have been welcomed home like soldiers from war used to be. Though there is a little distrust lingering. I don't blame them. We *were* running around looking like demons for a bit. But a lot of people saw us get healed by the angel, and even more saw me flying around. Witnessed my dramatic return to Earth, flying through the gate just before it closed, crashing to the ground, wingless and powerless once more.

I climb into a hammock stretched between two pines at the back yard's periphery, clutching my paper plate with both hands. The bed of ropes rocks back and forth for a moment. Balance regained, I lift my foot, swing myself into the hammock, and nearly flip over. "Shit!"

I splay my legs wide and stretch an arm out. The move keeps me from flipping, but it knocks the hot dog over. The bun topples. The meat rolls out and across the plate like an ink roller, leaving two lines of red before leaping onto my shirt and sticking. "Shit, shit, shit."

After a moment of wriggling, I'm balanced enough to pluck the hot dog from my chest and place it back in the bun. Fully recovered, I glance at the gathering of people, and find an audience watching me, all of them smiling, including several men and women who haven't fully trusted me yet. The guy who can't manage a hot dog and a hammock is probably not a threat.

Then again, I'm the guy who, prior to the Three Days, wore all black, went heavy on the eyeliner, and drove a loud, old, red Trans Am like I was David Wooderson from *Dazed and Confused.* I was untrusted. A stain on the pristine neighborhood. Then I went and turned into a demon. And finally, into an angel with inhuman powers.

My face confuses people, but they're coming around. Now I just need to spill a drink on my pants and trip into the pool.

Speaking of...I turn to the sound of laughter. Bree, Sung, Allie, Emma, and Dave are splashing around with other neighborhood kids, getting in a final swim before autumn beckons the winter and a crap-ton of snow. This Christmas is going to be hard for everyone, and not just in our neighborhood.

The Three Days was a localized event, stretching from Strafford to the seacoast, enveloping Southern Maine and stopping just short of Massachusetts. Just over five thousand people are missing and presume-ed dead—or worse. Would have been five hundred more if we hadn't staged our revolt when we did.

The rest of the world watched from a distance, marveling at the massive object orbiting the planet, plunging a quarter of the country and some of Canada into a shaded penumbra, while New Hampshire's seacoast was locked into a persistent umbra, blocking out the sun's light, and somehow disabling artificial light sources. Theories abound, but no one has answers. Several claim to, but scientists with the rare combin-ation of brains and humility admit it will be generations before we have any hope of understanding what happened, and how it was accomplished. Based on a reexamined historical record, it seems likely that the Dark visit Earth every five-hundred years or so, striking less populated areas and leaving few left alive to tell the tale. This time, we won't forget, and it's possible we'll be ready for them if they come back again.

All we really know for sure is that multiple species of aliens exist and they're not all friendly. But some of them have our backs. I think. It was hard to get a true sense of the angels' agenda. The Dark are their enemy, of that there is no doubt. But was the attack on the meat factory a rescue, or a coincidence? The angel I encountered felt cold and emotionless, but not indifferent. It cared enough to heal those of us on the verge of being claimed by the darkness, and it gave me the power to save my family. I'm choosing to believe they're the good guys, and that if the Dark return, the angelic aliens will have our backs again. Because if Hell returns to Earth for a round two anytime soon, we'll be mostly helpless again.

The United States military attempted to enter the darkness for three days. Jets fell from the sky. Vehicle lights and night vision failed. Everyone who entered the darkness was never seen again, including three special ops teams. Best of the best, they say. None of them managed to do what our neighborhood did. I'm now proud to call this my home, even if the houses are a little gaudy. The people are New Englanders, through and through, pulling together in times of crisis, overcoming hardships, and bonding over backyard barbecues. Wish I'd been able to see it before.

Aside from brief encounters at the grocery store, with Brad, who is now with Laurie, I was missing out on an expanded family. On friendships. On life.

I won't make that mistake again.

A napkin appears in front of my face. Mom smiles down at me. "That was slick."

I take the napkin, wiping my shirt. "Thanks."

"Nervous about tomorrow?"

I shrug. "Are you?"

About two weeks after the Three Days ended, our house had become home to two orphans—Sung and Dave. Mom rose to the occasion, caring for both. Allie and I do our best to help, but neither of us have the parental acumen of our own mother. As a result, she's officially adopted both Dave and Sung, who now calls her 'Mom,' and me 'Dad,' which might be the strangest thing to come out of this mess. I'm going to do my best to help raise Sung and Dave, but I'm not ready to be a full-time father.

There are other things I need to take care of first.

In the event's wake, there are a lot of broken families. Parents without kids, and kids without parents. To help alleviate the crisis, adoptions are being pushed through at record speed, flattening the litany of speed bumps that would normally keep Sung from being adopted.

"I'm looking forward to it," Mom says. "Feeling okay about living with three women?"

"Me and Chezy have enough testosterone to go around."

She shakes her head at me, and then raises her eyebrows toward Jen as she loads a cooler with fresh soda cans. Jen's dressed in a rainbow striped bikini. Absolutely stunning. We've spent a lot of time together, helping with kids, participating in rebuilding projects, but we're rarely alone. The spark is there, but it hasn't had a lot of time to build into a fire. "Gonna put all that testosterone to good use?"

"Oh! Mom. God. Stop."

She has a laugh at my expense. "They're rushing marriages, too, you know."

I choke on my response when Jen approaches and says, "Hey."

"I'll leave you two to it." Mom places a hand on Jen's shoulder and gives her a wink.

"Scooch," Jen says, motioning for me to move over.

"Uhh," I say, trying to make room on the hammock without turning myself into a circus act.

Jen all but throws herself into the hammock, perfectly balancing it with minimum effort. "It's easy once you get used to it."

"Practice makes perfect, huh?"

She turns to me, our faces inches apart. "That's what I've heard."

I'm frozen. Powerless in her gaze. After a few seconds, I gasp a breath. She laughs, then kisses me on the forehead where my death rune turned life rune used to be. Her fingers find mine, our hands interlinking.

I feel at peace, no marijuana necessary, despite the horrific events that led me here. Not because the effect of either rune is lingering. My emotions are my own again. Complex and a struggle, on occasion. But I'm no longer facing my demons alone—real, imagined, or in the past. I fled to Mary Jane when all I really needed was to let the right people past my defenses.

"Room for one more?" Allie asks. "Or would that make things weird?"

I lift my free arm and invite my towel-wrapped sister onto the hammock. She climbs in with the same grace as Jen, no risk of overturning.

"How are you all so good at hammocking?"

"A basic sense of balance is a good start." Emma climbs in beside Jen, snuggling up to her sister.

"This thing have a weight limit?" I ask.

"If that was a fat joke," Emma says, "we can take this to the parking lot."

"No way I'm messing with you." I lift a fist, and she bumps it.

We settle in, relaxing, rocked back and forth by a cool breeze that forces squealing kids back under the pool's water. We watch the shifting maple leaves overhead, luminous in the sun's light, framed by a wonderfully blue sky.

EPILOGUE

I wake in bed, soaked with sweat, chest heaving with something like panic...but not. It's a sense. Of wrongness. Of evil. Powerful enough to wake me from a dream involving me, Scarlett Johansson, and a pair of taco print socks.

My phone reveals the time. 3:00 am.

I rise from bed, wide awake. I'm already dressed in shorts and a T-shirt, so I throw on my shoes and do a quick inspection of the house. Nothing amiss.

The new front door opens smoothly. I sneak out into the night, not wanting to be seen...which is hard, in the well-lit neighborhood. But I welcome the electric glow. It's the first sign that things aren't as bad as they could be. I turn my head up to the sky. The Moon shines down on me.

Good, I think. *That's go—*

"Took you long enough."

"Holy shit!" I shout, turning around to find Bree crouched on the porch's railing, all ninja-like. "Geez, kid. Nearly gave me a heart attack."

"I'm almost eight, you know," she says.

"Can you get off the railing, please?"

She rolls her eyes at my concern. "Is Jen your girlfriend now? I saw her kiss your head today."

I smile at the memory. "I hope so."

"But you don't know." She scoffs at me, shaking her head. "You need to grow a p—"

"You need to spend less time with Emma," I say.

Bree shrugs. "She gets me."

She's got me there. Emma is the only other person Bree can talk to about what it was like to be a demon.

With one significant difference. "You sure about this?" I ask. "I mean, you're still a seven-year-old."

"I'll be eight in two months," she says.

I already know there's no talking her out of this, so I head down the steps and say, "Let's check it out."

She hops down from the railing, chases me down the steps, and follows me across the street. We pause at the edge of the woods, by the house that used to belong to Larry, but was recently bought by people we have yet to see. They come and go on occasion, parking in the garage, but they don't come outside, and they don't answer the door.

"C'mon," Bree says, stepping into the darkness and leading the way. We move through what's left of the forest, not speaking, but nothing close to silent, crunching and snapping charred twigs. That changes when we reach the clearing containing the now defunct gate. I tear apart the yellow tape cordoning the area off, and I step through the field of fallen trees.

Everything is quiet now.

The gate hasn't so much as flickered since the Three Days ended. The government is studying several of the nearly one hundred gates, but all they've been able to discern is that they're identical. As a result, most of them are now abandoned, to be dissected and removed at some future date.

"You feel that, right?" I ask. It's like the gate is emanating energy, like it's excited about something.

"Uh-huh." She sniffs. "We're not alone."

I test the air, but I smell nothing, relieved by the absence of sulfur.

"Up ahead," Bree says. "In front of the gate."

I see him. A young man, dressed a bit like me—shorts and a lime green T-shirt. On the outside, he's nothing special, but I sense power within him. So does Bree.

"Switch me on," she says.

"Not yet."

"He's not the only one." Bree's instincts are sharp. If she says there's someone else, there is. But we don't know if they're a threat, and I'm not going to exacerbate the situation.

Yet.

"Hey," the kid ahead of us says. "You guys whisper loud." He's got an edge about him, and a slight Bostonian accent.

"What are you doing here?" I ask, approaching cautiously.

"Live here," he says. "The new neighbors."

"This isn't part of the neighborhood," Bree points out.

"Yeah, but we bought it, too. The land." He's got a smirk on his face and a gleam in his eye. Mischief personified, and something else. Like confidence, but different. Like he's not afraid and has no concept of what it means to feel afraid.

"Going to ask one more time," I say, "and then I'm going to assume the worst about you."

"That'd be a mistake," says a woman from the darkness behind us.

"Told you," Bree says. "Two of them."

"Kid has a good nose," the young man says. "Probably best to keep it out of our business."

Our business?

I'm about to throttle this dude. Then I see his T-shirt.

"Poison, huh?" I motion to my KISS shirt. "I prefer a little more make-up, but 'Nothin' But A Good Time' is hard to beat."

"Sweet talk won't work." He squints at me. "What are you doing here?"

"I asked first."

"Put your dicks away, boys," the young woman says, stepping around me and Bree, giving us a wide berth. She's black, her hair done up in two pom-poms. And she looks tough as hell, full of actual confidence. "I think we're on the same side."

"As long as you're human," I say.

"Does *kind of human* count?" the young man asks.

I consider our own situation. "Good enough for me."

"You sure?" he says, and then he hovers a few feet over the ground. I'm surprised, but I don't flinch. I've seen stranger.

"Seriously, Henry," the young woman says, "you don't need to measure dicks."

"She talks about dicks a lot," Bree says.

"Sorry," the young woman says. "How old are you, anyway?"

"Seven," I say.

"Almost eight," Bree adds.

"Why do you have an almost eight-year-old out here in the middle of the night?" The woman squints at me, suspicious.

"Because she's not a normal almost eight-year-old," I say.

"Can we measure dicks?" Bree says, bouncing from foot to foot. "Please, oh please, oh please."

I sigh. "I'm Miah. This is Bree."

The woman steps closer. Holds out her hand. I shake it, and she says, "Sarah. You're the ones who helped save a bunch of people, right?"

"How do you know about that?"

"People talk," she says.

"Internet mostly," Henry adds.

"Why are you here?" I ask again. "Really."

"We're not sure," Sarah admits. "We felt...drawn to this gate."

"It knows you're here," Bree says.

"Well, that's creepy AF," Henry says.

"What makes you different?" I ask. "Why would the gate respond to your presence?"

Henry and Sarah share a look. She shakes her head at him, giving him a wide-eyed, 'Don't you dare' stare. Then he blurts out, "We're gods! Zeus is our father! Helen of Sparta is our mother! Oh my god, that felt good. Do you know how long I've waited to tell someone that?"

Sarah thrusts her hands at us. "Well, why did you tell *them*?!"

"Because they're like us," he says. "I mean, not gods, but not human, either."

Bree's 'oh, please' dance gets more frantic.

"Fine," I say to her, and then to Sarah I ask, "Can you fly? You might need to give us some space."

Sarah shakes her head. "I'll be fine."

"Oookay." I turn to Bree. "Try not to hurt anyone."

She nods, lifts her face to me, and closes her eyes.

I share one last concerned look with Sarah, who looks unsure. Then I press my thumb against Bree's forehead. Light flares. Bree cringes in pain. And then I swipe my thumb to the left, revealing her hidden death rune. Bree's body transforms, going black and crusty. She drops to her hands and feet, claws extending. Frenzied energy overtakes her. She sprints away on all fours, dashing around the three of us, and then lunging for Sarah.

"Look ou—"

Bree reaches Sarah before I finish my warning, swiping her claws across Sarah's cheek and lunging off her shoulder. Bree then lands and springs away again, calming down a little bit.

"That. Was. Awesome!" Henry shouts. "What is she?"

"Demon," I say.

Bree leaps to my side, able to fully control herself around me. "Demon Dog," she says, and she looks up at me. "And Laser Chicken!"

"Laser Chicken?" Sarah asks, her cheek unharmed by Bree's razor-sharp claws.

"Fine..." I look down at Bree. "Give me some space." She dashes away, and I flex my back, extending the bright blue laser wings I've been hiding from everyone but Bree since the gate closed behind me. I lift off into the air opposite Henry, wings buzzing with energy.

He's elated. When the laser blades extend from my arms, he breaks out laughing.

"These guys are great!" Henry said.

"What's on your foreheads?" Sarah asks.

I point to Bree. "Death rune." I point to my forehead, and say, "Life rune." Ever since leaving Hell, whenever I use my newfound abilities, the rune on my forehead glows blue, like I've been filled with some kind of supernatural energy. I think it's probably some kind of technology, like super-advanced nano-bots, but I have no way to prove it.

"So," Sarah says, "A demon, an angel, and a couple of gods." She smiles. "It's fate, I guess."

"You're serious about the god thing?" I ask.

"Zeus is our father. Apparently, it's in our DNA."

"Maybe...the DNA that makes you gods isn't...supernatural," I say. "Maybe it's..." I turn to the sky. "Maybe that's why the gate is responding to you. Can we try something?"

"Long as it ain't freaky," Sarah says.

Henry raises his hand. "I can do freaky."

I land and sheath my laser appendages. I head for the gate while Bree hops around me. She'll need to burn off some energy before she lets me change her back. We've been testing our abilities most nights for the past month. So far, there don't seem to be any negative side effects, but Bree needs to work on self-control. I get the impression Henry does as well.

I stop before the defunct gate, looking up at the two tall spires.

"Now what?" Henry asks.

"Touch it," I say. "One of you on each side."

"Uhh," Sarah says.

"I don't know why," I say. "It just feels right."

"C'mon," Henry says, already placing his hands against one of the two spires. Sarah heads for the second, pauses for a moment, and then places her hands against the rock-like surface.

Nothing happens.

"Don't know what to tell you, dude. But I don't think—"

The gate flares to life, a sheet of red energy spreading between the columns.

Sarah and Henry think their DNA is from the gods, but I think we've just proven the gods weren't from this planet, and they're not entirely human, just like Bree...and me.

"Don't let go," I tell them, stepping toward the gate.

"What are you doing?" Sarah looks about ready to abort.

"I need to see. What's on the other side."

"We need to close this," Sarah says. "Before they come back."

"Thirty seconds," I say, and then I turn to Bree. "Stay here."

She frowns, but she doesn't disagree.

I step through the gate, and out into Hell...reformed.

A smoldering crater is all that remains of the facility. Most of the gates have been destroyed, but a few still stand. The battlefield is littered with bodies. I'd like to believe the angels did this, that they wiped the Dark out, but the warzone is littered with bodies—human, demon, and angel alike. The wreckage of several angelic battleships smoke in the distance.

Whatever did this was more powerful than either alien species, leaving no trace—or bodies of their own.

Well. Shit.

Time up, I step back through the gate and emerge in the dark woods. The moment I appear, Sarah yanks her hands off the column, closing the gate.

"What did you see?" Sarah asks.

I crouch down in front of Bree, feeling overwhelmed. She lowers her head and allows me to swipe my thumb back across her forehead, changing her back into her sweet seven-year-old human self.

"What's it like?" Henry asks. "It's hell, right?"

"What did you see?" Sarah asks again, hand on my shoulder, demanding an answer.

"Something bad," Bree says, reading my emotions.

"We've heard the stories," Sarah says. "Hell is pretty bad."

I meet Sarah's brown eyes, wondering if the four of us meeting was fate, and I say, "It's something worse."

AUTHOR'S NOTE

As many of you know, my personal struggles (which I talk about openly and publicly) sometimes find their way into my novels. *Infinite* and *Alter* in particular are pure expressions of the physical and psychologyical... discomfort I've been experiencing over the past five years. Miah's journey is yet another parallel, as I've searched for solutions to PTSD and nerve pain that may or may not be connected. Having ruled out a brain tumor, cured Bartonellosis, and tested negative for a litany of other things—there are two remaining theories: an autoimmune disease and... it's all in my head—which honestly feels right. That doesn't mean I'm crazy (though everything else in *The Dark* might), or making it up, it means that the Bartonella might have rewired my nervous system so that when I am exposed to emotional stimuli experienced during my illness (stress, anxiety, fear), I experience the same symptoms as though I am still sick! Brains are weird.

I have yet to try marijuana as a solution, but I have attempted many of the other techniques Miah utilizes in this novel—with little success. And yes, laughter yoga is a real thing! Google it. While Miah's story might be viewed by many people as a tragic horror tale, for me it was a journey toward the hope of one day overcoming PTSD and this B.S. nerve pain. As much as I would love for an angelic maybe alien-thing to wipe its thumb across my forehead and cure what ails me, healing will come from finding peace, loving my work and spreading my madness around a little bit. If you're dealing with PTSD or chronic illness, I hope you share in my hope for a pain free future, or at least making peace with the possibility that this might be life from now until the end. Doesn't mean we can't experience joy, enjoy a good novel, or pursue our dreams.

Over the past year, which has been rough for everyone, the growing fan community at facebook.com/groups/JR.Tribe has been a great source of positivity, encouragement and camaraderie for me and other members.

If you're a fan looking for an amazing group of like-minded peeps, come on over. If you just want to stay up to date on the novels and other things, visit bewareofmonsters.com and sign up for the newsletters. And, as always, if you want to help The Dark become a hit, be sure to post reviews on Amazon, Audible and Goodreads. Every single one helps a ton.

If you didn't recognize the characters, Sarah and Henry, in the Epilogue, you definitely need to check out my novel, *Tribe*, narrated in the audiobook edition by R.C. Bray, just like *The Dark*. And while you're out and about on the Internet, visit bewareofmonsters.com/thedarkart to view a color version of the mock comic book cover and character sketches for Demon Dog and Laser Chicken! Finally, if you're tired of hearing about my deep emotional connections to my darkest stories, have no fear, the book I'm writing now—*Mind Bullet*—is gleefully bonkers. Until then...

—Jeremy Robinson

ACKNOWLEDGMENTS

Over the past few years, for a variety of reasons, the majority of my sales have shifted from Amazon e-books to audiobooks, which has led to my books receiving several awards, me becoming a *New York Times* bestseller, and me snagging the #1 spot on Audible several times. All of this is made possible by ACX.com and the good people there supporting my continued success. I'm looking at you, Otto and Scott. Thank you! And we can't talk about audiobooks without addressing the man responsible for making this audiobook sound as good as it does—R.C. Bray, who is reading this for the audiobook and probably feeling a little awkward about it. Thanks for continuing to support indie writers despite your meteoric fame.

Kane Gilmour, as always, your diligent work and endless support keeps the books on schedule and as good as they can be, despite whatever faults I bring to the table. Roger Brodeur, Heather Beth, Julie Cummings Carter, Philip Clinton, Paul Condon, Elizabeth Cooper, Dustin Dreyling, Joseph Firoozmand, Donna Fisher, Dee Haddrill, Justin Hoer, Andre Jenkin, Becki Tapia Laurent, Jennifer Lynne, Rian Martin, Stefanie Maubach, Kyle Mohr, Steven Newell, K.L. Phelps (Get well soon!), and Jeff Sexton, you guys continue to make me look like I understand grammar and know how to spell and type better than I do. Thanks for the awesome proofreading. Thanks also to Rian Martin and Rene Ramirez for Spanish language translation, so I could get some art instructions to Columbian artist Juan Kijo, who did the great illustration for the mock comic cover of *Demon Dog and Laser Chicken*. Tori Paquette, huge thanks for translation help on the Hebrew in this book. I have a habit of using other languages in my novels and then worrying about whether or not I got it right. This time, I'm not worried at all!

—JR

ABOUT THE AUTHOR

Jeremy Robinson is the *New York Times* and #1 Audible bestselling author of over sixty novels and novellas, including *Infinite, The Others*, and *NPC*, as well as the Jack Sigler thriller series, and *Project Nemesis*, the highest selling, original (non-licensed) kaiju novel of all time. He's known for mixing elements of science, history and mythology, which has earned him the #1 spot in Science Fiction and Action-Adventure, and secured him as the top creature feature author. Many of his novels have been adapted into comic books, optioned for film and TV, and translated into fourteen languages. He lives in New Hampshire with his wife and three children.

Visit him at www.bewareofmonsters.com.

COMIC BOOK ART

Behold! *Demon Dog & Laser Chicken*, the new comic book from...no one yet. Sometimes while I'm writing a novel, I get inspired by the characters and want to see what they'd look like. So, I reach out to an artist and have some sketches done. This time, the end result was a cover for a comic book that is *not* in the works, though I'd definitely like to see it. Pencils and inks on this piece were done by Juan Kijo out of Columbia, and colored by myself. If you're reading the print edition, or the black and white Kindle edition, and you want to see the full color version, or you are interested in the sketches that led to this cover, visit the URL bewareofmonsters.com/thedarkart to check it out! And if you've got fan art for the book, send it to jrobinsonauthor@gmail.com and I'll add it to the page!